Dear Reader,

*Tempted. Seduced.* Those two words conjure up all kinds of shameless possibilities, don't they? Sensual temptations. Erotic persuasions. Forbidden pleasures. You'll find all that and more between the pages of this two-in-one collection.

I'm thrilled that Harlequin has decided to reprint two of my favorite Temptation stories! In *Tempted* my sensible heroine, Brooke Jamison, finds herself stranded with her sexy brother-in-law, Marc, and she can't resist the temptation to shed inhibitions and indulge in erotic fantasies. Two days of blissful confinement changes everything between them, but can she risk her heart on a man who has no intention of committing to any one woman?

In *Seduced* you'll get to meet Brooke's sister, Jessica, and the man who'll go to any lengths to seduce her! Ryan Matthews is a man who knows what he wants, and he's wanted sassy, sexy Jessica Newman in his bed for over a year. Now, he's going after her, and he'll do whatever it takes to make her his...including seducing her in the most delicious, sinful ways! His very innovative "cake scene" is sure to make you crave something sweet, and his inspiring "couple's gift" will no doubt leave you restless and breathless. Seduction has never been so hot!

I'd love to know what you thought of *Tempted* and *Seduced*. For a list of upcoming releases, be sure to check out my Web site at www.janelledenison.com.

Fondly,

*Janelle Denison*

Signature Select™
MINISERIES

# JANELLE DENISON

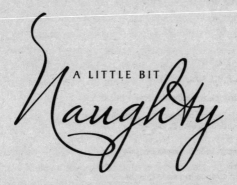

A LITTLE BIT
Naughty

HARLEQUIN®

TORONTO • NEW YORK • LONDON
AMSTERDAM • PARIS • SYDNEY • HAMBURG
STOCKHOLM • ATHENS • TOKYO • MILAN • MADRID
PRAGUE • WARSAW • BUDAPEST • AUCKLAND

ISBN 0-373-83701-1

A LITTLE BIT NAUGHTY

Copyright © 2006 by Harlequin Books S.A.

The publisher acknowledges the copyright holder of the individual works as follows:

TEMPTED
Copyright © 2000 by Janelle Dension.

SEDUCED
Copyright © 2000 by Janelle Denison.

www.eHarlequin.com

Printed in U.S.A.

# CONTENTS

# TEMPTED

To Carly Phillips and Julie Elizabeth Leto, for your extraordinary friendship and unending encouragement. Viva las Divas!

And to Don, for understanding that our astronomical long-distance phone bill is a legitimate business expense.

# PROLOGUE

"THIRTY-FIVE YEARS of marriage. Are you as impressed as I am?"

The deep, masculine baritone murmuring into her ear from over her shoulder caused Brooke Jamison to shiver. She turned and faced the owner of that sexy voice—her former brother-in-law, Marc Jamison. She met warm gray eyes framed in sooty lashes, and a mouth tipped in a lazy, sexy smile that was as natural as his gregarious personality. His thick, black hair, looking as soft and enticing as midnight, had been tousled by the slight breeze cooling the early August evening. In an attempt to maintain an executive image for his electrical contracting company, he wore his hair short, but the ends that curled over the collar of his sports jacket bespoke the rebel he was.

Startled by the unexpected flutter of awareness that tickled her belly, Brooke focused on his question and her answer. "Your parents' marriage is amazing, and inspiring."

Sliding his hands into the front pockets of his chocolate-colored trousers, Marc looked briefly to the guests gathered in his parents' lavishly decorated backyard to celebrate Kathleen and Doug's thirty-fifth anniversary. "So, are you having a good time?"

"Yeah, I am," she admitted, glad that she'd accepted his mother's invitation to join the celebration. She'd been hesitant at first, considering her and Eric's divorce had been finalized two weeks before, but Kathleen and the rest of the Jamison family had made her feel welcome, including her ex-husband. Despite the inevitable end to their marriage, she and Eric still maintained an amicable relationship, rare among divorced couples. Still, Kathleen's invitation had initially taken her off guard.

"I have to confess I'm surprised your family wanted me here, considering I'm technically not part of the family anymore."

A small frown pulled at his dark brows, her admission obviously causing him concern. "Hey, once you're a Jamison, you're part of the family forever, didn't you know that?"

Brooke smiled, liking the way that sounded. Unfortunately, in her experience families divided when couples split up. The dissension and emotional upheaval her own father had caused when he'd ended his marriage to her mother had been monumental. Without compunction, he'd shattered fragile family ties, forcing Brooke to mature beyond her thirteen years and leaving his other daughter hurt and disillusioned.

"That's not usually the way a divorce works," she returned, taking a sip of her drink.

"You divorced Eric, not the rest of us," he countered easily. "My parents adore you, my mother thinks of you as the daughter she never had, and I think you're pretty special, too."

His complimentary words were simple and sincere, yet she was suddenly, inexplicably entranced by the warm glow in his gaze. Ignoring the odd racing of her pulse, she looked away and found her ex-husband trapped in a steady stream of one-sided dialogue with his uncle George, a boisterous man who reveled in dominating the conversation. The beefy hand resting on Eric's shoulder guaranteed he wasn't going anywhere anytime soon.

Eric's hazel eyes met hers over Uncle George's balding head and silently pleaded, "Have mercy on me, please." He flashed her one of the endearing smiles that had won her over when she'd first met him, but now failed to elicit any stirring of desire or the inclination to help him out of his predicament.

Marc followed her line of vision to his brother and groaned. "Eric looks miserable, and we both know how long-winded, and boring, my uncle can be. Think we ought to go save him?"

An amused smile tipped the corner of her mouth as she considered Marc's question for all of two seconds before breaking eye contact with Eric and leaving him in his uncle's clutches. "No, I don't believe I will," she said without a hint of remorse. "It's no longer my job to rescue Eric, or play the doting wife." He was on his own, as she was. And she was pleased to discover she was fine with that.

Marc studied her expression intently. "You're doing okay, then?"

"More than okay," she verified, nodding. "Though after a two-year marriage, it seems strange to be single and available again."

"I'm sure that status won't last long." He leaned toward her, so close she caught the faint scent of mint on his breath. "Between you and me, Eric never knew a good thing when he saw one. I was really hoping you'd be 'The One.'"

She blinked up at him, not quite understanding what he meant. "'The One'?"

"Yeah, the one woman who could make Eric settle down."

Now it was her turn to frown. There was something in the depth of Marc's eyes she couldn't quite decipher. A hint of disappointment, she realized, but didn't understand its source.

"I'm only one woman," she said. "And that obviously wasn't enough for Eric."

Eric had tried to conform to their wedding vows, but ultimately he'd realized and admitted that he was a man who couldn't commit to any one woman. A genetic flaw, he'd told her, passed on from father to sons. Except Eric's father, Doug, had chosen to make his marriage work after his one indiscretion. Judging by the closeness Doug and Kathleen now seemed to share, their relationship had endured.

Resignation flickered across Marc's lean features. "If that's the case, it doesn't leave much hope for me."

His words held a longing she found curious. In the years that she'd known Marc she'd discovered that he steadfastly avoided serious relationships, didn't commit himself to any one woman and preferred to play the field. He *embraced* bachelorhood.

So why, then, did she get the impression that he wished differently?

Placing her empty glass on the corner of the rented bar, she decided that talk of anniversaries and marriage was getting the best of her and making her come to absurd conclusions about her brother-in-law. Making her feel things she had no business feeling.

She called up a smile. "It's getting late. I'd better say my goodbyes and be on my way."

He nodded, his charming grin lightening the moment. "I'll walk you to the door."

Half an hour later, after an endless round of hugs and farewells from the entire Jamison clan, Marc escorted her to the foyer. He rested his hand lightly at the base of Brooke's spine, the heat of his fingers penetrating through the black linen pants she wore. Her heart thundered in her chest, and she couldn't help but wonder how a simple touch from Marc could evoke such a startling response.

She stepped away from him as inconspicuously as possible when they reached the carved front doors, effectively dislodging that overwhelming contact that had her body tingling. Granted, she'd been without a man for a year, and Marc was extremely attractive, but she'd *never* thought of him as anything more than her husband's brother.

Until now…

His gaze found hers, and the muted sounds of the party faded into the background, making Brooke aware that they were very much alone.

A smile eased across his lips, but his expression was more serious than she'd ever seen it before. "Don't be a stranger, okay?"

Tamping a sudden rush of emotion, she whispered, "Okay."

He gathered her into a warm hug she hadn't even known she needed until she was enveloped by his hard body. Closing her eyes, she breathed deeply, inhaling the scent of warm spice and male heat. Greedily, she leaned into him and absorbed his comforting embrace, reluctant to let the moment go.

As much as she was over Eric, the past year had been difficult, and at times, lonely. She'd moved into her sister's apartment after her separation, and though Jessica provided female companionship, it wasn't enough. With Marc's arms around her, his hands stroking her back, Brooke realized how much she missed something as simple as a man's embrace, a man's touch. Eric had never been very demonstrative in their marriage, believing it wasn't masculine to exhibit tender feelings. Marc had always been one to openly express his affection.

Too soon he pulled back, and she lifted up on her feet to place a chaste kiss on his cheek—the same time he turned his head. Their lips met, momentarily startling them both. Over the past four years she'd shared many platonic kisses with her flirtatious brother-in-law, and this one started as innocently as any, his mouth brushing hers lightly…except somewhere along the way the tenor of the kiss changed, for both of them.

This time his lips lingered a little longer, and his mouth gradually, instinctively, exerted a gentle pressure that surpassed those chaste kisses they'd shared in the past. To her shock, a soft, unexpected moan of pleasure tickled her throat, and his tongue stroked along her bottom lip in tentative exploration.

Her mind spun, her senses reeled and she struggled to keep her perspective on the situation. Desires and denials clashed, confusing her. Nerve endings that had lain dormant for too long sizzled and came alive. And then she did something incredibly shameless—she touched her tongue to his.

She heard him groan deep in his chest, felt Marc's large hands on her hips guide her backward...until her spine pressed against the wall, and the two of them were shrouded in a shadowy corner. The heat surrounding her was incendiary. She caught a quick glimpse of the sensual hunger glimmering in his eyes and shivered at the thought of being the recipient of all that wild, frenzied electricity.

She didn't protest when he framed her face in his large, callused hands, didn't object or struggle when he lowered his mouth to hers once again. Without preamble, he parted her lips with his, glided his tongue into forbidden territory and seduced her with one of the hottest, most shockingly intimate kisses she'd ever tasted.

*And she let him.*

His fingers threaded through her hair, and his thumbs caressed her jaw. Her body swelled, and for a brief moment she felt reckless and wild. The feeling was liberating, exciting...until her conscience rudely reminded her who she was kissing—her bad boy, live-for-the-moment ex-brother-in-law.

Panic edged out pleasure, and she jerked her head back, effectively ending the rapacious kiss, but there was nothing she could do about the slow throb pulsing through her body, making her ache for primitive, erotic things she'd never, *ever* contemplated with Eric. Unfortunately, her ex-husband had never inspired such consuming lust, such excruciating need.

And that knowledge frightened her most of all.

Frantically, she pushed Marc away, and he immediately stepped back. They were both breathing raggedly, and judging by his bewildered expression, he was just as stunned as she was by the instantaneous flare of desire that had leapt between them. *And intrigued*—she recognized the thrill of a challenge in his quicksilver eyes.

Knowing that the dangerous, frivolous kind of interest she saw there could only cause trouble to her heart and emotions, she moved around him in a frenzied blur of motion and fled from the house. She sucked cool night air into her lungs, berating herself for a fool.

"Brooke, wait," she heard his voice, then his clipped steps as he followed her down the brick walkway.

Shaken by what she'd allowed to happen, and refusing to engage in a conversation about her brazen response, she nearly ran to her car. Disengaging her alarm, she slid behind the wheel of her Toyota 4Runner, wincing as his low, exasperated curses reached her. Slamming the door shut, she started the engine, drowning out his voice, then left him standing at the curb with his hands jammed on his hips and his features creased with frustration.

She experienced a twinge of guilt for her abrupt departure, but knew her actions spoke louder than any words possibly could. No matter how much she might want Marc, she wasn't interested in falling for another Jamison.

# CHAPTER ONE

*Three months later*

"HERE'S TO YOUR NEW single status, Brooke." Stacey Sumner lifted her strawberry margarita in a toast to mark the beginning of their weeklong "girls' retreat" in the Colorado Rocky Mountains.

Brooke grinned at her best friend and co-worker. Clinking her glass with Stacey's and then her sister's, she took a drink of the frothy beverage. "How about a toast to seven days of skiing, soaking in the hot tub, girl talk and eating everything we shouldn't?" At the grocery store on the way up to the time-share cabin she still maintained with Eric, they'd bought enough to satisfy every craving they might have—junk food had definitely been on their agenda.

"Oh, yeah," Jessica agreed, her pale blue eyes sparkling mischievously. "Sounds like heaven."

Stacey reclined on the matching love seat cornering the sofa and crossed her long legs. "Seven days of doing what we want, when we want. Spontaneity is the word for the week."

"And relaxation," Brooke interjected, thinking of all the novels she'd been wanting to read for the past six months and had brought along to curl up with at night.

"Aw, Brooke, you're no fun," Stacey lightly chastised. "This week was supposed to be about spontaneity and shedding inhibitions in celebration of being single again, remember?"

Averting her gaze to the fire crackling in the hearth, Brooke took another drink of her potent margarita. Yeah, she remembered the lecture Stacey had imparted on the drive up to Quail Valley for their ski vacation. But Brooke had always been the quintessential good girl—responsible, dependable and virtuous—thinking long and hard about consequences before acting. She'd even accepted her job as an accountant for Blythe Paints because the position was staid and reliable.

Being reckless wasn't in her psyche…unless she counted that very spontaneous, uninhibited kiss with Marc three months before. Try as she might to forget about that impetuous embrace, the incident, and the man, invaded her thoughts on a daily basis. And at night, well, she'd never had such erotic dreams, had never woken up so on edge. It might have been her own ministrations that had brought her the release her body sought, but it had been Marc who'd starred in the forbidden fantasies she'd woven.

Dismissing the kiss should have been relatively easy, considering she hadn't heard from Marc since that night. It was the way of the Jamison men, to seize the moment, then move on before the situation got too complicated. In this case, it was probably for the best.

Ignoring the heat flushing her skin—from the combined effects of tequila, the warmth of the fire and her sensual memories of Marc—she met Stacey's gaze. "You're the impulsive one, not me," she retorted.

Stacey made a sound of mock disgust. "You're just too exciting for words, Brooke."

She shrugged unapologetically, casually studying her nails. The pale pink polish was chipped and in need of a fresh coat—she planned on treating herself to a manicure and pedicure sometime this week. That's about how exciting her life got. Predictable…and *boring,* she realized.

"Let's try something different, in the way of girl talk," Stacey suggested. "If you could create the perfect, ideal male to be stranded up here with, what qualities would he have and what would he look like? Use your imagination. Fantasize a little."

Unbidden, Brooke's imagination conjured up thick black hair rumpled deliciously, a hard male body made for sin and pleasure, and eyes that darkened from silver to charcoal with a kiss. The fantasies that crowded her mind were something she refused to share with anyone.

Curling her legs beneath her on the sofa cushion, she shoved Marc from her mind and decided to give her ideal male her best shot. "Looks don't really matter," she said honestly, "as long as he's intelligent, warm and humorous."

Stacey braced her elbow on the armrest of the love seat and propped her chin in her hand, giving Brooke and her description of her exemplary mate her undivided attention. "And sexy?"

"In an understated way. Nothing presumptuous or arrogant." She finished off her margarita and thought about one of the things that her own marriage had lacked, and that she had often wished for. "His sole focus would be on me and my needs."

"Oh, yeah," Stacey said in a throaty purr.

Brooke caught her friend's drift right away. "And I don't mean just sexually."

Stacey wriggled her brows suggestively. "Though being focused on sexual needs doesn't hurt."

"I'm talking about emotional needs." She sounded practical and dull, but didn't care. After witnessing what her mother had gone through with her father, and her own experience with Eric, those qualities were important to her. "He'd be a good listener, and not afraid to show his feelings. He'd be secure in his masculinity so he didn't need other women to stroke his ego. And that goes hand in hand with him being monogamous. That's an absolute must."

Which certainly left love-'em-and-leave-'em Marc out of the competition.

"That's very sweet," Jessica said, a bit of awe in her voice. "Do you think men like that actually exist?"

Brooke glanced at her sister, regretting that Jessica's illusions about men had been shattered at such an early age by their father's actions. "Yeah, I do," she said softly, knowing at the same time that it was only her fantasy.

"You're so serious about men." Stacey drained the last of her drink and set her glass on the coffee table in front of her. "Ever thought of just going out and having a wild, mindless affair? Finding some guy that turns you on and having your way with him?"

Brooke imagined ripping Marc's shirt off, buttons flying. She imagined dragging those tight jeans he wore down his hips, pushing him onto his back and straddling his thighs, then seducing him…

Swallowing a groan, she tried to force those erotic images right out of her head, but she couldn't ignore that she *had* wondered a time or two what it would be like to be as sexually liberated as Stacey. To enjoy a man's attentions without pouring a lot of emotion into the relationship. To just lose herself in mutual pleasure with no expectations, no strings and without the risk of investing that deep, significant part of herself she could never recover once it was offered.

Men did it all the time. Her ex-husband had been guilty of playing that game, but then again, Eric hadn't invested the same emotions that she had into their relationship. She'd learned, belatedly, that he'd been incapable of doing so. She'd discovered, belatedly, that she'd been little more than a challenge for her husband, one he'd conquered, claimed, and quickly grown bored with. She'd determined, belatedly, that commitment wasn't an attribute the men in the Jamison family took seriously.

She *knew* that, so why was she allowing a bad boy like Marc to get under her skin and consume her thoughts?

"I don't think Brooke is that kind of girl," Jessica said when Brooke didn't answer Stacey's question.

The corner of Stacey's mouth tipped up in a lazy, confident smile. "*Everyone* has a wild side. It's just a matter of whether or not they tap into it."

"Very enlightening," Jessica said with a giggle. "And on that note, I think I'll go blend the next batch of margaritas."

Once she'd disappeared into the kitchen, Stacey glanced at Brooke, purpose glimmering in the depths of her eyes. "Ever looked at a guy and thought, I wonder if he's any good in bed?"

Brooke kept her thoughts centered and focused. "No."

Stacey considered that for a moment. "Ever looked at a guy's hands and wondered what they'd feel like sliding over your body?"

Marc had nice hands, large, callused, hot. Her body

thrummed at the thought of those palms stroking over her flesh, touching her in sensitive places. "Never."

"Ever looked at a guy's lips and imagined the slow, deep kisses he could give…or maybe the different ways he might use his mouth?"

"No, never." *Liar, liar, liar,* a voice inside Brooke's head chanted.

"Ever heard the phrase, 'just do it'?"

Brooke shrugged. "Yeah."

"It was meant for people like you."

Brooke frowned. "People like me?"

"Yeah, people who are too serious and self-controlled. You need to loosen up so you can get in touch with your feminine needs. 'Just do it' needs to be your new motto—at least for this next week. Then when we return to civilization you can resume looking for that fantasy man of yours."

"Just do it, huh?" Brooke repeated, testing out the words, not sure she could be so unreserved and direct— not when she'd spent her life being responsible and sensible in her approach.

Stacey grinned, looking pleased with herself. "Yeah, whenever you're unsure of something, but you want it really bad, repeat those words. *Just do it.*"

"Just do what?" Jessica asked, returning with a fresh pitcher of strawberry margaritas.

"Anything that strikes your sister's fancy this week," Stacey said, holding up her glass as Jessica refilled it with the slushy liquid. "Especially when it comes to men."

"Brooke is going man-hunting?" Jessica asked, intrigue infusing her voice.

Brooke winced. "That sounds so…*reckless.*"

"*Impetuous* is a better word, I think." Stacey took a sip

of her drink, her eyes bright with sensual knowledge. "You just kind of have to go with the feeling and not analyze the situation from every angle like you do those columns of numbers you work with. If it feels right, just do it."

Brooke chewed on her bottom lip and pondered her friend's suggestion. When it came to men, she'd always been cautious and selective, even analytical. Even her marriage to Eric had been based on practicality rather than uncontrollable passion—on both their parts, she now knew. They'd both had different expectations of their relationship, and each other, and in the end those individual needs had driven them apart emotionally and physically.

Ultimately, she wanted passionate love, a marriage based on mutual respect and the kind of solid family unit she'd grown up without. She wasn't like Stacey, who dated a slew of men, enjoyed the moment while it lasted and didn't think about the future. Brooke wanted a future with a man.

*One week.* Which wasn't a whole lot when she thought of it in terms of the rest of her life stretching ahead of her.

Brooke took a gulp of her margarita, her mind spinning. Could she shed her inhibitions and have a hot, wild, unemotional fling with a stranger before returning to her stable life and dependable job?

"Tell you what," Stacey said easily, as if sensing her doubts, "starting tomorrow, we'll check out the prospects on the slopes and see what's out there. If sparks happen, then go for it. If they don't, no loss."

Sparks, like the kind Marc generated. She shivered at the thought.

"Since I don't ski, you two are on your own," Jessica

said, settling back on the couch. "I'm going to enjoy the peace and quiet in the cabin and get caught up on my medical transcripts."

"Then it's you and me, Brooke." Stacey grinned, lifting her glass in another toast. "And a mountain full of men to choose from."

Brooke groaned as three glasses clinked together, trying to keep an open mind about Stacey's man-hunting plan and her new motto for the week.

*Just do it.*

"JUST DO IT," Brooke murmured to herself, trying to inject some enthusiasm into her voice as she wiped the coffee table of the remnants of their afternoon margarita-fest while Stacey and Jessica cleaned the kitchen. The words sounded flat and dull, too much like her personal life.

She snorted in disgust. For the past year she'd buried herself in her work, grasping on to the monotony of her job to counterbalance the stress and disappointment of her divorce. And now here she was, starting a new phase in her life…and still clinging to the safe and familiar.

Dull. Boring. Too damned predictable.

She sighed and straightened the sofa cushions. What Stacey was suggesting went against her grain and all those good-girl qualities she'd lived with her entire life, but much to her own surprise, she was gradually warming to the idea of finding a guy who turned her on and indulging in a sexy interlude. And she hoped in the process she'd finally banish Marc from her mind and ease the sexual frustration he'd caused her for the past three months.

Yeah, that particular idea definitely had merit. And

maybe she'd return to Denver with a new attitude and a new outlook on her future.

A beam of headlights slashed through the windows facing the front of the small cabin, cutting through the shadows of twilight. She heard the crunch of snow beneath tires, an engine rumbling as it idled, then everything went quiet.

Curious, she headed toward the window next to the front door and pushed aside the curtain to peer outside. Even bathed in early November dusk, she immediately recognized the vehicle parked next to her 4Runner, a black Suburban with the Jamison Electrical logo emblazoned on the door in bold, white print.

Her heart dropped to her stomach as the object of her lustful fantasies slid from the driver's side of the vehicle. Another male figure emerged from the passenger side, and finally, a third stepped from the back door, his boots crunching on the snow. Marc said something to the two other men, and while the duo moved toward the back of the utility vehicle, Marc started for the cabin's front porch.

Brooke's pulse tripped all over itself. Abruptly, she dropped the curtain and groaned, unable to believe her private refuge was about to be invaded by roughly six hundred pounds of gorgeous male testosterone, two hundred of which was trouble with a capital *T.*

Of all the possible ironies!

Knowing it was inevitable she face him, she opened the door before he had a chance to insert his key into the lock. His hand stopped midair, and their gazes met. A slow, intimate smile claimed his mouth, and his gaze drifted down the length of her with a slow, natural ease that came from years of assessing a woman in a single glance.

Not only did he assess her, he seemed to brand her

with a breathless heat wherever his gaze roamed—and it covered plenty of territory in an amazingly short span of time. She found his bold perusal unnerving; the fluttering deep in her belly was equally disconcerting. There was something different in the way he looked at her now, something that was distinctly male, a trifle dangerous and a whole lot predatory.

Her skin tightened, and to her dismay her breasts responded to his visual caress. They swelled within the lacy cups of her bra in a purely feminine way, pushing her taut nipples against the soft cotton of her University of Colorado sweatshirt. Even her thighs and legs seemed to become sensitized to the soft, faded denim of her jeans.

She blamed her body's response on the cold, brisk air filtering into the cabin, but had no such excuse for the contrasting heat warming her in more intimate places—a feverlike flush generated by a pair of smoky-gray eyes. That gaze radiated a sexy, unmistakable kind of message that told her the kiss they'd shared three months ago was a prelude to a deeper kind of magic.

"Hello, Brooke," he greeted her warmly. His voice was deep, rich, and sent a delicious shiver shimmering through her. Good grief, one kiss and now his voice had the ability to seduce her senses and make her weak in the knees.

She struggled to shake the awareness that had her in its grip. "What are you doing here?" she asked, part demand, part curiosity.

Marc lifted black brows over amused eyes. "I should be asking you the same thing. We're here because we borrowed the cabin from Eric until next Tuesday to go skiing. Business is slow right now, so we thought we'd take advantage of the prime skiing conditions."

One glance at the top of his Suburban revealed

three pairs of skis strapped to a rack. "Oh, no you don't," she said, shaking her finger at him. "The cabin is *ours* for the week."

He tipped his head and a dark, unruly lock of hair slipped over his forehead. "Did you tell Eric you were coming up?"

A sigh unraveled out of her, fringed with frustration. "Of course I did."

"That's odd." He absently rubbed his thumb along his jaw. "I asked him just this morning if the cabin was free, and he said since he hadn't heard from you, that it must be."

Unease slithered through Brooke, settling in her stomach like a rock. "I left a specific message with his secretary three days ago that I was taking the cabin for the week."

Marc's broad shoulders lifted in an apologetic shrug. "He obviously didn't get it, Brooke. His secretary is new and, well, she's more beauty than brains, if you get my drift. You know Eric wouldn't deliberately sabotage your plans if he knew you'd be here."

Brooke knew Marc spoke the truth. For all her ex-husband's faults, he wasn't one to do something so underhanded.

Marc's two friends climbed the porch stairs, duffel bags in hand and congenial smiles in place. They flanked Marc and waited for her to invite them into the warmth of the cabin.

She stood guard at the door, certain once the trio invaded the cozy, two-bedroom time-share her chance at a relaxing vacation would vanish. "You can't stay here."

"We don't really have a choice," Marc replied easily. "I called all the resorts in the area, and because of the recent snowfall, everything is completely booked up this weekend. That's why I asked Eric if I could borrow the cabin."

His argument was solid, and believable. Still, Brooke didn't budge.

"Who's here, Brooke?"

The sound of Jessica's curious voice loosened some of the tension building within Brooke. She glanced over her shoulder, watching as her sister exited the kitchen, followed by Stacey.

*"Men,"* Brooke said, the word escaping like the curse it was.

Marc's deep, familiar chuckle strummed down her spine like caressing fingers. Shaking off her reaction, Brooke turned back to the trio, her gaze locking on Marc's. "I don't know what you find so amusing, Jamison, considering you and your friends might be camping in your Suburban for the weekend."

That earned her a sexy grin that made her stomach dip and her toes curl. "You wouldn't do that to me."

He sounded too sure of himself. And her.

Before she could issue a retort, Stacey moved to her side, too much enthusiasm glimmering in her eyes. "Aw, come on, Brooke. These guys have obviously been on the road for a few hours, the least we can do is let them rest before sending them on their way." Her friend extended her hand and introduced herself, beating out any argument Brooke could have issued. "By the way, I'm Stacey Sumner. I work with Brooke at Blythe Paints."

Marc slipped his hand into Stacey's. "Marc Jamison," he said, nodding in acknowledgment.

Stacey flashed a grin. "Ahh, the ex."

"Excuse me?"

"Ex-brother-in-law," Stacey clarified.

A smile quirked his too-sensual mouth as his gaze slid back to Brooke. "I'd like to think I'm still a friend."

*Friends don't kiss friends the way you kissed me.* Squashing the frisson of heat spiraling toward her belly, despite the chill filling the room from outside, Brooke gave him a tight smile in return. "You're currently a pain in the ass," she muttered.

One of the men standing beside Marc grinned in amusement, and the other coughed to cover up a laugh.

Marc blinked, not the least bit offended. "But a darn loveable one."

"That's debatable," she countered swiftly, refusing to let his compelling charm soften her.

"That's exactly what Brooke needs these days. A good debate." Stacey grabbed Marc's arm and tugged him across the threshold. "Come on in, so we can continue this conversation without the threat of frostbite."

Before Brooke could protest, the cabin was filled with three overwhelmingly masculine bodies, and the small living room seemed to shrink in size.

Marc shrugged out of his jacket and went about introducing his friends, mostly for Stacey's and Jessica's benefit. "This is Shane Hendricks, who works for my company as an electrical engineer," he said of the blond-haired guy who'd seemingly captured Stacey's attention, then nodded toward the other dark-haired man. "And this is Ryan Matthews, a divorce attorney for Haywood and Irwin."

"Nice to meet you all," Stacey said gregariously.

Jessica greeted Shane politely, then turned to Ryan. "An attorney, huh?" A sly smile curved her mouth as Ryan confirmed her question with a nod. "What's black and brown and looks good on a lawyer?" Before he could respond to her odd, unexpected question, she offered the punch line. "A Doberman pinscher."

Brooke groaned, Marc chuckled, and Ryan stared at Jessica in bafflement, taken aback.

Then he shook his head and laughed, too. "Nice greeting. I have to admit I haven't heard that one before."

"Oh, I have one for just about every occasion." With a jaunty spring to her step, Jessica went to the coffee table, picked up her laptop computer and glanced at Brooke. "I'll be up in the loft working on my transcripts until you get everything settled with Marc and his friends."

Interest gleamed in Ryan's gaze as he watched Jessica climb the stairs to the cabin's only second-story bedroom. Once she was out of his line of vision, he looked back at Brooke, a grin quirking his mouth. "Was it something I said?"

Brooke rubbed the slow throb beginning in her temple, and offered the man a reassuring smile. "It's not you, personally. Lawyer jokes are Jessica's specialty. She finds them…amusing." But Brooke knew where Jessica's comments came from. Ryan's profession made him an easy target for the pent-up emotions Jessica had kept deeply buried since their childhood.

As for her own emotions, they were currently under siege, as well. She thought about her forbidden attraction to Marc, her sister's arsenal of lawyer jokes and Stacey's preoccupation with Shane as he helped her rekindle the fire in the hearth. Combining all that volatile sexual energy and masculine appeal and cramming it into one tiny cabin was not conducive to the rest and leisure she'd envisioned. No, it was more suited to insanity.

Desperate to see the trio on their way, she turned back to the leader of the pack. "Can I talk to you, Marc, alone?" Before he could refuse her, she headed purposefully toward the kitchen, the only room that would provide them a modicum of privacy.

She was determined that, within the next hour, Marc and his friends would be gone and her relaxing, weeklong ski retreat would resume as planned.

## CHAPTER TWO

MARC RELEASED a low, deep breath and watched Brooke
head toward the kitchen. His gaze was unerringly drawn
to the subtle sway of her slim hips, and the way her soft,
faded jeans contoured to her curved bottom…which, admittedly, was his favorite part of the female anatomy—
long, slender legs taking a close second. But her deeper,
less superficial qualities were what tied him up in knots
and had his conscience warning him to put her, and the
spontaneous kiss they'd shared, out of his mind.

Intensely loyal and infinitely giving, Brooke was
exactly the kind of woman he steadfastly avoided. She
was so completely opposite from the enjoy-the-
moment-while-it-lasts kind of woman he usually dated.
Granted, he was very particular about whom he pursued,
but his motto was always the same—no strings attached.
The women knew up front what to expect, and he
*always* bailed before the relationship turned demanding.
One fateful night had proved he wasn't cut out for commitment and forever promises, and he wasn't willing to
risk a woman's emotional stability to give any kind of
long-term relationship a try.

Nope, if his own brother hadn't been able to find contentment with the one woman who embodied the perfect
wife, then Marc had little hope for himself.

"Well, buddy," Ryan said, slapping him good-naturedly on the back and cutting into his thoughts. "I know finding your sister-in-law here puts a glitch in our personal plans, but we're depending on you to pull this off."

Marc lifted a brow at his friend. "After Jessica's odd brand of humor, you don't mind sharing the cabin?"

Ryan's gaze drifted toward the loft. "No doubt I'll be dodging a barrage of lawyer jokes, but I figure we'll be spending more time on the slopes than here. And if I don't find an enticing ski bunny to hook up with, I figure it's a place to sleep. It wouldn't be the first time I've crashed on the floor."

Marc glanced at Shane, who was currently flirting with Stacey as they knelt in front of the fireplace. It seemed the other man didn't have any objections to the cramped quarters, either. "I'll see what I can do."

He headed into the kitchen and found Brooke standing across the small room, near the oak table with six matching chairs—a convenient number given the current occupants of the cabin. He doubted Brooke would appreciate him using that fact as part of his argument for letting them stay.

Their gazes met, held, melded.

She folded her arms over her chest and lifted her chin, showing him the more stubborn side to her personality. Her thick, shoulder-length hair swayed with the movement, prompting him to remember the feel of his fingers tangling in those rich, luxurious, honey-blond strands as he'd angled Brooke's head for a deeper kiss. Wispy bangs touched her forehead and set off her expressive eyes, currently an intense shade of blue.

Despite her determined demeanor, her gaze revealed the wariness and caution she was really feeling. He knew those emotions were present because of the boundaries he'd unintentionally overstepped at his parents' house that night of their anniversary party.

Unfortunately, the three months that had passed since he'd last seen Brooke had done nothing to diminish the deep, sensual craving he'd developed for her. He'd tried to tell himself that moment had been instigated out of flirtatious fun, but he now had to admit that the soft, warm feel of her lips under his had seduced him, had forced him to acknowledge that flawed part of him that had coveted his brother's wife. Sweet, hot desire had gripped him, and he'd done the unthinkable and stolen a sample of what he knew would never be his—oneness, stability, eternity.

The discovery of what forever tasted like had shaken up every rule and restriction he lived by. He'd thought, he'd *hoped,* that time and distance would put their relationship back on track, as friends. He'd spent the past three months trying to get Brooke out of his mind, knowing she wasn't his kind of woman, knowing he was the last kind of man she'd go for, especially after what she'd endured with his brother. Especially when his own past track record was less than sterling.

Their time apart had only intensified their awareness of one another.

"I'm sorry, Marc," she said with an adamant shake of her head. "But having you and your friends here just isn't going to work."

He entered the room at a leisurely pace, closing the distance between them. "All of us have taken time off work until Tuesday, and there are no other lodgings available. I'm hoping we can come to some sort of compromise."

"Eric needs to hire himself a competent secretary," she muttered, more serious than joking. "We were here first, and this place isn't big enough for six. My sister and I are sharing the loft, and Stacey is taking the only other room downstairs."

"The sofa pulls out into a sleeper," he countered, stopping a safe distance away from her—for both their sakes.

She smirked, the first hint of humor dancing in her eyes. "And you and your buddies will sleep on it together?"

He visibly winced. "Uh, no. Two of us can take the floor."

"There's only one bathroom."

"That's not important to the male species," he said with a grin. "Besides, we'll be up and gone before anyone wakes up in the morning."

She released a sigh brimming with uncertainties, which he knew had to do with the subtle shift in their relationship. "Marc—"

He cut her off before she could issue an argument. "Look, Shane, Ryan and I came up here to hit the slopes, and for the most part, that's where we'll be. Or at the lodge. We just need a place to sleep at night. We'll do our own thing, and you can do yours. If you or your friends need your own time, I'm certain we can find something to do to occupy our time. In fact, we were planning on grabbing dinner at the lodge. The place will be yours tonight until nine, at least."

The determination in her gaze wavered, but then held strong, fueled by convictions only he understood. If it was anyone but him, he knew he wouldn't be reduced to groveling.

"C'mon, Brooke," he cajoled in his best persuasive

tone. "I'll talk Eric into giving you the next week that the cabin is free to make up for this fiasco."

Before she could respond, Stacey entered the kitchen. Shane followed close behind, appearing well on his way to harmony with the raven-haired beauty in front of him.

"Well?" Stacey asked impatiently. "Has the head-mistress given her approval for you to stay?"

Three pairs of eyes stared at Brooke expectantly, and Marc watched her shoulders slump in defeat. "Fine, you can stay." Her tone was hardly gracious. Neither was her gaze as she leveled a pointed looked at Marc. "But no extra guests allowed. You guys are on your own for any extracurricular activities."

"Fair enough." He stifled a grin at her militant attitude. "I promise, you won't even know we're here."

BETWEEN THE HARD, carpeted floor, the chilled living room and the erotic thoughts of the woman sleeping in the upstairs loft filtering through his mind, Marc couldn't sleep worth a damn.

Rolling to his back, he stretched his stiff muscles and cursed Ryan for drawing the longest toothpick at the Quail Valley Lodge last night, thus giving his friend the pull-out sofa bed for the night. It had been the fairest way to claim the only mattress left in the cabin, but for him and Shane who were in sleeping bags on the floor, it was hell.

Sighing, he stacked his hands beneath his head and stared up at the high-vaulted ceiling. Gradually, the first shades of dawn crept through the curtainless window, throwing shadows along the wall. He heard a rustling sound from the loft's bed, a sleepy sigh and his gut tightened at the thought of Brooke lying in that bed, all warm and soft and sensual.

Just like she'd been when he'd kissed her. An eternity ago, it seemed, yet he could still remember every nuance of her body's response as she'd melted against him, every silky glide of their tongues, the revealing and very sexy moan that had escaped her when he'd delved even deeper, wanting more of her.

The memory prompted a slow, aching throb through his body.

He'd convinced himself that the embrace had been a fluke, a flirtatious encounter that had accidentally escalated from the kind of platonic kiss they'd shared for three years, into a swift, indulgent seduction of senses. He'd convinced himself he'd only imagined the heat and incredible need that had flared between them. He'd believed it, until he'd seen her yesterday and experienced the urge to kiss her again, to see if what they'd shared had been as explosive as he remembered.

Dangerous, crazy, insane thoughts.

He'd deliberately stayed at the lodge until after midnight, but he'd known he was in deep trouble when he couldn't summon the slightest bit of interest in the women who'd approached him, and there had been a bevy of them to choose from. While Shane and Ryan had enjoyed dancing and flirting with the female population, Marc had found himself comparing those women to Brooke…and found them all sorely lacking. Physically, any one of them could have sufficed. Mentally, none had stimulated him beyond a token smile.

He wanted to taste Brooke again. Badly. Even though he knew he shouldn't. Knew he was completely wrong for her. And that she was completely wrong for him.

Somewhere along the way, those issues had ceased to matter.

And that's when he knew he was in big, deep trouble. The kind that tripped a guy up inside. The kind that defied logic. The kind that overruled common sense and rational judgment.

The kind that made a usually sensible, intelligent man make incredibly stupid decisions.

Ever since a relationship with a woman during his senior year in college had turned disastrous, and made Marc realize he was too much like his own father, he'd never allowed another woman to get too close emotionally—for both their sakes. The guilt that had plagued him after that incident had been excruciating. But beyond the remorse, his actions had cemented in his mind his greatest fear, that he didn't have what it took to sustain a lasting commitment—that fidelity was a chromosome missing from his family's gene pool.

For the past eight years he'd devoted his time and energy to his electrical business, and dated women who didn't make demands he knew he'd never be able to satisfy or fulfill. He'd never allowed his relationships to turn serious, and ended them before something deep and emotional developed.

One kiss, and he felt emotionally connected to Brooke—a revelation he found both scary, and exhilarating.

*Not with her,* his mind chided.

Listening to the voice of reason in his head, he determined that sooner or later they needed to discuss that kiss, to put things between them back on track, and into proper perspective. They'd always been friends, and maintaining that easy, casual relationship they'd shared during her marriage to his brother was of the utmost importance to him.

With that plan firmly in mind, he unzipped his sleeping bag, got up and made his way to the bathroom. Closing the door, he flipped on the light, and decided he'd get his shower out of the way before the women woke up and the men lost their chance at any hot water.

Half an hour later, feeling more refreshed and his aching muscles more relaxed, he slipped on a pair of long thermal underwear and shirt, and overlaid that protective warmth with jeans and a flannel shirt. Quietly exiting the bathroom, he grabbed his ski jacket and made his way to the kitchen. He found the keys for the outdoor shed on the peg by the back door.

Since it appeared his friends were sleeping off a night of too much fun, he had plenty of time to take one of the two snowmobiles parked in the shed and enjoy the light snowfall that had coated the ground during the night.

He suddenly craved something sweet. Since Brooke was out of the question, he'd just have to head down to Quail Village to the quaint bakery there and settle for confections of the pastry kind.

WHEN MARC RETURNED an hour later, the other snowmobile was gone, the lights in the cabin were on, and the kitchen was filled with the rich aroma of freshly brewed coffee. Tugging off his gloves, he stepped into the warm kitchen and closed the door to the mudroom behind him.

Brooke and Jessica turned from the counter to face him, and he smiled. "Good morning, ladies," he greeted them, setting the pink box of pastries on the oak table.

"Morning," Brooke replied in her normal, good ol' sister-in-law tone, then turned her attention back to pouring the steaming brew into the two mugs on the counter.

Ryan walked into the kitchen, and Jessica instantly honed in on the other man. "What could be good about waking up to a lawyer trying to negotiate time in the bathroom?" she asked, stirring cream and sugar into her coffee.

A lazy smile creased Ryan's lips, and he lifted a brow over a dark brown eye glimmering with amusement. "I did *not* try and negotiate time in the bathroom."

"What was I thinking? You're absolutely right," Jessica conceded humorously. "Divorce attorneys don't know how to negotiate, they *trounce* their opponents, which is exactly what you did to me." Wandering over to the table, she peeked into the pastry box and selected a bear claw. "And just to set the record straight, Mr. Matthews, your 'I'll only be a minute' turned into twenty."

Marc met Brooke's gaze, and they both suppressed a grin at the obvious undercurrents between the sparring couple.

Retrieving a cup from the cupboard, Ryan filled the mug with coffee. "I didn't take *that* long," he countered mildly.

Jessica crossed the room and stopped beside Ryan. "How can you tell when a lawyer is lying?" she asked sweetly, then replied before Ryan could. "His lips are moving."

With that victorious remark hanging in the air, she left the kitchen.

Marc chuckled and shook his head, feeling a twinge of sympathy for his good friend who was more used to women sweet-talking rather than mocking him.

Ryan joined him with his own deep laughter. "She's not much of a morning person, is she?"

Brooke grimaced in apology. "No, she's not."

Picking a jelly-filled doughnut from the bakery box, he took a big bite, chewing contemplatively. "You know, as crazy as it sounds, I find her very stimulating." On that note, he headed back into the living room, a grin curving his mouth and a challenging light sparking in his eyes.

As soon as Marc was alone with Brooke, silence, and a slow building awareness, settled between them. He still stood across the room, near the table, and she leaned against the far counter, looking at him over the rim of her mug as she casually sipped her coffee, but the charged energy that arced between them was unmistakable.

The instantaneous, intimate connection still startled him on an emotional level. Physically, he wasn't so surprised at his reaction. He'd always thought of Brooke as beautiful, and sensual in an understated way—her marriage to his brother hadn't blinded him to her allure. He was first and foremost a man who liked and appreciated women, and as such it was difficult not to notice the curves that made her intrinsically female—especially now, when the turtleneck sweater she wore clung to firm breasts, and black leggings molded to the swell of her hips and those long, slender legs that had consumed too much of his thoughts lately.

But it was the warmth in her blue eyes that made his heart beat faster and caused a riot of emotions to clamor within him—wants and needs he'd denied himself for eight long years. Wants and needs he had no business contemplating now, or ever, not when he'd resigned himself to the kind of lifestyle that didn't include the kind of commitment a woman like Brooke demanded… and deserved.

But those sensible thoughts did nothing to douse the undeniable desire that had taken up residence in him since that kiss they'd shared. While Brooke currently displayed admirable restraint and nonchalance regarding their situation, Marc experienced a contrary surge of recklessness that battled his willpower to resist her.

Shrugging out of his jacket, Marc laid it over the back of the chair, and turned to direct his gaze at Brooke. "Got enough coffee left for me to have a cup?"

"Uh, sure," she said, a bit breathless, he suspected, from the rippling heat they'd generated in the short span of time they'd been alone.

He watched her retrieve another mug from the cupboard and pour in the last of the coffee, her hand trembling ever-so-slightly while she tried to regain her composure. Crossing the small space that separated them, he pushed his fingers through his tousled hair and away from his face, the strands still chilled from his morning ride to the village.

She turned back around, startled to find him standing beside her. With a remarkable recovery, she handed him the cup, her gaze holding his.

"You lied," she said, the accusation low and husky.

The mug stopped halfway to his lips. The very notion that he might have deceived her about something unsettled him. For all of his faults, he valued honesty, *demanded it,* in himself and others. It was a personal trait he'd insisted upon after that crisis in his life eight years ago.

"I did?" His confusion was evident in his voice.

"Yep." She nodded slowly, seriously, though there was a twinkle in her blue eyes that softened her complaint. "I thought you said you and your friends would be gone before we got up."

Relief coursed through him, and he grinned. "My intentions were honorable, I swear. But we got in after midnight, and I had no idea that the guys would be slow-moving in the morning."

She strolled over to the table and surveyed the baked goods, selecting the chocolate French cruller he'd picked specifically for her. "Wild evening at the lodge?"

"We had a good time." He took a long swallow of coffee, then shrugged, knowing he could have had a better time, if he'd been in the right frame of mind. If his mind hadn't been on Brooke. "Dinner was decent, and they've got a great band in the bar. What did you girls do last night?"

"Talked and relaxed," she said vaguely, then took a bite of her doughnut. Her eyes closed for a brief moment. Sheer enjoyment etched her features, and a tiny moan curled up from her throat.

Her tongue darted out to catch the chocolate at the side of her mouth, and he experienced an overwhelming urge to lick the icing off himself and nibble at the smear on her bottom lip.

Marc's gut clenched tight, his reserve of willpower quickly dwindling. She had no idea just how erotic she made eating a French cruller seem, and her lack of self-consciousness or inhibition made him wonder about her response in bed, beneath him, with him sliding deep inside her—

*Whoa.* He cut off those intimate, forbidden thoughts, but the image lingered vividly in his mind.

On a satisfied sigh, she blinked her lashes open, saw him staring at her and a becoming shade of pink colored her cheeks.

He leaned a hip against the counter, his gaze lingering on her damp lips. "It looks good." He had first-hand knowledge that her lips, and the heated depths of her mouth, tasted equally sweet.

"It's wonderful," she admitted. "You remembered that I liked French crullers."

Lifting his gaze to her eyes, he allowed a rogue grin to grace his lips. "How can a man forget something that brings a woman such pleasure?"

The twist in his words wasn't lost on her. Her eyes widened at his sexy innuendo, but surprisingly, she made no attempt to counter his brazen comment. Finally, she drew a deep breath and looked away, breaking that irresistible, tantalizing pull.

He was flirting, crossing that invisible line he knew he ought to respect even though she was no longer married to his brother. They were both bound to get tangled up in the sensual web he was spinning if he didn't stop this madness. He tried like hell to rein himself back, to dismiss the attraction that intrigued and enticed him beyond reason or his better judgment.

He took a sip of his coffee. "You plan on skiing today?" he asked, striving for innocuous conversation.

She smiled, seemingly grateful for the change in subject. "Stacey and I are heading to the slopes in about an hour. Jessica doesn't ski, so she'll stay here." She took another bite of her doughnut, this time careful not to display her enjoyment of the pastry.

"I could give her a few basic lessons." Pushing off the counter, he slowly crossed the small space separating them. "She'd be skiing in no time."

Wariness reflected on her face as he approached, and she smoothly slipped around him and went to the sink to wash the sticky icing from her fingers. "Thanks, but I think Jessica prefers to just hang out in the cabin."

Lifting the lid on the bakery box, he grabbed a glazed buttermilk and bit into it, contemplating Brooke's sudden skittishness. "I noticed that the other snowmobile was gone. Who's using it?"

"Shane and Stacey went out for a morning ride."

"They've seemed to hit it off well," he said, guessing from the various comments Shane had made the previous night that he wouldn't mind pursuing something with the other woman. "In fact, I think my friend likes your friend."

"What's not to like?" Brooke asked, rinsing her coffee cup. "She's got a great personality, a perfect body and she's naturally sensual."

He tilted his head, and let his gaze take stock of her attributes. "You've got a great personality, a perfect body and you're very sensual."

She rolled her eyes at that, clearly disbelieving him.

Obviously, his brother hadn't appreciated what an enticing wife he'd had. "It's all in the eye of the beholder, I suppose." He finished off his doughnut, and sucked the glaze from his fingers, then shrugged. "I happen to think you're very sexy. Always have."

A wry grin quirked the corner of her mouth. "Interesting, considering my packaging didn't hold your brother's attention for long."

And judging by the guarded look in her eyes, she believed she couldn't hold his attention for long, either. Though his short-lived relationships verified her unspoken opinion, he found himself unjustifiably annoyed that she'd lump him into the same category as his brother.

He started toward her, and she automatically skirted to the side again, away from him and back toward the table. He turned to face her, and jammed his hands on his hips, his exasperation mounting. "You're acting as though you're afraid I'm going to pounce on you…or kiss you again."

There, he'd said it, finally brought the forbidden kiss out into the open so they could discuss it, and move on.

She seemed just as relieved to be offered an opportunity to talk about what had so obviously caused tension between them. "About that kiss—"

"Something happened between us, didn't it?" he asked, stepping toward her from the side, so she couldn't bolt around him.

"Yes, but I think it's best if we chalk it up as a mistake." Her chin lifted as he neared. "A casual kiss that accidentally flared out of control."

*Like wildfire.* "No, I don't think it was a mistake or an accident," he refuted, trapping her against the solid oak table so that her bottom hit the edge. His body crowded her from the front, but didn't touch her…yet. "I think we both knew what we were doing, but then you panicked."

"I came to my senses," she argued, pressing a hand to his chest to stop him from coming any closer. One more inch and they'd be more intimate than he'd been with a woman in too many months to count. One more inch and she'd discover just how badly he wanted her, despite the dozen reasons why he shouldn't.

"Marc, this is all so complicated." She shook her head, confusion clashing with the wanting in her gaze. "If it was anyone but you…"

The honorable intentions he'd vowed earlier, to leave her alone, dissolved in that moment. Suddenly, he had a point to prove.

She gasped as his hands clasped her hips, then lifted

her a fraction so her bottom slid onto the flat surface of the table. "That doesn't sound like a compliment."

She frowned at him and his bold move, but the arousing shade of her eyes contradicted her prim attitude and countered the silent reprimand in her gaze. "It wasn't meant to be a compliment, or an insult. It's the truth."

He grinned lazily and flattened his palms on her slender thighs. She sucked in a swift, shocked breath, and before she could guess his next intent, he pushed her legs apart and moved in between so her knees bracketed his hips, leaving her no possible escape.

Incredible heat shimmered between them. The initial panic touching her expression was quickly eclipsed by a thrilling rush of excitement that flowed hot and molten through Marc's veins, as well, spiraling straight toward his groin. His erection strained against thermal and denim, full and hot and heavy.

No doubt, she felt his desire and hunger for her. She swallowed convulsively. "You're my brother-in-law," she attempted.

"Ex," he breathed, dipping his head near her ear, squashing her paltry argument. Before she could issue a more obvious objection, that he was a *Jamison,* he distracted her by sliding his lips against the silken skin of her neck. "I haven't been able to get you out of my mind since that kiss."

A tiny moan caught in her throat, and she gripped the edge of the table with her fingers, seemingly trying desperately to resist him. "Me, either," she admitted, sounding miserable.

He slid his hand to the nape of her neck, curling his fingers just beneath the French braid she'd twisted her hair into. He touched his lips to her jaw, dragged them to the corner of her mouth, which was parted and trembling. He lifted his head, just enough to look into her soft blue eyes, brimming with anticipation, despite her protests.

That was the only assurance he needed to take this encounter to the next level. "You're curious," he murmured huskily, "I'm tempted, we both want it, so let's try another kiss and see what's really there."

She shuddered, resisting, her body stiff with tension. He waited for her to give him the permission he sought, because this time he wasn't about to take something she wasn't willing to give.

This time, he wanted no regrets, no excuses.

Through half-mast lashes, he watched her struggle with her conscience, and prepared to let her and this fleeting moment go—probably the smartest thing for him to do.

He started to step back, but she suddenly reached out and gripped his flannel shirt in her hands, pulling him back—close. Determination fired her blue eyes, and she drew a deep, fortifying breath.

*"Just do it,"* she ordered.

## CHAPTER THREE

MARC BLINKED, surprise registering in his gaze at Brooke's ardent demand. "Excuse me?"

Brooke dampened her bottom lip with her tongue. Her heart pounded frantically in her chest, and her entire body was charged with a nervousness she couldn't deny. "Just do it!" *Before I change my mind,* she thought desperately.

He tilted his head, a curious smile canting the corner of that sensual mouth she knew was capable of giving her great pleasure. "Demanding thing, aren't you?" he murmured.

*He had no idea.* Right now, she didn't want to think about what she was about to do, or her reckless, irresponsible behavior, or the excitement spiraling low in her belly. She had a point to demonstrate, to him and herself…that she *could* just do it.

Forcing herself to be the aggressor, she released her grip on his flannel shirt and slid her palm around to the nape of his neck. Her fingers glided through the silky length of his black-as-midnight hair. The strands were cool, contrasting with the fevered heat radiating from his body and the smoldering intensity darkening his eyes.

She shivered, and before she came to her senses, she pulled his mouth toward hers. His head dipped willingly, without hesitation, and his soft, warm lips settled over hers with a gentleness that threw her plan for a mindless seduction off-kilter. She'd wanted, *expected,* fast, wild and unemotional. He gave her slow, lazy and tantalizing, catering to her doubts and uncertainties…and the tension thrumming through her.

His large hands stroked down her back, encouraging her closer, making her spine arch until her breasts brushed his wide, hard chest. The delicious friction caused her nipples to tighten and ache. He gripped her hips and slowly pulled her bottom to the very edge of the table, spreading her legs wider and pressing against her until the only thing separating them was heavy denim and cotton leggings.

He sucked her bottom lip into his mouth, nibbled on the soft flesh with his teeth, and a moan slipped past her throat before she could catch it. Her mind spun, and her thighs clenched against his lean hips.

"You need to relax," he murmured against her mouth. She felt her lips gradually soften and part for him. "Yeah, that's it," he said, then exerted a more provocative pressure with his mouth. "Now give me your tongue…"

Shivering at the husky, rich tone of his voice, she did as he ordered. Completely meshing their lips, she slid her tongue into his mouth and instantly tangled with his, silky slow and lush with promise. The flavor of hot male and honey glaze from the doughnut he'd eaten overwhelmed her, excited her, and made her melt and relax against him.

Three months ago the kiss they'd shared had been a thrill ride neither one of them had expected, giving them little time to explore and enjoy taste and textures. This time, he was entirely too thorough, incredibly indulgent and generous in catering to her pleasure.

This languorous kiss, as titillating as it was, suddenly wasn't enough. The need to be a little bit wild and a whole lot uninhibited swept through her. Framing his jaw in her hands, she opened her mouth wider beneath his and took control before she came to her reliable, responsible senses. The pace of their kiss immediately quickened, grew wetter and deeper and shockingly suggestive as their tongues entwined and stroked and mated.

Amazed that she could feel so physically needy, so intensely aroused so quickly, she gave into the sensations lapping at her feminine nerves, screaming for a more sexually charged contact. Locking her calves at the back of Marc's muscular thighs, she pulled him even closer, welcoming the heat and pressure of him against her newly aroused, swollen flesh.

Marc groaned deep in his throat, the sound reverberating against her lips, her breasts, her belly, *between her thighs.* Unable to help herself, she tilted her hips and deliberately rubbed against the hard ridge straining the fly of his jeans. She rubbed sinuously again and gasped as he instinctively pushed back, a slow, purposeful stroke that seemed as intimate as him being inside her.

That shameless friction triggered a rush of dampness, a deep clenching of her body, and stole her breath. Their hot, openmouthed kiss turned ravenous and urgent, and he did it again, sliding rhythmically against her, as if he couldn't help himself.

Desire rippled through her, coiling tight in her belly. An explosive, wondrous climax beckoned, and she whimpered, struggling between holding on and letting go of those restrictions and good-girl tendencies that had ruled her life for so many years.

And just like the first time they'd kissed, she came to

her senses and *panicked.* Physically, he thrilled her, turning
her on faster than any man ever had. But it was the complex
emotions he evoked that threw off her balance.

The sound of the snowmobiles approaching the cabin
escalated Brooke's alarm. Wedging her hands between
them, she pushed her palms against his shoulders frantically, and he immediately came to his senses and
pulled away.

Stumbling back, Marc plopped down in the nearest
chair, looking dazed and undeniably aroused. "Wow,"
he murmured, scrubbing a hand over his jaw. "That was
incredible."

Scrambling down from the table, Brooke pressed her
palms to her flaming cheeks, unable to deny his claim. Her
body buzzed with unfulfilled desire, throbbing for the
climax that had been so, so close. She'd been so primed
he could have taken her on the table—and how would she
have explained her torrid embrace to her sister, who was
only a room away? No doubt Jessica would call her a fool
for getting involved with another Jamison, for allowing
hormones to reduce her to a mass of nerves and sensations
with only a need for ultimate satisfaction on her mind.

What made her believe she could indulge in a mind-
blowing kiss with him and not want more?

She shook her head, afraid to think of what might
happen with all that volatile passion if they ever made
love. Not that she was contemplating getting naked with
him! "Marc, we can't do this."

"I know," he agreed, his voice tight and strained. He
shifted in his chair to find a more comfortable position.
Clearly unable to accommodate the bulge straining the
zipper of his jeans, he instead clasped his hands strate-
gically in his lap.

She straightened her sweater with a yank, and nearly groaned as the rasping sensation tantalized her sensitive nipples. "Well, don't worry, it won't happen again."

His gaze narrowed perceptively, a spark of Jamison challenge glimmering in his eyes, as if she'd issued him a dare. "You don't think so?"

"I *know* so," she said adamantly.

The sound of Shane's deep voice and Stacey's flirtatious laughter drifted from just outside the kitchen door leading to the back area of the cabin. Brooke willed the couple inside, fervently hoping they'd interrupt what had become a very awkward conversation.

Marc glanced at the door, then back at her, knowing his time was limited. "Brooke, two people don't kiss like that unless there's a certain chemistry and a strong attraction between them."

One she couldn't afford to explore further. Not with him. "Call it a release of sexual frustration. It's been a long, celibate year for me."

Irritation creased his expression at her flippant tone. "So you're insinuating that you would have responded to *any* man the same way?"

No, she thought miserably, knowing that a faceless stranger wouldn't have evoked such a startling heat, hunger and *need*. But that was part of the problem with Marc. She'd never responded so shamelessly, so eagerly to a man in her entire life. Neither Eric nor her one sexual encounter in college had prepared her for this. Marc's magnetism and appeal seemed to strip away every proper, responsible characteristic she'd honed since the age of thirteen, reducing her to a sensual creature who couldn't get enough of that blend of excitement and ecstasy Marc's kisses promised.

She shrugged indifferently, letting the gesture speak for itself, since she couldn't bring herself to lie to him.

His lips at first pursed, then he opened his mouth to argue—just as the back door opened and Stacey and Shane entered the kitchen, thankfully intercepting his rebuttal.

"That morning ride was incredibly exhilarating!" Stacey said, sounding like a giddy schoolgirl in the throes of her first crush.

Ignoring the extra occupants in the room, Marc swallowed back whatever words he'd been about to impart, but boldly held Brooke's gaze. Indeed, she couldn't look away. Through the slight haze of frustration and confusion, his eyes conveyed a startling message—they weren't finished with this particular issue. And he wasn't finished with her.

The silent claim he staked caused Brooke's internal temperature to spike, despite the gust of cool air Shane and Stacey's arrival had invited into the room. Her traitorous pulse fluttered, stoking the desire simmering just beneath the surface. Did she even stand a chance if Marc followed through with that sexy threat to pursue her?

"Umm, are we interrupting something?" Stacey asked, too much interest infusing her voice.

The last thing Brooke wanted was Stacey speculating over her relationship with Marc, and coming to conclusions she didn't want to discuss with a woman who had a fearless, fabulous sex life.

Before she could formulate a response, Marc stood, the evidence of what had transpired between them earlier not nearly as obvious now that his body and libido had time to cool. "You're not interrupting anything that Brooke and I can't resolve at another time." Though he answered Stacey, his gaze never wavered from Brooke's.

In her opinion, there was nothing left for them to resolve. Of course the rogue knew she wouldn't oppose him with an audience listening in on their debate.

Finally, he glanced at Shane. "You ready to head over to the lodge for the day?"

Shane exchanged a reluctant look with Stacey that made it clear they would have preferred to spend the day together. "Yeah, I'm ready."

Stacey winked at Shane as she casually pulled off her lined gloves. "I'll catch up with you on the slopes later," she promised.

The two men left the kitchen, and an unnerving silence settled over the room.

Stacey unwrapped the colorful scarf from her neck, a knowing smile curving lips stung red from the cold. "Well, well, well," she murmured.

Brooke knew exactly what those three simple words meant, knew precisely what was tumbling through Stacey's mind. She held up a hand to ward off her friend's interrogation. "I don't want to talk about it."

"All right," Stacey conceded, but her gaze sparkled with mischief and a wicked provocation. "You ready to put last night's plan into action?"

*No.* Without the buzz of the margarita giving her courage and with the taste of Marc still lingering on her tongue, going out on a man-hunt held little appeal. But she desperately needed the distraction, and there was always the possibility that flirting with another man, and enjoying his attentions, would make her forget about Marc and that luscious, earth-shattering kiss they shared.

Pulling in a deep breath, she fabricated an optimistic smile. "I'm ready. Let's do it."

STACEY NUDGED BROOKE with her elbow and gestured to a good-looking blond-haired guy making his way to the end of the line for the ski lift, where the two of them were waiting their turn.

"What do you think of him?" Stacey asked out of the corner of her mouth. "He has a great body, and a nice smile."

Brooke tried to regard her friend's newest quarry objectively, and like every other man Stacey had singled out, she found herself comparing him to Marc, whose body proved to be a perfect fit for hers, and who owned a lazy smile that seemed to stroke her senses as intimately as a caress. This guy's physique didn't spark even a glimmer of interest, and his smile was a shade too cocky for her liking. And she was coming to realize that she preferred dark hair over light.

A curvaceous woman crossed the man's path. Without an ounce of subtlety, he craned his neck around and lowered his sunglasses to gawk at her retreating backside, a wolfish smile transforming his features.

Brooke rolled her eyes, completely turned off by the guy's arrogance and playboy image. "He looks like he's on the prowl."

Amused laughter bubbled out of Stacey as they moved closer to the head of the line. "Oh, and we aren't?" she asked wryly. "I thought finding a man for you was the purpose of today's expedition."

"It was. I mean, it *is*," she amended, trying to sound enthusiastic. "I just haven't seen a guy yet that makes me want to tap into that wild side you're so sure I'm suppressing."

The ski lift attendant motioned them into position, and both she and Stacey held tight to their poles as the next chair swung around, swooped them up and began its ascent to the top of the intermediate slope.

"You've rejected about a dozen prospects so far just at a glance, without giving any of them a fair chance," Stacey said, continuing their conversation without missing a beat. "There are only so many single men on the mountain, Brooke, and you've narrowed the field considerably."

Brooke made a playful face at her friend. "The day is young, and we still have all afternoon." She shrugged. "I don't want to 'settle.'"

A sudden, dreamy sigh drifted from Stacey. "I, personally, would settle for Shane, and be perfectly happy for the rest of our vacation."

"I think the feeling is mutual." Brooke grinned at Stacey's obvious intentions. "I take it you're going to 'just do it' with Shane?"

"Oh, yeah." Stacey waggled her brows lasciviously. "The first chance we get."

Brooke chuckled and shook her head. Glad that she'd managed to reroute Stacey's thought process, she glanced down at the crowd of people below enjoying the recent snowfall, and promptly frowned when she caught sight of Marc at the base of the beginner's slope. He was hard to miss, with his shock of thick black hair, those wide shoulders she'd clung to this morning and black Lycra coveralls that defined his lean, honed body and sexy male attributes.

He was helping a little girl about the age of eight learn to ski, and alternating his attention to the very grown woman accompanying the child. The redhead appeared completely captivated with Marc and had no qualms about touching him at every opportunity.

She released a disgruntled snort that did little to alleviate the growing pressure in her chest. Their kiss wasn't even cold and Marc was already moving on to another more willing female. As the lift climbed higher, she twisted around to keep him in sight, disgusted with her weakness for yet another Jamison. And she fiercely resented that the lusty embrace they'd shared in the kitchen had meant very little to Marc, while her body was still trying to deal with the shimmering after-effects of that encounter.

"For crying out loud, Brooke, I can't take this anymore."

Stacey's exasperated tone had Brooke straightening in her seat so fast she nearly gave herself whiplash. The carriage rocked precariously, and Brooke gripped the safety bar for support. "You can't take what anymore?" She blinked in wide-eyed innocence at Stacey.

Her friend raised a perfectly arched brow. "What's going on between you and Marc?"

"*Nothing,*" she said, then winced at the too-adamant tone of her voice, as if she were trying to convince herself of the fact.

Stacey scoffed. "Yeah, right. There were enough sparks in the kitchen this morning to light up the sky on the Fourth of July." A humorous smile curled the corners of her mouth. "Maybe you don't need to look any further than our own cabin for your *prospect.*"

"Are you nuts?" Her high-pitched voice echoed in the high altitude, and she lowered her volume when she realized she'd garnered the attention of the couple ahead of them. "Marc is my brother-in-law!"

"Ex," Stacey reminded her oh-so-helpfully, making the excuse a flimsy one. "Which makes him just as eligible for your vacation fling as any other man in Quail Valley."

Brooke sucked cold mountain air into her lungs, which only served to make her light-headed. "Except for the fact that he's not a stranger I can just leave behind." She had a feeling if she sampled a taste of mindless sexual gratification with Marc there would be no going back, that she'd want more than he was capable of giving—like sentimental desires and expectations. She wasn't willing to risk the staid, orderly existence she'd adopted after her divorce for that kind of emotional upheaval.

The chair headed toward their drop-off, and Stacey flipped up the fur-lined collar of her jacket around her neck while slanting Brooke a mocking look. "Jeez, it was just a suggestion. You don't have to get so defensive."

"I'm not getting defensive," she argued, then immediately softened her tone. "I'm trying to be reasonable."

"I thought we agreed that was part of your problem, that you're way too analytical and pragmatic." She tugged on her gloves, and gripped her ski poles in her right hand in anticipation of exiting the lift. "Judging by that flush I saw on your face this morning in the kitchen, I'm guessing that Marc turned you on."

Brooke's cheeks burned, and it had nothing to do with the cold or stinging breeze, and everything to do with Stacey's accurate summary of her morning episode with Marc. She didn't bother issuing a futile denial when the truth remained, that she was *still* turned on.

Stacey grinned in her own personal victory. "Why pursue some stranger if the guy who turns you on is standing right in front of you?" Having imparted those pearls of wisdom, Stacey released the safety bar and glanced at her one last time. "Now, if you don't mind, I've got my own prospect to pursue."

Brooke slipped her sunglasses back on to cut the glare from the sun and snow. "Shane doesn't stand a chance."

Stacey's laugh was throaty and very confident. "Of course he doesn't. Ta-ta for now." And then she was off.

Brooke hopped down from the lift after Stacey and skied down the slope at a leisurely pace. By the time she reached the base, Marc and the redhead were nowhere to be found. Brooke wasn't surprised. Attempting to put him out of her mind, she forced herself to enjoy the great skiing conditions and exercise.

The afternoon passed quickly. At a quarter after three Brooke decided on one last run before heading to the lodge for a latte, and to wait for Stacey so they could head back to the cabin. She trudged toward the ski lift line to wait her turn.

"Mind if I share a chair with you?"

Every nerve ending tingled to life at the deep, masculine timbre of Marc's voice. She glanced over her shoulder and found the object of her fantasies standing there with an adorable grin tipping the corners of his mouth. He wore reflective sunglasses, and she disliked being at a disadvantage, unable to read that bold gaze of his.

She gave an indifferent shrug, though she was feeling anything but. "No, I don't mind."

Once they were situated on the lift and the chair began its climb skyward, Brooke slanted him a casual glance. "Did things not work out with the redhead?" she asked, and immediately chastised herself for being so blunt.

Finally, he removed that barrier in front of his expressive eyes, letting the nylon cord around his neck catch the sunglasses as they dropped against his chest. Tilting his head, his brows puckered thoughtfully. "The redhead?"

As if he didn't know who she was talking about! "The one with the little girl."

Understanding dawned, and the knowing grin spreading across his handsome face crinkled the skin at the corners of his eyes. "Ahh, the *redhead.*"

Brooke bit the inside of her cheek, too affected by the teasing glint in his smoky-gray eyes. Despite herself, she marveled that Marc was so different in personality from his older, more serious brother—so fun-loving, carefree and playful. But there was one similarity the two brothers shared, a significant characteristic she couldn't discount. "You move on quick, Jamison."

Stretching his arm across the back of the chair, he touched his gloved fingers to her jaw, his bemusement fading into something far more resolute and sincere. "And you're jumping to wrong conclusions, honey."

A head-to-toe shiver coursed through her. It had nothing to do with the cold weather, but was provoked by the rumbly sound of his voice, the heat in his gaze, and the raspy feel of his glove against her skin. *Honey.* The endearment was intimate and personal, a pet name even Eric hadn't used with her. It made her feel special and cherished and too close to falling for Marc's innate charm.

Trying not to let his sweet-talk distract her, she responded to his statement with a challenge of her own— even as her mind whispered that she shouldn't care what his intentions with the redhead had been. Unfortunately, their kiss had struck a possessive bone in her body she hadn't known existed. "Am I jumping to the wrong conclusion?"

"Yeah, you are." He held her gaze, his eyes clear and

honest, offering her something Eric never had—a keen sense of trust. "I know how it probably looked, but I was teaching the little girl to ski. She'd taken a couple of hard spills and was crying because she was frustrated, and I didn't want her to give up when I knew once she got the hang of it she'd have a blast."

"Ahh," she murmured, striving for a humorous note. "A very clever way to get to know her mother better."

He laughed, the rich, unfettered sound wrapping around Brooke like a warm, fuzzy blanket on a chilly day. "Oh, the woman was definitely interested, but I wasn't. But don't worry, I let her down gently." He blinked those long, sooty lashes of his lazily. "I spent about an hour with Amber, showing her the basic moves, and before long she was mastering the bunny slope and I had a line of about half a dozen other kids begging for lessons."

"So you spent the afternoon teaching kids how to ski?" She couldn't keep the incredulity from her voice.

"Pretty much." He gave her French braid a gentle tug. "Don't look so shocked. I enjoy kids."

Brooke pictured the scene, with Marc surrounded by six or more eager children, all vying for his attention. Judging by the wide grin on his face, he'd reveled in playing ski instructor to the little imps.

"I have to admit that I *am* surprised. Eric was never really comfortable around children."

Marc's lips thinned. Obviously, the comparison didn't please or flatter him in the least. "And you just automatically assumed the same applied for me?"

She glanced away, toward the approaching unloading station, ashamed to admit that she'd done exactly that—unfairly painting Marc with the same brush as

Eric when there was so much she didn't know about Marc. She owed him an apology.

Meeting his troubled gaze, and wondering about the emotions swirling in the shadowed depths, she attempted to explain. "I'm sorry—"

"I don't claim to be perfect, Brooke," he cut in quickly, seeming to want to state his own argument before they reached the ramp and he lost the opportunity. "I've made mistakes I'm not proud of, but I'd like to think that I've learned from them. I just want you to know that what you see is exactly what you get. I don't pretend to be anything more or less."

Brooke swallowed, hard. What she saw was someone who was caring and *honest*, a trait she'd learned to value above all else at a very early age. A quality she'd realized too late had been absent in her marriage to Eric. She appreciated that characteristic in Marc, along with his ability to speak openly and candidly without fearing what others might think. She was learning that he was a man who didn't hide behind pretenses...as his brother had.

The chair made the connection into the station and the safety bar unlatched under the pressure of Marc's gloved hand. He glanced at her one last time and flashed her a quick smile that dissolved the serious moment and put their relationship back into familiar territory—as friends.

"Thanks for the ride." Slipping on his glasses, he moved to the edge of his seat until his skis skimmed hard-packed snow. "I'll see you back at the cabin."

She watched him go, then followed behind. While Marc navigated the hill with finesse and speed, Brooke opted to take her last ride down the slope slow and easy.

*What you see is exactly what you get.* Marc's comment echoed in her mind, along with Stacey's remark about him being a suitable prospect. The two went hand in hand, she realized with sudden insight.

She'd automatically discounted the idea of having a wild fling with Marc as ludicrous, but now she reconsidered that option. He might not be a stranger she could leave behind, but he was a man who wouldn't expect anything more from her than the good time she was determined to have before returning to her dependable job and her responsible, *boring* life. Separating her feelings for Marc from her quest for physical gratification wouldn't be easy, but she was determined to have this, and him, and for once in her life ignore her practical, sensible nature.

Their undeniable attraction was a bonus, and they'd proved with two kisses that the chemistry between them would be explosive. Awesomely so. She didn't doubt that he'd be an attentive, focused lover…and she could depend on him to keep their liaison discreet.

A slow smile curved her mouth. He *was* the perfect candidate. She knew and trusted him, which made more sense than taking a risk with someone she truly didn't know. She and Marc were beyond first kisses, so there would be no awkward moments to worry about, no wondering if *she* turned *him* on. She already knew.

*Oh, yeah,* she thought with a renewed surge of excitement. If she indulged in all Marc had to offer without any expectations besides pleasure and fun, she'd walk away satisfied and Marc would have enjoyed the challenge—a win-win situation.

She wanted this. For once, she wanted to please *herself,* without analyzing the outcome or worrying about consequences. She wanted to shuck her reserved, practical nature, forget insecurities, and experience lust and passion in its fullest measure. Marc had given her a taste of that particular ecstasy, and she was determined to devour the entire sensual feast.

Only one issue stood in her way...figuring out a way to proposition Marc.

# CHAPTER FOUR

MARC TOOK THE SEAT across from Ryan in the cabin's living room and glanced at his friend's swollen foot, which was propped up on the coffee table. "Hey, buddy, how's the ankle doing?"

Ryan shrugged and settled himself more comfortably on the sofa cushion, wincing as the movement jarred his injury. "Okay, but I'm still ticked off at that jerk who cut me off," he grumbled. "I'm pretty sure it's nothing more serious than a slight sprain."

Jessica entered the living room from the kitchen on the tail end of Ryan's comment, holding a bag of ice. "Slight?" she repeated, then rolled her eyes incredulously. "You'd think he'd had his leg amputated by the way he's been complaining and acting completely helpless."

Marc hid a grin, suspecting Ryan's helpless act was strictly for Jessica's benefit. No doubt, he was playing up his injury in hopes of gaining some attention and feminine sympathy, and surprisingly, his ploy had worked to a small degree. "Well, it's nice of you to help him out."

Jessica bent over and arranged the makeshift cold compress on the puffy, purplish skin around Ryan's ankle. "I was passing through the living room and he caught me at a weak moment."

Ryan eyed Jessica's curvaceous backside appreciatively. "Yeah, I'm feeling really weak, and a little feverish, too."

Straightening, Jessica cast Ryan a guileless smile that belied the sassy glint in her gaze. "I'd be happy to get you another ice pack…for your lap."

Shane, who sat on the opposite end of the couch from Ryan, chuckled. As soon as Jessica disappeared into the kitchen again, he addressed Ryan. "You asked for that, Matthews."

"She wants me," Ryan responded confidently. "And it's gonna take a whole lot more than a bag of ice to cool me off where she's concerned."

Marc leaned back in his seat, silently echoing Ryan's sentiment as it pertained to Brooke and himself. Ever since that morning's sexy kiss he'd been feeling hot and bothered, and more than a little restless. The first kiss they'd shared had been a shocking revelation. Their second had been explosive and beyond anything in his experience. The emotional fallout had left him reeling, and completely tied up in knots.

He wanted Brooke more than he'd ever wanted another woman. His need for her was basic and elemental, yet he was smart enough to know that a relationship with her was way too complicated to consider—because of her past with his brother, and his own past mistake that kept him from committing to any one woman.

For longer than he cared to recall he'd harbored a secret attraction toward Brooke. All through her marriage to Eric he'd kept their relationship friendly, flirtatious, and not too personal, infinitely careful not to cross those matrimonial boundaries. Now, he had an overwhelming urge to discover her as a woman, to tap into the thoughts that filled her head, and explore the full extent of their compatibility in bed.

Dangerous, insane, *impossible* thoughts. Yet that knowledge didn't stop him from fantasizing about her, and them, and spinning numerous "what if" scenarios that made him feel hotter than he'd been as a teenager.

Female voices from the loft captured Marc's attention and drew his gaze to Brooke and Stacey as they descended the stairs to the lower level of the cabin. He and Brooke hadn't talked since their conversation on the lift, and as their eyes made contact he detected something different about her.

He'd expected polite reserve and a whole lot of distance after his honest, "what you see is what you get" spiel. Yet she exuded a new kind of confidence in the smile lifting the corners of her lush mouth and in the easy, sensual way she moved. The sway of her slender hips mesmerized him, her lithe legs encased in those form-fitting leggings provoked wicked, sinful thoughts that, unfortunately, would never play out in real life.

"So, what do you think, Marc, do you still want to grab dinner at the lodge?" Shane asked.

Marc blinked and transferred his gaze to his friends. "Are you okay with that, Ryan?"

"Hey, don't let me stop the two of you from having a good time," he replied sincerely. "I'll be fine."

"Grabbing dinner at the lodge sounds good to me," Marc agreed, figuring he'd be better off in a crowd of people than alone with Brooke in this tiny cabin. "And since there are only two of us going, we can take the snowmobiles."

"Sounds like fun," Stacey said as she and Brooke

strolled over to the couches, just as Jessica exited the kitchen with a mug of hot tea. "Brooke and I were just talking about heading to the lodge for dinner, too, and maybe some dancing afterward. Would you two mind if we hitched a ride on the snowmobiles?"

"Not at all," Shane replied quickly, his tone as enthusiastic as his smile.

Marc fully expected Brooke to balk at the bold way her friend invited them along, and the obvious fact that she'd be partnered with him for the ride. But again, that new poise and self-assurance presented itself, making him wonder what she was up.to.

Brooke cast a concerned look her sister's way. "Are you okay with me going to the lodge for the evening, Jess?" she asked, her insinuation clear. With the four of them gone, Jessica would be alone with Ryan.

Jessica took a sip of her tea, her eyes gleaming mischievously over the rim of her mug as she considered the question. "No, I don't mind," she said after a moment. "I kinda like the thought of having a crippled lawyer at my mercy."

Ryan groaned good-naturedly. "Go easy on me, sweetheart."

"See, he's already pleading for deliverance," she quipped, a triumphant smile curving her mouth. "Don't worry about us, we'll get along *just* fine."

Twenty minutes later, the four of them were dressed in their snowsuits over their regular clothing to keep warm during their ride to the lodge. Outside, they paired up to each snowmobile.

"See you there," Stacey called out and waved back at Marc and Brooke before wrapping her arms securely around Shane's waist. The snowmobile's engine rumbled, and then they drove off with the illumination of the full moon leading the way.

Brooke watched them go, then glanced up at the night sky. "Looks like there are some heavy clouds moving in," she commented, tugging on her gloves. "Have you heard what the weather is supposed to be like for the next few days?"

"Nope." Marc sat astride the long seat and slipped his insulated helmet over his head. "When I come up to the mountains, I try to leave all aspects of civilization behind, including radios and TVs. As far as the weather is concerned, I just go with the flow and hope for lots of fresh snow."

She approached the snowmobile, a wry smile on her lips as she buckled her helmet strap beneath her chin, leaving the face shield open. "If you claim to leave civilization behind, what excuse do you have for the cell phone I've seen you talking on a few times since you've been here?"

He absently patted his jacket, checking for the compact phone he kept tucked inside the breast pocket. "That's one thing I don't leave home without. I'm up here to relax, play and have a good time, but bottom line, I've got a business to run and I like to stay in touch with my secretary, and my foremen."

He slapped his gloved hand to the space behind him, beckoning her with a lazy smile. "Hop on."

The Brooke he knew would have scrutinized the situation, deemed the proximity of their bodies too intimate and possibly bowed out at the last minute with a convenient excuse. Without delays or the uncertainties he'd come to associate with Brooke when it came to *them,* she straddled the leather seat behind him. Her spread thighs bracketed his, and her pelvis cradled his bottom with snug precision.

Gulping cold air, he turned on the engine and let it idle and warm while marveling at her daring demeanor. He had no idea where or when the transformation had occurred, but he couldn't deny that Brooke's newfound confidence and sensuality tightened his gut and made resisting her difficult as hell.

It also made him want to see just how far she was willing to go with her blossoming, sexy, arousing attitude. The challenge was too appealing to pass up. He revved the engine, making the seat beneath them vibrate as the RPMs climbed, then turned his head to the side so she could hear him. "What kind of ride are you looking for? You want to take it slow and easy, or do you want it fast and wild?"

The question startled her—the slight stiffening of her body gave her away—but she recovered quickly. She leaned forward, so that her chest pressed against his back and the sides of their helmets touched. "If you think you can keep it up, I'll take it fast and wild." Her breath was so warm, the night so cold, that her breath evaporated in a puff of white that seemed to glow in the darkness.

He chuckled, enjoying their sexy banter too much. "I've never had a problem keeping it up before." He switched on the headlamp and tossed out a last safety precaution. "Hold on tight, honey, and get ready for the ride of your life."

She did as he instructed, wrapping her arms around him and aligning their bodies from shoulders to knees. Her arms rested low on his hips, and her gloved and entwined fingers settled in his lap. His clothing was layered, but even through thermal, denim and the insu-

lated down of his snowsuit pants he could feel the tantalizing pressure of her hands.

In an effort to cool his response, he took off toward
the lodge, giving Brooke the thrill ride he'd promised
her. He hit every slope on the way, making her squeal
in a combination of delight and fear. They arrived at
their destination almost half an hour later because he'd
played along the way, laughing and breathless, and
Marc felt more in control of his libido.

He planned to keep things that way for the evening,
even if being chivalrous killed him. For as much as
Brooke was sending off those sensual, flirtatious
signals, for as much as he wanted to give free license to
that mutual attraction and desire, he knew too much
about regrets to take advantage of what she was subtly
intimating. He wasn't about to compound the guilt he
carried by adding Brooke to his unrelenting conscience.

He parked the snowmobile in the designated area,
and they met up with Stacey and Shane just inside the
lobby of the lodge. The heat inside engulfed them,
warming their faces and thawing cold body parts.

Men's and women's changing areas and locker
rooms flanked the long ticket desk in the lobby, and
Marc deliberately headed toward the men's room while
unzipping his jacket, forcing Shane to follow. The
women automatically drifted to their side, too.

"We'll see you two around the fire pit in the bar after
dinner," Marc said, effectively establishing the distance
he needed between him and Brooke, while Stacey and
Shane exchanged a look that promised they'd meet up
with one another later.

But it was the disappointment he saw in Brooke's
gaze that made him feel like a heel. Telling himself he

was doing them both a big favor by not pursuing what she was inviting did nothing to ease his conscience, or his need for her.

HOW WAS SHE supposed to seduce Marc when another woman had gotten to him first and was busy attempting the same thing?

Brooke tried not to glare at the pretty blonde bestowing a dazzling smile upon Marc as the two of them engaged in a conversation at the bar in the lounge. Instead, she wrapped her fingers around her mug of Irish coffee and took a drink. Warm liquid settled in her belly, and only seemed to stoke the flames of jealousy flickering inside her.

She shook her head at that thought—she'd never been the possessive sort and was more than a little disgruntled that Marc was the one to evoke such a covetous emotion. And twice in one day!

Even with Eric she'd maintained a level head and sensible attitude about his indiscretions. She hadn't ranted, raved, or made an ugly scene when he'd confessed, just calmly came to the realization that their marriage had been based on false expectations on both of their parts, and that neither one of them had been able to live up to the other's high hopes.

Now that she'd had time to analyze the situation, she'd come to the conclusion that an emotional connection had been lacking in her relationship with Eric. From the beginning they'd been friends. Gradually, they'd become lovers, and from there, they'd each stepped into their role as husband and wife. Despite all that, they'd never shared all the intimacies that most married couples did. Passion hadn't been a part of their union, either. Their relationship had been superficial, with no real substance to hold it together.

She'd fallen for Eric's charm and pursuit and expected a lasting marriage, a house in the suburbs and strong family values that they'd pass on to their children. As for Eric, he'd attempted to deny his playboy tendencies behind the pretense of marriage, but in the end his true nature had prevailed and he'd admitted that he couldn't suppress the urge to be with other women.

They'd opted for divorce, and she'd parted ways with Eric experiencing more disappointment than resentment over the end to their marriage. It had been a mistake, on both their parts. She'd accepted that and was ready to move on to the next phase of her life.

And that phase included seducing the sexy, good-looking man who made her pulse race with desire. Except Marc had his own agenda tonight, which didn't include flirting with *her*.

Sighing, she found Stacey and Shane out on the dance floor having a good time together. At least Stacey had landed *her* man, Brooke thought with a small smile. She saw the blonde at the bar grasp Marc's hand and laughingly insist he dance with her. When he obliged, Brooke decided it was time that she did the same and accepted the invitations of the men she'd been turning down for the past half hour.

Unfortunately, she couldn't drum up any enthusiasm for her partners beyond mild interest. None made her feel desirable or caused that undeniable feminine reaction Marc could elicit with just a grin. There was no instantaneous attraction, no sizzling awareness. No excitement or sexy thrill just by looking into their eyes. Every one of those responses was reserved for the gorgeous bad boy who'd offered her a few token smiles from across the lounge in the past hour.

"Hey, folks," the band's lead singer cut in after the song had ended, garnering everyone's attention. "An emergency weather report just came in and it seems we have a blizzard heading our way and we're going to be in for white-out conditions, possibly through tomorrow. We'll be closing the lodge early so our employees can make it home safely. I suggest you all do the same."

Everyone took the weather report seriously, and the crowd in the bar area immediately dispersed and thinned. Stacey had informed Brooke twenty minutes ago that she and Shane were heading back to the cabin to take advantage of the Jacuzzi, so that left her and Marc to follow behind on their own.

She spotted Marc across the room talking to the blonde, who pouted in disappointment over whatever he was saying. Brooke imagined Marc regretted bringing her along on the snowmobile, which put a definite crimp in any evening plans he might have entertained with the other woman.

After a moment, he strolled over to her, parting ways with the blonde. "You ready to go?" he asked.

She slanted him a meaningful glance, while squashing that green-eyed monster swirling within her. "You know, I'm more than capable of taking the snowmobile back to the cabin by myself if you'd like to spend your evening elsewhere."

He smiled and lightly grasped her elbow as he ushered her toward the lockers. "I'm not going to let you out there on your own with a blizzard heading in."

Concern for her welfare. Nothing more. His indifference toward her the past few hours nipped at her, provoking her, making her irritable and frustrated on too many levels.

By the time they were bundled up in their snowsuits and headed outside, the winds had kicked up and fat flurries were falling. The full moon that had guided them earlier was now covered by dark, menacing clouds. Even the temperature felt as though it had dipped drastically in the few hours they'd been at the lodge. As she trudged behind Marc, the fierce winds stung her cheeks, a warning of more temperamental weather to come.

"It doesn't look like we have a whole lot of time before the brunt of the blizzard hits," she called out to him as she took her place behind him on the leather seat.

He turned his head so she could hear his reply. "I know a short cut. We'll be back at the cabin in no time at all."

She opened her mouth to tell him that she thought they should stick to the familiar trail, but decided against arguing. All she wanted was to get back to the cabin so she could head up to the loft and wallow in her failed attempt to seduce Marc. The sooner they arrived, the better.

She held on as he took off, but this ride lacked the fun and excitement the first one had. There were no sexy innuendos, no laughter, just a straight trek through territory she didn't recognize. The swirl of snow from the oncoming storm reduced their vision and slowed their speed considerably. The path he'd taken was dark and shadowed, and the only sign of civilization she saw was the one unoccupied cabin they'd passed. Tall, snow-encrusted pines loomed over them, adding to the eeriness. Closing her eyes, Brooke rested her head against Marc's shoulders and waited for them to arrive at the cabin.

Unexpectedly, the snowmobile came to a slow, sputtering stop. Brooke lifted her head and frowned when she realized they were sitting out in the middle of nowhere, with the wind howling in the trees and cold chips of snow mingling with the flurries.

"Damn," Marc muttered, the one word as ominous as the elements surrounding them.

Brooke's heart leapt in her chest. "What's wrong?"

"I think we're out of gas." His tone was grim.

"What?" Unable to believe that could be true, she flipped up her face shield and peered over his shoulder at the illuminated panel between the handlebars. "The gauge says you still have a quarter of a tank."

"I know." He opened the gas cap on the metal tank in front of him and rocked the snowmobile with his thighs. They both listened intently for the slosh of liquid, and heard nothing. "The gauge must be stuck or broken, because we're completely empty." Unzipping his jacket, he pulled out his cell phone, pressed the on button, but didn't look hopeful as he stared at the digital display. "I can't call for help. We're out of range."

"Great," she said, dismounting the machinery and yanking off her helmet as adrenaline flowed through her. Fear, dread, and the accumulation of frustration from that evening's events mingled into a potent combination, and she jabbed an accusing finger his way. "Just great, Jamison! Here we are stranded somewhere off the beaten path of God knows where, without anyone knowing where we are. Even on the off chance that Shane or someone else came looking for us they wouldn't find us because you didn't take the normal route!"

He removed his helmet and stabbed his fingers through his hair. "Stop yelling," he said, his voice even and composed.

"Like it matters!" she shouted even louder, and threw up her arms to emphasize her point. "It's not as though there is anyone around to hear me."

"I hear you just fine, and you're making it difficult for me to think."

"If you were *thinking*, we wouldn't be in this predicament in the first place." She paced in front of the snowmobile, dismayed to realize that with each step she was sinking up to her calves in the fresh layer of snow. Not a good sign.

Trying to keep a clear head and her perspective on the situation, she glanced ahead, where the beam from the headlight barely penetrated the sheet of white in front of them. "How much further ahead do you think our cabin is?"

Hooking his helmet on the handlebar, he swung a long leg over the seat and stepped off the snowmobile. Very carefully, and without meeting her gaze, he said, "I'm not sure."

Brooke's stomach dropped to her knees and she gaped at him. "What do you mean, you're not sure? You said you knew a short cut. We should have been to the cabin by now, or at least be close enough to walk there in a few minutes."

"I agree, but I think I veered off too far to the right at that cutoff a ways back." He braced his fists on his hips and worked his mouth in thought. "I don't remember seeing that cabin we passed when I took this short cut yesterday."

"You mean you don't know where we are?"

"I know *approximately* where we are."

"Approximately?" Her voice rose to a hysterical pitch when she realized the ramifications of his statement. "We have a major storm heading in and you're not even sure where we are or what direction it is to our cabin?"

He cast her a placating look. "Brooke, calm down."

Furious at him for numerous reasons, most of which stemmed from her lousy evening at the lodge, she bent down and scooped up a gloveful of snow and packed it into a solid ball. Then she vented. "Don't...tell... me...*what to do!*" She pitched the snowball at him and gained a measure of satisfaction when it splattered on his chest.

An annoyed frown creased his brows. "Dammit, Brooke, stop it."

Rebelliously, she immediately formed another one and threw it, and he ducked as her icy bullet came precariously close to his head. She continued her assault on Marc, heedless of the frigid air and the large, moist clumps of snow eddying around them. He cursed and held his arms up to ward off her blows, but she managed a few good shots.

She ranted and raved, and irrational or not considering the circumstances, the release felt so, so good. She'd learned from an early age to keep her feelings bottled up inside, not wanting to burden anyone else with her emotions when she was supposed to be the strong one. Now, the irritation she'd experienced at the lodge took precedence, making Marc an easy target.

He tried to reason with her, but she was too intent on making him suffer. She cursed him and his short cut that had stranded them. She insulted his lousy sense of direction. She addressed every issue but the one that really had her riled.

And then the rogue started laughing, which increased her temper. As she dipped down to scoop up more ammunition, he unexpectedly lunged toward her. Eyes wide in surprise, she tried to escape him, but her boots felt heavy, her legs like rubber. She turned, only to have him snag her around the waist and tackle her. She twisted in his embrace and cried out as she fell, burying her backside a foot deep in snow. Marc landed on top of her with a muffled "oomph." His ragged breath was blessedly warm on her face, and his large body sheltered her from the wind and falling snow. The weight of his body, however, threatened her sanity and caused a liquid rush of desire to spread through her veins.

Before she could react, his mouth came down on hers, hard, demanding and incredibly possessive. She gasped as the shocking contrast of his cold lips gave way to the delicious heat of his mouth, then the incendiary stroke of his tongue against hers. He kissed her deeply, aggressively, possibly punishing her for her numerous hits with those snowballs.

Reminding herself that she was mad at him, she jerked her lips from his and pushed at his shoulders. She struggled beneath him, but he wouldn't budge. In frustration, she blurted out, "I bet you're sorry you didn't leave with that blonde, aren't you?" As soon as the words left her mouth, she instantly regretted the outburst.

It was dark outside, darker still cocooned beneath him, but she saw the corner of his mouth hitch up in a cocky grin. "Ahh, now we're getting to the crux of your attitude."

She set her jaw and said nothing. She'd revealed too much already.

"You're jealous," he murmured, his tone oddly affectionate.

"I am *not*," she refuted adamantly, unable to admit

the truth to him. It was difficult enough admitting the truth to herself! "Being jealous would imply that I care about your sex life and who you date."

"And you don't care?" he asked, amusement threading his rich, husky voice.

"No," she replied primly.

"Liar." His expression softened, and a gust of air left his lungs, rife with resignation. "Just for the record, that other woman at the lodge was just a diversion from all those sexy signals you were sending off earlier. But it didn't work. I still don't want any woman but *you*."

With that startling revelation, he pushed off her and stood, then offered her his gloved hand. "Come on, we need to find shelter."

Knowing now was not the time to pursue his comment, she accepted his assistance. Ducking her head against an onslaught of flurries, she followed him back to the snowmobile, where he opened the compartment under the seat and withdrew a flashlight and a small emergency survival kit containing flares, matches, dried food and other necessities.

Now that the heat of her anger had been purged, the severity of their situation hit Brooke full force. Her teeth began to chatter and a chill slithered down her spine. She reached for her insulated helmet and slipped it over her head, knowing she'd need the added warmth. "If you're not sure where we are, or what direction the cabin is in, what are we going to do?"

He switched on the flashlight then turned off the snowmobile's headlamp. Pocketing the keys, he swung the small replacement beam back toward the way they'd come. "Our choices are limited. Staying here isn't an option, so we're going to have to head back to that cabin we saw and stay there for the night, or until this storm passes."

## CHAPTER FIVE

"THERE'S THE CABIN, just up ahead," Marc said to Brooke as his flashlight beam finally lit on a small structure coated in snow, a welcome sight that would provide them with the warmth and shelter they desperately needed. His thighs burned with the effort of trudging through knee-deep snow and leaning against the fierce gusts. He imagined Brooke was experiencing the same agony, but she hadn't issued any complaints.

"Thank God," came her muffled response through the shield of her helmet as she plodded along next to him. "I was beginning to think you'd misjudged your sense of direction again."

Though her tone held a wry note, she clearly sounded relieved, as was he. What had taken minutes by snowmobile had taken nearly an hour by foot. The winds, icy snow, and poor visibility had worked against them, and though he'd never admit it to Brooke, Marc *had* started to worry that he'd gotten them completely lost.

The emergency survival kit was tucked securely in his jacket, but the last thing he wanted was to test its reliability against the fury of a blizzard. Despite the fact that they were protected from head to toe in insulated gear and that the walking had kept their blood heated and flowing, the freezing temperature had managed to creep through seams and small openings, sending an occasional shiver coursing through him.

Once they were under the awning of the tiny porch and deemed the place deserted, Marc looked around for the best way to break into the cabin. Knowing he had little choice, he busted open one of the four small panes of glass that made up the front window, then reached inside with a gloved hand and unlatched the lock. He shoved up the wooden casing, and brushed away the sharp remnants of glass.

"You'll fit through that space better than I will," he said, motioning Brooke over.

She nodded in agreement, and seconds later she'd slipped safely inside the cabin and had the front door open for him to enter. He shoved the door closed behind him, and they both removed their helmets and looked around.

It wasn't much warmer in the cabin, but at least they had a roof over their heads and amenities for the duration of the storm. The structure wasn't anything fancy, definitely a vacation retreat. One sweeping glance of his flashlight encompassed a carpeted living room with a single couch in front of the fireplace, a kitchen with a small table, a bathroom off to the left, and an upstairs loft.

Marc hit one of the switches on the wall, and they both grinned as the lamp on the end table illuminated the room, indicating that the owners kept the electricity supply on. Heading into the kitchen, he turned on the sink's faucet, and wasn't surprised to discover the water had been turned off so the pipes wouldn't freeze. They checked the cupboards and found them stocked with bottled water, canned and packaged foods, and airtight containers holding other staples.

"See what you can find to cover up that hole in the front window," he said, heading back through the adjoining living room to the front door. "I'm going back outside to see if I can locate the valves to turn on the water."

Within an hour, the place was as intimate and cozy as their own cabin. They had running water, along with gas for the water heater and stove. While Marc had been scouring the perimeter of the cabin for those valves, he'd discovered a crate of wood. Against the fierce elements, he'd hauled every last log into the house, and Brooke had patched the window with a piece of cardboard and nails she'd discovered in the back utility room. Though they could hear the wind whistling through cracks and still feel an occasional draft, it was nothing compared to spending the night outside in the company of the storm.

After stripping off his snowsuit and gloves, Marc joined Brooke by the fire. Rubbing his chilled hands together, he glanced at her, immediately picking up on the worry lining her features.

The urge to touch her was strong, and with effort he restrained the tender impulse. He'd revealed way too much after that kiss in the snow, more than he'd intended. If she hadn't known before, she certainly realized now that she had him confused and frustrated, and completely tied up in knots, despite his attempt to divert their attraction by fraternizing with another woman. The only thing his efforts had accomplished was to make him more aware of Brooke.

Maintaining distance during their seclusion and not taking advantage of their attraction was going to zap every bit of restraint and control he possessed. She knew as well as he did that nothing could come of them being together, no matter how much they both wanted one another. Above all, he treasured his friendship with Brooke, and the possibility of heartache and other emotional complications was too high to risk. They'd already skirted that particular danger with the seductive kisses they'd indulged in, and he knew making love would only up the ante to a level he wasn't prepared to invest in.

And since he wasn't the kind of guy to carry an emergency condom in his wallet, keeping his hands off her was a matter of principle as well as practicality. Never mind that there were a dozen other ways he imagined making love to her that didn't require a prophylactic.

He watched her chew on her full lower lip and ignored the deep clenching of desire in his belly. "Hey, you okay?"

She inhaled a deep breath, momentarily drawing his gaze to the way her breasts rose and fell beneath her tightly knit sweater. "Jessica is probably frantic right about now," she said, turning her deep blue gaze his way. "I really wish there was some way we could reach her and let her know we're both okay. It would make the next day or so easier to get through knowing she wasn't worrying about us. There's a CB radio back in our cabin that Jessica knows about for emergencies. I'm sure she's turned it on by now since we haven't returned, but I guess that does *us* little good."

He grasped a way to ease Brooke's concern. "Unless I can call out on my cell phone." He hated to offer false hope, but he couldn't discount the chance that he might be able to transmit from this area.

Heading back to his snowsuit by the door, he retrieved the unit from his jacket and turned it on. The signal remained non-existent. Not willing to overlook any realm of possibility, he meticulously strolled around the cabin, covering every inch of space…and finally found a two-foot area near the front window that afforded him a signal, albeit a weak one.

"Got it," he said, grinning victoriously at Brooke, who returned the smile. He dialed 911, and after he explained their predicament, the dispatcher forwarded his call to the ranger's station for help.

Five minutes later, he disconnected the line and headed back toward Brooke, who was kneeling in front of the fireplace and tossing more logs onto the grate. "Now that the ranger station has your CB channel, they'll keep trying to call our cabin until they get hold of someone and assure them that we're safe and okay."

"Good." After arranging the wood with the poker, she stood and set the screen back in place then brushed off her hands. "What about us?"

He placed his phone on the coffee table, next to a small pile of magazines. "They know our location—"

*"Approximately,"* she cut in, her voice infused with a teasing note.

"Yeah, approximately," he reluctantly agreed. Like any other male, he was loathe to admit that he wasn't exactly certain of their whereabouts. "The guy I spoke with said that as long as we aren't in an emergency situation we need to stay put until the white-out conditions improve and they can send out their rescue team."

"And when did they think that would be?"

"According to the National Weather Service, there's another storm right behind this current one. They're expecting four to six feet of snow in the next day or two, without much relief in between."

The implications of his statement couldn't be more obvious. Instead of the apprehension or reservation he would have expected from Brooke, his sister-in-law, an alluring smile curved the mouth of Brooke, the newly confident woman. "Then it's just you and me alone until the blizzard passes."

Marc's heart thumped hard in his chest. The sudden sexy gleam in Brooke's gaze didn't bode well for him, his libido or his willpower.

THEIR SITUATION WAS RIPE with opportunity, and teeming with endless possibilities. Marc, however, wasn't cooperating with Brooke's plan for seduction. Ever since calling the ranger station and imparting the news of their two-day confinement, he'd opted for light and amicable conversation, and avoided close proximity.

That arrangement would change, and soon, considering they'd be sharing the makeshift bed they'd made in front of the fireplace. Neither one of them felt comfortable sleeping in someone else's bed, so they'd opted to spread open a large, flannel-lined sleeping bag they'd found in the closet, and use the pillows and blankets from the loft. The bed was soft, comfortable, and afforded them both their own separate space—*if* they wanted it.

Marc apparently did, considering how neatly he'd aligned his own blanket and two pillows on *his* side of the sleeping bag.

Luckily, she had two days to sway and convince him, to wear down his resistance and lead them both astray.

Releasing a deep sigh to waylay the desire curling low in her belly, she glanced toward the gorgeous, tempting man in the kitchen who'd insisted on making them each a mug of prepackaged hot chocolate before they turned in for the night. She wasn't the least bit tired. Now that her adrenaline surge from their hike through the storm had dissipated, and her initial worry about the others back at their cabin had been eased, her thoughts were focused on the various ways she might entice Marc into accepting her proposition.

Unfortunately, he was being way too chivalrous, and though the old Brooke would have appreciated his gallant attempt to resist her, the newly blossoming Brooke had decided to have this affair and enjoy every aspect of it. Stranded in this little cabin, she didn't have a care in the world, just a burning desire to explore the depths of her sensuality and passion with Marc…no promises involved.

The arrangement should suit Marc perfectly, just as soon as she broke through his reserve.

Figuring tonight was a bust considering everything they'd been through, she sat up and peeled her sweater over her head and tossed it onto the couch, then shimmied out of her leggings, leaving her clad in her long-sleeved thermal top and bottoms etched with tiny pink hearts—nothing remotely sexy or appealing about that! Then she wrangled her way out of her confining bra through her top, and added that to the pile. Removing the elastic band at the base of the French braid she'd worn, she unraveled the strands and massaged her tight scalp. When she turned around, she gasped to find Marc standing by the sofa, two mugs of steaming cocoa in his hands and a lopsided grin on his face that belied the dark, smoldering gray of his irises.

His gaze took in her form-fitting underwear. "I think I have a new appreciation for thermals," he murmured.

This was the flirtatious Marc she knew and felt comfortable with. The inherently sexual man who'd accommodate her request when the time came. "Uh-huh," she said, rolling her eyes at his claim, no matter how complimentary. "I find it hard to believe any man would find thermal appealing. It ranks right up there with flannel."

Marc chuckled, the rich sound filled with relaxed amusement. "It's what's underneath all that thermal that counts. Peeling away all those soft, warm layers to reveal even warmer, softer skin could prove to be a very exciting experience."

*Oh, yeah,* she thought, knowing she wouldn't object if he decided to do just that with her.

He reached out…and handed her one of the mugs of hot chocolate. "This ought to warm your belly before you fall asleep."

She accepted his offering and grinned when she saw the smooth white blob floating on top of her drink. "Hey, where did you find marshmallows?"

"It's marshmallow cream, the kind that comes in a jar." He placed his mug on the coffee table in front of their makeshift bed. "It was in the cupboard."

Settling back down on her side of the sleeping bag, she crossed her legs facing the hearth and waited for Marc to join her.

The lamp behind her snapped off, but the bright fire provided more than enough illumination to make up for the loss of light. She glanced at her watch—it was ten after eleven and definitely bedtime. After the day they'd had she should have been ready to crash, yet she decided if Marc was going to be noble and not touch her, then she wouldn't mind just talking for a while.

Wrapping her fingers around her mug, she brought it to her lips and took a sip. She savored the luxuriant flavor of chocolate filling her mouth, then licked off a smudge of marshmallow that clung to her upper lip.

Behind her, she heard the arousing rustle of Marc removing his sweater, the heart-pounding sound of his jeans' zipper and the scrape of that rough material dragging down his legs before he stepped out of it.

When he joined her in front of the fire, his attire matched hers, minus the pink hearts. She couldn't resist teasing him. "You don't look half-bad in thermal, either." On the contrary, the nubby fabric molded to every hard contour of his body. Judging by the lack of bumps or lines around his hips and thighs, he wasn't wearing any briefs.

He retrieved his hot chocolate off the coffee table, and he flashed a sexy grin.

She watched as he stretched out on his side and propped himself up with his elbow. Taking another drink of the warm liquid, she decided on more stimulating conversation. "I'll bet Stacey and Shane wish they were the ones who were stranded in this storm, instead of us."

He slanted her a curious glance over the rim of his mug. "How so?"

She grinned. "They'd definitely make the most of the seclusion."

He said nothing, though she knew Marc had followed the implication behind her statement—why weren't *they* taking advantage of the isolation that had so conveniently presented itself?

Since he wasn't cooperating with her discussion, she continued. "I have to admit that I've always been a little envious of Stacey, and how she can just enjoy having an affair with a man she's attracted to, no strings attached."

He considered that for a moment. "And you wish you could be like that?"

"In some ways." She shrugged, and set her empty

mug on the coffee table. "I've only recently given it any thought, but it doesn't seem as easy for a woman to just have a physical relationship with a man without gaining a certain kind of reputation."

A smile tipped up the corner of his mouth. "Ahh, the old double standard."

"Yes. It's unfair how it seems acceptable for a man to play the field, but when a woman does the same thing she risks her virtue or respectability."

He mulled over her comment while staring into the depths of his mug, then glanced her way. "Are we talking about the double standard within the bonds of marriage, or being single and unattached?"

"Both, actually." She drew her slender legs up and wrapped her arms around her knees. "I know society has come a long way and we're living in the twenty-first century, but it just seems easier and more acceptable for men to go out and have a fling than for a woman to do the same thing."

"I don't believe in double standards when it comes to sex and relationships," he replied. "A good sexual chemistry should be enjoyed by both partners, for as long as the attraction lasts."

"No commitments, huh?" she asked softly.

He met her stare evenly. "No commitments, Brooke," he said, the statement sounding too much like a warning. "I *avoid* serious relationships."

She rested her chin atop her knees, a compelling blend of curiosity and tenderness weaving through her. "Why?"

He scrubbed a hand over his stubbled jaw, his frown giving her the distinct impression that he'd rather ignore her question. She waited patiently for his reply, wanting to know the reasons why he'd chosen the bachelor route and was so against something permanent with a woman.

As if realizing she wasn't going to let the subject slide, he finally answered. "I learned early on that I don't have what it takes to sustain a lasting commitment." A muscle in his cheek ticked with irritation. "The women I've dated know my rules right up front. I don't make promises I can't keep."

Brooke knew there was more to Marc's statement than a cavalier attitude about relationships. There was something deeper and infinitely emotional behind his words—the misery creasing his expression told a tale of its own. Whatever he'd been through had affected his ability to believe he could be the kind of man a woman wanted for a husband.

"What I see is what I get, huh?" She tossed his own words back at him, suddenly seeing them as an emotional shield he hid behind when things got too intense. Didn't he realize that he'd given her too many glimpses past the surface of that carefree, flirtatious demeanor for her to think him so shallow? She'd seen a side to Marc she hadn't known existed until this weekend, a man with integrity whom she trusted, a man very different from the one he believed himself to be, or the one he presented to everyone else.

"That just about sums it up, Brooke." Abruptly, he stood and picked up her mug from the coffee table. "It's late, it's been a long, exhausting day and I think we both need to get some rest."

He stalked off toward the kitchen, and Brooke let him go, seeing his exit for the diversion it was. She'd touched on personal issues and struck a nerve somewhere. She'd also broached the subject of an affair in a subtle, but unmistakable way. In return, he'd set down his unbendable rules with her, letting her know under no circumstances did he waver from his convictions.

She was forewarned, but not discouraged in the least. She understood and accepted his rules, and she still wanted him and the culmination of pleasure that his kisses evoked.

But for tonight, she'd give him a reprieve. They were both exhausted, and she wanted to be at her freshest when she seduced him. Tomorrow was another day of seclusion, and she wouldn't be as easily denied.

BROOKE GRADUALLY WOKE to the smell of freshly brewed coffee, and the sexy sight of Marc standing in the kitchen by the sink, holding a mug in his hand while he stared out the window. There wasn't much to see outside except a swirl of white, which confirmed they were in the throes of the furious storm sweeping through the Rocky Mountains.

Seemingly deep in thought, he sighed heavily and shifted his stance. The muscles bisecting his back rippled with the movement beneath his thermal shirt, and his jean-clad hip rocked to the side. A small smile played around her mouth as she enjoyed the masculine view—until he turned around and glanced her way, meeting her sleepy gaze. His ebony hair was damp, and the dark stubble lining his jaw and cheeks made his eyes appear black and intense.

A feathery sensation coursed through her, prompting instantaneous awareness. Indeed, the erotic fantasies that had invaded her dreams last night had deepened her aching need for him.

"Morning," she murmured, her voice husky with the remnants of sleep.

"Morning," he returned, then took a drink of the steaming brew in his mug. "How are you feeling?"

Tossing off her covers, she stood, then groaned as muscles she didn't even know she possessed screamed in protest. "Oh, man," she breathed in agony.

The corner of his mouth quirked with amusement. "I think you just answered my question. I woke up in the same sorry condition."

She smiled. "I feel like every tendon from my neck to calves is going to snap if I straighten too fast." Slowly, she reached her arms over her head and arched her back, and winced as her body reluctantly distended. The exercise caused her breasts to thrust forward and her top to lift, exposing a two-inch strip of flesh. He noticed, his gaze lingering, searing her skin.

An annoyed frown creased his brow and he averted his gaze, placing his mug on the counter. "A hot shower will help relax your muscles."

"Sounds wonderful," she agreed, gratified to see that despite his lecture and good intentions last night he was struggling with his own desire. Heading into the kitchen area, she glanced at her watch. It was twenty after eight. "Have you been up long?"

"For a while," he said vaguely, giving her the impression that he'd had a restless night. "I called the ranger station this morning. They confirmed that they got a hold of Shane late last night and gave him the message that we were fine and safe."

"I'm glad." Knowing that Jessica wouldn't spend the next day or so panicking over their whereabouts was a big relief. "Any change in the weather?" she asked, dragging a hand through her disheveled hair.

His jaw tightened. "No." He didn't sound happy

about that fact. Turning away from her, he retrieved a frying pan from below the gas stove and set it on a burner. "Why don't you go take a shower while I make us some breakfast? I found some shampoo, soap, toothpaste and mouthwash, and I left it out for you to use."

"Thanks." Heading into the bathroom, she turned on the water, stripped off her clothes, and stepped beneath the shower spray.

Her head fell forward, and a groan of relief purred in her throat as the hot, pulsating water pounded across her stiff shoulders, loosening muscles and gradually relaxing her body. She shampooed her hair, then soaped up a face cloth and washed from neck to ankle. She turned around to rinse, and gasped as the hard stream of water pelted her sensitive breasts, causing her nipples to peak, then flowed down her belly and trickled between her thighs like the tantalizing stroke of liquid silk.

She shuddered as a shameless kind of pleasure beckoned, swirling around her as feverishly as the steam from the hot water. Closing her eyes, she cupped her hands over her heavy breasts and kneaded the firm flesh, brushed her fingers over the taut crests. Her breathing grew shallow, and her heart pounded hard in her chest.

The need Marc had ignited with his sexy kisses was just as vibrant, just as demanding. Biting her lower lip, she slowly slicked her palms down her stomach, let her fingers graze the thatch of soft curls at the apex of her thighs. Her belly tightened, and her thighs trembled in expectation of that first touch, a deeper caress, and the incredible, shuddering release that would follow.

It would be so easy to take the edge off the desire thrumming through her. Instead, she stopped before indulging in the intimate touch that would end her torment, opting to let the ache and anticipation build.

Marc had roused that sensual hunger within her. *He* would be the one to appease it.

## CHAPTER SIX

"I MADE A PIG of myself." Brooke set her fork on her empty plate and pushed it aside. "I've never eaten six pancakes in one sitting before."

Seated across from Brooke at the small table in the kitchen, Marc chuckled as she pressed a hand to her full stomach, her expression dismayed. "I guess you were hungrier than you'd realized." There certainly hadn't been anything spectacular about the pancakes he'd made from the mix he'd found in the cupboard, or the butter flavored syrup they'd poured on top.

"Hmm," she replied, the sound rumbling sensually in her throat. A slow smile graced her lips, and her gaze took on a shimmering quality that tempted and teased. Hunger took on another meaning altogether.

The insinuation behind that vague response and her body language wasn't lost on Marc. Ever since she'd returned from her shower, she'd been openly flirting with him, heightening the awareness between them.

The woman had seduction on her mind, and he feared his sanity and libido wouldn't survive the length of the storm. Obviously, openly admitting to a love-'em-and-leave-'em attitude hadn't deterred her campaign to tempt him, as he'd hoped.

She stood and leaned across the table, reaching for

his plate, unerringly drawing his gaze to her breasts, which swayed forward with the movement and pressed full and round against her top. The chafe of fabric caused her nipples to peak and his groin to stir. She hadn't put her bra back on after her shower, and wore only her leggings and thermal shirt. The cabin was warm enough that they didn't need more than that.

She stacked his dish and utensils on top of hers. "Since you made breakfast, I suppose the least I can do is clean up the mess."

He swallowed the offer to help along with the last of his coffee, knowing it was best if they kept their distance. The entire day stretched ahead of them, impossibly long and filled with too many appealing scenarios he was determined to avoid.

"Great." He abruptly stood. "I'll go start another fire."

Kneeling before the brick hearth, he removed the screen. He stacked pieces of wood on the grate, stuffed pieces of crumpled paper beneath the logs, and struck a match to ignite the flame. Despite his resolve to resist Brooke, that didn't stop his gaze from continually drifting her way as she cleared the table and washed dirty dishes.

Though she'd towel-dried her hair and combed the strands away from her face, the ends were still damp from her shower. Her skin had been scrubbed clean of makeup, and she looked natural and wholesome, and more beautiful than any of the sophisticated, cosmetically enhanced women he'd dated over the years. She attracted him on too many levels, but it was the way she tugged on his emotional wants and needs that completely disarmed him.

He shook off the sentiment and focused on stoking

the fire. Too soon, she joined him, sitting on the sleeping bag a few feet away from him. Neither one of them had folded their blankets or made their beds—why bother when they'd be there at least another night?

She reached for one of the women's magazines on the coffee table and absently thumbed through the glossy pages. After a moment of skimming the contents, she said, "Now here's an interesting quiz. 'Take our sizzling sex survey and tell us about your sex life.' What do you say you and I fill in the blanks and see how we measure up?"

After placing the poker on the brass rack, Marc straightened the screen in front of the blazing fire, then sat across from her, unable to miss the daring light in her eyes. He turned the magazine his way and perused the article. "You sure about that? Some of these questions are really personal."

"I'm game if you are." She grinned impudently. "It'll pass time, which we have plenty of, and our answers could prove to be quite entertaining."

*And enlightening,* he thought, and knew that was the purpose of her challenge. Knowing she was intent on seducing him regardless of his efforts to resist her, he decided to play into her scheme. He'd be aggressive and push her as far as he could, until she realized she was engaging in a risky game with irreversible, emotional repercussions. Hopefully, she'd rethink her plan to tempt and tease him before she made a big mistake she would regret later.

And most important, this way he'd maintain control of the situation right from the start.

"All right, I'll take the survey with you. And there'll be no cheating or fibbing," he said.

She wrinkled her nose at him and affected an amusing, prim attitude. "I don't cheat or fib."

"That's good to hear." He stretched out on his side, propped his head in his palm, and patted the sleeping bag in front of him. "And you need to come down here so I can look you in the eyes while we're answering our questions."

She hesitated for a brief moment. He supposed she felt a semblance of security sitting upright, elevated above him, but he wasn't going to allow any distance between them. If she planned to push boundaries, he was going to push right back.

She scooted low, until she lay on her side facing him. They weren't touching physically, but a keen sense of intimacy surrounded them.

"Better?" she asked.

Smiling his approval, he nodded. "Much. Let's get started." Pushing the sleeves of his thermal shirt up to his forearms, he glanced at the magazine open between them. "When was your last sexual encounter? Yesterday, last week, one to six months ago, six to nine months ago or over a year?"

He lifted his gaze, meeting Brooke's expectantly, and her stomach took a steep, unexpected dive. Embarrassed to admit just how long it had been since she'd been with a man, she said, "You go first."

He squinted up at the low-beamed ceiling and thought for a moment. "My last sexual encounter would fall in the category of six to nine months ago."

Without a doubt, his reply shocked Brooke—the man was so earthy and physical she'd always imagined he indulged freely in sex. She liked that he was discriminating when it came to whom he slept with. She also realized he hadn't been with a woman since before their first kiss three months ago.

His candid response eased the way for hers. "Mine was over a year ago."

His gaze glittered with too much heat. "Abstinence and the anticipation of wanting someone makes for some of the best sex."

A delicious shiver lapped at her nerve endings, the compelling sensation spreading through her like warm molasses. "I suppose it does," she said breathlessly.

Grinning as if he was enjoying himself, he bent his head back over the test, causing a thick shock of black hair to fall over his forehead. With the light from the fire casting shadows over his face he looked like a sexy renegade.

His body tensed as he perused the next question, and his flirtatious smile faded. "Have you ever engaged in a one-night stand?"

"No." Her reply was immediate. "Have you?"

Slowly, he lifted his head. "Yeah," he admitted with obvious reluctance. "Once. Years ago."

The guilt and regret etching his lean features concerned and bewildered her. "Was the incident that bad?"

He hesitated, scrubbing a hand over the stubble lining his clenched jaw. "It was the circumstances surrounding the one-night stand. It never should have happened."

Whatever had occurred, whatever the reasons, the encounter had affected him deeply. Curiosity stirred within her, as well as the knowledge that despite his carefree bachelor appearance, Marc didn't possess the cavalier attitude toward women and sex that she'd thought he did…that his *brother* did. The revelation was stunning, and reassuring in a way she didn't want to contemplate.

Curving her arm around her pillow, she tucked it more

fully beneath her head. "Next question?" she prompted brightly, anxious to change the subject for his sake.

He looked grateful for her move to dispel the too-serious mood that had settled between them. "Hmm," he said, considering the next topic up for deliberation. "If you weren't in a relationship, would you be willing to have a hot, wild fling with someone who completely turned you on?"

Brooke's skin tightened and tingled at the underlying insinuation in that simple survey question. The statement addressed an issue they'd been avoiding since yesterday morning's kiss and challenged her new dictum to *just do it*. It also tested that wall of resistance Marc had erected between them.

He hesitated, seemingly struggling with his answer. Finally his long, sooty lashes swept upward, revealing eyes that had darkened to charcoal. "As much as I wish I could say no, I'd be lying. I've considered it."

*With you.* The unspoken words hung in the air. Brooke's pulse raced, and her lips parted on a rush of breath. A foot of distance separated them, but that made little difference in her body's reaction to those sultry bedroom eyes, the rich, warm tone of his voice. His deliberate words. Her breasts swelled, and she grew moist between her thighs, which she pressed tightly together. His direct, masculine stare definitely turned her on, seducing her mind, making her ache to feel those callused hands of his skimming her naked skin, to feel his lips and tongue exploring *everywhere*.

A moan slipped past her throat at the provocative image filling her head. Mortified that she'd gotten so carried away, she reined in her lustful fantasy.

His smile turned sinfully confident, too knowing. "I take it you agree?" he asked huskily.

She nodded mutely, not trusting herself to speak. Especially when she realized how aroused he'd become just by watching her face, her expression and hearing the frustrated sound she'd made. His erection jutted against the front of his pants, full and long and incredibly thick.

Without a hint of embarrassment, he angled his leg toward her on the sleeping bag to adjust his position to a more comfortable one. "Shall we go on?" he asked nonchalantly.

A subtle dare, though he was giving her the opportunity to call a halt to this crazy game. Electrifying heat poured over her and shimmered between them, prompting her to explore the depths and boundaries of the sensuality Marc was awakening.

"Go ahead," she whispered.

Lowering his gaze, he skimmed his index finger down the numbered sentences on the page. Dark brows raised with interest as he read, "Would you be open to experiencing new and different sexual positions and techniques that your partner might suggest?"

That sexy grin of his made another appearance. "Sure. Variety is a good thing. It keeps a couple's sex life fun and exciting."

"I'll take your word for it," she said, then grimaced when she realized exactly what she'd revealed—that her sex life hadn't included much variety. There hadn't been much fun or excitement, either. Eric had been just as serious in the bedroom as he'd been outside of it.

Marc splayed his big hand on the opposite side of the survey page, his long, tapered fingers reaching the edges. "You didn't answer the question," he said, not allowing her to retreat on any level. "Yes or no to shedding inhibitions?"

He couldn't have known about her vow to explore her sexuality, yet his eyes glimmered with a hot, intense perception. She swallowed hard and replied, "Yes, I'd do it."

The corner of his mouth curved with lazy humor, and he continued on. "Have you ever brought yourself to orgasm?"

Brooke's pulse thudded, and she pressed her palms to her burning cheeks. "You can't be serious!"

A warm, deep chuckle filled the cozy space between them. "I wouldn't make up something like that. It's right here, see?"

She leaned close, verifying his claim. Her face flamed brighter.

"I'll go first," he offered, his breath warm against her cheek since she hadn't moved back.

She lifted her head and rolled her eyes. "Considering most boys discover at an early age how good *that* feels, I already know *your* answer."

"I think this magazine is referring to a *man* gratifying himself." He worked his mouth back and forth in thought. "Why don't we rephrase the question? How about...have you brought yourself to orgasm within the past six months?"

She gaped at him. "Can we just *skip* this question?"

"No, now you've got me curious—unless you'd rather stop the survey altogether?"

She got the distinct impression that he was hoping for just that, but she wasn't willing to call it quits. "No, go ahead."

Amusement gleamed in his eyes. "Well, since it's

been almost nine months since I've been with a woman, and we are being *honest,* I'd have to say yes, I've brought myself to orgasm in the past six months."

An erotic mental image popped into Brooke's mind before she could stop it, of Marc magnificently naked and aroused, on the verge of ecstasy as his fist stroked his erection in a tight, wet rhythm...

"I guess that blush on your face speaks for itself, huh?"

If he only knew! Her arm clenched the pillow tighter, and she cursed the heaviness between her thighs. She shifted her legs, and nearly gasped at the exquisite friction against her swollen, inflamed flesh. "Yes," she said, her voice raspy.

"Yes, what?"

The man had no shame! "Yes, I've resorted to self-gratification in the past six months," she said between gritted teeth.

His breath left his chest in an audible whoosh. He blinked heavily, scrutinizing her with eyes gradually glazing over with lust. Suspecting that he was entertaining his own personal fantasy, starring *her* in the same role she'd just imagined *him,* she tapped the magazine to redirect his attention. "Next question, Marc."

He shook himself back to the present, then searched to find where they'd left off. "What is your favorite sexual position?" He rubbed his thumb along his chin before answering. "Whatever feels good at the time."

She drew a deep breath that did little to help her regain her composure. "I like being on top."

"Oh, yeah," he agreed, his devastating grin matching his dark good looks. "That feels good *anytime.*"

His eyes went downcast again as he consulted the survey. "Have you ever had multiple orgasms with one partner in a single night?" His chest puffed out a fraction. "Yeah, though I do need time to recuperate in between."

She stifled a grin at his typical male pride, even while she appreciated that he was a generous, giving lover. "I'm impressed."

He lifted a dark brow, silently turning the tables on her. *Have you ever had multiple orgasms?*

At the moment, she was so aroused she felt as though she could have a dozen in rapid succession. She shook her head. "No."

He glanced down at the page, then back up again. "Would you like to?"

Her stomach pitched sideways and a flood of liquid desire weakened her limbs. She eyed him warily, wondering if the man could read minds. "Is *that* on the survey?"

His gaze searched her face, too intently. "No, personal curiosity."

She bit her bottom lip as a slow swell of excitement pounded through her at the thought of indulging in such luxurious, all-consuming pleasure…of freeing her body of all mental restrictions and wallowing in wave after wave of the purest ecstasy a woman could experience. To be greedy, and revel in a man worshiping her body with his mouth and hands, caressing her in carnal ways, discovering sensitive regions and plying her with sensual delights beyond her comprehension.

Brooke tugged at the collar of her thermal top, suddenly burning up. She felt hot and achy and needy…and wondered if she'd have to go outside and roll in the snow to cool off. The icy bath might help the fever spreading across her skin; unfortunately, it wouldn't do much to soothe the fretful knot pulling tighter and tighter inside her. She couldn't remember ever feeling so hot and bothered. So sexually aware of her body.

He waited patiently, *shamelessly,* for her answer.

She cleared her throat. "I don't think it's that easy for a woman to achieve multiple orgasms." Her reply was deliberately evasive, a testimony of her own personal inexperience and an attempt to usher them on to the next phase of the quiz.

"Depends on the woman's partner." The rumbling, seductive undertone to his voice mesmerized her, as did his eyes. "Most women are incredibly sensitive after their first orgasm, but if they relax and you touch them just the right way, soft and slow and gradually build up to a steady rhythm again…"

Brooke's breathing grew ragged, and she held up a hand to halt his outrageous, stimulating monologue, certain she couldn't take much more without embarrassing herself. "I don't think this is relevant to the survey."

A satisfied smile played around the corners of his mouth. "Last question," he murmured, moving on, leaving her frustrated and her body throbbing with an excruciating need. "What arouses you the most?"

She groaned deep in her throat as a multitude of answers bombarded her. *Him. His words. His body. That promise of ultimate pleasure blazing in his eyes.*

He didn't mull over the question for long. "I get really turned on when I'm with a woman who isn't afraid to be aggressive and tell me what she wants or what feels good. How about you?"

Oh, she was feeling *very* aggressive. Shamelessly so. She was tempted to prove her assertiveness, to climb on top of him and kiss him senseless and let him do all those wicked, delicious things to her and

anything else that entered that salacious mind of his.
The reckless urge was so strong it took all her effort to
restrain herself.

Emboldened with sexual confidence, she allowed a
naughty smile to grace her lips. The man liked a woman
who wasn't afraid to tell him what she wanted. This
week, she was supposed to be that kind of brazen
female. Tonight, she'd test her wiles.

Slowly, provocatively, she dampened her bottom lip
with her tongue, and noticed that his eyes watched, and
his body tensed. "What arouses me the most?" she
repeated throatily, reveling in the power she possessed
to excite him. "The way you kiss me," she whispered.

His nostrils flared at her admission, and his eyes
flickered with something dark and predatory. As if she'd
unleashed a sleeping tiger, he moved, quick and precise,
a blur of tan cotton, fluid muscle and virile heat. In less
than a heartbeat he had her pinned beneath his stun-
ningly large body with his elbows trapping her arms at
her sides, and a knee wedged between her thighs.

Their gazes locked, and their ragged breaths came in
unison. They'd avoided touching one another all
morning, instead arousing each other with words and
mental images, which made this contact all the more
electrifying. His unmistakable erection prodded her hip,
throbbing with desire, matching the same pulse deep
within her.

His callused fingers reached her mouth, stroked
across the soft, sensitive flesh of her bottom lip. The
smile that eased across his face was strangely tender, as
if he coveted what he touched. "You're extremely easy
to please," he murmured.

"I've never been kissed like that before," she

admitted, baring herself and unearthing deeply buried secrets she hadn't intended to share with him. Despite all the sexy, personal things the survey had revealed, she suddenly felt very vulnerable and exposed. Somewhere along the way they'd gone from fun and playful, and crossed that forbidden line to something deeper and more serious.

An agonized groan rumbled up from his chest, and he buried his face in her neck, as if he, too, were struggling with some internal battle. His silky hair tickled her jaw, and his hot, moist breath caressed her throat. He shifted his weight, which caused his thigh to press against her sensitive core.

She inhaled sharply as sensations clamored within her. "Marc?" Her voice trembled with undeniable need.

The one word seemed to snap him out of his sensual haze. With a fierce curse, he rolled off her and moved away. Immediately, Brooke missed the warmth and intimacy of him lying on top of her.

He sat with his back braced against the couch and scrubbed both hands down his face, his features haggard with frustration. "I think our conversation has gotten *way* off track."

Brooke disagreed. They were finally *on track,* and she wasn't about to let this opportunity slip out of her reach.

She shifted to her knees, but didn't move closer. Not yet, anyway. "Remember that question on the survey?"

A startling combination of suspicion and sexual heat glowed in the depths of his gaze. "There were *many* questions on that survey," he said cautiously.

She touched her tongue to her upper lip, which had grown dry from a sudden bout of nerves. Seduction had never been her forte. "I'm talking about the one that asked if you'd be willing to have a hot, wild fling with someone who completely turned you on."

"Yeah, I remember," he said, his tone low and rough.

The thudding of her heart couldn't be calmed. "We both said yes."

His hands clenched into tight fists. "I said I've considered it."

"With me?" She needed to hear him say it.

He didn't disappoint her. "Yeah, with you."

A shudder passed through her, igniting her blood with anticipation. "Then we're even. I've considered it with you, too."

A harsh hiss of breath escaped him, and his big body tensed. The very air around them seemed electrified, sizzling with energy and keen awareness.

"I think we've established that we turn each other on." A needy ache tightened her throat, her skin tingled, and her pulse quickened. "I want you, Marc. I want that hot, wild fling with *you*."

Shaking his head in denial, he pressed the heels of his palms against his eyes and gritted his teeth. "Brooke, I'm not sure this is a good idea." Doubts infused his gruff voice.

Feeling desperate, she crawled over to where he sat and knelt in front of him. Gently, she grabbed his wrists and pulled his hands away from his face, undeterred by his fierce expression. "I'm a big girl, Marc. We're both adults, and I'm going into this with my eyes wide-open, with no expectations other than fun and pleasure."

She looked at his big hands next to hers, his long fingers, and trembled at the thought of him touching her, caressing her. "I'm willing to take this as far as you're willing to go. No commitments, no promises and no regrets." She was offering him every bachelor's dream. Where most men would have leapt at her proposition, without conscience, thought or hesitation, Marc's internal struggle proved that he didn't take sex with her lightly.

"Brooke…" Her name on his lips sounded so sweet, so intimate, conflicting with the regret etching his lean features. Reaching out, he brushed her hair away from her cheek, then skimmed his knuckles gently along her jaw. "Not only is this not a smart idea, I don't have any protection with me."

Initial disappointment curled through her, and she immediately squashed the emotion. She wasn't going to give him any excuses to deny her. "A minor technicality I'm sure we can work around. I'm willing to be as creative as our surroundings allow, and as innovative as you want to be."

His eyes darkened, and she imagined he was thinking of all the erotic ways they could pleasure one another. Still, he resisted, wavering between holding back, or accepting her sexy proposal.

She planned to push him over the edge, straight into bliss.

Moving closer, between his legs, she pressed her palms to his chest. Even through his shirt she could feel the heat and strength of him, and his wild heartbeat. Holding his gaze, she boldly slipped her hands down his torso, past the waistband of his jeans and let her fingers trail lightly over the erection straining the fly of his pants.

He sucked in a swift breath, but didn't move, touch her, or try to remove her playful hand.

His willpower amazed her, and challenged her.

Letting her lashes fall to half-mast, she smiled lazily, determined to shatter his control to obtain what she wanted. Recalling the words he'd used on her yesterday morning in the kitchen, she decided to turn the tables on him.

She leaned into him, until her mouth hovered near his ear and she cupped the proof of his desire for her more fully in her palm. "You're *definitely* curious," she murmured, then shivered as his hot, erratic breath stirred against her neck. "I'm tempted, we both want it, so let's do it and enjoy the time together."

He grasped her hand to stop her tantalizing caresses. Lifting her head, she looked in his smoky-gray eyes, expecting a gentle rejection, not the ruthless glint she encountered.

"All right," he agreed, surprising her. "We'll have that hot, wild fling you want. But I want something in return." Bringing the hand that had stroked him to his lips, he placed a kiss in her palm and flicked his soft, warm tongue against the center.

She gasped, feeling that sensual lap all the way to the tips of her breasts. The sensation he evoked was delicious, and incredibly sinful. "What do you want in return?" she asked breathlessly.

"While we're here in this cabin, there is no saying no." He nibbled on the tip of one finger, then another, taking his sweet time toward her pinky. "No restrictions, no inhibitions. *Anything* goes."

Her belly tumbled at his frank request. His gaze was daring, and a trifle dangerous, but she refused to back down now that she'd come so far. Tilting her head, she injected a teasing note into her voice. "Aww, darn it, and here I left my padded handcuffs at home."

A dark brow arched wickedly. "Oh, I'm sure we can

find a way to improvise on that fantasy, or any other you or I have in mind. Anything goes, Brooke," he reiterated, his gaze very direct and wholly male. "Agreed?"

She nodded. "Agreed."

He looked momentarily taken aback at her easy acquiescence. "You're willing to do anything I ask?"

She almost smiled at the surprise in his tone, and realized he'd fully expected her to refuse his outrageous terms. "*Anything,* Marc."

He released her hand, locked gazes, and put her new sexual bravado to the ultimate test. "I want you completely naked."

Her breath whooshed out of her. So much for the slow, tantalizing seduction she'd envisioned. "You want me to get undressed?"

The barest hint of a smile played around his mouth. "Yeah, that's usually how a person gets naked."

She hesitated, feeling a twinge of uncertainty, and modesty. "What about you?"

"Anything goes, Brooke," he said, reminding her of their pact. "This is *my* fantasy. You can have yours later."

She swallowed, hard, and wondered what he intended. "And what fantasy is that?"

"There were two questions on that survey that captured my interest. Or rather, your answers did. The first question asked if you'd be open to experiencing new and different sexual positions. You said yes. Do you still feel that way now?"

She heard the subtle warning in his deep voice, but the thrill of the forbidden was too strong to resist. "Yes," she whispered. "You did say variety is a good thing."

He dipped his head to hide a grin, and a shock of black hair fell across his forehead. "So I did," he murmured. "I just want to be sure you won't object to experimenting now that we're down to the nitty-gritty."

"No," she assured him. Feeling antsy and anxious, she rubbed her damp palms down her thighs. "And the other answer of mine that intrigued you?"

"When I asked you if you'd like to have multiple orgasms, you didn't give me a straight answer." His glittering gaze was hot and intense and filled with the same raw desire pouring through her veins. "I'd like one now."

*Most women are incredibly sensitive after their first orgasm, but if they relax and you touch them just the right way...*

Marc's blatant, outrageous claim echoed through her, stealing her breath and making her head spin.

"Yes or no, Brooke," he asked, his voice a husky growl that rumbled seductively along her nerve endings. "It's a very easy question."

Closing her eyes, she touched her hand to the fluttering pulse in her throat, and imagined his fingers there, on her breasts, and lower...giving her more pleasure than she'd ever had in a single night, in ways she'd only entertained in her mind.

A flush stole across her face, and she lifted her lashes, meeting his smoldering gaze. "Yes, I want those multiple orgasms," she said brazenly.

"And it's my fantasy to give them to you." An incredibly sexy smile lifted his mouth. "And I want you completely naked when I touch you. Those are my terms."

A breathtaking excitement seized her as she imagined the ways he might give her that release. He was being forceful and candid, and obviously believed she wouldn't follow through with her end of the bargain...to do anything he asked.

He was wrong.

Slowly, she stood up and straightened. His gaze leisurely traveled up her legs to her face, his stare bold and earthy and unapologetically sexual. There was no mistaking what he wanted from her. And there was no doubt in her mind that she was going to give him free access to her body, and enjoy every erotic moment. She only hoped that in the end she'd walk away with her heart intact.

Taking a deep breath to banish any last doubts, she reached for the hem of her top and drew it over her head.

## CHAPTER SEVEN

MARC BLEW OUT a harsh breath as Brooke acceded to his demand and slowly stripped off her thermal shirt, peeling away that soft, warm layer of material, baring her pale, firm breasts to his gaze. His heartbeat thundered in his chest, in his ears, and a hot rush of blood surged to his groin, increasing the pressure behind his fly.

She wasn't overly large, but perfect in size to match her slender hips and those long, shapely legs of hers encased in form-fitting thermal leggings. As he watched in silent appreciation, her breasts grew full and taut, and her rosy nipples peaked. His hands itched to plump that flesh, to draw those tight crests to his mouth and use his lips and tongue to taste her.

He remained seated, with his hands clasped over his updrawn knees, unable to believe that she was actually following through with his shocking request, which had been a sexy, shameless dare he'd fully expected her to back down from at the last minute. True, he wanted to do all those things he'd told her, but he never thought she'd allow him, or them, to go so far.

And now that she was holding up her end of the bargain, the game was over and the ultimate seduction was about to begin. He'd promised her pleasure, in a very explicit manner, and that sensual gratification was something he could deliver, even if it meant sacrificing his own physical desires in the process.

In some ways, he was grateful that he didn't have any condoms with him. Touching her so intimately was risky enough to their emotions, but he suspected being deep inside of Brooke would be too intense an experience, and more complicated than what either of them agreed to.

But, Lord, how he wanted her. More than was wise. More than was ever possible. In ways that defied his mind and the restrictions he'd put on his heart and emotions.

Their time together in this cabin would have to be enough to satisfy his craving for her.

He lifted his gaze to her softly flushed face, ready to proceed with the fantasy he'd woven. *"Everything comes off, Brooke."*

The top dangling from her fingertips dropped to the ground, and she drew a deep breath that caused her breasts to tremble. Dampening her bottom lip with her tongue, she hooked her thumbs in the waistband of her leggings and pushed the stretchy material over her hips, then bent to drag the pants down her thighs and long legs. Straightening, she kicked them aside, leaving her clad in a pair of pink silky panties trimmed in lace. Without hesitating, she slid those off, too, and stood before him gloriously naked.

Desire gripped him hard, overwhelming him with the fierce need to possess her as *his*. She was beautifully sculpted, and he took his time looking his fill. With the firelight flickering behind her, her skin shimmered with a vibrant warmth. The hair spilling across her shoulders looked soft and feathery and golden. His gaze trailed lower, over her shapely breasts, her curved waist, then stalled at the soft curls concealing softer, sensitive folds of flesh.

He thought of all the various ways he planned to give her those orgasms, and wondered how he was going to be able to touch her, feel her response as he brought her to that exquisite peak, listen to the sexy sounds she made as she climaxed and not embarrass himself in the process.

Gathering every ounce of willpower at his disposal, he lifted his gaze to her face. His heart squeezed tight at the barest hint of insecurity he detected in her eyes—she obviously wasn't used to being so openly scrutinized. By the time he was done with her there would be nothing left of her inhibitions.

Shifting more comfortably against the couch, he straightened his legs and widened his stance, creating a space for her in between. He crooked his finger at her, and eased the tension in the air with an irresistible grin. "Come over here and sit between my legs."

She hesitated for a split second, then glided toward him, the sway of her breasts, the sensual movements of her hips and thighs, mesmerizing him. At the last possible moment she turned around, just quick enough to give him a tantalizing glimpse of her smooth, rounded bottom, before lowering herself to the flannel sleeping bag between his spread thighs. She sat straight, not touching him, her spine too rigid.

He ran his fingers down the silky skin of her back. She shivered in response, but didn't move. "Sweetheart, in order for this to work, you're going to have to scoot closer, lean against me, and relax."

She glanced over her shoulder, the smile touching her mouth relieving him. "It's very disconcerting to be completely naked, while you're fully dressed."

Resting his wrists on his knees, he merely shrugged.

"This is my fantasy," he reminded her. Also his barrier of clothes acted as a safety precaution, a way for him to keep his perspective on the situation without losing complete control.

She settled more fully against his chest, until her buttocks nestled against his rock-hard groin. She placed her arms on his thighs, but kept her knees bent and closed primly.

That wouldn't do at all.

Gently hooking his bare feet against the inside of hers, he drew her ankles a good twelve inches apart, opening her to him, and letting the heat of the fire warm every inch of her naked flesh. She didn't resist, but the gooseflesh rising on her skin was enough to indicate her brief bout of self-consciousness.

Starting slow, he spanned her waist with his hands and brushed his fingers along her belly. She flinched at that sudden contact, and an unpredicted swell of tenderness filled his chest. Despite the sexy bargain they'd struck, he wanted this to be good for her. The best she'd ever experienced.

"Close your eyes, Brooke," he murmured, grazing his mouth against her ear. "Just focus on your body, and what you're feeling."

Listening to his advice, she let her lashes fall and relaxed her head against his shoulder. He sensed the last of her nerves drain away, and her limbs grew heavy and complacent. Taking advantage of her acquiescence, he nuzzled the side of her neck at the same time he cupped her breasts in his palms and kneaded the firm flesh. He flicked his thumbs over the nipples that had stiffened for him, then rolled those tight, velvety crests between his fingers, wishing he could do the same with his tongue.

A throaty moan purred in her throat, and she reached up and tentatively pressed her hand to his stubbled cheek. She rolled her head to the side, giving him greater access to the column of her neck, and he placed a hot, openmouthed kiss just below her ear.

She gasped, and squirmed restlessly against him. Deciding she was ready for him to move on, he flattened his palms and slid his hands down her quivering stomach then along both of her thighs, leisurely stroking the skin the fire had heated. Slowly, languorously, he petted her, drawing out the pleasure, heightening her need, strumming his fingers everywhere except where she burned the most for his touch. His thumbs met at her juncture, grazing the soft downy hair there, tantalizing her with the promise of something far more exquisite.

She turned her head toward his and opened her eyes. Her irises were a dark, aroused shade of blue, and unbridled sensuality etched her expression. "No more teasing, Marc," she said, her voice husky with impatience. "Touch me, please." Her hand slid from his cheek around to the nape of his neck. Her fingers tangled in the strands curling against the collar of his shirt, and she inexorably drew his mouth to hers. "Touch me now."

Their parted lips met, and she clung to him, drawing his tongue into her mouth. He let her dictate the pace, and followed her lead into a slow, deep, hot seduction. One kiss melted enticingly into another, and he surrendered to the sweetness of her mouth taking his.

And then he touched her intimately, where she was wet and eager and so incredibly primed. At his first gliding stroke, her groan vibrated against his lips. After all the mental stimulation they'd endured, along with his physical caresses, he knew she was beyond ready and right on the edge. Knowing there was much more to come beyond this initial release, he didn't bother drawing this climax out, which would have been pure torture for her.

With one hand splayed on her stomach, he deepened his exploration, rubbed his callused thumb over her swollen, needy flesh, once, twice…the third time sent her straight into the realm of pleasure. Her orgasm hit her fast and furiously, the buildup so intense her entire body convulsed. She wrenched her mouth from his as a lusty cry ripped from her throat. Burying his face against her neck, he wrapped his free arm around her waist and held her as waves of pure, blissful fulfillment engulfed her.

With a final shudder and a repleted sigh, she slumped back against his chest, her breathing as ragged as his own. Though a pulsing, throbbing need settled low, Marc couldn't deny the sense of masculine satisfaction he experienced in making her come apart for him.

A log on the fire settled, sending sparks filtering up the chimney. Outside, the storm howled and snowflakes pelted the windows. Inside, they were in a world all their own, where there were no rules, or boundaries, or anything beyond their own sensual desires.

He placed a tender kiss on her temple, and watched her mouth tip up in a positively delightful smile. "I take it that felt good?"

Her head rolled on his shoulder, and she tilted her face up to his. The wonder in her gaze did enormous things for his ego. "Mmm, that was absolutely decadent."

He chuckled and laced his fingers with hers, preparing for the next installment in his seduction. "One down, several more to go," he murmured wickedly. With her hands secured beneath his, he placed her palms on her breasts and squeezed her fingers gently around the plump flesh.

Her eyes widened. She sucked in a startled breath and resisted fondling herself. He could feel her heart beating erratically in her chest, and the pulse at the base of her throat fluttered madly. "Marc…" The tremor in her voice relayed her uncertainty.

He had no doubts that she'd touched herself before— she'd admitted as much when they'd answered those survey questions—but a certain male intuition told him she'd never done so in front of another man. Excitement escalated within him at the thought of being the first to share and witness such an erotic act.

Lifting one of her hands to his mouth, he lapped his tongue across the center of her palm and over her fingers, dampening the surface. "I want to show you how much pleasure you're capable of experiencing, all the different ways you can enjoy your body, and I don't want you to hold anything back. Be greedy, Brooke."

He dragged her slick hand back over a taut breast and administered the same provocative treatment to her other palm. She moaned and rubbed her thumbs over her beaded nipples, arching into her own touch, her reserve rapidly fading.

"Yeah, just like that," he praised, his voice thick and rough as he watched. "It's just you and me and hours stretching ahead of us. Whatever feels good, just do it."

This time around, she offered no resistance when he gently skimmed her palms lower, over her ribs and abdomen then along the inside of her thighs. Fingers still entwined, he splayed her hand at the apex of her legs and trailed her fingers along the moist, silky cleft in between.

She flinched at the direct contact, and whimpered, telling him she was still sensitive after her recent orgasm. "Soft and slow," he whispered. Determined to give her more, he directed her touch, applying a delicate, rhythmic pressure with her fingers to that responsive bud, until he was no longer instructing her and she'd found her own personal rhythm that rekindled the acute sensations.

Her face was flushed, and her hips undulated against her caressing fingers. Her breathing deepened, grew choppy, and within moments her climax beckoned.

The eroticism of the act shook Marc to the core. Feeling primitive and predatory, he filled his hands with her breasts, then bent his head and sank his teeth into the flesh between her neck and shoulder, claiming Brooke with a passionate love bite.

That's all it took to release the floodgates a second time. The breathy, intimate sounds she made nearly had him coming right along with her.

Before she had the chance to float back to earth, Marc moved around her, pulled her all the way down on the sleeping bag and straddled her hips, careful to keep his weight off her. She was weak and so dazed in the aftermath of experiencing such luxurious pleasure all she could manage was a drowsy, satisfied smile. Her hair was dishevelled around her face, and her hands rested beside her head in complete and open surrender.

Returning her smile, he gently ran his fingers over her breasts and teased the pretty tips with featherlight strokes. "Ready for more?"

She bit her bottom lip, arching restlessly into his hands and the thighs bracketing her hips. "Yeah," she said, thrilling him with her easy capitulation, and her trust.

Burning up from the inside out, he yanked his shirt over his head. Her hands followed right behind, skimming up his hard, jean-clad thighs, and fluttering over his taut belly, exploring unabashedly. Her finger dipped into his navel, then followed the dark trail of hair that whorled southward and disappeared into the waistband of his jeans. Glancing up at him with a hunger that stole his breath, she moved her flattened palm lower and massaged the fierce erection begging for freedom. Unable to help himself, he groaned and thrust against her splayed hand.

Every muscle in his body flexed and strained toward the heady, tingling sensation coursing through his blood. Knowing his control was too close to shattering, that her touch threatened his good intentions, he grasped her wrists and stretched her arms above her head.

Their faces were inches apart, and he dropped a soft kiss on her lips, then allowed a sinful grin to ease across his features. "This is where we improvise on the padded handcuffs."

Her eyes widened in surprise, but she issued no protest when he leaned over her, wrapped his shirt sleeves around her wrists, and tied the ends to the leg of the coffee table. She'd agreed to "anything goes," and he'd told her there was no saying "no," but he found himself searching her expression for the slightest hint of hesitation or objection, and found none. Her eyes were bright with anticipation, eager for whatever he had planned.

He lowered his head and started slow, with long, deep kisses that thrilled and aroused. Tongues tangled rapaciously, damp lips slid silkily, and beneath him he felt her grow lethargic and pliant. Finally, he moved on. His lips glided over her jaw, then down her throat, searing her skin and blazing a hot, moist trail to her breasts.

He brushed his lips across her nipples, teasing her, tempting him, then flicked his tongue over the stiff crown, tasting her for the first time. Her sharp intake of breath echoed in his ears, along with the whispered word *"Please."*

Lifting her breast, he enclosed her in the heat of his mouth and suckled gently, then more urgently, until she moaned long and low and writhed beneath him. She was sweet and warm and irresistible, and he couldn't seem to get enough of her.

In time, his hands and lips moved lower, scattering kisses along the slope of her belly and sampling the curve of her hip with his tongue. He made a place for himself between her legs, and with a gentle touch to her bent knees, she opened wider for him, giving him free rein to her body, and every sensual secret she harbored. His nostrils flared as her feminine scent played havoc with his senses and provoked raw, primitive instincts no other woman had ever roused in him.

The emotions caught him off guard, made what he was about to do with Brooke more than just simply satiating physical urges. *Need* consumed him. The strong, undeniable sentiment clawed at his insides, squeezed tight around his heart, making him feel desperate and impatient.

He glanced up at her face, knowing this wasn't only his decision to make. Blue eyes dark with passion boldly stared back. Without any doubts, she knew what he wanted, knew his intentions and craved this ultimate intimacy as much as he did.

Brooke tugged on the bonds restricting her arms, aching to touch Marc. As he devoured her with his smoldering gaze, she'd never felt so vulnerable—or so connected—to a person in her life. A storm raged between them, a sensual tempest that excited as much as it frightened because she feared she wouldn't survive the emotional impact.

At the moment, none of that mattered. The ache spreading through her body couldn't be denied, nor could the soul-deep hunger he'd awakened. They'd come this far, and she'd given him everything else. He'd stolen more than any other man ever had, had given so selflessly in return, there was no reason not to trust him with this, too.

"Anything goes," she whispered, giving him the consent he sought.

He needed no more encouragement. Eyes turning slumberous, he slid even lower, curved her legs over his broad, muscled shoulders and settled in for an unhurried exploration. His dark head moved down, and he pressed a sizzling, openmouthed kiss against the quivering skin of her inner thigh. She gasped as his stubble chafed her, and shivered and moaned when he soothed the burn with his hot, wet tongue. He nibbled leisurely on her thighs, lapped her skin and spent an inordinate amount of time discovering erogenous zones she never knew she had.

She thrashed and moaned, begged and pleaded, frustrated by her inability to thread her fingers through his hair and direct his mouth to a more explicit kind of touch.

But he knew. His fingers caressed her slick folds first, seconds before his hot breath washed over her and he laved her with the velvet heat of his tongue, feasting on her as if she were some sweet, rare delicacy for him to enjoy and savor.

Despite her husky pleas, and because he knew he could, he took his time and learned everything about her body. The feather-soft stroke of his tongue that made her whimper, the teasing flick that drove her mad and the gentle suckling that pushed her closer to the edge.

The assault became more than she could bear, and he seemed to sense that, too. Without preamble or further preliminaries, he spread her with his thumbs and pressed his mouth hard against her, rasping her sensitive flesh with his tongue, over and over, then delving deeper, making love to her the only way possible. Two fingers slipped within her tight channel, filling her, touching off a whole new series of sensations as he ruthlessly pushed her higher. The contractions in her womb built, then exploded, catapulting her straight over the precipice. Her hips shot upward, and she screamed as she came in a fiery, liquid rush that shook her entire body.

With a low, primitive growl, he reared back to his knees and fumbled with the snap on his jeans, then struggled to lower his zipper over his straining sex. The muscles in his abdomen rippled with his abrupt, anxious movements, and he cursed the thermal underwear he'd put back on after his shower, which now provided a frustrating hindrance.

Startled by his abrupt change, and uncertain of what he meant to do, she attempted to capture his attention before they went further than either of them intended. "Marc?"

The caution in her soft voice was unmistakable, and he immediately lifted his head, his gaze dragging up the length of her, from her splayed thighs, to her breasts, and all the way up to the shirt that still confined her wrists. Pure, male instinct glittered in his eyes, and his chest rose and fell with deep breaths.

She drew a steady breath, though her limbs still quaked. "I thought you said you didn't have any protection with you."

He closed his eyes as a shudder wracked his body. "I don't," he said, seemingly struggling with some internal battle. When he looked at her again, his expression was a curious blend of agony and hope. "I just want to feel you against me, with nothing between us. Will you let me do that?"

Impossible as it seemed, an electrifying thrill ignited deep in her belly. She smiled invitingly, and nodded. "Yes." After everything they'd shared today, she couldn't refuse his request. Didn't want to, because she yearned to feel him, too.

She watched him shove his pants and thermals over his hips and eagerly divest himself of the restricting garments. Naked and inflamed, a gorgeous, masculine work of art, he moved over her, bracing his arms at the side of her head to support his weight. Gradually, he lowered his body…chest to lush, swollen breasts, taut stomach to plush belly, muscular legs to the welcoming cove between her thighs. Finally, he flexed his hips, nestling his arousal firmly, intimately between her legs.

They both groaned in unison at the exquisite pleasure that washed over them.

He raked his fingers through her hair, and dragged his thumb across her bottom lip. "I don't think I've ever felt anything more perfect." Awe infused his voice.

Her throat grew tight. "Me, either," she said, knowing it to be true.

He moved, sliding his hard, pulsing shaft against her slick, feminine folds. Her breathing hitched, and she arched into him.

His gaze darkened, and a cocky grin canted his mouth. "Feel good?"

"Yeah," she admitted, beyond being bashful. "For you, too?"

"Incredible." He bent his head and kissed her cheek, her jaw, then nuzzled her ear. "The only thing that could feel any better is being deep inside you."

With his words, she experienced a profound sense of emptiness, a loss she couldn't account for. "I'm sorry," she whispered.

He met her gaze and shook his head. "No apologies, Brooke. This is the next best thing." He dragged a hand down her side and cupped her bottom, tilting her hips so the next time he thrust he created a delicious, breathtaking friction.

She gasped, and he growled deep in his throat, the sound vibrating against her chest. "You're so warm, and soft, and wet." His gaze turned hot and possessive. "Move with me, Brooke. I want to feel you come, just like this."

She wriggled her hands, wanting freedom to indulge in this experience without restrictions. "Untie me, Marc. I want to touch you."

Reaching up, he slipped a finger in the knot, and the soft shirt sleeves unraveled, setting her free. With a sigh and a smile, she closed her eyes and caressed the taut slope of his back, his toned buttocks, and back up his muscular arms, learning the feel of *him*. Every time he moved, sparks of heat skittered through her, and she suddenly couldn't get enough.

Tangling her fingers in his silky hair, she brought his mouth to her parted lips and kissed him in a brazen manner that would have shocked her if he hadn't already shed her of her straightlaced demeanor. There was nothing demure left, and she reveled in the sexual abandon that was hers. Rocking with the steady movement of Marc's hips, she embraced the sheer erotic sensation of sleek, male flesh gliding provocatively along the hot, liquid center of her. Impossibly, another swell of tension coiled inside her, tighter and tighter…

With a raw curse, Marc jerked back, and Brooke mourned the loss. Before he could completely leave her, she wrapped her legs around the back of his thighs, holding him hostage.

Their harsh breathing mingled, and she ignored the savage frown creasing his brows. "Where do you think you're going?"

His jaw clenched with restraint. "I'm too close."

She caressed a hand over his cheek and smiled seductively. "So am I," she said, her meaning clear.

Despite the severity of the moment, a glimmer of amusement sparkled in his eyes. "Greedy wench."

"Your fault," she murmured. With the strength of her limbs, she drew him as close as possible, arching upward to deepen the contact, to increase the incredible friction. "You did promise me multiple orgasms, and I want them all."

A low, strangled moan caught in his throat, and he gave up the fight, surging strong and sure, and with deliberate purpose. His lips crushed hers, and he took control of their kiss, slanting his mouth over hers, again and again. Sensation spiked through her blood, centering between her legs, and she slid her body sinuously, erotically against his in a rhythm that matched the thrust of his tongue, the frenzied pumping of his hips.

Brooke's climax built, and she writhed frantically

beneath him, clawing at his back to get closer. He held her mouth captive, swallowing her moans, pushing her toward yet another stunning, unparalleled peak. The feelings he evoked were too intense, too strong…and she couldn't deny the sensations that exploded within her, or her lusty response.

A guttural groan ripped from Marc's chest as he rode the crest with her, wringing every drop of pleasure from her body. At the last possible moment he raised up and over her, sliding his throbbing manhood against her soft belly. Tossing his head back, he ground his hips into her, over and over, shuddering with the violent force of spilling his own release.

He collapsed on top of her, burying his face against her neck, their damp bodies still entwined, but satiated. Closing her eyes, she wrapped one arm around his back and threaded the fingers of her other hand through his hair, absorbing his warmth, his weight, and inhaling the musky scent of their lovemaking.

A smile found its way to her lips. The heavy beating of his heart echoed hers, and the sheer magic of what they'd just shared saturated her with unbelievable contentment. Nothing had ever seemed so completely natural, so extraordinarily perfect, as this moment. A sense of rightness settled over her, as did the startling realization that the pleasure Marc had given her had not only dissolved her inhibitions, it had stripped her to the very essence of her soul.

So MUCH FOR willpower and discipline, Marc thought, glancing down at the napping woman cuddled against his side. Obviously, he had absolutely none where Brooke was concerned, and that revelation caused a frisson of unease to sneak up on him and rattle the convictions he'd lived by for the past eight years. He'd meant to give her pleasure, and without a doubt he'd executed that plan in spades, but he'd *never* anticipated that she'd switch the tables on him and demand his own acquiescence in return.

Resisting her hadn't been an option and he'd gone wild, surrendering to the most intense, mind-blowing orgasm he'd ever experienced. The connection between them had been extraordinary and consuming, all without even being inside her. Incredible didn't even begin to describe what they'd shared, and now he was trying to sort through the conflicting, confusing emotions that had swamped him in the aftermath of such an amazing encounter.

The fire he'd rebuilt in the hearth after their sensual love play snapped and hissed at the wood stacked on the grate. A soft sigh escaped Brooke in her sleep and she snuggled closer to him on their makeshift bed in front of the fire. His arm automatically shifted around her shoulders to accommodate her position and keep the warmth of her body next to his. Her cheek rested on his chest, her arm spanned his waist and a slender leg draped over his thigh, entwining their naked bodies as familiarly as the lovers they'd become.

Except he'd always steadfastly avoided this particular intimacy with the lovers he'd slept with in the past, and for very good reason. In his experience, sticking around after sex gave a woman the wrong impression, and was too easily construed as an invitation to something deeper he had no intentions of offering, not when he knew he lacked the ability to offer that kind of lasting commitment.

But instead of feeling suffocated or antsy to put

distance between him and Brooke, he was filled with a
tenderness and affection that warred with the subtle
warnings slipping through his mind—that he'd fallen
deeper, and more emotionally, than he'd ever intended.
He'd always secretly desired Brooke, but acknowledging the awesome need she stirred was a very dangerous
thing, because nothing could ever come of it beyond
their short, private time in this cabin.

*No commitments, no promises and no regrets.*

They'd established the terms of their brief fling
before they'd crossed that line of no return. She knew
up front that this was a temporary affair, that a future
was impossible, and forever wasn't something he'd
consider. Despite how compatible and in tune to each
other they were physically, he had to believe that
they'd both abide by those rules and leave this cabin
without unrealistic expectations, guilt or other emotional entanglements.

She'd said no regrets, and she hadn't shown any signs
of shame or doubts after they'd made love. Indeed, she'd
appeared downright pleased with herself, and the
lengths she'd driven him to. As for his own loss of
control, that was something he'd be more careful to
keep a tight rein on next time.

Snow continued to fall outside and showed no signs
of stopping anytime soon. The last time he'd glanced at
his watch, it had been only half past noon, with the rest
of the day and night stretching ahead of them—along
with tomorrow, if the storm didn't abate.

That meant long, endless hours filled with anything
their imaginations might conjure. With Brooke having
just discovered the sensuality that had obviously lain
dormant within her, Marc had no doubt that she was far

from done experimenting with him, and indulging in forbidden, innovative adventures.

The thought made him instantly hard and he entertained a fantasy or two of his own. The woman seemed insatiable, and though she'd exhibited a few reservations at first, she'd gradually blossomed, eager to learn and experience the exciting wonders of her body, and his.

She'd pushed him over the edge as no other woman ever had. Now that he knew what she was capable of, he was prepared for her brand of passion and the way she wreaked havoc with his mind. For the rest of their stay he'd give her anything and everything she asked for, and then some, but ultimately, he'd be in control of each situation—mentally *and* physically.

## CHAPTER EIGHT

"WHAT ARE YOU in the mood for?" Marc asked.

"Just about anything you have in mind," came a throaty, feminine reply.

Marc instantly responded to the sultry invitation in Brooke's voice. His stomach clenched with need, and his body grew hard with incredible, astonishing ease. Glancing from the cupboard of canned goods, he cast his gaze over his shoulder, watching as Brooke approached from the living room. A suggestive gleam sparkled in her blue eyes, and the alluring glide of her body spoke a hedonistic language that said she was his for the taking, despite that she should have been exhausted and sexually depleted from their earlier tryst.

Her nap had obviously restored her ardor and enthusiasm.

He fought the primitive urge to haul her over his shoulder and spread her back down on the sleeping bag in front of the fire for another sumptuous feast. But since they'd skipped lunch, they needed sustenance of the nutritious kind. "I'm talking *food,* Brooke."

"So am I," she said, all innocence.

Marc knew better. With his earlier encouragement, the sensual creature within Brooke had been unleashed, and she was enjoying the benefits of being so winsome, of basking in the glory of physical liberation. Her new, brazen attitude showed in her soft expression—the come-hither look in her heavy-lidded eyes, and the I-want-*you*-for-dinner smile curving her mouth.

No way could any healthy, red-blooded male resist that kind of ambush.

He drew a deep, steady breath to calm his raging hormones. This was a fascinating side to Brooke he'd never seen before, and he couldn't help but wonder how this sexy, exciting woman hadn't been more than enough to satisfy his brother. Obviously Eric hadn't taken the time to discover all that passion simmering beneath the surface, hadn't taken the care to coax her desires and needs to their full potential.

Or maybe Eric hadn't wanted *his wife* to be that kind of woman. The sudden, fleeting realization slipped through Marc's mind, making sense in a warped kind of way. Before he could analyze the thought further, it was quickly obliterated by the press of Brooke's body up against his chest, and the bold way she dragged her palms down his belly and tugged on the waistband of his thermals. Without hesitation, her fingers slipped inside.

Groaning deep in his throat, he grasped her wrists before she took him in her hands and erased his good intentions to make her dinner. With obvious regret, he withdrew her shameless touch. "We really do need to eat."

She buried her face against his neck and breathed deeply of his scent, then nibbled on his throat. "*You* taste good enough to eat."

Abrupt laughter escaped him. "*Food*, Brooke."

She lifted her head and looked up at him. A sigh unraveled from her, the sound rife with regret. "You're right, of course, especially since I want to make sure you've got plenty of energy for later."

He lifted a brow. "Later?"

A feline smile curved her lips. "*My* fantasy," she whispered, reminding him that she had a score to settle. "So, what are my choices? For dinner, that is."

Trying not to think of the ways she might extract her revenge, he turned back to the cupboard and perused their selection. "We've got beef stew, chicken noodle soup or ravioli."

She reached for one of the bigger cans. "Let's go for something hearty and filling, like beef stew. It's going to be a *long* night."

He watched her sashay toward the stove, exuding too much confidence, and knew he was in big, big trouble.

They worked together to prepare dinner, all the while talking companionably. There wasn't an ounce of tension between him and Brooke after what had transpired earlier, just a special closeness that they'd never shared before. She flirted and teased impetuously, exhibiting all the unmistakable signs of a woman attracted to a man. She touched him often and with abandon, and he liked every aspect of their new, intimate relationship. Way too much. More than was wise.

They settled across from one another at the small table, along with their bowls of stew, saltine crackers, and the apple juice Brooke had found in the pantry. Nothing gourmet, but definitely a tasty and filling meal.

He picked up his spoon and pushed around the steaming chunks of beef and vegetables, resuming their casual, easy conversation. "So, how do you think Jessica and Ryan are surviving being confined together during this storm?"

She spread her napkin on her lap and slanted him an inquisitive look. "How do you mean?"

"We've both noticed the verbal sparring and sparks flying between the two of them." He grinned. "I'm just wondering if they'll come out of this as friends or enemies."

"I'm not worried much about Jessica," she replied wryly, and bit into a saltine cracker she'd dipped into her stew. "She can definitely hold her own with Ryan, as you've seen."

He nodded. "And I can vouch for Ryan enjoying the challenge she presents."

A brief show of regret entered her eyes. "Unfortunately, that's all Jessica will ever be for him."

Curiosity got the best of him, prompting him to delve deeper into their discussion. "Why? They're obviously attracted to one another."

Her spoon stilled over her stew, and she met his gaze steadily from across the table. "Just as we are, but that doesn't mean anything will come of our attraction beyond the here and now, right?"

Marc's gut clenched. He had the distinct impression she was testing him and his answer, possibly hoping for more than they'd originally agreed to. As much as he wished he *could* promise her more than their pact as temporary lovers, he knew it wasn't possible. Not with him. And he refused to offer her false hopes.

"You're right that our time together is limited to this cabin, but our circumstances are different than theirs." He chased that lame statement down with a long drink of apple juice, then concentrated on finishing his stew.

She had every opportunity to turn the tables on him,

to confront their circumstances, challenge his excuse, but she didn't. He exhaled a breath of relief.

"Ryan doesn't stand a chance with Jessica," she replied, putting their conversation back on track. "There might be some kind of attraction between them, but he's a lawyer, and a divorce attorney at that. Those are two major strikes against him."

"What, exactly, does Jessica have against Ryan being an attorney?" He reached for a few more crackers. "And what's with Jessica's wisecracks? I've never heard such a colorful assortment of lawyer jokes."

She laughed lightly, but there was an odd tightness to the sound. "Collecting them is a hobby for her and has been since she was a teenager. As for her aversion to attorneys, well, that stems from lingering anger over our parents' divorce."

Marc didn't know much about Brooke's parents, or her past, and found himself interested in that aspect of her life. "What happened?" he gently prodded.

Her brow creased with reluctance. Setting her spoon in her nearly empty bowl, she hesitated, giving him the strong feeling that it had been a long time since she'd talked about her childhood. He waited, giving her the time she obviously needed to sort through memories.

She rewarded his patience, her release of breath seemingly releasing that tight hold on her thoughts. "Jessica was only nine when our parents separated—I was thirteen—but our father's actions made a huge impact on her. She was his little girl, and she idolized him, so when he left the family for a younger woman and filed for divorce, Jessica was just as devastated as my mother."

Finished with his meal, he pushed his dish aside. "And what about you?"

"Oh, I was definitely crushed," she admitted, absently running a finger over the rim of her glass. "But someone had to be strong and keep a level head during the separation."

So she'd been the sensible, reliable one of the trio—at a startlingly young age. "I take it the divorce was a nasty one?"

"Yeah," she said grimacing, the recollections he'd evoked obviously unpleasant ones. "Everything about the split was awful. Our mother was a stay-at-home wife, always had been, and when our father left she was forced back to work and had to keep two jobs in order to support us, which left me to take care of Jessica and basically take over our mother's duties at home."

He frowned, not caring for the image of her at thirteen, taking on the responsibilities of an adult when she should have been enjoying her teenage years. He silently absorbed everything Brooke and her sister had gone through, grasping a better understanding of Jessica's emotional state, as well as why Brooke was so sensible, levelheaded and stable. She'd had to be, for her sister's sake, and to support her mother's mental well-being, as well, he suspected.

"What about alimony and child support? Didn't that help your mother?" he asked.

"This is where the animosity toward attorneys comes in," she explained with a faint smile. "When our father walked out, he wiped out their savings account and took all the money they had. Come to find out, his new girl-friend liked pricey things and was very high-mainte-nance. He hired a cutthroat lawyer who had no compunction about taking advantage of my mother's emotional shock. He raked her over the coals, so to speak, and since my mother couldn't afford to hire a decent attorney, she lost everything. She was forced to sell our house, and after my father took his portion of the proceeds, my mother barely had enough to move us into a one-bedroom apartment and buy herself a used car to get her to her two jobs."

She glanced away toward the fireplace, but she wasn't done recounting her disturbing tale. "Somehow, my father got out of paying alimony, or he just didn't pay it at all. Child support payments were sporadic, and then they just stopped, as did his infrequent calls and visits." Her gaze found his again, the hurt in her eyes running deep—deeper than she allowed anyone to see, he'd hazard to guess. "It's been over thirteen years since we've seen or heard from him."

He shook his head in astonishment. "I can't imagine how things would have been if my parents had gone through something similar when my father had his one brief affair. Granted, Eric and I were eighteen and sixteen at the time, but if my parents hadn't worked through their problems and decided to make their marriage work then Eric and I would have been casualties of divorce, too."

Sighing, she stood and began stacking their dishes. "Consider yourself lucky. Your mom and dad obviously believed they had a marriage worth saving, despite your father's one indiscretion." A fond smile lifted the corner of her mouth at the mention of his parents, but he caught a brief glimpse of sadness in her eyes before she turned and moved toward the sink. "My father wasn't willing to work through the problems he'd created, or give up his new love interest. His family hadn't been a priority for him. His only concern was his own selfish wants and needs."

Marc cleared the table for Brooke while she filled the sink with hot, sudsy water, giving him a few quiet moments to reflect on the turmoil her father had inflicted on so many lives. His own father had strayed and caused Marc's mother emotional distress, but his family was fortunate in that his parents had worked hard to repair the problems in their marriage, and avoided becoming a statistic. Most couples weren't so lucky.

Marc had learned from his father's mistake, along with his own past transgression with another woman. That one incident in his life was a vivid reminder of why he avoided serious, complicated relationships. He had concrete proof that he had his father's wild blood running through his veins, just as Eric did, and he couldn't, *wouldn't*, risk the possibility of breaking a promise as sacred as wedding vows. Eric had tried, but those impulsive urges had destroyed his own marriage, had made Brooke a casualty of divorce not once, but *twice*. Yet she didn't seem to harbor any resentment.

He came up beside her and set their glasses on the counter, searching her expression. "After everything you've been through with your father, you don't seem bitter at all," he commented, fascinated by her acceptance when she had every reason to be cynical.

"I dealt with the situation differently than Jessica, and I couldn't afford to wallow in those hostile emotions." Shrugging, she pushed up the sleeves of her thermal shirt and dipped her hands into the soapy water. "I was too busy learning to cook and clean, raising Jessica for my mother, and keeping myself in school, too. I think I just came to accept the circumstances because I had no choice, but my sister was so young and my father's actions really disillusioned her."

His hand clenched into a fist against the crazy urge to reach out and touch her, to offer some kind of physical comfort for what she'd endured. He ached to pull her against him, hold her close and give her everything she'd been denied. Except he was the last man who had the right to stake such a claim, to make promises he feared he'd break.

Instead, he reined in his desires to the best of his ability and opted for the consolation of words. "It sounds as though the men in your life haven't exactly been pillars of security, or fidelity."

Regret fluttered across her features as she scrubbed a bowl, rinsed it, then placed it on the dish rack. "Yeah, I'd hoped that my own marriage would be different from my parents, that I wouldn't get divorced." Her gaze captured his, the deepening color of blue revealing a puzzling culpability. "But honestly, I'm partly to blame for my marriage to Eric not working out."

His brows shot up in surprise, and he grabbed a terry towel to dry their dishes. "And how's that?"

"My expectations of Eric, and our marriage, exceeded what he'd been capable of giving me." Resignation laced her voice. "I should have seen that *before* the wedding, but I was so swept up in Eric's single-minded pursuit that I didn't take the time to analyze the situation, or the fact that I'd let his charm seduce me. Despite knowing about Eric's wild ways, I wanted to believe that he could be the kind of man to give me everything my own father hadn't given my mother. Like unconditional love. Respect. Security."

Something within him softened perceptively. Behind all that strength of hers hid a wellspring of vulnerabilities. "But you never had any of that in your marriage to Eric."

It was a statement, not a question, but she answered him, anyway. "No. But that doesn't mean I don't believe I can find a man who *will* give me those things. Next time, I just need to be more careful, and selective." An indulgent smile brightened her expression. "Even after everything my father put my mother through, she managed to find a terrific man who treats her like she deserves. They live in West Virginia and have been happily married for the past seven years."

He dried a bowl, then replaced it in the cupboard. "I guess it's just a matter of finding the right person."

She nodded in agreement. "Yeah, along with compromise and lots of open communication."

"Which you obviously didn't have with Eric." He knew that personal observation should have remained unspoken—the problems Brooke and Eric experienced in their relationship were none of his business—yet he wanted to know the details that had driven his brother toward other women, when his own wife should have been more than enough to satisfy him, emotionally and physically.

His comment didn't seem to bother her. "I tried to be a good wife, and I suppose in some ways Eric tried to be the kind of husband he *thought* he should be." Reaching for the pot on the stove, she submerged it in the water. "In the end, we both discovered we weren't meant to be together. I married Eric wanting a house in the suburbs, a dog, two or three kids and the whole family kind of thing. Eric *said* he wanted those things, too, but he was forcing himself into a role that didn't fit *him*."

He frowned at her explanation. "What do you mean?"

"I think Eric married me because I was safe for him, a way for him to deny his true nature." She unplugged the sink, and stared out the window as the water swirled down the drain. It was completely white outside, the banks of snow nearly four feet high and they still had another day to go.

She transferred her gaze back to him. "There was an attraction between us when we first met, but once we got married, there was no real emotional intimacy between us. Eric played the part of a hardworking, serious husband, and he treated me like, well, a wife."

He put away the last of the clean utensils, not sure he was following her. "As opposed to?"

"A woman. A lover." She bit her bottom lip, a becoming blush spreading across her cheeks. "Eric and I…well, we never would have done the kind of things you and I did earlier. Our sex life was okay, but very predictable. Nothing hot or wild or exciting, and Eric seemed to prefer it that way. None of that really mattered to me, probably because I didn't know what I was missing."

*Until now.*

The tempting words hung between them, making him too aware of the sensual, sexy woman he'd had the pleasure of awakening within Brooke…and wanted to again.

He realized his earlier assumption had been correct. It wasn't as though Brooke hadn't been enough to keep Eric content, but that his brother had pegged her into a demure, domestic role that didn't include erotic intimacies. It had been Eric's way to keep his distance emotionally and maintain the stability of a proper marriage, while his affairs had offered the fantasy of hot sex.

Unfortunately, Eric hadn't realized he could have had the best of both worlds with Brooke.

Dragging a hand through her hair, she shook her head and grinned ruefully. "Where did all *that* come from?"

He hadn't meant for them to embark on such a serious conversation, but it was apparent their discussion had been good for Brooke—and very educating for him. "Sounds like you needed to let it all out."

As if she'd just realized all the personal things she'd confided about herself and her marriage to his brother, she slid a sheepish glance his way. "I've never really talked about my marriage to Eric to anyone. I adore your mother, but I'm not about to discuss Eric with *her,* and Jessica has her own opinion about the matter and is too quick to accuse instead of just listen. And I really shouldn't be discussing my relationship with Eric with you, either."

Tossing the towel aside, he leaned his hip against the counter and crossed his arms over his chest. "Nothing we talked about will go any further than this cabin," he promised.

"Thank you." She looked immensely relieved, believing his word without question, making him feel absurdly pleased that she trusted him so completely.

Tipping her head, she regarded him teasingly. "Do you charge by the hour for your therapy sessions, Mr. Jamison?"

He winked at her and grinned, liking this playful side to Brooke. "For you, I'll waive the fee."

"No, that won't do at all." A provocative gleam entered her gaze. "I don't have a whole lot of money on me, but I insist on paying up in other more *inventive* ways."

His libido twitched as she moved toward him. "Such as?"

"I think we've talked too much." Aligning her body

against his, she twined her arms around his neck and brought his mouth down to hers. "How 'bout I show you?"

Her parted lips meshed with his, and she compensated him with long, rapacious kisses that threatened his sanity, made him wish for impossible things, and proved that she had plenty more newfound passion and desire to put to use.

## CHAPTER NINE

BROOKE STARED at her reflection in the bathroom mirror, wondering how she'd lived her entire adult life without experiencing the freedom and abandon she'd discovered here in this cabin with Marc. Mentally, she felt alive, energetic and impetuous. Sexually, she felt liberated and unfettered, willing to explore desires and push limits that a few days ago she would have never dreamed she'd challenge.

And at the center of her transformation was a generous, selfless man who'd coaxed her to her full potential, made her feel enthusiastic and incredibly feminine. Marc helped her realize what she'd been missing for too many years, that she'd *settled* for certain things when she should have been much more selective and demanding about her needs.

She'd never resented that she'd been a good, responsible daughter, a reliable sister and a faithful, dependable wife. She'd sacrificed her childhood to take care of her family without complaint. She'd raised Jessica, doing her best to keep her out of trouble, and despite the clashes they'd had when Jessica had been a stubborn teenager, Brooke was proud of the woman her sister had become. And when she'd married Eric, she'd done so knowing on some level she'd be taking care of him, too, just as she'd mothered everyone else in her life. For as long as she could remember, she'd suppressed her own personal wants and desires for others, and had never begrudged her choices.

Until now, when she'd discovered all that she'd forsaken. Now, she had a wealth of wants and desires to make up for, and she planned to do so with Marc, who stirred passions that ran deeper than just superficial needs.

She'd once believed that Marc and Eric possessed too many similarities as brothers, the most predominant of which was the inability to nurture and sustain a committed relationship. But in the past few days she'd discovered too many differences between siblings to judge them as equals. While Eric had treated her formally, with his own reserved ideals of how a wife ought to be stereotyped, from the very beginning Marc had been warm and openly affectionate. He was sincere, honest and candid, and didn't pretend to be anything more than what he presented. Except she didn't think he gave himself enough credit for who he was—a man with a big heart, selfless intentions, and an endless capacity to care.

He'd shown her all that, and more.

Reaching for the hem of her thermal shirt, she drew it over her head and let it drop to the bathroom floor, shivering as the cold air caressed her warm skin. With cool fingers she touched the chafe marks on her neck from Marc's stubble, then followed the abrasive path down to her bare breasts, loving this newfound freedom to touch and enjoy her body, which Marc had introduced her to. Shucking convention and thumbing her nose at the restrictions that had ruled her life never felt so wonderful.

And being bad never felt so good.

Closing her eyes, she let a slow smile curl the corner of her mouth as she remembered the kiss she'd instigated in the kitchen after their serious conversation about her father and Eric. The kiss had led them to the couch, where they'd necked and petted and fondled each other like sex-starved teenagers. She'd intended to focus all her attention on Marc and test her seductive wiles on him, but he'd too easily managed to distract her. With a skillful caress, a deep, wet kiss, he'd reduced her to putty beneath his hands and mouth, making her a willing, wanton slave to his carnal desires.

He'd pleasured her, twice, and before she could regain her breath and restore her stamina to seduce *him*, he'd moved away and settled himself in front of the hearth, where he'd proceeded to add logs to the grate, then muttered the excuse of calling his secretary at home since there was no way he was going to be leaving here until Wednesday and Marlene had been expecting him back in the office tomorrow.

Clearly, that particular episode was over for him.

She'd been miffed that, while she'd been shameless and greedy in taking her pleasure, Marc clearly meant to maintain a tight hold on his own control.

Well, she planned to shatter his restraint.

While he'd been on his cell phone with Marlene, Brooke had retrieved a pillar candle she'd seen in one of the kitchen cupboards, a book of matches, and sequestered herself in the bathroom.

Now, it was time to execute *her* fantasy.

She no longer heard the deep rumble of Marc's voice as he talked to his secretary, and assumed he'd disconnected the call. Stripping off the rest of her clothes until she was completely naked, she lit the candle she'd brought with her and turned off the light, throwing the tiny room into seductive shadows and tingeing her skin with a golden, shimmering glow.

Drawing a steady, fortifying breath, she opened the door a crack, then called out, "Marc, can you come here for a sec?"

"Is everything okay?" came his concerned voice.

"I need you, please." It wasn't a lie. She needed him in ways that should have frightened her, but didn't. The connection they shared felt right, and too wonderful to question. The feelings he evoked were rich and vibrant and exciting, and while she'd come to acknowledge the gradual shifting of her emotions, she knew she had to tread cautiously with Marc, who'd built barriers against his innermost thoughts and feelings.

Ultimately, she trusted him, and knew, despite his fierce belief in no commitments, he was a man with integrity. But for some reason, he didn't see that goodness and decency in himself, believing instead that he was better off alone. Before they left this cabin, she was determined to unearth those reasons, and possibly take a huge risk of her own.

She heard him padding across the living room, then the door pushed open and he appeared, as did an instantaneous frown when he saw that she was naked. "What's wrong?"

"I need someone to scrub my back." Smiling invitingly, she crooked her finger at him. "Come inside and close the door."

A rush of breath escaped him. "Brooke—"

"Anything goes," she interrupted, not allowing him the chance to refuse her, or turn the situation around so he was the one in charge again. "I've done everything you've asked me to. Now it's time for you to return the favor."

He conceded by stepping closer and shutting the door, cocooning them in flickering, soothing candle-light. "You mean to tell me you want *more* after what we just did on the couch?" His tone was amused and in-credulous at the same time.

"Oh, yeah, a *whole* lot more. I'm making up for everything I've missed. And I've missed an awful lot, as you know." Her lashes fell to half-mast. "Since I plan to get you *very* wet, you need to take off your clothes."

He groaned at the provocative slant to her words. "Are you gonna help?"

She shook her head, shivering as her silky hair swayed around her shoulders, brushing her sensitive skin. "Nope. I'm going to watch you while you strip, and enjoy myself, so make the most of it."

He chuckled as he pulled his shirt over his head, and though the sound was strained with desire, the depths of his eyes glimmered with too much confidence. Brooke knew if she wasn't careful and didn't stay on guard, he'd steal this seduction right out from under her and make it his own—with her acquiescence being the ultimate prize. While she certainly didn't mind being the recipient of the luxurious pleasure Marc so easily wove, she wanted him to let go again, physically and emotion-ally, as he had the first time they'd made love.

"Don't be so cocky, Jamison," she murmured as he pushed his thermal pants over his hips and down his muscular legs, then stepped from the nubby fabric, com-pletely at ease with his own nudity. And why not, when he had a magnificent body? "This time, it'll be *you* begging, not me."

He stood in front of her, large and gorgeous and every inch male, including that arrogant grin on his face illuminated by the candle's glow. "I'll certainly enjoy your attempts."

She rolled her eyes and pushed aside the shower curtain to turn on the hot water. "Has anyone ever told you that you're way too presumptuous?"

"Has anyone ever told you that you have a nice ass?" His cool, callused palm stroked her bottom, sending a wave of gooseflesh rising across her skin.

"You're the first," she said, straightening, then cast him a playful frown. "And keep your hands to yourself. This is *my* fantasy."

"Don't you think I know what really turns you on?" he asked, his rich voice infused with unwavering certainty.

He knew too much, every wanton desire even *she* hadn't known she possessed, and intimate secrets she'd never shared with anyone else. She wanted the same from him. "Well, maybe it's my turn to discover what turns *you* on."

"That's easy," he murmured as his gaze drifted down the length of her, lingering on feminine dips and curves along the way. "You turn me on."

That much was obvious by his body's reaction to her. His arousal grew full and thick, and she hadn't even touched him yet. The knowledge bolstered her confidence, made her feel *very* sexy, restoring her determination not to lose her advantage in this seduction.

"Sweet-talking me isn't going to work." Stepping beneath the hot, steaming spray, she grabbed his hand and pulled him in. He followed willingly, but she didn't trust the wicked gleam in his eyes and knew maintaining control would be a challenge in itself.

Intending to emerge the victor this time, she closed the curtain and drenched herself from head to toe, letting him watch as the water slicked back her hair, then sluiced over her taut breasts, her belly, and down her thighs, until her entire body glistened wetly. Then she pushed him beneath the shower and let him do the same while she poured shampoo into the palm of her hand.

The fiberglass stall was small, which made for more intimate contact, and amusing and innovative ways to get clean. Their laughter and chuckles mingled as she scrubbed his hair and he did the same for her, then they helped one another rinse, chasing the suds down their limbs with slick palms. Their bodies brushed erotically, glided silkily, turning their frolicking fun into sizzling arousal and excruciating awareness.

Soft sighs and low groans coalesced. Lips met, damp and soft and hot. Their tongues tangled with delicious indulgence while her soapy hands slid over sleek sinew, discovering fascinating male contours, both hard and soft but undeniably virile.

Hunger and need coiled deep within Brooke as long, callused fingers touched and teased and tormented. Her mind spun, her pulse raced, and just when she made the silent decision to do some exploring with her mouth, he broke their kiss and eased her around so her bottom tucked against his groin and his throbbing erection nestled between her thighs.

Her breath hitched in her throat and a rush of liquid heat greeted the sleek glide and subtle pressure of his arousal *there*. Realizing this position put *her* at *his* mercy, she tried to turn to face him again, but he snagged a muscular arm around her waist, holding her secure and tight against his heaving chest. He stepped back, until the hard, warm stream of water hit her thighs, heightening the ache between her legs, and deeper inside.

On a soft cry, she arched her back, sliding her hips intimately closer to his, but still feeling too empty. She'd sworn she wouldn't be the one to beg this time, but the need he evoked was too great, and she was helpless to deny what she wanted so badly. She craved not only physical fulfillment, but a spiritual, emotional connection that threatened the rules they'd established for their brief affair.

Turning her head, she looked up into his face, clenched with restraint, and widened her stance for him. "I want to feel you inside me, just like this." Her voice quivered, as did her whole entire body.

He pushed forward as if he couldn't help himself, creating a breathtaking friction. She gasped, and he shuddered, his expression agonized. "We can't, Brooke. I won't put you at risk that way."

Frustration blossomed within her. She wanted to argue that this was another way for him to remain dominant and disciplined with her, but how could she when his reasons were solid and rational? As much as her feelings for him were becoming deeper and more serious than she'd anticipated, an unplanned pregnancy was a complication neither of them were prepared to handle.

Her thoughts scattered the moment he slid his hand low, spread her with his fingers, and the shower jet made a direct hit on swollen, sensitive flesh. Her knees buckled, but he held her secure in his embrace. His breath was hot on her neck, as sporadic as her own.

And then he filled her the only way he could, two fingers burrowing incredibly deep while the rhythm of his stroking thumb and the tantalizing spray of the water sent her careening swiftly over the edge. She soared straight in the realms of an explosive orgasm that sapped her of energy and strength.

When it was over, she turned in Marc's arms and sagged against his chest for support. One arm curled around his neck, and the other pressed against the strong beating of his heart.

Lifting her heavy head, she glanced up at him, her backside tingling from the pelting water. "You did it again," she accused.

"What? Made you come?" That cocky grin of his reappeared.

Unable to help herself, she laughed, surprised that she was comfortable enough with Marc to indulge in humor after sex. It was a new experience for her, and she liked it. "That, and you're not allowing yourself to enjoy the moment and just let go."

"I already had my fantasy. This one was yours." He dragged his thumb along her jaw, his touch infinitely gentle. "Besides, I enjoy watching you. Immensely."

Her face flushed at the reminder of her abandon. "It's not the same thing, and you know it." She wouldn't be deterred from her original purpose. "You're holding back, and I want to know why."

She felt him stiffen, and his heart thudded beneath her palm. "I'm not holding anything back," he said evenly, though his shadowed gaze contradicted his words.

Her eyes narrowed on him. While she'd opened up and revealed emotional, personal, intimate secrets, he was very stingy in reciprocating. He was afraid, of giving too much, of needing much more in return. She knew, because she felt it, too, and was just as scared, but was prepared to accept the possibility of something more.

Shifting against the fiberglass wall under her

scrutiny, he grasped the hand resting on his chest and guided it downward, over his lean belly and lower—his purpose, she knew, to divert her barrage of questions.

He curled her fingers around his pulsing shaft, and dipped his mouth near her ear. "Here, I saved this just for you."

Oh, he was so bad, and so, so *good*. How could she resist such a gift? She stroked him lightly, feeling him grow in her palm, and marveled at the heat and size and strength of him. Rubbing her breasts against his chest, she looked up into his eyes. "How do you like it?"

"Tight. Slow and easy," he murmured. "And we've got wet covered." Fisting his hand over hers, he showed her the rhythm that turned him on the most, and she learned quickly.

With sinuous movements, his hips undulated, and he groaned low and deep at the pressure and friction they created together. "Yeah, just like that," he said huskily.

His head fell back against the wall, and she placed openmouthed kisses on his neck and shoulder. Experimentally grazing her thumb over the tip of his penis, she gleaned a slick pearl of moisture that made her eager to discover his taste and essence, to offer him the kind of mindless pleasure he'd so selflessly given her. She wanted to show him how much he'd come to mean to her with that gesture. That what they were experiencing together, no matter how fleeting, was special.

Dipping her knees, she slid her lips across his nipple, flicked her tongue over his wet abdomen, lapped the trickle of water that streamed lower…

Seemingly realizing her intent, he cursed and grasped her arms, hauling her back up before she could take him in her mouth.

She frowned at him, startled by the flare of panic that etched his features. "Marc…"

He shook his head in denial, but there was no disputing the stark need burning in the depth of his eyes, the same sentiment that clutched at her heart. Crushing his lips over hers, he swallowed her protest, attempting to drive his own fear far, far away.

She wanted to reassure him, let him know that he wasn't the only one swamped with confusing emotions, but there was no stopping the demands of his body. His thrusts quickened against her grip, and his breathing grew choppy. His hips bucked, the muscles along his stomach and thighs clenched and then he climaxed—long, hard and furiously.

The empty sensation that settled in the pit of Brooke's stomach didn't completely surprise her. Neither did the sting of frustration. He'd given her incredible pleasure, and she'd driven him to his own release…all on his terms. Despite her best efforts, he'd maintained ultimate control.

The water continued to rain down upon them, and a shiver coursed through her. He wrapped his arms around her back, warming her skin but not her soul.

"The water is getting cold," he said after a long, quiet moment had passed. He shut off the valve and opened the curtain, which made her even chillier.

Grabbing one of the fluffy towels she'd set on the counter earlier, she handed it to him, then retrieved the other for herself. "Let's go out by the fire where it's warm," she suggested, as she towel-dried her wet hair. "I'm not done with you yet."

Doubts and an unmistakable reserve dropped over his features, as if he dreaded the possibility of her pursuing the silent conversation that had transpired between them minutes ago. She did plan to find out what kept him and his emotions at arm's length, but not tonight, when he was already on the defensive.

Turning on the light, she blew out the candle and smiled at him as she wrapped her towel around her chest and tucked the end between her breasts. "I was thinking of giving you a nice, long massage, and you can repay the favor by cuddling with me." Nothing threatening at all, just lots of intimacy she hoped to use for emotional artillery later.

A hint of a smile lifted his mouth. "Sounds like a fair trade."

"I think so." Taking his towel from him, she slung it around his waist and secured the end at his hip. "Don't bother putting any clothes on. You go build another fire, and I'm going to see if I can find some lotion to use."

With a nod, he left. She perused the items in the medicine cabinet, but didn't find what she was searching for. There were various toiletries beneath the sink, and just as she reached for a bottle of moisturizer, she knocked over a small, flat rectangular box and read the universal word Trojan emblazoned across the front. She picked up the carton, turned it upside down, and a foil packet fell into her hand.

A single condom. Feeling giddy at the resource she'd discovered, and the ammunition it provided toward shattering Marc's control, she decided to save her treasure for a very special moment. She knew exactly where she'd hide the prophylactic, so it would be handy and nearby when she needed the protection.

An elated smile spread across her face. When the time came, none of Marc's excuses would suffice, and he wouldn't be able to deny her.

# CHAPTER TEN

ANOTHER NIGHT HAD PASSED with Brooke, and Marc was barely hanging on—to his rapidly slipping control, his valiant intentions and his conflicting emotions. All were conspiring against him, and like a man sinking with no life preserver in sight, he was struggling to keep a firm grip on reality—which meant no future with Brooke, no matter how much he was beginning to wish otherwise.

He *had* to keep that fact in mind, along with maintaining a clear division between fantasy and reality, despite how difficult she was making it for him. Physically, separating himself from her was easy, since they weren't going to make love in the traditional sense. Emotionally, he didn't think he'd ever be able to isolate himself from her, not when everything about her was indelibly etched in his mind. Especially the way she'd looked at him in the shower last night when he'd stopped her from taking her caresses one step further. Too many expectations had shone in her eyes, coupled with a longing that exceeded the hot, wild fling they'd agreed to.

The anxiety he'd experienced in that moment had shaken him to the core, because he'd had the overwhelming urge to just let go and give Brooke everything she wanted, everything she demanded. But the fear of ultimately hurting her later, of not being able to give her everything she deserved, of breaking promises he had no right making, kept him from letting her lavish that particular intimacy on him. He'd felt vulnerable enough without surrendering to her silent supplication to accede to *her*.

"Your turn, Jamison," Brooke said.

Squinting at the cards fanned in his right hand, he tried to concentrate on the game of Rummy they'd been playing for the past hour. He was losing, which wasn't a huge surprise—he'd lost every game they'd played so far with the deck of cards she'd discovered in one of the kitchen drawers, from poker, to crazy eights, to twenty-one and now this.

And still, the rest of the afternoon and evening stretched ahead of them.

They'd slept in late that morning, almost to noon, and after waking up and verifying that the storm hadn't passed through yet, Brooke had coaxed him back beneath the warmth of the covers so she could snuggle with him a little longer. Their cuddling had been very relaxing and satisfying, and surprisingly, had remained platonic. The contentment and rightness of waking up with Brooke was unlike anything he'd ever experienced, and something he knew better than to get attached to.

They'd talked about inconsequential things while they lay entwined, sharing favorite movies, foods, activities, likes and dislikes, and they discovered they had a lot more in common than either of them realized. While idly skimming his hand down her side, he'd found a ticklish area right at the curve of her buttocks that sent her into a fit of gasps and giggles when he added a tantalizing pressure to that direct spot. Finding that sensitive region had been purely an accident, but one he couldn't resist exploring further, making her writhe and squirm until she breathlessly pleaded for him to stop the torment.

He did, only to have her grab a pillow when he wasn't looking and pummel him over the head. With a low growl he'd tackled her to the sleeping bag, seen the mischievous glint in her eyes, and seconds later found himself embroiled in a pillow fight. They'd rolled around naked, the moment playful and teasing and filled with raucous laughter and shrieks of indignation—until he'd rolled to his back to escape her and she'd leapt on top of him, straddling his hips to hold him down.

All teasing and fun ceased, and the pillow she'd raised to gain retribution fell to her side. The mischief in her expression faded, replaced with a soft, sensual look he was coming to know too well, and a wanting that stirred his soul. Slowly, she'd splayed a hand on his chest and dragged her palm down his belly toward her spread thighs, until her fingers met the moist heat and silken skin trapping him, teasing him, tempting him. All she had to do was lean forward, slide lower, and she'd impale him right at the heart of where he wanted to be. The urge to touch her, fill her, was so strong his blood had roared in his ears.

*What is your favorite sexual position?*

*I like being on top.*

He didn't like it. Not at all. He'd felt vulnerable under her spell, her feminine power stripping away the tenacious hold he had on his control until the only thought filling his head was being deep, deep inside her and forgetting everything else…like that he was all wrong for her.

She'd bit her bottom lip and glanced toward the couch for some unexplainable reason, as if debating what to do and how to handle their current predicament.

His stomach chose that moment to growl, loudly, obnoxiously, declaring that he'd missed breakfast and it was past time to eat. Much to his relief *and* disappointment, she'd relented to his belly's hungry demand and moved off him, though there was a look in her eyes that proclaimed she'd only given him a brief reprieve.

Marc grunted to himself. She had no clue how close she'd been to his complete capitulation.

She peeked at him from above her cards, amusement dancing in her eyes. "Does that grunt mean you're holding a lousy hand?"

"Like that should surprise you," he muttered. Picking a card from the stack, he discarded the five of hearts, then winced when he realized he'd just given away the card he needed to complete a run.

Without hesitation, she retrieved his card and tucked it into her hand, then tossed out one she didn't need and he couldn't use. "You know, you're not providing much in the way of friendly competition." And she seemed delighted that she had him completely distracted, the little minx.

Other than that one incident earlier, they hadn't touched or kissed or indulged in any more fantasies. After eating a combination lunch and dinner of ravioli, they'd each taken a shower, alone this time. While she'd been in the bathroom, he'd checked in with Marlene and made a call to the ranger station for a weather update. He'd confirmed that the storm would be gone by late that night, and was told they'd send someone out in the morning to pick them up when the roads were clear.

They had all evening and night, and so far, not one sexual advance. Although she'd been on her best behavior since that pillow fight, he didn't trust her demure act and was prepared for a surprise attack…

along with a bold attempt to maintain control of whatever erotic scheme she conjured up.

"I hate to do this to you again," she said, spreading her hand out on the coffee table with a triumphant grin. "Rummy."

Rolling his eyes, he tossed his cards onto the pile. "I give up. My pride can't take any more abuse."

Laughing throatily, she crawled around the coffee table toward him. "Aww, poor baby," she crooned. "Maybe I can help soothe that male pride of yours."

He eyed her gradual approach, unable to miss the wicked, purposeful gleam lighting her blue eyes, or the anticipation curling deep in his belly. "What, you're gonna let me win the next hand?"

She lifted a blond brow. "*Giving* you the win wouldn't be any fun, now would it?" Settling onto her knees in front of where he sat on the middle of the couch, she held his gaze. "No games this time, Marc. We only have this last night left together, and I want to make the most of it."

Suddenly, so did he. As selfish as it was, he wanted what he could take from her, one last time. "Come up here on the couch," he said huskily, wanting her at eye level and within touching distance.

She shook her head and pulled off her thermal top. Her breasts were already swollen, her nipples tight. "I'm fine where I am, thank you," she countered politely, keeping things *her* way and not allowing him any advantages. "Take your shirt off for me."

Dragging the hem up and over his head, he tossed the thermal aside, baring his chest. He watched her stand and shed her bottoms and panties, then kneel again, grasping the waistband of his long underwear. "Now let's get rid of these."

He lifted his hips as she tugged and removed the last barrier of clothing. Pressing her hands to his knees, she widened his legs and moved in between that cove, and leaned more fully into him, so his thighs bracketed the sides of her ribs and her breasts rubbed against his taut belly. She reached up, curled a hand around the back of his neck, and pulled his mouth down to her parted, waiting lips and kissed him, slow and deep, and decadently sensual. She initiated an unrushed, seductive journey of lips and tongue, as if they had the rest of their lives together, rather than just this last night.

The thought made him desperate to touch her, to memorize the feel of her, the sweet, giving taste of her mouth, the texture of her skin—for all those long, lonely nights ahead. He trailed his hands over her shoulders and along her smooth, silky back, pulling her closer still, but not near enough, not deep enough, not intimate enough. His sex pulsated between them, burning with the need to be a part of Brooke in ways that he knew were impossible—for so many reasons.

Her lips left his, trailing kisses along his jaw, the stubble long since softening to a two-day beard, then she nuzzled his neck and inhaled deeply of his scent. Her hands charted a path down his chest, and her mouth followed leisurely behind. Fingers grazed his nipples seconds before she tasted him with a wet lap of her tongue. He groaned and closed his eyes as she teased him with her lips, tantalized him with her teeth, then continued on her descent, tormenting him with the erotic feel of his erection sliding between the warmth of her breasts as she lavished attention on his belly, his navel, and the point where hip met thigh.

Then she surrounded the hard length of him in both hands, and knowing what she meant to do, he tangled fistfuls of her soft hair in his fingers and gently held her intentions at bay. His heart raced, and he battled with the urgent, excruciating need ripping through him.

She looked up at him, her eyes glazed with desire, her expression as vulnerable as he felt. "Tonight, don't tell me no," she whispered, a desperate quality infusing her voice. "I want to share this with you, *please.*"

He knew what she wanted, his complete and total surrender, and there was no denying her, or himself, this intimate pleasure. This time, when she lowered her head, parted her lips over the tip of him, he didn't stop her, resigned to giving her this final fantasy and letting her have her way with him.

He watched her through heavy-lidded eyes, but was unprepared for the wild, primitive onslaught of need that gripped him when the wet heat of her mouth enveloped him. He sucked in a sharp, swift breath as fiery hunger ripped through his body. He shuddered as she stroked him rhythmically, the silky textures of her lips and tongue heightening the incredible sensations. And because there was nothing else he could do, he tightened his fingers around the silky strands of her hair and rode with the exquisite pleasure, until it became too much to bear and his release beckoned.

He swore, and pulled her away before he climaxed, feeling the loss as acutely as the frantic beating of his heart. Breathing hard, he flung his head against the back of the couch and squeezed his eyes shut, trying to regain a semblance of control.

He heard a crinkling sound, felt Brooke's fingers brushing over his fierce erection, then something tight sheathing him. Frowning, he glanced down to find her rolling a condom over his straining shaft.

He choked on hoarse, disbelieving laughter. "Where in the hell did that come from?"

A sultry smile curved her lips as she finished her seductive task. "I had it tucked between the cushions. I found one in the bathroom last night and I was saving it for the perfect moment."

The moment *was* perfect, *too* perfect, rich with possibilities, and swirling with the dangerous prospect of going all the way with Brooke, of consummating emotions he'd spent the past two days avoiding and denying.

She crawled on top of him, straddling his waist. Her slick wetness grazed him, and he grasped her hips before she could take him inside her.

He gritted his teeth against the instinctual urge to drive within her in mindless abandon. "God, Brooke, are you sure about this?" he asked, his voice low and rough. "*Really* sure?" He had to know, because once they made love, there would be no retracting the intimate act…and no experiencing it again.

Like the condom, this was a one-shot deal, reserved for this time in the cabin only.

Framing his face between her palms, she gazed into his eyes, searching so deep he could swear she could see straight to his soul. "I've never been more sure of anything in my whole entire life."

Neither had he. But that changed nothing. "No regrets tomorrow?"

She shook her head, graceful and beautiful and certain. "Never."

"No promises?" He forced the words out around the painful vise tightening his chest.

Her fingers slipped into his hair, curved around

the nape of his neck and she smiled. "Just the promise of pleasure."

The last rule got stuck in his throat, and he felt as though he'd ripped out a piece of his heart when the words finally emerged. "No commitments?" He had to make sure she understood and agreed.

She didn't answer, and instead kissed him, contradicting his final stipulation with so much passion and emotion he was helpless to resist her, despite what her eloquent silence had stated.

She wanted what he couldn't give.

"Make love to me, Marc," she breathed against his lips, and reached down to surround him with hungry hands, guiding him toward the heart of her. "I need you."

The honest statement tore at his resolve, shattered his restraint. There was no denying this woman, or the powerful longing she evoked. He was too far gone, beyond reasoning. He was hers for the taking, a willing partner in this primitive desire to mate and be one.

With a shivery little sigh, she sank down on him, flowing over him like honeyed heat. With a deep, guttural groan, he thrust upward, burying himself to the hilt in her sleek warmth. Too many heartbeats to count passed as they absorbed the feel of one another. Then they gradually began the sinuous movements and gliding rhythm of two lovers completely in sync.

With the intensity of the emotions swirling between them, he expected wild and rushed. She gave him slow and tantalizing, drawing out this one and only joining for as long as possible, taking as well as giving. Threading her fingers through his hair, she tugged his head back, leaned into him and brushed her nipple across his lips. He took her into his mouth, suckling her breast, nipping gently, lapping indulgently, greedily feasting on the sweet taste of her.

It wasn't enough. Not nearly enough. His hands grew restless, and he filled his palms with her soft, supple flesh, caressing her spine, across her buttocks, along her gently rocking hips. He skimmed his fingers down the length of her sleek thighs, then back up again, grazing his thumbs where their bodies joined, pleasuring her with an illicit, knowing touch.

Her breathing deepened, and he looked up into her flushed face, met her drugged gaze and knew he was lost.

Possibly forever.

Knowing he wouldn't last much longer, he increased the pressure to that pulse-point of hers, building the tension they'd kept harnessed for too long, until her ragged breathing indicated just how close she was to that sharp edge.

Taking hold of her hips, he surged powerfully, filling her completely, again and again, until his thrusts turned into an uncontrollable extension of his need for her.

Rapture finally swept her up in its wild, tempestuous current. He heard the excitement of it in the moan that escaped her throat, saw the thrill of it in her eyes before they rolled back in ecstasy, felt the elation of her abandon in the way her body arched toward his and her inner muscles clenched so exquisitely around him.

But it was his name on her lips as she reached that crest that unraveled his control, shattered his restraint, and made him shudder with the incredible force of his own release.

And this last time, he came with her, and held nothing back.

STANDING BY the cabin's front window, Marc stared out at the blackness that had descended with the onslaught of midnight, no longer glimpsing the occasional glow of snowflakes drifting by the glass pane. The storm outside had finally passed through the Rocky Mountains. He wished the upheaval within him would abate just as completely.

Unfortunately, he suspected the memory of these past two days with Brooke would haunt him for the rest of his lonely, solitary life.

He scrubbed a hand down his face, unable to stop thinking of the woman he'd left sleeping on their bed in front of the dying fire, soft and warm and replete from their lovemaking. An occasional cold draft drifted his way from the covered hole in the window, but it wasn't enough to numb him—his mind, his body or the pain in his heart. It ached with wanting Brooke. Stung with the knowledge that the one woman he craved in ways even *he* didn't understand could never, ever be his…not in that deep, intrinsic way that mattered most.

Unease tightened his belly. When had those emotional issues started to make a difference to him? And how in the hell had he allowed Brooke to breach barriers and convictions he'd erected after discovering he was a man who lacked the ability to commit? For the past eight years he'd effectively dodged romantic entanglements and intimate relationships, and poured most of his time and energy into building his business. No single woman had distracted him from his goals and personal creed to embrace bachelorhood. No one woman had tempted him to question his vow to live a solitary life.

Until Brooke. She inspired tenderness and affection. She roused passion and desires he never knew possible.

She kindled a hunger that surpassed anything he'd ever imagined, or felt. She provoked needs that sex alone couldn't quench. In just one wonderful weekend she'd dragged him deeper than he'd ever gone with any woman.

And he had no idea what he was going to do about her hold over him once they left this cabin.

"Marc?"

Brooke's sleep-husky voice drifted from behind him, and he glanced her way. She'd propped herself up on her elbow, and her disheveled hair spilled over her bare, smooth shoulders. The blanket slipped low, revealing perfect breasts tipped with taut, rosy nipples. There wasn't a hint of inhibition about her now, and he loved that about her, and that he was directly responsible for her sensual transformation.

*Love.* The word surged through him like a 220-volt shock, paralyzing him on many levels. Denials came swiftly, and he grasped each one, using them as a means to shore that unexpected flood of emotion.

*It couldn't happen.*

She tipped her head, her brow creasing with concern. "Are you okay?"

No, he didn't think he'd ever be the same again. "I'm fine." His voice cracked, and he swallowed hard to clear it.

"Come back over here." She patted the space beside her. "It's getting cold and I miss you."

His chest tightened. *He was going to miss her, too.* Forcing the thought from his mind, he moved across the room, irresistibly drawn to her.

"You put your thermals back on," she complained with an adorable pout when he neared. "Take them off."

"Yes, ma'am." He shucked his underwear, and she

lifted the blanket for him to slip inside next to her. She turned so he could spoon his body along the back of hers—wanting nothing from him but to simply be held.

And he did just that, all night long—it would be his last chance to do so.

## CHAPTER ELEVEN

SHE'D BROKEN their rules, Brooke acknowledged the next morning as they attempted to restore the cabin to its original order. While she harbored no regrets for what she and Marc had shared in this cabin, she'd discovered that she wanted promises from Marc. But she also knew she had no right to ask for something more lasting and definite, not when he'd made his terms of this affair abundantly clear from the very beginning.

*No commitments.* And because she'd openly agreed to that condition, she had to respect the pact they'd made and let him go, no matter how much her heart wished otherwise.

Straightening the place mats on the table, she slanted a glance at Marc, who was folding the blankets in the living room while she cleaned up the kitchen. Outside, she could hear the snowplows clearing the roads. Within the next hour, someone from the ranger station would be there to pick them up, retrieve their snowmobile, and take them back to their place.

Their chores gave Marc the perfect excuse to avoid her. All morning, he'd kept his distance, keeping conversation to a minimum and physical contact nonexistent. It was as though he'd shut down in the hours before dawn. She'd thought, *hoped,* that their intimate lovemaking the night before had breached the barriers between the flirtatious, carefree man she'd always known, and the caring, complex man she'd glimpsed here in this cabin. She was wrong.

When she'd embraced the idea of an affair with Marc, she hadn't considered anything more than the pleasure, fantasies and fun she'd requested. One wild fling to enjoy and savor before returning to her responsible job as an accountant, and her staid, predictable life. He'd given her all those thrills she'd sought, and so much more. But she'd never expected to discover herself as a woman because of Marc's coaxing, never expected to feel so liberated and free.

And she never, *ever,* expected to fall in love with him.

The realization didn't send her into a panic like it would have a week ago, just as she'd panicked the night he'd kissed her at his parents' anniversary party. Ever since that evening, she'd been struggling against the inevitable, denying what had been so patently obvious in that magical embrace. There was a chemistry between them, an instantaneous connection that transcended sex or lust and touched on something special. She knew Marc had felt it, too, despite his current aloof attitude.

Finished wiping down the kitchen counter, she rinsed the dish rag, drew a deep, fortifying breath…and finally broke the strained silence between them. "Since we've made ourselves at home here, we'll have to find out who owns this cabin so we can reimburse them for our stay, and for the damage to their front window."

"I'm sure the ranger station can help with that information." He rolled up a sleeping bag and secured it with the ties, keeping his gaze on the task. "I'll take care of everything when I get back to the office later today."

His business could have waited a day or two for his return, but she knew he was grasping any excuse to put distance between them. Clearly, he had no intention of pursuing her beyond today, and that knowledge hurt in ways she doubted would ever heal.

Struggling to keep her own emotions under wraps, she put the last of their breakfast dishes away. "I'll split the cost with you, so be sure to let me know what I owe."

He glanced at her, his frown fierce. "*I'll* pay for it."

His insistence on footing the bill made her curious about his reasons, and provoked her to find out. Deeming the kitchen spotless, she headed toward the couch, stopping behind it. "Are you insisting on taking care of any charges because you want to, or are you doing it to ease your conscience?"

He jerked his head back up again, and glared at her. The short, dark beard lining his jaw added to his brooding appearance and made his eyes a piercing, glittering shade of gray. "What the hell is that supposed to mean?"

She crossed her arms over her chest, refusing to allow his gruff tone to discourage her. "You're feeling guilty."

The muscles beneath his shirt tensed, and he immediately averted his gaze to the other sleeping bag, confirming that her suspicions had been accurate. Relief poured through her. His guilt, no matter how misplaced, meant that he cared about her. It wasn't a declaration of his feelings by any stretch of her imagination, but it did give her a slim glimmer of hope.

Then he crushed her optimism with his next announcement. "I'm thinking that maybe this wasn't such a good idea."

She knew without asking what "this" referred to. Them. Together. Intimately. "Kinda late for second thoughts or *regrets,* don't you think?" she said, referring to the conditions he'd insisted on.

He winced, but didn't back down from his own personal crusade to dissuade her. "Yeah, I suppose it is." Scooping up the blankets topped with their pillows, he turned and headed up the loft stairs, effectively severing their discussion.

Easing out a taut stream of breath, she took her aggravation out on straightening the sofa cushions. Unfortunately, touching the couch only served to remind her of the passion that had consumed them last night when they'd made love, his needy response to her aggressive approach, the desperation in his touch and the emotion in his ultimate surrender. What had transpired between them was rare and wonderful and unique, and for some people, a once-in-a-lifetime opportunity. Having experienced a monotonous, passionless relationship with Eric, and having witnessed her own parents' desolate marriage, she refused to settle for less than mutual desire, excitement, and soul-deep devotion.

She and Marc had experienced all three, so why couldn't he admit that what they'd shared was worth exploring beyond today?

She watched him descend to the lower level and cross the room to the fireplace. Removing the screen, he prodded the logs with the poker, making sure that all the embers had burned out. His movements were brusque and filled with restless energy.

She resisted the urge to come up behind him and knead her fingers along the taut sinew bisecting his spine. Certain he wouldn't welcome her touch—not when he was using that tension surrounding him as armor—she kept her hands to herself.

Dragging her fingers through her hair, she stared at his back and continued the conversation he'd tried to divert minutes ago. "Are you going to tell Eric about us being stranded together?"

He hesitated for a few heartbeats. "Yeah." His tone was gruff, but resigned. "I'm sure he'll find out about it one way or another, since he knows Ryan and Shane. It's best if the news comes directly from me so he doesn't think we're hiding something."

She bit her lip to keep from reminding him that they *were* hiding something—the fact that they'd had a wonderful, thrilling affair. "Will you tell him about *us?*" she asked, more pointedly this time.

He shook his head, and kept jabbing the ashes in the grate. "I don't think our being together, or what we did in this cabin, is anyone's business but our own." Setting the poker back in its brass stand, he replaced the screen, giving the task way too much attention.

Resting her bottom on the couch's armrest, she wondered if there would always be this awkward tension and unease between them now. She wanted to know what to expect from Marc in the future when they encountered one another at his mother's house, which was bound to happen sooner or later.

She voiced her concern. "What about us seeing one another?"

Finally, he turned around and faced her, his expression a heartbreaking combination of anguish and fierce control. "I don't do relationships, Brooke," he said roughly. "Nothing long-term or serious. You knew that going into this affair."

He'd misunderstood her question, but that didn't stop her heart from giving an odd little twist. She couldn't refute his claim. He *had* warned her, and she'd blindly agreed to his terms. But that had been before she knew an affair with him would alter her expectations, and make him one of the most important people in her life. Unfortunately, he didn't want to be a part of hers.

Very calmly, she replied. "All I meant was that I'm sure we'll run into one another at some point. Thanksgiving is coming up, and you know your mother usually invites me over since my mother lives out of the state. Is that going to be a problem for you?"

He thought about that for a quiet moment, and it was obvious to her that he hadn't considered the possibility of the two of them being thrown together, having to make polite talk, while trying not to think of all the intimacies they'd shared. After these past two days, nothing would ever be the same between them again.

"I don't know," he replied honestly.

His candid response gave her an opening she hadn't anticipated, an opportunity she wasn't going to let slip through her grasp. Scooting off the edge of the couch, she closed the physical distance between them. Emotionally, the gap seemed to widen. He watched her approach warily, but didn't bolt around her like she half expected him to when she stopped inches away.

Lifting her hand, she pressed her palm over his heart, absorbing the rapid pulse, and the warmth radiating off him. She inhaled his unique masculine scent, and her stomach curled with an acute desire and longing.

He stood statue still, giving her the impression that he wanted to prove that he was immune to her touch, to *her*. She'd give him an A for effort, but he ultimately failed to conceal his own need. She watched his pupils dilate into dark orbs, observed the slight flare of his

nostrils that indicated just how aware of her he was…
and just how hard he was struggling to keep that attraction and fascination confined.

Satisfied that she'd gotten to him, even just a tiny bit,
she pushed her advantage, ignoring for the moment the
promise she'd made—to be satisfied with nothing more
than pleasure and erotic memories. "You might not
know if you can handle seeing me at family gatherings,
but I can tell you that after all we've shared, it won't be
simple or easy for me. Not when I know what we had
here in this cabin is worth taking a chance on."

Swearing viciously, he paced to the other end of the
couch. "Dammit, I *knew* this would happen."

She tipped her head and regarded him cautiously.
"You knew what would happen?"

His accusatory eyes burned like hot coals. "That
you'd confuse lust with other sentimental emotions and
want more from me than I can give you."

His anger and denials inflamed her own ire. All her
life she'd been a mediator, rushing to diffuse angry
flare-ups instead of dealing with whatever conflict or
problem she encountered. It started with her parents,
and gradually shaped her personality as she was
growing up. She'd always been the one to soothe upset-
ting situations, restore peace and avoid opposition.

Being passive no longer held any appeal for her. Nor
was she going to let Marc blame her for his own insecurities. He was battling his own fears and personal
demons—she couldn't fight them, too, not unless she
knew what they were.

Her chin lifted a determined notch. "If I learned one
thing in this cabin with you, I now know the difference
between satiating lust and making love. We did both,

and I'm not confused about which took place when." She softened her tone, but not her candid words. "I'm not asking you for anything, but after our time together, and what we shared, I think I have the right to tell you how I feel."

"I do care for you, Brooke. And these past two days with you have been incredible, beyond anything I've ever experienced with any other woman." He scrubbed a hand over his jaw, looking torn. "As for taking a chance and pursuing this relationship any further than this cabin, I *can't*."

She hadn't outright asked him to take that chance. She'd promised herself, and him, she wouldn't. But she couldn't suppress her curiosity. "Why not?" she countered. "And this time, give me a good, solid reason *why*."

His brows snapped together, and his features swirled with dark, dangerous hostility. Unease slithered through Brooke. She'd never seen him this way before, never knew he possessed such depth and multi-faceted layers…and a secret he was very reluctant to share.

But then she'd never provoked him before. "Why not?" she asked again, forcing him to acknowledge her and the question.

His mouth flattened into a grim line. The emotions in his eyes were raw and frayed. "You want a good solid reason why? How about the fact that I'm just like my father, and Eric?"

The pit of her stomach clenched at his insinuation, but she refused to believe the worst, not after glimpsing shadows of old pain and regret in his eyes. "What, that you enjoy flattering women?"

"I wish it were as simple as that." Marc's shoulders slumped in defeat. He'd never meant for their special time together in this cabin to end on such a dreadful note, but she was leaving him little choice except to be brutally honest with her. "How about the fact that I have a problem remaining faithful?"

Her eyes widened and her hand fluttered to the collar of her sweater. "What?" she whispered, her soft voice colored with incredulity.

"It's true," he confirmed, and watched as a mixture of horror and disbelief creased her features. God, he hated hurting her. Hated that he was about to shatter the chivalrous image of him she'd believed in.

The fantasy was definitely over. They'd gone from friends, to lovers, and would quickly revert to polite acquaintances when she discovered he was too much like his brother.

Ignoring the growing pressure in his chest, he said, "Just like my father, and Eric, I've been unfaithful to someone I was seeing."

Slowly, she sank onto a sofa cushion. Her deep blue gaze, so filled with confusion, searched his expression, seemingly wanting to know more.

"That one indiscretion is enough to convince me that I'm not cut out for a monogamous, committed relationship, Brooke. Not long-term, anyway. Not when I take into consideration my father and brother's track record and what Eric put you through. I won't take that risk with *any* woman again. Especially you."

End of discussion for him, he stalked toward the front windows, searching for signs of the ranger's vehicle coming up the drive. No such luck. After two days of seclusion, he was feeling boxed in, edgy, and restless for wide open spaces. Though cabin fever would have been a logical excuse for his anxiety, he knew this unwanted conversation with Brooke was the real culprit.

"What happened?" she asked after long minutes passed.

Hanging his head, he shut his eyes, reaching deep for calm and patience. "You don't need to hear the sordid details." And he sure as hell didn't want to relive that awful night he'd spent the past eight years trying to forget.

"I want to know what happened," she persisted. "We've been nothing but honest with one another in this cabin. Before we leave, make me understand why these two days together are all we can have. I think you owe me that."

Yeah, he owed her an explanation for the brusque ending to their affair. And by the time he was done recounting his appalling tale, not only would she understand his reasons, she'd definitely keep her distance. Bracing his arm on the frame above his head, he kept his gaze trained on a snow-covered tree outside, unable to look at Brooke, not wanting to see the pity in her eyes when he revealed the whole truth.

He inhaled a ragged breath, exhaled slowly. "Remember that survey question about one-night stands?"

"Yes," came her quiet reply from behind him.

"Well, that incident was it. One sexual encounter with a faceless stranger when I was still seeing another woman." He shook his head in disgust over his actions, and how that event had changed his entire view on serious relationships, as well as served to shore up the belief that short-term affairs were more his style.

He continued. "I was twenty-two at the time, and a senior in college. I'd been dating Dana Ramsey for about three months. She was ten years older than me, *very* experienced, and we spent most of our time together in bed. At first, I thought it was great. I mean, what healthy, hormonal twenty-two-year-old wouldn't?"

Brooke didn't answer him, but he wasn't expecting a reply to his rhetorical question. "Dana came on strong, was very possessive, clingy even, and I started feeling stifled. I told her I wasn't looking for anything serious, but that didn't seem to make a difference to her. If anything, my attempts to back out of the relationship intensified her demands."

He paused, remembering the panic he'd first experienced at Dana's pressure tactics, then the defiance that had settled in. "When she started dropping hints about us getting married, I just lost it and completely rebelled. I was at a frat party one night drowning my anxiety in beer. When some coed I didn't even know came on to me, I followed along and slept with her."

Silence settled over the room for several heartbeats, then Brooke spoke. "I take it that ended your relationship with Dana?"

He jerked his head around, unable to believe that she could be so apathetic about his infidelity. "Good God, Brooke, I felt like crap the next morning, knowing that I *cheated* on her. She didn't deserve that, no matter how uptight I was about her demands about marriage."

"True," she conceded, "but at least you experienced guilt and remorse after the fact."

He frowned. "What difference does that make?"

"You were young, you weren't ready to settle down, and you tried to tell Dana that, but she wouldn't listen," she said. "You made a mistake, Marc. One you obviously regret and haven't repeated."

How could she sit there and be so reasonable when

he despised himself for what he'd done? "That doesn't excuse what I did."

"No, it doesn't," she agreed, but there was no condemnation in her expression.

"It's no better than what Eric did to you," he persisted.

"Don't compare yourself to your brother." Her gaze held his, filled with steely conviction. "You're two very different men, and the circumstances are completely different."

He gaped at her. "How can I *not* compare myself to Eric when I'm guilty of the same thing he did to you?"

"We were married, which makes a big difference. He *vowed* to be faithful to me." She stood, but didn't close the distance between them, opting instead to remain by the coffee table. "You were dating Dana, and she ignored your attempts to keep your relationship from getting too serious. And Eric cheated more than once, whereas this is your one and only indiscretion, an error of judgment that I'm guessing has been eating you up inside since it happened."

She knew him well. Too well.

Drawing a deep breath, she slid her fingers into the back pocket of her jeans. "And the biggest difference between you two? Eric and I never had the kind of openness and honesty and trust that you and I have shared in just two days."

And he'd never had that with any other woman, either, because he'd never let himself get close enough to establish those emotional bonds. Yet with Brooke, those intimacies had come naturally, and had felt incredibly right and good.

Turning back to the window, he pressed his fingertips to the cold pane. "I watched Eric get married to you, and I prayed that you'd be the one to keep him monogamous. And when it didn't happen, I lost all hope for myself." He swallowed the tight knot gathering in his throat. "I don't want to offer you false promises when I don't know if I can make that kind of commitment." But how he wished he *could* give her something more lasting and permanent.

"I'm not asking for a commitment, Marc," she said.

He laughed, but the harsh sound grated along his sensitive nerve endings. "Right at this moment, maybe not, but you will eventually. That's the kind of woman you are, and it's what you deserve." Pushing away from the window, he moved across the room toward her, prepared to issue more blunt and irrefutable honesty if that's what it took to make her understand, and leave this cabin with her own pride intact. "The sex between us was spectacular, but it won't be enough for you months down the road. You'll want more, and my biggest fear is that I'll panic again when things get too intense."

Her mouth quirked with the barest of smiles. "Things are already intense."

"And I'm *panicking!*" He felt himself physically trembling, and he pushed his unsteady hands through his disheveled hair. "I'm afraid of disappointing you, Brooke."

She bit her bottom lip, her eyes shining with a wealth of vulnerabilities. "And that's my same fear, that I'll disappoint you, too. That maybe I won't keep you satisfied in the long run. You don't own the market on insecurities."

He remained mute, stunned by her admission. Tenderness swelled within him, but before he could reassure her that she'd keep any man well gratified, she stepped toward him and pressed her palm to his bearded cheek, her touch, her eyes, unbearably gentle.

"But I'm most afraid of giving you up, of letting you go, of feeling empty and alone when you're gone." Her fingers grazed his jaw as if memorizing his features. "All my life I've done for everyone else. Now, I want to please *me*. There's more between us than incredible, mind-blowing sex. We both know it, feel it, even if you won't admit it out loud. I saw it in your eyes last night when we were making love. I see it in your eyes now."

Instinctively, he tried to turn his head away so she couldn't see straight to his soul, but she framed his face between both hands, not allowing him the luxury of that escape.

She stared deep into his eyes. "You want more than just an affair, I know you do. And I know you're afraid to take that risk, so I won't ask for more than you're willing to give. Making a relationship work isn't easy, but you have to want to try and make it happen. We could start out slow and simple, by seeing one another, and dating, and spending quality time together."

Overwhelming frustration gripped him. "To see if I'm capable of remaining committed in a relationship? To make sure I don't screw up again and hurt someone I—" He sucked in a swift breath, catching himself before the word *love* slipped past his lips and he gave her the leverage she needed to sustain her argument. His heart thudded in his chest, and he quickly amended his remark. "I don't want to risk hurting you."

"You make it sound like some kind of lab test," she quipped lightly.

"In a way, it would be a test. What if I discover that I can't handle being in a serious relationship? That I find I'm too restricted and I just can't commit? Where does that leave *you?*"

Instead of backing down, retreating or giving up on him like she should have done, she continued to fight. "I don't believe you'd deliberately hurt me. I don't believe you'd deliberately seek out another woman in an act of rebellion. Maybe when you were a young man of twenty-two who just wanted to have a good time in college and didn't want the responsibility of a relationship, but not now."

She paused, as if gathering her thoughts. Then she shared them. "I'll admit that I once believed you were like Eric, too, but that was before I really took the time to get to know you. I've discovered that you're a man who has patience and likes to be around children. You're warm, and caring, and you don't try to hide who you are or try to be something you're not. The Marc I know would cherish a wife and kids and work through problems rather than shirk them."

*Wife and kids.* The very things he hadn't allowed himself to think about, but had always wanted. "You don't know that."

"I *believe* it," she said with so much faith he almost believed it, too. "The Marc I've learned about these past two days isn't selfish. The Marc I've discovered would put his family first, just as you're thinking of me now, trying to protect me from something that may never happen." She smiled, though the sentiment held a tinge of sadness. "If your brother was half the man you are, maybe Eric and I would still be married. And maybe if I was the woman I am *now,* Eric never would have felt the need to cheat."

"Eric was a damn fool," he said, meaning it.

A delicate brow lifted. "Then what does that make you?"

*An even bigger fool.* "It would destroy me if I hurt you, and I'm not willing to take that risk. For both our sakes. If anything, I've learned from my father and brother, and my own mistake." He headed over to the front door, where they'd left their gear.

She trailed behind, more slowly. "Your father is still married to your mother, and they're happy together. They worked through whatever problems they had."

He slanted her a cynical look. "As you know from your own parents' situation, it doesn't always end happily."

She stopped behind him, and crossed her arms over her chest. "What I do know, what I've learned, is that there's no guarantees in love and marriage. But if two people care enough to compromise and communicate, then love and a good, strong marriage *can* work."

The sound of a vehicle pulling into the drive echoed in the quiet cabin, followed by two short honks to announce the ranger's arrival.

*Finally,* Marc thought, welcoming the interruption, which saved him from issuing more arguments. "Sounds like our ride is here." He turned away, but she grabbed his arm and forced him to look at her.

"What if…" Her voice cracked, and she swallowed to ease her throat. "What if I tell you that I've fallen in love with you?"

He stared at her, seeing the devotion and hope shimmering in her eyes. Her sweet declaration nearly sent him to his knees with his own avowal, but he kept his emotions and his expression firmly battened down, even though he was dying inside. Anxiety banded his chest, but this time the pressure wasn't a result of feeling stifled, but because he dreaded the thought of spurning that love he ached for so badly.

He dredged up the words he knew he had to speak. "All the more reason to end this now." Scooping up her snowsuit and helmet from the floor, he handed them to her, then busied himself collecting his own gear.

Unable to look her in the eyes, he added, "I know this is difficult now, but in the long run, you'll thank me, Brooke."

*THANK YOU VERY MUCH.*

Brooke was thanking Marc, all right, for leaving her with a heartache she was certain would never ease. Two days, and she loved the man. Two days, and she was back to being alone again.

The emptiness and loss that consumed her was unlike anything she'd ever encountered. Her divorce from Eric had been inevitable. Losing Marc had been a one-sided choice she'd had little say in. He'd thwarted every argument, and ultimately rejected her, her love, and her belief in him—as if he knew what was best for her, all because he couldn't forgive himself for a past mistake.

Her gratitude was overwhelming.

When they'd returned to their cabin, he'd wasted no time in informing Shane and Ryan that they needed to hit the road so he could get back to his office since they were a day behind in returning. Within an hour, the men had vacated the place. Within five minutes of their departure Brooke knew her life would never be the same, not without Marc to complete it.

He'd taught her all about love and passion and embracing the woman inside her. And that woman wanted him, with the very depths of her heart and soul. She no longer wanted to live her life conservatively, and dreaded the boring, practical and predictable lifestyle awaiting her at home. Not when she'd tasted something far more exciting and thrilling with Marc.

She berated herself for her naiveté, for thinking she was capable of enjoying a fling with Marc and chalking the incident up as an unforgettable affair. She *did* crave more, more than he was willing to give.

"Come on, fess up, Brooke," Stacey cajoled. "We want all the steamy details."

Taking a deep breath and shaking off the desolate feeling swirling within her, Brooke sank down on the living room couch across from her friend and Jessica. "There's not much to tell," she hedged, not willing to divulge intimate details and sully what she'd shared with Marc. "Like I said, we got lost coming home from the lodge, ran out of gas and had to break into someone's cabin for the duration of the storm."

"Sounds...*adventurous.*"

Her friend's meaning was clear, but Brooke chose to ignore the underlying question in her comment. "We were lucky we found shelter, considering how brutal the blizzard turned out to be."

"And?" Stacey persisted.

Brooke affected nonchalance. "And what?"

Stacey blew out an exasperated stream of breath. "Well, did you two take advantage of the situation?"

In erotic, provocative ways she'd never imagined possible or would ever forget. Feeling Jessica's inquisitive gaze on her, as well, she laughed lightly to diffuse the anticipation seemingly quivering in the air. "Marc was a perfect gentleman." It wasn't a lie. He'd been generous with her pleasure, and entirely too noble about protecting her from himself.

Jessica didn't look completely convinced, and

Brooke quickly averted her gaze from her sister's knowing one.

Stacey groaned in disappointment. "I can't believe you let a perfect opportunity like that go to waste!"

She shrugged as though to say "oh well" and quickly changed the subject. "What about you and Shane?"

A dreamy expression softened Stacey's features. "Oh, we definitely took advantage of the situation."

Jessica rolled her eyes. "The two of them only came out of the downstairs bedroom to go to the bathroom or to the kitchen to get something to eat."

"Well, we certainly know who had the most fun on this trip." A grin lifted the corners of Stacey's mouth. "*And* I have a date with Shane when we return to Denver on Sunday."

Shaking her head in amusement, Brooke stood, ready to move past this conversation. "I think I'll make myself a sandwich. Anyone else?" The thought of food hitting her stomach made her queasy, but it worked as an excuse.

"None for me, thanks," Stacey said, reclining languorously on the couch. "I'm discovering that love has a way of eclipsing hunger."

"Love?" Brooke stared incredulously at her friend, who'd always avoided serious relationships in lieu of just having a good time. "You're in love with Shane?"

"Don't look so surprised. I know I come across as this wild, single woman, but when the right guy comes along there's no mistaking when it's the real thing."

Brooke felt a knot form in her chest, wishing that Marc could have had faith in the real thing. In her. "I'm happy for you."

Stacey's adoration for Shane shone in her eyes. "Thanks. I'm hoping it'll work out between us."

Heading into the kitchen, Brooke retrieved the lunch meat, cheese, bread and mayonnaise from the refrigerator and started making herself a sandwich. Admittedly, she wasn't really hungry, but starving herself over Marc wasn't something she'd allow herself to do.

"I'll take one," Jessica said from behind her as she entered the kitchen. "*My* hunger is still intact."

Brooke managed a smile at her sister's meaningful comment. She obviously hadn't fallen for Ryan Matthews's charm while she and Marc had been stranded. "How were things between you and Ryan during the blizzard?"

Jessica propped her hip against the counter next to Brooke. "Interesting, considering he didn't take much offense to my lawyer jokes." She sounded disappointed.

Slathering a piece of bread with spread, Brooke slanted her sister a sly look. "Hmm, smart guy." She gave Ryan credit, for seeing past Jessica's sassy mouth and attitude that kept men at arm's length.

Jessica reached for a slice of cheese and peeled off the plastic wrapper, her brows pulled into a troubled frown. "He asked me out," she said quietly.

Her confession took Brooke by surprise. "And?"

"I said no, of course," her sister replied quickly, layering slices of meat on their bread.

"Aw, Jess, you like him, don't you?" She'd always been able to read Jessica's moods and thoughts and felt pretty certain she'd accurately assessed her sister's problem.

"Maybe," she said nebulously. "I mean, he is a—"

"Lawyer," they finished at the same time.

"End of story," Jessica said succinctly. "I'm particular about who I date, and lawyers top the list of automatic no-gos."

Arguing Jessica's reasons was futile, Brooke knew. "That's really too bad, because he seems like a nice guy."

She shrugged noncommittally as she finished stacking their sandwiches with ham.

Brooke brought down two small plates from the cupboard and Jessica set their lunch on them. "You know, you really shouldn't hold the guy's occupation against him."

"No matter how gorgeous, sexy or amusing I find Ryan, I don't like what he does for a living." A deep hurt shimmered in Jessica's eyes, brought on by old memories. "Why let myself get attached to him when it'll never work out?"

Just as Brooke had with Marc. She was attached…by the heart. "You'd be amazed at the things you'd be willing to compromise on if you fell for the right guy." Suddenly unable to eat even a bite of her sandwich, she pushed her plate away.

Jessica took a bite of her lunch, scrutinizing Brooke as she chewed. "Ohmigod," she said, her voice infused with a startling revelation. "Something *did* happen between you and Marc at that cabin. I knew it!"

She'd never lied to her sister, and she wouldn't do so now. "Yeah, something happened, but it's over before it's even had a chance to begin."

Jessica's brows rose in astonishment. "Did you two, um, *you know?*"

Brooke found the blush staining her sister's cheeks endearing. They'd talked about guys and sex, and from what Brooke knew, Jessica's experience was limited. "Yes, we made love, and it was the most incredible, intimate experience of my life." No doubt, no other man would ever compare to Marc.

"Wow," she murmured, envy tingeing her voice.

Brooke drew a deep breath, along with a healthy dose of fortitude. "And I love him."

"Oh, wow," Jessica said again, this time her eyes wide with concern. "What are you going to do?"

"There's nothing I can do. Marc knows how I feel about him, and he's decided that we're better off, that *he's* better off, not pursuing our relationship."

The compassion Brooke had offered Jessica so many times over the years was now returned by her sister. "I'm sorry, sis."

A bottomless sadness engulfed Brooke, tightening her vocal cords. "Yeah, me, too," she whispered.

## CHAPTER TWELVE

MARC GLANCED at his watch, noted the time, and knew he couldn't avoid the inevitable much longer. He would have preferred spending Thanksgiving day holed up in his office, working on electrical estimates and generally being alone in his miserable state. Instead, he would soon be with Brooke at his parents', feigning that they were just friends and pretending that they hadn't spent two incredible days together that were indelibly etched in his mind. Regretting, too, the way he'd severed their affair and hurt her with his uncompromising conviction that ending their relationship was for the best.

*Best for whom?* his conscience taunted. The question had haunted him, tangling up his emotions with uncertainties and a yearning that tugged at his heart twenty-four hours a day.

*Best for her,* because he couldn't give her all that she deserved.

*Best for him,* to save himself from confronting fears he'd lived with for eight long years.

Tossing his pen onto his desk, he leaned back in his leather chair and stabbed his fingers through his disheveled hair. When had he become such a damn coward? Like a man who'd perfected the art of avoiding entanglements, he'd run hell-bent from the mere mention of commitment. Except no matter how hard he tried, he couldn't escape the fact that he'd fallen in love with Brooke.

The knowledge only compounded his misery. She was everything he'd ever wanted, and everything he knew he'd never have. While she might be willing to take risks with her future, and them, he was not. He knew he wasn't a smart investment for her, even if she wouldn't acknowledge that for herself.

Two weeks had passed since they'd been stranded together, and he hadn't heard from her. Not that he'd expected her to call when he'd given her no reason to hope that he might make room for her in his life. True to their agreement, she'd made no demands on him, and while he should have been grateful for her acquiescence, all he felt was a huge, gaping loss.

He straightened the contracts and files on his desk into neat piles. He reviewed bills, signed checks and pitched wadded-up pieces of paper into the wastebasket. When he could stall no longer, he headed out of his office to his Suburban. On the way to his parents' place, on a whim he bought a bouquet of flowers from a roadside vendor to surprise his mother.

Once he arrived, he parked behind Eric's sports car. Brooke's vehicle wasn't in the drive, and he experienced relief that he'd been spared that initial awkward encounter, and disappointment at the thought that she might have decided to forgo the holiday with his family because of him.

Without knocking, he entered the two-story house he'd grown up in, hung his coat in the foyer closet and followed the delicious aroma of Thanksgiving dinner toward the back of the house. He passed through the family room, and stopped at the glass slider leading to the back porch, where his father and Eric were practicing their putting skills on the strip of green his father used in the wintertime to perfect his short-range shots. Marc knocked and waved a greeting.

He started on his way, then paused when he caught sight of the family portrait that still hung on the paneled wall. The picture had been taken when he was sixteen, and Eric eighteen, about six months before his parents' marriage had hit its lowest point, if he remembered correctly.

He stepped closer to the portrait, noticing how he and Eric were positioned between their mother and father. His parents were both smiling at the camera, but their eyes held no joy, and their expressions were more strained than relaxed. He shook his head, amazed that he'd never noticed those small telltale signs before now, and realized what they'd signified. Amazed, too, that the man and woman in the portrait didn't resemble the loving couple his parents were now, despite the rough times they'd endured. All these years he'd taken his parents' marriage for granted, never giving much thought to how much work they'd put into the relationship to make it last, when they easily could have opted for a divorce during that crisis.

Mulling that over, he continued through the house and found his mother in the kitchen. She was standing by the stove wearing an apron over her casual khaki pantsuit, stirring a simmering pot of what looked and smelled like gravy. He approached quietly from behind and presented the flowers first.

"Happy Thanksgiving, Mom."

Kathleen whirled around, surprise lighting her features when she saw him. "Happy Thanksgiving to you, too." She gave him a hug and a kiss on the cheek, then reached for the bouquet and inhaled the floral fragrance. "Oh, honey, they're beautiful, but you shouldn't have!"

Her words meant she was thrilled that he'd thought of her, he knew. "I wanted to." He shrugged and grinned, and for the first time in two weeks felt a lightness in his heart. "I like seeing you smile."

She beamed, her blue eyes sparkling with pleasure. "You're just like your father," she said, and turned away to retrieve a vase from the cupboard.

After the heavy discussion he and Brooke had had at the cabin, his mother's comment initially startled him, and made him wonder, exactly, what she meant by her comparison. He wanted to ask, but wasn't sure how to phrase the question without sounding defensive.

Heading to the refrigerator, he retrieved a bottle of beer, screwed off the top, and took a drink of the malty liquid. "Is Brooke coming today?" he asked as nonchalantly as possible.

"Yes." She filled the cut crystal vase with water, and unwrapped the flowers, arranging the stems just so. "And I invited Jessica, too, so she wouldn't have to spend the day alone. Brooke called just before you got here and said she was running a little behind. She should be here in about half an hour."

His stomach did a tiny flip. Automatically, he glanced at the clock on the wall and gauged the time, and just how long it would be before he saw her again.

Kathleen glanced his way. "Do you plan on going outside to visit with Eric and your father?"

He shook his head, still trying to figure out a casual way to ask his mother why she thought he was so much like his dad. "I saw them on my way to the kitchen and waved hello."

Picking up the vase, she passed him to the adjoining dining room, where she set the arrangement in the center of the formal mahogany table they used on special occasions, then returned. "Well, if you plan on staying in here, I'm going to put you to work."

He set his beer aside, and pushed up the sleeves of his cable-knit sweater. "That's fine, just so long as you don't make me wear an apron."

"Why not?" Her eyes sparkled playfully. "Your father looks very cute wearing my aprons." She laughed. "Of course your father would never admit that he's ever worn one, but, well, baking with your father can get really messy, but fun."

To his dismay, he felt his face warm. "I'm *sure* I don't want to hear this."

She retrieved two pot holders from a drawer and handed them to him, then opened the oven for him to retrieve the turkey. "What, you think just because we're an old married couple that we don't have any fun together?"

That sobered him, because there had been a time when his parents hadn't enjoyed one another's company. Hefting the huge, golden-brown turkey from the oven, he set it on the stove top. "I'm really glad that you and Dad have each other." He meant that sincerely, and couldn't imagine his parents apart...*now.*

She shut the oven door, her expression softening. "Me, too, though I'm sure you know our marriage wasn't always so pleasant."

He'd never discussed with either his mother or father the obvious problems they'd endured years ago, though at the time he and Eric had been old enough to decipher their arguments, and figure out the gist of what was going on. They just hadn't known the details, the reasons why their parents had drifted apart or what had brought them back together.

"What happened?" he asked, surprising both of them with his frank question.

She didn't shy away from his personal query, but then he knew she wouldn't. Over the years his mother had developed a strength and candidness he now appreciated.

"Well," she said, taking a deep breath, and keeping her gaze steadily on him. "Do you remember the hysterectomy I had when you and Eric were in high school?"

Marc nodded. "Yes."

"Well, that's where the problems started in our marriage." She gave a small smile, and uncovering the fresh yams she'd baked, she layered the top with pecans. "After the surgery, I experienced some depression, mostly because I didn't feel desirable anymore. I'll admit that your father was very understanding at first, but I kept pushing him away and wouldn't talk to him about how I was feeling. Eventually, we grew apart, emotionally and physically, and instead of working on the problem together, I completely shut out your father because of my own insecurities. Before long, we were like two strangers living in the same house."

Marc was surprised to learn of the deeper issues that had contributed to his parents' troubled marriage. As a teenager, he'd noticed his mother's mood swings, but had never known the extent of her illness, or how it had affected his father. All he'd seen and learned of had been the affair that had ultimately brought his mother and father to a crossroad in their relationship.

Kathleen's delicate brow wrinkled as she pulled out more memories to share. "And then one night your father came home and told me he'd had an affair. He was so wracked with guilt and remorse, and of course I was completely devastated."

"How did you get through that?" Marc asked.

"It wasn't easy, that's for sure." She gave a little laugh, but Marc knew that incident must have been a very painful time for both of them. "I wanted to blame your father for the affair, but the truth was, I was more at fault for pushing him away and forcing him to look elsewhere for what his own wife wouldn't give him. It's not an excuse for what he did, but it was his honesty about the situation that made me realize just how close I was to losing him. He could have kept that one night a secret or continued with the affair or had numerous ones, but he didn't. It wasn't what he wanted."

She sprinkled brown sugar on top of the yams and pecans, and continued. "The experience made us reevaluate our marriage and forced us to decide what we were going to do. When I suggested a divorce, thinking that's what your father wanted, he broke down and told me that he wanted me, and us, the way we were when we first got married."

Marc reached for the bag of marshmallows on the counter and placed them on the top of the candied yams. He recognized the true meaning of commitment in the way his parents had worked through their troubles, instead of opting for the easy way out. "And you wanted that, too."

"Yes, I did." She smiled without an ounce of regret for the choice she'd made. "But first, I had to get help for my depression, which I did. And as we talked and worked through the mess we'd made of our marriage, we discovered that we had never stopped loving one another. With everything that happened after my hysterectomy, I just lost track of what was most important, and that was your father, our marriage, you and Eric, and being a family."

Once again, she opened the oven, and he placed the baking dish on the rack so the marshmallows could melt over the yams. They'd been open about everything else, now he wanted an answer to the question he hadn't been able to voice earlier.

He tipped his head toward his mom. "What did you mean about me being just like Dad?"

She rummaged through a cupboard and brought down the box that held the electric knife for carving the turkey, and cast a smile his way. "I only meant that you're thoughtful, sweet and sensitive."

"Sweet? Sensitive?" He blanched. "Uh, that's not usually how guys like to be described."

She laughed as she unrolled the cord to the knife. "What, you want me to tell you how macho and strong and handsome you are?"

He grinned. "I'll take strong and handsome."

"All the men in this family are that, but you, well, you take after your dad in so many ways." Warmth and affection touched her features. "I love Eric, but he just doesn't have that sensitivity to other people's feelings that you and your father do, which I think is part of the reason his marriage to Brooke didn't work. I also believe that he gave up so easily and settled for divorce because it just wasn't true love between them. Otherwise, he would have fought for her."

Undying, true love. Marc loved Brooke and he hadn't fought for her. His chest tightened with too many emotions, too many fears...the biggest one of which was living the rest of his life without Brooke.

"Being thoughtful, and considerate and caring is a compliment, Marc," his mother continued, oblivious to his internal turmoil. "It makes you the kind of man a woman can trust and rely on because you'd never intentionally hurt her, just like your father never set out purposely to hurt me all those years ago. And someday, when the right woman comes along, those qualities will make you a wonderful husband and she'll be very lucky to have you."

Marc leaned against the counter as his mother turned away to check on the gravy. He absorbed her words, feeling as though he'd been sucker-punched in the stomach.

*God, what had he done?* Hadn't Brooke tried to tell him essentially the same thing his mother was telling him now? And just like his mother, Brooke believed in him, too—saw the goodness and honesty and integrity he swore had been stripped away that night he'd made the wrong decision.

He'd been so wrapped up in the past, so fearful that he'd repeat that same mistake with Brooke, that he couldn't bring himself to trust his true instincts, or grasp that unending faith she had in him. Instead, he'd used that youthful mistake and his father's indiscretion as a barrier, intent on punishing himself for the guilt and regret that had consumed him. And in the process he'd lost the one and only woman he'd ever loved.

For eight years, he'd considered being like his father a curse, not knowing his dad's affair had been prompted by emotional issues with his mother. Now, he saw the qualities he'd inherited from his dad for the blessings they were, and was grateful for the strength it gave him to trust himself, to know that he *could* endure the hard times…with the right woman to complement him.

The doorbell rang, and his mother's face lit up. "That must be Brooke and Jessica. Why don't you go answer the door while I check the yams and call your brother and father inside?"

Marc couldn't move. That damnable fear again. But this time he dreaded the worst, that his blunder in doubting Brooke, in not trusting her, in rejecting her love, would result in the biggest mistake of his life.

What if he'd hurt her so badly she no longer wanted him? Could he blame her? Could he live without her? Did he even stand a chance at reclaiming her love?

The doorbell rang again. "Marc?" his mother said, frowning at him. "Would you please get the door?"

"Uh, yeah," he said, and forced himself to move toward the foyer. Heart hammering wildly, he opened the door, and time stood still as he devoured the sight of Brooke.

Their gazes met, hers a soft, velvet shade of blue. He searched for a sign that she still wanted him, that she forgave him for not believing in her. Before he could witness anything to give him a glimmer of hope, she glanced away, as if it pained her to look at him.

His heart dropped to his stomach.

Jessica cleared her throat, breaking the silence and the tension that thrummed in the air between him and Brooke. "Happy Thanksgiving, Marc. Do you plan on inviting us in?"

"I, uh, yeah, come on in." He opened the door wider so they could enter.

Jessica stepped through the threshold first and gave him a sisterly hug in greeting. He turned toward Brooke, who watched him warily. Then, with amazing fortitude and frustrating detachment she gave him a hug, too—but she was holding a pumpkin pie in the crook of her arm and used it to her advantage, to keep a discreet distance between them. He couldn't wrap his arms around her waist and pull her close like he ached to, not without crushing the dessert she'd brought. The only part of their bodies that touched was the hand she settled lightly around his back, and the press of their shoulders. Quick, impersonal, but her scent, mingled with the fragrant scent of cinnamon and spice, lingered long after she moved away.

"Can I help with your coat?" he offered, dying for an excuse to *really* touch Brooke, to feather his fingers along her neck, to run his hands down her arms, and see if there was a spark of anything left between them. Lord knew just the sight of her made his pulse race and desire heat his blood.

She quickly shook her head and moved out of his reach, as if remembering the kiss that had transpired the last time he'd helped her with her coat in this very foyer. "No, thank you."

Handing the pie to Jessica, who slanted him a look that said *sorry, buddy, but you blew it,* Brooke shrugged out of her coat and hung it in the closet next to Jessica's.

"It looks and feels like it might snow tonight," Brooke said, her voice holding no real emotion that he could grasp. Nothing to bolster his optimism that he might still stand a chance with her.

The weather? She was talking about the *weather?* So formal. So polite. So distant and reserved. Aggravation flowed through him, along with an acute sense of loss. The flirtatious banter and easy conversation he'd once enjoyed with her was a thing of the past. As were they, it seemed.

What did he honestly expect after the abrupt way he'd ended things with her? She was holding up her end of their agreement, making no demands, acting as though they hadn't spent two days stranded together, pretending that she hadn't learned more about him than any woman had ever taken the time or care to discover.

And he hated her aloofness. He wanted the warm, sweet, generous Brooke back. The one who gave of herself so freely. The one who'd pried open his heart and given him the faith and love he'd so desperately needed.

But he'd shunned her selfless offering, her priceless trust, and he had no idea how to repair the damage he'd done.

COMING HERE hadn't been a good idea. Brooke forced another swallow of stuffing and gravy, wishing that she'd followed her original plan to call Kathleen with the excuse that she wasn't feeling well, and skip Thanksgiving dinner with the Jamisons. Except Jessica wouldn't let her take the easy way out, and promised her it would get easier in time to be around Marc if she didn't avoid situations with him now.

But it hurt like hell to be near Marc, to even look at him, because all she could think about was how much she loved him, with everything she had within her, and that she had to live the rest of her life with the knowledge that he'd never be hers.

She'd spent the past hour since arriving avoiding eye contact with Marc and casually skirting him when he came near. It had been awkward enough at the door; she could only imagine how strained and uncomfortable it would be if they were caught in the position of being alone. Any conversation with him had been in a group with other members of his family, and very superficial on her part.

She'd smiled and endured, as she was now at the dinner table while everyone else carried on a lively conversation. She had no clue why Marc was brooding across from her when she'd abided by their agreement to resume their friendship. No pressure, no demands, no promises.

She was going to leave just as soon as it was politely possible, she decided as she took a bite of her buttered roll. And she would arm herself with a multitude of excuses to avoid Christmas with the Jamison family.

A lull came over the current conversation, and Eric transferred his gaze from Marc to Brooke. "You know, you two seem awfully quiet this evening," he commented. "And I don't think I've seen you say two words to one another. Did you guys have a fight while you were stranded together?"

"No," she and Marc answered in quick unison, hers a soft reply and his a rough bark.

Eric quirked a brow at Marc, scrutinizing his brother with his direct look. "What has *you* so uptight?"

Marc stabbed his fork into a slice of turkey and scowled at his brother. "I am *not* uptight."

"Yes, you are," Kathleen cut in, agreeing with Eric. "You were fine earlier when we were talking in the kitchen…until, well, Brooke arrived."

Four pairs of eyes glanced her way, and she felt her skin prickle and heat. She managed an impish shrug. She couldn't imagine what she'd done to make him so upset, unless he resented that she'd come at all. What else could it be?

"We're fine, really." Her reassurance only seemed to annoy Marc more.

His father redirected the conversation, recounting an amusing tale of a Thanksgiving when Eric and Marc had been kids and the two of them hid a few of their plastic army men in the hollowed-out turkey when Kathleen hadn't been looking, and what a surprise it had been to find them in the stuffing. Everyone laughed but Marc.

Eric continued to watch Marc, and Brooke knew that stare—it was the kind of look that said he'd found an intriguing mystery he wanted to decipher.

Finally, Marc bristled. *"What?"* he snapped at his brother, surprising everyone with his abrupt outburst.

"Man, I've never seen you like this before." Eric shook his head in bafflement. "It's got to be a woman that has you so on edge and moody."

Marc dropped his fork onto his plate. "So what if it is?"

Brooke's stomach churned at the challenging note in Marc's voice, but Eric merely chuckled at his brother's dark tone and slapped him on the back. "It's hell when women aren't cooperative, isn't it?"

"It's not her, it's *me,*" Marc admitted, sounding just as miserable as Brooke felt, though he never looked her way. Indeed, it was as though she wasn't even in the room. "I'm the one who blew it, and I'm afraid that nothing I say or do will change her mind about me, or us."

The thudding of Brooke's heart roared in her ears as she tried to make sense of his comment and this little drama playing out before her—which made no sense at all. Reaching numbly for her glass of wine, she took a big gulp to drown the swarm of unease churning in her belly.

Kathleen gazed at her youngest son, her eyes filled with gentle wisdom. "Have you told her how you feel about her?"

"No," Marc replied, his voice hoarse with regret. "I was too much of a coward the last time we were together."

"A woman needs to know how her man feels about her." Kathleen shared a loving look with her husband, who sat at the other end of the table from her. "The next time you see her tell her exactly how you feel."

Marc stood, and Brooke fully expected him to leave the dinner table with his dignity and pride still intact— and her heart in shreds. It was all she could do not to bolt herself.

He looked straight at her, his gray eyes brimming with an odd combination of nerves and gentleness. "I love you, Brooke," he said in a voice so clear and pure she knew she had to be dreaming.

The commotion that erupted at the table assured her she was not.

"Oh, my goodness," his mother exclaimed softly.

"I'll be damned," his father said in surprised amusement.

*"Finally,"* Jessica muttered.

"No kidding?" Eric asked, his expression amazed.

"No kidding," Marc affirmed softly, hopefully. "I love you, Brooke." He waited anxiously for her response.

An overwhelming rush of emotion swelled within her, joy, anticipation and stunned disbelief that he'd blurted out his feelings in front of his family. Not willing to discuss something so personal with everyone watching and listening, she stood and calmly set her napkin on the table. "I think this is something that would be better discussed in private."

Marc watched Brooke leave the dining area and head toward the family room, his chest tightening with an awful, heart-stopping pressure. Her composed, formal attitude wasn't the reaction he'd been expecting or hoping for, and he couldn't help but fear that he was too late with his declaration.

Eric broke the strained silence that had descended over the dinner table with Brooke's departure. "I have to admit, Brooke was the last woman I expected you to be tied up in knots over."

Marc glanced at his brother, realizing how ironic it was that he'd once envied his brother for having Brooke, and now had fallen deeply, irrevocably in love with that same woman. "She's an incredible woman," he said, though he knew that one adjective didn't do Brooke justice.

"Yeah, she is pretty incredible," Eric agreed quietly, but sincerely. "So make sure you treat her better than I did." Smiling, he held out his hand toward Marc in a gesture of respect and consent to the relationship.

Marc shook his brother's hand, and one quick look around the table affirmed that everyone else approved, as well.

"Just as a father-to-son piece of advice," his dad offered, casting an affectionate glance toward his wife. "It's been my experience that women like it when men wear their heart and emotions on their sleeve. You've made a good start of that here in this room, but it doesn't stop once you've got her. Make sure she knows that you love and cherish her…every day."

Kathleen smiled. "I can attest to that excellent advice."

The support and encouragement of his family went a long way in restoring his fortitude with Brooke. Heading into the family room, he saw Brooke standing there looking so achingly beautiful, so vulnerable and uncertain, and did the only thing he knew would assure her that he meant the love he'd professed to her in the other room.

Closing the distance between them, he caught her up in his arms and wrapped her in his strength and warmth. And then he kissed her, from the very depths of his heart, body and soul. The embrace was like coming home after being gone for an eternity.

When he broke the kiss, he framed her soft, smooth cheeks in his hands and tipped her face up to his, so he could look into her eyes. "I meant what I said, Brooke. I *do* love you."

"I know," she whispered, a tremulous smile touching her mouth. "I knew you loved me at the cabin, and I was so afraid that you'd never admit it, or see it for yourself."

"What can I say. I was an idiot. I didn't want to hurt you, but I put us both through hell by pushing you out of my life." And now, he was ready to tackle the next hurdle with her. "Brooke…I want to take that chance with you."

A small frown formed on her brow. "Why?"

She had every right to ask, to know what had changed his mind. He settled his hands on her hips to keep her close. "For the past eight years I've carried around guilt and blame, and a whole lot of fear. It was easier for me to keep my distance and not get emotionally involved with anyone than risk screwing up again. And then you came along and blasted through every defense I had, believing in me, trusting in me, when I couldn't even trust myself."

He pressed his forehead to hers, inhaled a deep breath, then went on. "I have to be honest with you, Brooke. I'm not this miraculously changed person. I still harbor insecurities and I still have doubts, but I see that fear as a good thing. It makes me a stronger person, and more aware of how hard I have to work to make *us* work. I don't ever want to take you for granted, or lose sight of what's important to me, and that's *you.*"

"Don't you think all this scares me, too?" she asked, seemingly humbled by all he'd revealed. "But I do trust you, and I believe in you. But most of all, I love you, too."

"God, I don't think I'll ever get tired of hearing that." He kissed her, slow and deep and rich with promise.

Moments later, she insisted against his warm lips, "I want dates, lots of them."

He grinned as his mouth skimmed across her cheek, thinking of all the places he wanted to take her, of all the fun they'd have together. "I think I can arrange that."

She tilted her head back, giving him better access to nuzzle her neck. "I want to take things slow and easy."

"Hmm. Slow and easy can be good." He felt the shiver that coursed through her at the sexy, husky insinuation in his voice, and he wished they were back at the cabin, naked and alone.

"Nothing serious or restricting—"

"*No.*"

His firm tone startled her, and she looked up into his face. "What do you mean, no? I just thought…"

"That's what I wanted?" he cut in quickly. "That we'd see where all this might lead?"

She swallowed, confusion coloring her eyes. "Well, yes."

He shook his head adamantly. "Do you honestly think I'm going to date you, make love to you often, every day if possible, and not insist on a commitment from you?" He didn't wait for her to answer. "It's all or nothing, Brooke. When I make my mind up about something, I'm not a man who does it halfway."

"Another reason to love you." A slow, joyful grin blossomed. "All right, then how about we have a hot, sexy, *exclusive* fling?"

The grin he gave her was as wicked as the hands easing beneath her blouse, stroking her skin, making her melt and moan just for him. "Yeah, I like the sound of that, just so long as the fling lasts for the next fifty years or so."

She laughed, knowing they were destined for a future filled with happiness, love and incredible, unbelievable passion.

# SEDUCED

To all the readers who've written to let me know how much
they enjoy my stories. Thank you for your kind words
and friendship. This one's for you.

And to Don, whose support, encouragement and love
make each story a reality.

# CHAPTER ONE

"MR. MATTHEWS, Jessica Newman is here to see you."

The voice of Haywood and Irwin's receptionist drifted through the intercom on Ryan Matthews' desk, breaking his train of thought on the brief he was preparing for a client's divorce case.

Before he could recover from Glenna's unexpected announcement, she continued in her ever-efficient manner. "Ms. Newman doesn't have an appointment, but said she'd like to speak with you regarding a personal matter if you have the time."

Curiosity flickered through Ryan, as well as an undeniable spark of enthusiasm. He'd make the time for Jessica Newman—anytime, anyplace. That she'd sought *him* out was enough to pique his interest, especially when she'd made it abundantly clear the last time he'd seen her that there could never be anything between them. Although he'd sensed a mutual attraction at the time, she'd diverted it with a collection of lawyer jokes he'd found too amusing to be offensive.

"My afternoon is clear, Glenna." He didn't have any appointments or engagements, just a tedious pile of correspondence awaiting his attention. No doubt, Jessica would provide a much more exciting diversion. "Will you show her to my office, please?"

The line disconnected, and Ryan set aside the documents he'd been reviewing and straightened the scattering of folders and papers on his desk, all the while wondering what had prompted this unscheduled visit of hers.

He'd first met Jessica a year ago when he and his buddies, Marc and Shane, had headed up to the Colorado Rocky Mountains for a few days of skiing. But instead of the guys-only weekend they'd envisioned, they'd found themselves sharing the same cabin with Jessica, her sister, Brooke, and another friend, Stacey. A blizzard had stranded Brooke and Marc together for two days in a deserted cabin, which had been the beginning of a lasting relationship between the two. And while Shane had also connected with Stacey on a very intimate level, Ryan had struck out with Jessica, but not for lack of trying.

Over the past twelve months he'd seen her a handful of times, the last of which had been at Marc and Brooke's small, intimate wedding three weeks ago where they'd stood up as best man and maid of honor for the couple. Other than Stacey and Shane, only immediate family had been invited to the private gathering.

And once again, Jessica had opposed his flirtatious advances. She'd used her arsenal of lawyer jokes to keep her attraction to him at bay, and ultimately turned down his request to take her out to dinner sometime. He'd been prepared for her refusal—over the course of a year she'd rejected him more than any man's ego should have to endure. More than most men *would have* endured.

He wasn't most men, and possessed enough patience to believe that some things were worth waiting for. And

Jessica intrigued him with her efforts to resist him. She stimulated him with her sassy mouth and spirited debates. And it drove him nuts that he couldn't break through that reserve of hers and make her admit to the awareness simmering between them.

She'd become a challenge, one he enjoyed as much as it frustrated him—losing, in any capacity, wasn't something he liked to accept, and he'd never been one to admit defeat until he'd exhausted every effort available.

A slow smile curved his mouth. Maybe it was time he upped the ante with a more direct approach and *showed* her that their attraction could lead to a mutually satisfying relationship. He wasn't looking for anything deep, heavy or serious that would interfere with the goals he'd spent the past six years trying to achieve. No way did he want to disappoint his parents, who'd scraped and saved to send him through college and law school and were so proud that their only son had chosen such a distinguished career. Eventually, he wanted to make junior partner. There was also the possibility of him heading up the family law department, and he was biding his time, winning cases, and making a name for himself that would go a long way in impressing the higher-ups when the time came for that particular advancement.

Being a bachelor suited Ryan just fine—it freed him to pursue his career goals single-mindedly, without the distraction of a serious relationship to waylay him, as he'd seen with other colleagues. But he wasn't opposed to spending time with a woman who aroused him on all levels, and Jessica Newman certainly did that.

But first, he needed her to admit she reacted the same way to him.

His mind turned over tantalizing ideas just as his office door opened and Glenna stepped aside to let Jessica enter. Automatically, he stood, one of the many gentlemanly gestures ingrained by his mother since he was a toddler. Being the only son in a family with three sisters, he'd learned early to treat women with utmost respect. As a teenager, he'd grumbled about the unfairness of having to cater to his sisters, but had grown to appreciate being familiar with the formalities that women seemed to admire and value.

Not that he was counting on his social graces to make any difference with Jessica. No, it was going to take something more tangible and candid to make an impact on her. By the time she left his office, he planned to shake her aloof composure and, he hoped, put a fracture in her convictions to keep him at arm's length, too.

She strolled into the room, her winter coat draped over her arm with her leather gloves stuffed in the front pocket. He started around his desk and across the distance separating them, watching as her big blue eyes registered his gradual approach. He smiled, taking in her teal-and-black, thigh-length sweater over black leggings, which tucked into stylish boots. She always dressed conservatively, whether in jeans and loose blouses, or slacks and long flowing skirts—nothing to draw attention to the slender curves and full breasts merely hinted at beneath her choice of clothing.

Nothing sophisticated like the kind of worldly women his profession drew, but it was her wholesomeness that fascinated him and appealed to him. She wore little makeup to enhance the creamy perfection of her skin, just enough to intensify the drown-in-them-forever

blue of her eyes. Her hair was a rich shade of honey-
blond, all chin length in a no-fuss style, and parted on
the side with wispy bangs touching her forehead. The
strands were incredibly silky-looking, beckoning for
him to slide his fingers through them as he'd envisioned
doing a hundred times since knowing her.

Today, there would be no suppressing his urges.
Today, he was going to discover just how warm and
heavenly her hair felt wrapped around his fingers…and
he planned to discover a whole lot more.

"Can I bring either of you refreshments?" Glenna
asked.

"Would you like something from the coffee bar
downstairs?" he suggested to Jessica. "An espresso?
Mocha? Cappuccino?"

He fully expected her to say she wasn't staying long,
but she surprised him with, "I'd love a mocha, thank
you. I'm still chilled from the cold temperatures outside.
Maybe that will help warm me up."

Ryan thought of more traditional and fun ways to
generate heat. Long, slow kisses. The stroke of his
hands across her bare skin. His naked body against
hers. The possibilities were endless.

"A mocha it is," he said, glancing toward Glenna
with their order. "And I'll take a cappuccino."

With a nod, the receptionist was gone, closing the
door behind her.

"This is a pleasant surprise." Taking her coat and
purse, he hung both next to his suit jacket on the brass
hooks mounted on the wall just inside the room. "Dare
I hope that you've reconsidered going out on a date and
you're here to beg me for a second chance?"

A smile quirked the corner of her mouth, and she

slanted him that sly look he was coming to know so well. He knew what was imminent, and anticipated her brand of humor.

"Hmm, let's see," she murmured speculatively, as if giving his question serious consideration. "I'm trapped in a room with a tiger, a rattlesnake and a lawyer. I have a gun with two bullets. What should I do?"

He lifted his brows, indicating he was ready for her punch line, even though he knew it wouldn't bode well for him. "I have no idea. What should you do?"

"Shoot the lawyer. *Twice.*" She flashed him a quick grin.

He chuckled and shook his head, even as he wondered what had caused such a cynical attitude toward attorneys. "I take it that means no?"

"Ahh, a lawyer that catches on quick. Amazing." She moved away from him, to the wall holding his law degree and other various certificates, diplomas and credentials he'd acquired since college. He watched her examine each one, a tiny frown forming on her brow. Not sure what had caused the sudden mood change, he attempted to keep their banter light and flirtatious.

"You'd better be careful, Jessie. I have to confess that those lawyer jokes of yours are starting to turn me on."

She glanced over her shoulder at him, a hint of laughter dancing in her eyes. "Maybe I need to work on my delivery."

His gaze perused her lazily, thoroughly. "From my vantage point, your delivery is *perfect.*" He gained a bit of satisfaction at the temptation he witnessed in her eyes, the wanting. What he didn't care for was the struggle to curb her desires. "I think what we need to work on is your general opinion toward lawyers, and me."

She turned around and sighed, the sound rife with regret. "It's nothing personal, Ryan. I *do* like you."

"Just not that I'm a man who represents clients in a court of law."

"Yeah, something like that," she responded vaguely.

Pushing his hands into his trouser pockets, he slowly stepped toward her, watched as she subtly backed up to keep the same amount of distance between them. "Then maybe we should narrow it down to working on just you, and me...on a *personal* level."

She bumped into his cherrywood filing cabinet, glared at it for being in her way, then crossed her arms over her chest in a gesture he read as protective. "You don't give up, do you?"

"What can I say? Being a lawyer, I like to argue and prove people wrong. Especially when I know I'm right."

She rolled her eyes at his too-confident statement. "Well, this is one case you won't win, counselor."

He smiled lazily. "You don't think so?"

She shook her head, and that soft, enticing hair of hers swayed with the movement, teasing him, making the tips of his fingers tingle for direct contact. "I *know* so."

Very casually, as if it were a perfectly natural move, he braced his left hand against the edge of the filing cabinet, sealing off her one chance to slip around him. All amusement ceased, replaced by a shimmering heat. Her scent, an arousing combination of jasmine and innocence, curled around him, intoxicating and impossibly alluring.

Resisting the urge to bury his face against her neck and inhale deeply of the fragrance clinging to her skin, he tipped his head and said, "Give me a strong, valid reason why I *should* give up."

She swallowed, and the pulse at the base of her throat fluttered. "Number one on my list of dating rules. No lawyers. *Especially* divorce attorneys. It goes against my ethics."

He'd heard it all before, in so many words, and he didn't bother asking why, knowing by that guarded look in her eyes that he wouldn't glean the answer he wanted, just a brush-off. But he knew her reasons went much deeper than something so superficial, and the analytical part of him couldn't help but want to discover all her secrets.

"So, you're gonna hold my profession against me?"

"'Fraid so." She lifted her chin. "You know, despite knowing how much you enjoy provoking me, I didn't come here for an interrogation."

He stared deep into her eyes, filled with conflicting emotions. Denial. Defiance. Longing. It was the last emotion that struck a reciprocating chord in him.

"Maybe you came here for more than you realize," he murmured, and lifted his free hand. He moved slow and easy, catering to her apprehension, intending to brush his knuckles across her cheek, gently tangle his fingers through her silken hair, stroke along the warm nape of her neck…and let desire take its natural course.

He was determined to make this the defining moment between them. And judging by the deepening of her breathing, the parting of her lips, and the way her lashes drooped slumberously over her hazy eyes, he was fairly certain she wouldn't belt him for satiating the need to caress her supple skin, taste her honeyed lips, and draw her lithe form up against his hard, hungry body.

It never happened.

A brisk knock on the door interrupted his seduction. Jessica jerked back, shaken, her eyes widening in alarm. Inches away from touching her, he fisted his fingers in the air, and swore beneath his breath at Glenna's untimely return.

Frustration tightened his jaw. Another five seconds, and he would have finally kissed Jessica, as deeply and as intimately as she would have allowed. And in the process he would have put a serious crimp in her "ethics" against getting involved with a lawyer. He'd waited a year for this opportunity, only to have his proficient receptionist shatter the moment.

He gave Jessica the breathing room she suddenly seemed to need and opened the door, retrieving their hot beverages from Glenna. Out of the corner of his eye he saw Jessica move into the center of the room, where it was spacious and safe. She dragged a hand through her hair, looking flustered and as though she couldn't believe what she'd almost allowed him to do, what she'd almost openly participated in.

He nearly laughed at her naivete. If she knew the half of what he imagined doing to her, he was convinced he'd never see her again. Kisses and stolen caresses were only the beginning of what he wanted from her.

He turned back to the receptionist, who was awaiting further instructions from him. "Glenna, will you hold all my calls until I'm through with Ms. Newman?" At her nod, he added with a rueful grin, "And would you mind closing the door for me since my hands are full?"

"Of course." With a smile that told him she believed this was just another business meeting with a client, she enclosed them in the room. A tension-filled silence immediately descended over his office.

Jessica eyed him cautiously, and he hated that her wariness was back. "You don't have to hold your calls for me."

He held her cup out to her, and she took her beverage. "I prefer private, uninterrupted consultations."

A faint smile touched the corner of her mouth. "Are you going to charge me by the hour for your time?" She took a drink of her mocha, then her tongue darted out, catching the smear of whipped cream clinging to her upper lip.

His gut clenched, and he drew a deep, steady breath, unable to remember the last time a woman had him so tied up in knots. "For you, my fee is negotiable, and very flexible." He winked at her to put her at ease. "But we can discuss that later. Have a seat and let's get business out of the way first."

He waved to one of the two seats in front of his desk while he settled into his leather chair. He caught a glimpse of the gray-leaded sky out the floor-to-ceiling windows that dominated the Denver high-rise where Haywood and Irwin leased their offices, and wondered if they were in for another winter storm.

Taking a quick drink of his cappuccino, he set his cup on his blotter and reclined in his chair. "You have my complete and devoted attention, not to mention my curiosity. What brings you by my office in the middle of the day?"

"I wanted to discuss something with you." A sudden anxious light flickered in her gaze. "I suppose I should have called first, but I was the next block over having lunch with Brooke, so I thought I'd take a chance that you were in and available. I figured a half hour out of your afternoon might be easier and more convenient than taking time out of your evening."

He lifted a brow her way. Easier and more convenient for her, of course. "Don't be shocked, but my social calendar in the evenings is quite empty, though I wouldn't mind filling in a few of those nights with a date, or two, or three, with you."

She wrinkled her nose at him, and this time didn't bother responding to his flirtatious attempt to sway her. He chalked up another rejection, but wasn't the least bit discouraged.

She took another drink of her flavored coffee, then stated what was on her mind. "I want to do something special and fun for Brooke and Marc since they had such a small ceremony and no reception."

"From what I remember, they didn't want a reception," he interrupted, remembering his friend's request to keep their wedding small and simple, which had included no gifts from the guests.

"True. My sister felt that since this was her second marriage she'd keep things low key." Though Jessica's tone held mild reproach for her sibling's sensible characteristic, her affection for Brooke was unmistakable. "But I'd really like to throw a surprise reception party in their honor, to give family and friends the opportunity to congratulate them, too. And since you and I were best man and maid of honor at the wedding, I thought it would be appropriate if *we* hosted the party. I also thought New Year's Eve would be a romantic and fun evening to celebrate their marriage."

He glanced at the open engagement calendar on his desk for the month of December, noting that the new year was only four weeks away. "That sounds great, but aren't most halls and ballrooms already booked for New Year's Eve parties by now?"

"Well, this is where I need your help." Grinning impishly, she shifted in her seat, and crossed one slender leg over the other. "Brooke has mentioned in passing that your house is huge, and I was hoping that's where we could have the party. Obviously, we can't do it at my apartment, and yes, I did check into various halls and ballrooms and couldn't find any place that wasn't already reserved. You're my last hope."

He liked that she might have to depend on him for something, which meant he'd gain leverage to reap something in return…like her acquiescence for a date.

Unfortunately, he wasn't sure he could accommodate her request. "My house isn't *huge*." Granted, the twenty-five hundred square feet of living space he'd purchased a little over a year ago sometimes seemed monstrous and too damned quiet and lonely in the evenings. He had his cat, Camelot, to keep him company though, and she was the perfect roommate. Female and loving, she didn't make unrealistic demands on his time and never complained about his sometimes grueling work schedule and late nights.

Absently, Jessica tucked a swath of hair behind her ear, revealing a small diamond stud earring that sparkled with her slightest movement. Not surprisingly, Ryan found her lobe incredibly sexy, and wondered if he'd elicit a shiver or moan from her should he ever have the pleasure of nibbling on that soft, enticing piece of flesh.

"Can it accommodate about thirty people?" she asked, bringing his musings back to the present.

He rubbed his thumb along his jaw as he considered her question. "If they're spread out between the living room, dining room and family room on the bottom level. And if we move my furniture around to make more open space."

"We can make it work." The exuberance brightening her features made him realize how much this party meant to her, and just how close she was to her sister.

From the sketchy details Ryan had learned at Brooke's wedding, they had no other siblings. Their mother lived in West Virginia with her second husband, and when he'd casually asked Jessica about her father, he'd received a cool, emotionless response that their real father was no longer a part of their lives and hadn't been for some time. It was all the information he'd gleaned, but it had been enough for him to suspect that she'd had a rough childhood.

She set her nearly empty cup on the small table between the two chairs, her eyes brimming with excitement. "We'll send Brooke and Marc a separate invitation on the pretense of you having a New Year's Eve celebration so they'll be surprised and won't try and talk us out of the party."

He took a drink of his warm cappuccino and didn't reply to her monologue, since she wasn't really asking for his input. He hadn't said yes to using his house, either, but Jessica was obviously way ahead of him on that score and assuming that he'd agree. She had the party all planned out in her mind, and he was getting the distinct impression that he was just along for the ride.

He intended to veer her off course and make the excursion much more interesting.

"I'll take care of the other invitations, the decorations, catering and a cake, and if you have a stereo system I'll bring along some CDs with romantic music that we can play." She grinned, bowling him over with that guileless smile that lacked her normal sass or reserve. "And I'll find a gift that I know they'll both enjoy, which we can go in on together, if you'd like. You won't have to worry about a thing except writing up a speech to toast the newlyweds."

How convenient, he thought in amusement, knowing exactly what she was attempting to do—take complete charge and keep his interaction with her to a minimum. "And splitting the cost of the party with you, of course."

"I'll keep the expenses as minimal as possible. I promise. And if the expense of the party gets to be too much for you, I'll cover the costs."

Money wasn't a concern for him. Not in the least. "I can afford whatever you have in mind."

She leaned forward in her chair expectantly, her eyes hopeful. "Then the party is a go at your place?"

He saw this idea of hers as his last opportunity to insinuate himself in her life, to work past those barriers she put up with him, to spend quality time with her and tempt and seduce her, and see where their attraction might lead.

Picking up his favorite Mont Blanc pen, he rolled it between his fingers. "I'll agree to the party at my place on one condition."

She made a snickering sound. "You can't agree without striking some kind of bargain, can you?"

"I can't help it." He shrugged. "Making deals is part of my business. Why settle for less than what I know I can get?"

"Call it what it is, Matthews—wearing your opponent down."

He feigned a wince at her barb. "I'd like to think of

it as drive and ambition to succeed. I haven't gotten as far as I have without it."

Derision colored her gaze. "In your illustrious career as a divorce attorney, or with me?"

Somewhere along the way their conversation had taken a personal slant, and it seemed as though his ambitious nature was a source of contention for her. "With both, actually."

The leg crossed over her opposite knee bounced impatiently. "All right then, counselor, let's hear it. What are your conditions?"

He set his pen in its holder. "That I'm part of the planning, every step of the way."

Her jaw dropped, and she stared at him incredulously. "You're joking."

He blinked, and kept his face carefully blank. "I'm completely serious."

"You don't have time to do the planning," she insisted, obviously rattled by his suggestion and what it implied—spending time with him.

"How do you know what I have time for?"

She shook her head in an attempt to divert his interest. "I work out of my apartment with my medical transcripts, and can take care of calls and errands during the day. Why would you want to worry about any of this when I'm more than willing to handle everything?"

Knowing if he revealed his true motives he'd never stand a chance with her, he opted for the obvious. "Well, for starters, I'm paying for half of this party, which gives me the right to contribute my opinion on everything, yes?"

Very reluctantly, she said, "Well...yes."

"And I'm opening my house to thirty-something

people, so I'd like to know what to expect, and what you plan to do." He flipped through his daily calendar and summed up his schedule fairly quickly. "I do have some court appearances coming up and cases that I need to close, but for the most part my nights and weekends are wide open."

Frustration all but radiated from her—there was nothing she could refute. She sat back in her chair with a small huff. "Why don't sharks attack lawyers?"

Suppressing a grin, he reached for a piece of letter-head and retrieved his pen again. "Why?"

"Professional courtesy," she muttered.

He chuckled deeply as he drew a diagram to his house for her. "Is that your way of saying I got my way?"

"Yeah, you got your way." She didn't sound happy about the fact.

He added his address and home phone number to the piece of paper. Standing, he circled around the desk and handed her the stationery with his bold script on it. "Here are directions to my place. How about we start on the planning tomorrow since it's Saturday? I'm free—how about you?"

Tentatively, she took the heavy cream vellum from his outstretched hand, but didn't bother looking at it. "Unfortunately, I don't have any plans, either."

"Great. Why don't you come over around eleven and take a look at the layout of my house and see what we have to work with, and then we'll go from there?"

"All right." She folded the paper into a precise square. "I have a list of Marc and Brooke's close friends, and I have a program on my computer that can print up nice party invitations, so I'll do that this evening, get them addressed and drop them in the mail on my way to your place in the morning."

He leaned his backside against the edge of his desk and crossed his legs at his ankles. "Bring them over and we'll address them together."

Her lips pursed. "I can do it myself. It's really a one-person job."

"Regardless, I want to be a part of every aspect of this party, Jessie." He knew if he gave her an inch, she'd run a mile. "Including addressing and stamping the invitations."

Her chin lifted a stubborn notch. "It's *Jessica*."

"I like Jessie better." The nickname was soft, gentle, with just a hint of rebellion. "It suits you."

She clucked her tongue. "I suppose you could call me worse."

He dropped his voice to a low, husky murmur for effect. "Like honey, or sweetheart?"

Her cheeks flushed a sudden, telltale pink. "Those endearments *definitely* don't apply to me and you." Finishing the last of her mocha, she stood and pitched the empty cup into the wastebasket at the side of his desk.

"They could." He twisted around to keep her in his line of vision as a sudden thought dawned on him. "Unless you're dating someone else?"

"No," she admitted freely. "I'm single, available, but not interested…in you."

Then it was up to him to change her mind, because her lying words contradicted the wistful look in her gaze.

She broke eye contact first. "Well, I think we just about covered everything, and now that you've black-mailed me, I think I'll be on my way." She headed toward the door, and he followed right behind.

"Just one more thing," he said with a lazy, self-assured smile.

Her gaze narrowed skeptically as she reached for her coat. "What? Another condition?"

He gently grabbed her wrist before she could execute her move, startling her. Instantaneous awareness cloaked them. She sucked in a swift breath, but didn't struggle or pull back. Their gazes locked as he stroked his thumb over the pulse point at the base of her wrist. In gradual degrees, he eased closer to her, while she stood statue-still.

He watched as her irises turned as dark and sensual as crushed sapphire velvet, and a surge of heat sped through his veins. Their thighs brushed, and he heard her breath hitch in her throat. Unwilling to let this moment pass without indulging in one of his tamer fantasies, he lifted his hand and finally skimmed his fingers along her smooth cheek, savoring the suppleness of her skin.

She looked stunned by his boldness, mesmerized by the tenderness of his touch. Taking advantage of her uncharacteristic docility, he gave in to the impulse he'd been denied earlier and slid his fingers into her hair. Silky warmth engulfed him, like nothing he'd ever experienced. The sensation was so unbelievably erotic he shuddered with pleasure.

"Ryan?" she whispered, her voice holding a slight tremor.

"No more conditions," he said, his tone low and rough. Fisting his hand into the feathery mass, he tipped her face up, so she could look into his eyes and see his intent. "This has nothing to do with the party, and everything to do with you and me…and finally getting an answer to a question I've been wanting to ask for the past year."

And then he lowered his head and settled his mouth over hers.

## CHAPTER TWO

JESSICA NEVER COULD HAVE anticipated the impact of Ryan's kiss, or her open response to him. A year's worth of resisting his charm, teasing and advances dissolved the moment his mouth touched hers, unraveling every solid lecture she'd given herself on why she could never fall for a man like him…a man who made a career out of tearing families apart, just as her family had been ripped apart.

But none of that mattered at that moment, not when the man, not the lawyer, was gently coaxing her with the soft glide of his lips across hers, taking time and care to draw her into far more forbidden territory. She had no defense against his brand of lazy seduction, his hypnotic patience. And when he slid his other hand into her hair, gradually eased her back against the wall and slanted her mouth more firmly beneath his, she was totally and completely lost. She gripped his corded forearms for support, bared by his rolled-up shirt-sleeves, and held on.

Aching to experience more of this exquisite pleasure, she surrendered with a breathy moan. Her lips softened and parted beneath his, and his tongue swept inside to taste her, tantalizing her with silken, gliding forays that made her knees weak and her head spin. She brazenly sought a more intimate sampling, too, and shivered at the combined flavors of hot male and rich coffee.

She learned quickly that despite his straightforward manner, he was a man who took his time and did things thoroughly. He kissed her with delicious languor, as if he had all the time in the world to indulge in the taste and textures of her mouth. His hips pressed closer, making her all too aware of the unyielding masculine body pinning her to the wall, the citrus scent of his aftershave, and the voluptuous sensations coursing through her.

His thumbs brushed her jaw, and her skin caught fire. His wide chest grazed hers, and her breasts swelled and her nipples tightened and ached. A muscular thigh insinuated itself between hers, she felt the hard length of his erection against her hip and heated desire curled low in her belly. And when he deepened the kiss, she responded just as enthusiastically.

She'd never experienced passion like this—instantaneous and wild. Never wanted another man with such shameless abandon. Never allowed herself to be so reckless with her desires. Her one and only quick, awkward encounter with someone she'd briefly dated three years ago hadn't prepared her for such intense, thrilling pleasure and consuming need.

Ever since her sister's marriage she'd been feeling restless, wanting something that felt just beyond her reach. With a kiss, Ryan tapped into deeper longings, and made her crave *more*.

While her body wanted to see where all this irresistible ecstasy might lead, her sensible mind reminded her that any kind of relationship with him was impossible. Having witnessed the pain of her mother's separation, along with experiencing the anguish of abandonment, she'd learned to be cautious and selective when it came to men in general. By Ryan's own admission, his ambition to succeed was his main focus, and wouldn't leave much spare room in his life to cultivate a commitment to something other than his career. She'd spent the past year dodging his flirtatious overtures, turning him down, swearing never to court the kind of disaster imminent with a driven man like him, whose profession contradicted everything she believed in and wanted for herself...love, marriage and family.

A kiss, no matter how exciting and earth-shattering, wouldn't change her mind or her principles...or allow her to overlook the fact that he terminated families and marriages without thought to the injured parties involved in those cases.

As if sensing her sudden doubts, he slowly dragged his soft, damp lips from hers. His hot, ragged breath along her cheek added to the arousing sensations, and she bit her bottom lip to keep from releasing his name on a breathless, plaintive sigh.

"In case you're wondering, the answer was yes," he murmured huskily in her ear, then lifted his head and gently untangled his fingers from her hair.

Trying to regain her own equilibrium, she braced the flat of her palms against the wall behind her and forced her lashes open to look at him. Though his body no longer touched hers, he only stood a few inches away, and she could still feel the sizzling heat radiating from him. His eyes were heavy-lidded and dark, his irises a rich shade of brown rimmed in a glittering gold. Hungry eyes. Seductive eyes. His thick, sable hair was tousled around his head enticingly, and he looked very sexy and overwhelmingly male.

"What was the question?" she asked, her mind foggy and confused.

A crooked, full-of-himself smile curved his lips. "Do you want me as much as I want you?"

She'd forgotten all about his original quest to achieve an answer to his personal query. What she desperately needed was a lawyer joke to diffuse the too-intimate moment, but he had her so unbalanced she couldn't remember the simplest of her attorney witticisms.

Frowning, and without thinking, she touched her bottom lip, which was still moist, swollen and incredibly sensitive. "And you think I said yes with that kiss?"

"You most definitely didn't say no, and I always look for the positive." He slipped his hands into the front pockets of his olive-colored trousers. "Now that we have that awkward question out of the way, we can move on to the next logical phase of our attraction."

She laughed at his presumptuousness, but couldn't deny just how adorable he looked, and just how much he *did* appeal to her, physically and intellectually. He sparked something utterly shameless within her, made her want to throw caution to the wind and give in to that attraction he spoke of.

"And what do you consider the next logical phase?" she asked.

"A date."

Nothing she hadn't already heard and turned down before. She inclined her head and smiled. "Don't you think you're going about things backwards? A kiss first, date second?" Deeming it way past time she left, she reached for her coat.

He beat her to it, and held open the wool garment for her. "I've never been accused of being traditional."

She wasn't surprised. How could a man whose main objective was to split up married couples believe in romantic customs and idealistic sentiments?

She slipped into her coat with a murmured thanks, and turned around. His hands lingered, adjusting the collar, his thumbs grazing her neck. Of course her traitorous body shivered at that delectable caress, and her mind conjured up images of him gliding those long tapered fingers elsewhere.

He handed her purse to her, and she slung the long leather strap over her shoulder. "What if I'm a traditional kind of girl?"

An appropriately contrite look transformed his gorgeous features, though his eyes danced with a teasing light. "Then I apologize profusely for offending your delicate sensibilities with that kiss, and would like to make up for my atrocious behavior with dinner. How about tomorrow night?" He opened the door to his office and waited for her to precede him.

She stepped out into the hall, and realized he intended to escort her out—and felt ridiculously pleased by the gesture. "I'll be seeing you tomorrow morning, and we'll be spending the afternoon together."

"That's business. I'm referring to pleasure."

The word *pleasure* rolled off his tongue like a silken, seductive stroke along her spine. She drew a breath and resisted its allure. "No."

"Sunday night, then?"

He lightly rested his hand on the base of her back. Her coat was heavy and lined, yet that subtle pressure was enough to incite her feminine nerves and send a feverish awareness swirling within her. She held on to her standards and her respectability with both hands. "No."

"Okay," he said, unperturbed by her steadfast refusal. "You name the night, then."

His unwavering persistence amazed her. "How about never?"

They passed through the receptionist area, Ryan told Glenna that he'd be right back after escorting her to the lobby, and they continued to the alcove holding the bank of elevators.

He punched the down arrow and met her gaze. "You're going to make me work for this, aren't you?" He didn't seem at all bothered by that notion. In fact, Jessica suspected the challenge appealed to him and his lawyer instincts.

With his good looks and easygoing charm, she was certain he'd never had to work for a date in his life, and was ninety-nine percent sure his interest in her would wane once she capitulated to his relentless pursuit. No matter how easy it would be to surrender to Ryan despite his profession, it could never happen. She didn't intend to end up hurt and discarded by any man once he decided the fun was over—especially by one who affected her so strongly and threatened her emotions so severely.

The elevator pinged, signaling its arrival, and they both stepped into the lift. She pressed the button for the lobby, and waited until the metal doors closed. Her stomach dipped, from the descent of the elevator, or from being trapped in such a tiny cubicle with Ryan, she wasn't sure.

"I'm doing both of us a big favor," she finally said, infusing her voice with a suitable amount of regret that felt overwhelmingly real. "It would be ridiculous after that kiss to deny that I'm attracted to you, but I don't think we're looking for the same things in a relationship."

He flashed her a quick, tempting grin. "Chemistry is a great start."

They definitely had plenty of that, but she wanted something more permanent with a man, something more enduring and emotional. Stability and security— the very things she'd grown up without. "Which rarely lasts once the relationship turns physical."

He studied her too intently with those deep brown eyes of his. "Is that your experience?"

She shrugged vaguely and broke eye contact, unwilling to admit that her experience was limited, and did not evoke pleasant memories. "What's the longest relationship you've ever had?" she asked, turning the conversation back to him.

He worked his mouth in thought. "A little over a year."

Retrieving her lined leather gloves from her coat pocket, she pulled them on. "How long ago?"

"My senior year in high school."

She rolled her eyes at him, not at all surprised to discover that he'd spent most of his adult life avoiding a commitment with a woman, which was pretty much equivalent to him confirming himself as a bachelor. "You just proved my point about you and lasting relationships. They don't exist for you."

"You didn't prove anything," he refuted calmly. "After high school, I went to college while holding down a part-time job, then went straight into law school. Becoming a lawyer and establishing myself has taken precedence over a relationship."

"And your career is your number one priority." And that kind of focus didn't leave much time to nurture an intimate relationship.

*Not that she cared.*

"I haven't gotten as far as I have without working hard and making sacrifices." His words weren't at all defensive, just a statement of fact. "And quite honestly, I haven't met a woman who's made me want to give up being a bachelor."

The velvet timbre of his voice, the flicker of something far more promising in his eyes, shot a distinct and unnerving tingle through her. The elevator came to a whirring stop, and she opened her purse and dug through the contents, using the search for her car keys as a much needed visual diversion. "I doubt I'm that woman, Matthews, and you're definitely not someone I'd consider anything long-term with, either."

"Something short-term then?"

Unable to tell if he was serious or joking, she slanted him a quick glance. The sinful invitation in his gaze indicated his suggestion was, indeed, an earnest one. Temptation crooked its finger, and it took more than a little effort to abstain from accepting his beguiling proposal.

None too soon, the door whooshed opened, and she stepped into the marbled lobby. "You're a rogue, and I'm not interested."

"You're not a very good liar, Jessie," he said in that silky tone of his. "You're definitely interested."

He stopped in the middle of the lobby, and she continued on to the main entrance. Then he called out after her. "And just for the record, I plan to wear down that resolve of yours."

She turned and used her backside to push open the glass doors that enclosed the interior of the building. Her breath caught, at the afternoon chill that swirled around her, and at the vision of Ryan leaning against a tiled column, so utterly confident, so inherently sexual, so completely irresistible.

But resist him she would. She flaunted a grin full of fabricated sass. "You can certainly try, counselor, but don't expect me to make it easy on you. And don't expect to win."

He tipped his head, and a lock of dark hair fell across his brow, adding to his appeal. "You making it easy on me wouldn't be any fun, now would it?" he drawled. The devastatingly wicked grin claiming his lips told her he accepted her dare and anticipated the challenge. "See you tomorrow morning."

RYAN PUSHED HIMSELF to swim an additional ten laps on top of the fifteen he'd already accomplished, hoping the extra morning exercise would burn off the restless energy that had kept him tossing and turning for most of the night. Also to blame were the vivid fantasies that had invaded what little sleep he'd been able to snatch. Of Jessica beautifully naked and submissive in his bed. Of him discovering those curves she'd hidden beneath her bulky sweater, skimming his hands along quivering flesh, tasting her with his tongue, making her want him to the point of begging him for release.

And she begged so prettily in his fantasy, so sweetly. But before he could experience the ecstasy of burying himself deep inside her softness and warmth, he awoke from the erotic dream with a start. He'd been hard and aching, the sheets tangled around his bare legs, and sweating despite the cool night air washing over his body. Three times she'd brought him to the edge last night, until he'd finally dragged himself from bed at dawn and put himself through a rigorous workout regimen in hopes of diminishing the lust that gripped him.

The sharpness of desire had ebbed, but he still wanted her.

Reaching the deep end of the pool, he executed a flip, accelerated off the wall and continued his fluid, precise strokes across the surface. Curls of steam rose from the water he kept heated in the winter so he could use the pool on a daily basis, but his lungs burned from drawing in cold morning air. The muscles across his shoulders and down his back tingled from the exertion, while the warm water sluiced along his skin, his belly, his thighs, like a lover's caress.

Jessica's caress. And just like that, she'd joined him in the pool where he thought he was safe from those erotic fantasies with her.

The kiss they'd shared yesterday afternoon had ignited a dark, carnal craving he couldn't seem to shake, along with a deeper hunger that transcended mere sexual need, and emotions no other woman had ever evoked. For a year he'd let their desire for one another simmer, and now that he knew there was a warm and willing woman beneath that composed exterior, he wanted to discover everything about her, every sensual secret she harbored.

No easy feat, considering her maddening attempts to deny him, and her frustrating aversion to his profession. But that kiss had provided him with irrefutable evidence. Her vocal cords might be saying "no," but her lips had told him all he needed to know.

She wanted him, too.

Pulling himself out of the pool, he shivered as too-cold temperatures replaced the warmth of the water.

Grabbing the large, fluffy towel he'd left on a lounge chair, he dragged it over his wet head to remove the excess water from his hair, then wrapped the terry around his shoulders. He headed up the brick inlaid steps leading to his two-story house, and wasn't surprised to see his younger sister, Natalie, sitting at the small table in the kitchen nook that overlooked the landscaped backyard. As always, she'd made herself right at home and was reading his newspaper and drinking what he assumed was a mug of the coffee he'd made that morning. She saw him coming up the walkway, smiled gregariously and waved.

He lifted a hand in greeting, but entered the house by way of a back door that led to one of the downstairs bathrooms, where he took a quick shower, washed his hair and changed into the sweatshirt and jeans he'd left there earlier. Leaving his hair damp and finger-combed away from his face, he grabbed his socks and sneakers and headed into the kitchen to see his sister.

The unmistakable fragrance of the delicious buttermilk spice muffins his mother made assailed his senses. There was a cloth-lined basket on the table, and judging by the half-eaten muffin on the plate next to his sister, he'd identified the scent accurately.

"Morning, Nat." Taking one of the chairs across from her, he began pulling on his socks. "I'm glad to see that the house key I gave you for emergencies is coming in handy."

Unaffected by his wry tone, she set aside the paper he'd read earlier and shrugged. "I knocked, and no one answered. I didn't expect you to be out in the pool, for God's sake." She eyed him dubiously as she petted the fluffy gray ball of fur reclining on her lap. "How you

## OFFICIAL OPINION POLL

Dear Reader,

Since you are a book enthusiast, we would like to know what you think.

Inside you will find a short Opinion Poll. Please participate in our poll by sharing your opinion on 3 subjects that are very important to all of us.

To thank you for your participation, we would like to send you your choice of **2 FREE BOOKS** and a **FREE GIFT!**

Please enjoy them with our compliments.

Sincerely,

*Pam Powers*

Editor

P.S. Don't forget to indicate which books you prefer so we can send your FREE gifts today!

# What's your pleasure...

## Romance?

Enjoy **2 FREE BOOKS** that will fuel your imagination with intensely moving stories about life, love and relationships.

**OR**

## Suspense?

Enjoy **2 FREE BOOKS** that will thrill you with a spine-tingling blend of suspense and mystery.

Whichever category you select, your **2 FREE BOOKS** have a combined cover price of \$11.98 or more in the U.S. and \$13.98 or more in Canada.

Simply place the sticker next to your preferred choice of books, complete the poll on the right page and you'll automatically receive **2 FREE BOOKS** and a **FREE GIFT** with no obligation to purchase anything!

We'll send you a wonderful surprise gift, **ABSOLUTELY FREE**, just for trying our books! Don't miss out — **MAIL THE REPLY CARD TODAY!**

Order online at
www.FreeBooksandGift.com

# YOUR OPINION POLL
# THANK-YOU FREE GIFTS INCLUDE

▶ **2 ROMANCE OR 2 SUSPENSE BOOKS**

▶ **A LOVELY SURPRISE GIFT**

## OFFICIAL OPINION POLL

**YOUR OPINION COUNTS!**

Please check TRUE or FALSE below to express your opinion about the following statements:

**Q1** Do you believe in "true love"?

*"TRUE LOVE HAPPENS ONLY ONCE IN A LIFETIME."*
○ TRUE
○ FALSE

**Q2** Do you think marriage has any value in today's world?

*"YOU CAN BE TOTALLY COMMITTED TO SOMEONE WITHOUT BEING MARRIED."*
○ TRUE
○ FALSE

**Q3** What kind of books do you enjoy?

*"A GREAT NOVEL MUST HAVE A HAPPY ENDING."*
○ TRUE
○ FALSE

Place the sticker next to one of the selections below to receive your 2 **FREE BOOKS** and **FREE GIFT**. I understand that I am under no obligation to purchase anything as explained on the back of this card.

### Romance
193 MDL EE4P
393 MDL EE5D

### Suspense
192 MDL EE4Z
392 MDL EE5P

0074823 |||||||||||| ||||||| |||||||     **FREE GIFT CLAIM #** 3622

FIRST NAME          LAST NAME

ADDRESS

APT.#          CITY

STATE/PROV.     ZIP/POSTAL CODE          (TF-SS-06)

Offer limited to one per household and not valid to current subscribers of MIRA®, Romance, Suspense or The Best of the Best™. Books received may vary. All orders subject to approval. Credit or debit balances in a customer's account(s) may be offset by any other outstanding balance owed by or to the customer. Please allow 4 to 6 weeks for delivery.

**DETACH AND MAIL CARD TODAY!**

## The Reader Service — Here's How It Works:

Accepting your 2 free books and gift places you under no obligation to buy anything. You may keep the books and gift and return the shipping statement marked "cancel." If you do not cancel, about a month later we'll send you 3 additional books and bill you just $5.24 each in the U.S., or $5.74 each in Canada, plus 25¢ shipping & handling per book and applicable taxes if any.* That's the complete price, and — compared to cover prices of $5.99 or more each in the U.S. and $6.99 or more each in Canada — it's quite a bargain! You may cancel at any time, but if you choose to continue, every month we'll send you 3 more books, which you may either purchase at the discount price...or return to us and cancel your subscription.

*Terms and prices subject to change without notice. Sales tax applicable in N.Y.
Canadian residents will be charged applicable provincial taxes and GST.

If offer card is missing write to: The Reader Service, 3010 Walden Ave., P.O. Box 1867, Buffalo NY 14240-1867

BUSINESS REPLY MAIL
FIRST-CLASS MAIL     PERMIT NO. 717-003     BUFFALO, NY

POSTAGE WILL BE PAID BY ADDRESSEE

THE READER SERVICE
3010 WALDEN AVE
PO BOX 1341
BUFFALO NY 14240-8571

NO POSTAGE
NECESSARY
IF MAILED
IN THE
UNITED STATES

can go swimming in fifty-degree weather and enjoy it is beyond me."

The pool was one of the things that had appealed to him when he'd bought the house, along with the large whirlpool in his master bath. "I keep the water heated, and it's invigorating."

"Whatever rocks your boat." Green eyes twinkling, she lifted her mug in a toast to him, then took a drink of the coffee.

Finished tying his shoes, he glanced at the clock, noted that he only had a half hour until Jessica arrived, and realized he needed to move his sister along her way. Unfortunately, Natalie was one to do things at her own unhurried pace.

At twenty-seven, she was the baby of the Matthews clan, and five years younger than he. Though he was close to all his sisters, he was especially fond of Natalie, whom he'd formed a special attachment to from the day his mother had brought her home from the hospital and he'd first peered into her bassinet. They were also the only two siblings left who were single and unattached.

"So, what brings you by?" he asked, wanting to get to the crux of her visit—if there was even a reason.

She glanced down at the cat she'd given him six months ago as a gift, so he'd have company in his big house. "I just wanted to make sure that Camelot isn't wanting for anything, isn't that right, Cammie?" she crooned, scratching the feline under her chin.

He couldn't help but grin at her excuse. "And?"

She tipped her head up, and her rich brown hair, permed with soft waves, swirled around her shoulders. "I found her lapping at a bowl of cream, and judging by her very affectionate purrs, I think she adores her master."

The cat was truly an affectionate pet, very spoiled, and he was just as smitten. "Now that you know Camelot has me wrapped around her paw, what *really* brings you by?"

She tore a hunk off the crispy top of the baked good, sprinkled with cinnamon sugared walnuts. "Mom wanted me to deliver something to you, along with these delicious muffins she made." She popped the bite into her mouth and chewed.

"Which you've helped yourself to, I can see." Unable to resist, he took a chunk of her muffin for himself. It all but melted in his mouth.

She licked the sugar from her fingers. "Of course," she replied unrepentantly. "It's not as though you have anyone else to share the muffins with."

He lifted a brow at her direct comment, but didn't feed the curiosity glimmering in her eyes. "You mind getting to the *real* reason why you're here?"

"I'll give you a hint. "You need to start practicing your 'ho, ho, hos' for Christmas Eve."

Remembering what had transpired last Christmas Eve, he guessed right away. "You brought the Santa suit over?"

"Yep. Mom wanted to make sure you had it beforehand. Christmas is only three weeks away, and I heard Jackie, Jennifer and Alyssa talking about Santa stopping over at Grandma's again this year. Looks like you started a new tradition."

He smiled at the mention of his nieces, whom he adored, the three of which belonged to his oldest sister, Courtney, and her husband Dale. He also had two nephews by his other sister, Lindsay, and her husband Clive. The kids ranged in age from two to seven, and all still believed in the magic of St. Nick.

"I'd be happy to play Santa Claus." He glanced at the clock again, this time more meaningfully. "I hate to rush you off, Nat, but I've got company coming over." He ate the last of her muffin, then stood and started clearing off the table.

Natalie remained seated and continued stroking Camelot, watching as he tossed the newspaper into the trash, and took her mug and plate to the sink. "Hmm, if you're cleaning, your company must be female."

He slanted her a tolerant look. "Yes, she is."

Interest glimmered in her eyes. "Is it serious?"

If Jessica had her way, they'd remain platonic friends. If he had his way, she'd be warming his bed and fulfilling those fantasies that had him tied up in knots. But no matter how much he desired her, he wasn't about to rush her into something she wasn't emotionally prepared for. When the time was right, they'd make love. He'd waited a year for her to come around, so he could abstain a while longer, until he swayed her to his way of thinking. But until then, he planned to keep her just as aroused and inflamed as he was with touches and kisses and anything else she'd allow.

He wasn't sure how to answer his sister's question, so he kept his reply ambiguous. "I definitely like her."

"What's her name?"

"Jessica Newman." Rinsing the dirty plate and utensils in the sink, he placed them in the dishwasher. "She and I are planning a surprise party for Brooke and Marc on New Year's Eve, and she'll be here *anytime*."

She ignored his blatant hint to leave. "Are you going to bring her over to Mom and Dad's for Christmas Eve?"

Drying his hands on a dish towel, he thought of that

possibility. Christmas Eve at his parents' was a fun, cheerful, overnight affair, with baking, a buffet of food to snack on and his mother playing Christmas music on the baby grand piano his father had bought her years ago for an anniversary present. There was laughter and reminiscing, and before the stroke of midnight they'd all retire to the rooms that they'd grown up in and wake up the next morning to enjoy the delight of watching the younger generation tear through the presents Santa had left for them.

He thought of Jessica, possibly spending the better part of Christmas alone, with her mother living in West Virginia, and Brooke now remarried. Would she accept such a personal invitation when she turned down the simplest of dates?

He'd never taken a woman to the family gathering before, never had the desire or the inclination to share that special time with someone else. Although it wasn't difficult to imagine Jessica fitting in with his family, he wasn't certain if *he* was ready for that leap and what it implied.

"I don't know if I'll ask her," he replied, as honest an answer as he'd give.

The doorbell rang, and Natalie's expression brightened with curiosity. Gently, she pushed Camelot to the floor, then stood, brushing the cat hairs from her black jeans. "Since your lady friend is here, I guess I should go."

"How convenient," he said drolly, knowing this was exactly what his sister had been stalling for. "Let me walk you to the door and introduce you."

STANDING ON RYAN'S front porch at eleven o'clock to the minute, Jessica drew a deep fortifying breath and adjusted the strap of her tote bag over her shoulder. The canvas bag held the notepad on which she'd started to plan Brooke and Marc's New Year's Eve party, along with the invitations and labels she'd printed up last night.

With luck, and the feminine strategy she had in mind, she'd be here an hour, max. Once she droned on about the tedious, boring party plans that would have most men fidgeting and thinking about the football game on TV, she was certain he'd change his mind about helping and be grateful that she'd handle all the details on her own. From there, any decisions she needed from him could be taken care of over the phone, and she wouldn't have to see him again until New Year's Eve.

And that suited her perfectly, she told herself with a decisive nod. The less direct involvement she had with sexy Ryan Matthews, Esquire, the better. No matter how much he tempted her, no matter that a single kiss from him had the ability to arouse her to the point of making her feel reckless and wild, absolutely nothing could come of their attraction. So why put herself through the added torment of spending so much unnecessary one-on-one time with Ryan?

Her determination melted the moment he opened the door and stood there, filling her senses with the seductive, drugging hunger she'd managed to squash since leaving his office yesterday afternoon. The tantalizing awareness returned with a vengeance, contradicting the lecture she'd just given herself.

Gone was the professional lawyer attire. With seemingly little effort, dressed in casual jeans and a sweatshirt, he still managed to look gorgeous and exude way too much confidence. It was December cold outside, but the heat in his dark eyes set her body on fire. The sensual promise of his smile made her want to toss her better judgment to the wind and experience all that had gone unexplored in her previous sexual encounter.

No doubt, Ryan would be happy to accommodate her, and satisfy her every whim. The thought sent a strange thrill racing through her, and had her mind tumbling with shameless possibilities.

"Amazing, a woman who's right on time," he said teasingly, and motioned her into the foyer with a sweep of his hand. "Come on in."

Shaking off the impossible thoughts stealing through her mind, she stepped inside the warmth of his house and opened her mouth to issue a lawyer joke in response to his male cynicism. The flow of words stopped when she saw another woman standing just inside the entryway, shrugging into a coat with a fur-lined collar.

The pretty and petite woman smiled. "Hi, Jessica, I'm Ryan's sister, Natalie," she introduced herself. "And I believe that wisecrack of my brother's comes from his scarred childhood and having to wait on his three sisters for the better part of his life."

Ryan sent a mock scowl Natalie's way, but there was affection in his gaze. "You have no idea what it's like to have to get up at four in the morning in order to take a shower for school before the three of you woke up and commandeered the bathroom. I was done in ten minutes, then had to sit around for three hours for the bus to arrive while the three of you fought for mirror space." He turned back to Jessica, and continued his argument. "And no matter how much time they all had to get ready, they were *never* on time for anything. Lindsay and Courtney were even late to their own weddings."

Deeming it her duty to stick up for her gender, Jessica added, "Obviously, their husbands think they were worth waiting for."

Her reply earned her a brilliant smile from Ryan's sister. "Oh, I do like you."

Ryan groaned. "Weren't you just leaving, Nat?"

"I'm gone." Natalie pressed a quick kiss to his cheek, then grasped Jessica's hand in hers. "It was nice meeting you. I hope we have the chance to get to know one another better."

Jessica didn't bother to correct the woman's assumption that she was Ryan's girlfriend. "It was nice meeting you, too."

Ryan blew out a breath once he closed the door behind his sister. "Ya gotta love her," he said with amusement, and helped her out of her jacket. "Especially since my parents keep insisting that she wasn't adopted."

Despite his joke, it was obvious that he loved his entire family very much. It wasn't what she'd expected. A part of her had assumed that his career choice had been based on his own personal family history being less than stable. Now, she wasn't so sure, which made her wonder what had inspired his choice of career.

She swallowed the personal question and retrieved her notepad from her bag. "I brought the invitations, and I thought I could draw out a diagram of the bottom level of your house so that I…I mean, *we* can figure out what we need to accommodate the guests."

"Let's get started," he said, too eagerly, too helpfully. "You can make notes while I give you the grand tour."

The "grand tour" left Jessica breathless. His house *was* huge in her estimation, when all she'd known was the one small home her family had lived in before her parents divorced, then the cramped space of apartments. Being self-employed and making a decent living as a medical transcriber, she'd upgraded to a nice complex in a middle-class neighborhood which she'd shared with Brooke until recently, but it didn't come close to the luxury in which Ryan lived.

Obviously decorated by a professional, in masculine colors of royal blue, hunter green, and chocolate brown, the lower level was spacious and spread out, affording them enough room to set up rental chairs for the party. The formal table in the dining room would hold the buffet she had in mind, and if they rearranged the furniture in the living room and family room they could add more seats there, too. The kitchen was a caterer's dream, with a huge wooden center island for them to use to prepare the appetizers.

As she gazed up the spiral staircase to the upper level, she imagined entwining evergreen and twinkling lights along the handrail and throughout the house to make it more enchanting. Cinnamon-scented candles would add to the ambiance. Flipping the page of her pad of paper, she made a notation under "florist" for poinsettias, holly and greenery, along with a few table arrangements.

"Did you want to see upstairs, too?" he asked once they'd covered the first level of the house.

She lifted her gaze from her notes and quirked her brow at him, feeling a tad suspicious. Up until this moment, he'd been very well behaved. "Is there anything up there I *need* to see?"

"The master bedroom?"

She bit the inside of her cheek to keep from grinning

at the hopeful note in his voice, the inviting light in his gaze. "You plan on letting your guests mingle in there?"

A warm, private smile brushed across his mouth. "I'm only extending the invitation to you."

"It would be incredibly rude of us to leave our guests downstairs while we *mingle* upstairs," she said, deliberately misconstruing his meaning.

He followed her through the living room to the kitchen. "I'm sure our guests wouldn't miss us for an hour."

A delicious pressure tightened in her belly at his insinuation. An hour of pure ecstasy compared to the ten minutes of groping and fumbling she'd experienced three years ago.

Oh, wow.

Trying not to allow his sexy overture to entice her, she sat at the small kitchen table and withdrew the invitations, address labels and stamps. It was time to execute her scheme to discourage his interest in the party planning.

He didn't complain when she gave him the unpleasant job of licking the envelopes, and assigned him the monotonous task of affixing the return labels and stamps. Too cheerfully, he did as she instructed, not once shifting anxiously in his chair, or issuing an exasperated sigh.

Her ploy wasn't working. The man was impossible to dissuade. Not to mention that he had her completely distracted and unable to concentrate.

He was sitting so close, his leg occasionally grazed hers, the friction of denim against denim nearly electric. She could feel his eyes on her as he waited patiently for her to address the last two invitations.

And then he reached out and tucked the strands of hair behind her ear that had fallen against her cheek, exposing her neck to his gaze in the process. His fingers lingered for a few fretful heartbeats, then skimmed her jaw as his hand fell away.

A shiver coursed through her, and she calmly handed him the invitation and reached for the last one. "Am I boring you?"

"Not in the least." Without acknowledging that he'd touched her, he dampened a stamp and pressed it onto the corner of the envelope. "And why do I get the impression that you're disappointed about that fact?"

"More like amazed that you're actually enjoying this." Finished with the last invitation, she passed it to him to finalize the job. "Well, that's done." And now she could leave. "I'll drop them in the mail on my way home."

"All right." He gathered the other items for her to put into her tote bag, then stood, left the kitchen, and returned with her jacket, and a worn, masculine leather one.

Considering his sudden eagerness to help her clean up, and the fact that he was shrugging into his own jacket, she wondered if maybe she *had* waylaid his interest in party planning. Obviously, he had more exciting plans on his agenda, and was just politely going through the motions.

"Have you eaten anything?" he asked.

She grabbed her purse and tote bag and replied without thinking. "Not since breakfast."

"Me, either, and I'm starved. Come on, let's get out of here." He retrieved a set of keys off a hook on the nearby wall, and before she could gain her bearings, he had her hand enclosed in his and was guiding her out a back door to the garage.

He hit a button on the wall, a light went on and the garage door started rolling upward, revealing a gray sky and snow flurries. A gleaming black Lexus with rich gold trim sat waiting, and Ryan opened the passenger door and ushered her into the butter-soft, tan leather interior.

Marveling at how easily he could manipulate her, how easily she let him, she buckled up while he circled around the car. Once he was behind the wheel, she asked, "Where are we going?"

The engine turned over on a soft purr of sound, and he glanced her way, grinning with wicked satisfaction. "On our first date."

## CHAPTER THREE

"THIS IS NOT A DATE," Jessica reiterated once they'd arrived at the restaurant he'd selected and they'd placed their orders with the waitress.

Ryan glanced across the table at his *date*, and grinned. The sparkling laughter in her bright blue eyes belied her insistent tone and convinced him that she really didn't mind that he'd coerced her into having lunch with him. "You keep insisting that this isn't a date, but I think it all depends on how our afternoon ends."

Her features altered into mock suspicion. "What's the deciding factor?"

His gaze dropped to her soft lips, remembering the taste and lush feel of her. He could feast on her mouth for hours and still want more. "I think a kiss at the end of the day would determine whether this outing constitutes a date or not."

She dipped her head as she opened her napkin and spread it on her lap. "Sorry to disappoint you, Matthews, but this is strictly a *business* lunch."

He clasped his hands on the table and lowered his voice flirtatiously. "Ahh, but we haven't discussed any 'business' yet."

"But we *will*," she said, and dutifully pulled out her

pad of paper and a pen, along with a very diligent attitude. "We need to nail down the specifics for the party so I can make the appropriate calls and get everything set up and scheduled."

"You win," he relented, feigning a defeated sigh. "Business it is. For today."

How was it that she looked both relieved *and* disappointed? The conflicting emotions he glimpsed intrigued him, and assured him that the potential for something more than their business dealings looked promising. It was just a matter of taking things slow and easy, and he had four weeks to persuade her to his way of thinking.

Admittedly, he'd never taken such time and care with a woman, but then the sophisticated, career-driven women he'd dated in the past had blatantly pursued *him,* and they'd both gone into the affair with the mutual understanding that there were no strings attached. Satiating physical needs had been the mainstay of those relationships, and ultimately their jobs had taken precedence over cultivating anything lasting. When they'd parted ways, they'd done so without regrets or emotional entanglements, and that type of arrangement had always suited him just fine.

Ever since meeting Jessica, he'd found himself growing more selective, to the point that he'd turned down a few offers from beautiful women he knew wouldn't make demands on his time. Attracting willing females had always come easily, but somewhere along the way indulging in a purely sexual relationship had lost its appeal.

Jessica stimulated not only his body, but his mind, and a woman hadn't accomplished such a feat in a long time, if ever. She made him think of things he'd put aside for his career, made him wonder if combining a real, lasting relationship with his job was do-able. Made him wonder if there was some kind of way to strike a balance between achieving success and maintaining traditional values.

*Not with her,* his conscience mocked, reminding him of her ultimate aversion to his profession. She was tolerating him because of the party she wanted to throw for Brooke and Marc, and no doubt would say good riddance come New Year's Eve, unless he could convince her otherwise.

Yet there was no denying their attraction—or her reluctance to let their desire for one another take its natural course. And that meant he needed to help things along at a gradual, coaxing pace, in a way that would entice Jessica to give him a chance.

"…I thought appetizers would be more practical, instead of a full-course dinner," he heard Jessica say. "Quiches, chicken fingers, stuffed mushrooms, buffalo wings. Those kinds of things that everyone seems to like. I can call a few caterers, get their suggestions, too, and an estimate for the party." She took a drink of her soda, her gaze expectant. "What do you think?"

He pretended to mull over her suggestion. "That sounds fine to me."

"Great." Seemingly pleased with his easy acquiescence, she scribbled a note on a piece of paper with the heading "Caterer." Meanwhile the waitress arrived with their meal, setting a bowl of potato cheese soup in front of Jessica, and a cheeseburger in front of him.

They both started in on their respective lunches. After a few spoonfuls of soup, Jessica continued with her agenda. "I was going to contact Wilson's bakery to order a cake, and I was thinking we should go with white cake with a butter cream frosting."

He chewed on a bite of cheeseburger and thought about her bland suggestion. Not wanting to outright discount her opinion, he chose his words carefully. "I'm not a cake connoisseur by any stretch of the imagination, but what's wrong with a flavored cake, like chocolate, or lemon or even something more exotic like Black Forest?"

She wrinkled her nose at him, silently rejecting his idea. "Not everyone likes those flavors, and vanilla is pretty safe."

"But not very exciting or different," he pointed out, and saw her brows pucker ever so slightly at his argument. "I mean, why do we have to go with just one cake?"

"Because..." Her jaw snapped shut when no other words emerged, then she tried again. "Well, I just thought..." Seemingly unable to find a solid answer to dispute his creative concept, her shoulders slumped. "I guess we could get a variety," she said reluctantly. "What do *you* suggest?"

He'd put her on the defensive, and he hadn't meant to do that. And she obviously wasn't happy about his interference in *her* plans, but it just wouldn't be any fun if he gave in to her every whim without adding a little spice to the mixture. If it was really important, he'd let her have her way—but first, he'd prove to her that plain and practical white cake didn't compare to a more exciting, tasty and pleasurable array of desserts.

She was waiting for his ideas, very impatiently if the tapping of her pen was any indication. Keeping his expression unreadable, he dragged a French fry through a pool of ketchup and met her gaze from across the booth. "Can I have a few days to think about it?"

He'd definitely caught her off guard with his request to take the time to consider their cake dilemma. As much as he knew she would have preferred settling the issue here and now, she conceded to his request.

"Sure." She smiled as if to placate him. "Can you let me know your ideas and suggestions by the end of the week so we can make a decision and get the cake, or cakes, ordered?"

He nodded. "We'll definitely have it covered by the end of the week." And she'd have a new appreciation for the different tastes, flavors and textures of cake.

Closing her notepad, she stuffed it back into her tote bag in an attempt to terminate their discussion. He wasn't about to let her retreat so easily.

"You mentioned going in together on a gift for Brooke and Marc," he said, sucking off a smear of sauce from his thumb. "What did you have in mind?"

She dabbed at her mouth with her napkin as she swallowed a mouthful of soup. "I was thinking along the lines of something for their bathroom, which Brooke mentioned she wanted to redo in peach and greens. We could get them towels, a vanity set, a matching hamper—"

"Well, that's certainly very practical and sensible," he drawled, not at all impressed.

She bristled, a flicker of annoyance finally making an appearance in her gaze. "And what's wrong with that?"

"Nothing, I suppose, for old married couples." Done with his cheeseburger, he wiped his fingers on his napkin. "They're newlyweds, Jessie. Why not get them something fun and sexy for the bathroom?"

She stared at him as if he'd spouted Latin. "What in the world could be fun and sexy for the bathroom?"

Did she honestly have no clue? He shrugged, thinking of the things that would appeal to a woman, and a man, as well. "Lotions, candles and bath products. I've even seen some flavored finger paints that couples can use to rub all over each other's bodies, then lick off."

Her brows rose in skepticism, contradicting the flush stealing across her face. "You're kidding, right?"

He searched her flustered expression, and wondered about her sexual experience. She didn't strike him as completely innocent, but he was beginning to suspect that she'd never experimented beyond basic sex. Had she ever really been seduced by a man? *Really* seduced, in a way that encompassed every one of her five senses?

Bits and pieces of their conversation yesterday at his office filtered through his mind:

*Chemistry is a great start.*

*Which rarely lasts once the relationship turns physical.*

*Is that your experience?*

She hadn't given him an answer, but he was beginning to believe that her sexual encounters had been brief, and inadequate.

"It's a romantic and playful gift," he argued lightly. "Brooke and Marc would enjoy it. Any couple would."

"I doubt it."

Stubborn woman, he thought. She wouldn't doubt his choice if she knew just how sensual and erotic bathtime could be when you had someone to play with in the tub.

"Tell you what," he said, more than willing to compromise. "You purchase the practical items, and I'll buy the fun, sexy stuff. We'll put it all together and the gift will be a great combination of both."

She crossed her arms over her chest, her mouth pursed with frustration. No doubt she was wishing she'd never agreed to allow him to help with the party and planning.

"You're not convinced?"

"I just don't think your idea is a very *useful* gift, and it's not what I had in mind." Her tone was prim, but her words undercut him as a man who knew what women liked. "Maybe we ought to just buy our gifts separately."

Without further comment, he let the issue slide—for now. It appeared he had something else to teach her— about the many creative ways to enjoy being intimate. And when he was done with her, she'd gladly admit to his expertise.

THE MAN WAS INFURIATING!

Jessica walked into her apartment, yanked off her jacket, and released a loud, aggravated sound that did nothing to dispel the frustration coiling within her. Why couldn't Ryan just be a typical male and leave the plans for the New Year's Eve bash to her? Why did he have to put a crimp in her plans and suggestions?

And why did he have to be so gorgeous and sexy and make her want him so much when she knew how foolish any liaison with him would be?

She sank into the old, soft chair that had seen her through many years of pain, anger, tears and confusion. Though the sturdy frame had been reupholstered three times since her parents' divorce when she was nine years old, the chair was the one thing she couldn't part with from her childhood. The softness and warmth had become a comfort zone for her, a place that swallowed her up and offered silent solace for her troubles, whatever they were.

Like her disconcerting attraction to Ryan.

It was silly to hang on to the chair, she knew, considering all the bad memories that came with it—but it had been the one constant in her life, other than Brooke. When her father decided that he preferred the single life with a younger woman over the family he'd created, which entailed nearly destroying his wife in the process, Brooke had been the strong one during the turbulent divorce that had ensued. Brooke had taken care of her, and their mother. The separation had been a nasty one, with her father hiring a powerful attorney who had no compunction about taking advantage of her mother's emotional shock. And since her mother hadn't been able to afford to hire a decent lawyer for herself, she'd lost most everything to her husband and his new lover.

Bitter memories swamped Jessica as she remembered the years after the divorce, of her mother struggling to make ends meet because their father never paid child support and alimony on time, and Brooke sacrificing her teenage years to help raise her because their mother had to work two jobs to keep a roof over their heads, clothes on their backs and food in their mouths.

An awful childhood, due to the abandonment of her father, and the insensitive, cruel nature of a divorce attorney more interested in his final take than a family's welfare.

She curled into the soft cushion and rubbed her hand over the powder-blue fabric. This chair had absorbed her tears and had taken all the angry pounding and abuse she would have unleashed on her father had he shown up to exercise his visitation rights. But ultimately, he hadn't cared for his daughters' emotional needs, just his own selfish desires. He'd never given a second thought to the family he'd left in shambles.

Neither had his cutthroat attorney.

When she thought of Ryan's profession, she thought of the lawyer who'd represented her father and coldly and cruelly demolished a little girl's dreams. A man who'd degraded a good wife and mother to benefit his client and pad his own pocketbook.

But Ryan wasn't cold and unfeeling and degrading. He was warm and caring and amusing, in a way that made her wonder how he was able to enjoy being a divorce attorney and accomplish all the necessary evils that went along with the profession when it was obvious that his own family ties were tightly woven. She wondered what had prompted his choice of occupation, then dismissed the thought because the answer really didn't matter—and *shouldn't* matter. Between his career and his drive and ambition, Ryan was completely wrong for her.

Closing her eyes, she burrowed her cheek against the plush headrest in an attempt to forget about her oppressive past, and the turbulent present. No matter the problems and afflictions that plagued her mind, the effect of the chair managed to calm her soul.

At the moment, Jessica was more concerned about the state of her heart…and Ryan Matthews easing his way into it. Despite everything he stood for, despite how frustrated and infuriated he'd made her today with the cake issue and his idea of a wedding present, she couldn't deny desiring Ryan Matthews, the man.

Her blossoming feelings for him were dangerous and could only lead to heartache. He himself had admitted that he wasn't looking for commitment, while she'd spent most of her adult life searching for just that, along with security and stability with a man. After living through her parents' nasty divorce, seeing her sister through a bad marriage, and making an error in judgment of her own in a previous relationship, Jessica was determined to make better choices. When she fell in love, she wanted it to last forever. When she married, she wanted to do it right the *first* time around.

And Ryan wasn't her vision of love and marriage material.

But he was a man who made her feel alive and desirable. He made her want to take risks and experience real passion. With him. The rest of the month stretched ahead of them, beckoning her to give in to that restless sensation swirling within her.

She drew a deep, shuddering sigh. She had no idea what she was going to do about her troubling attraction, and Ryan's unconcealed interest. She was struggling between holding on to her convictions, or letting go and tasting the bit of heaven his smiles, touches and kisses promised.

She feared the latter was winning the battle.

But no matter what happened between her and Ryan, no matter if she surrendered to the attraction she was finding increasingly hard to resist, two things were certain. She was holding firm to her decision about ordering a single vanilla-flavored cake for the party, and no way was she going to be a part of his outrageous, unconventional bathroom gift!

THREE DAYS PASSED before Ryan called Jessica to discuss his thoughts on the cake issue. He meant to call sooner, but work and late-night preparations for court appearances had interfered with his good intentions.

While she wanted to settle the disagreement over the phone, he'd insisted on coming by her place Thursday evening after dinner to resolve the matter— and made her suffer through another two days of wondering what he was up to and what he'd decided.

Finding a bakery who'd cater to his peculiar request hadn't been easy, thus part of the delay in seeing Jessica, but Ryan was confident that the end results of tonight's "taste test" would be worth the expense, and the wait. He planned to treat Jessica to her first seduction of her five senses.

After a long day filled with two depositions and a court appearance, Ryan headed home and changed from his suit into comfortable jeans and a long-sleeved cotton shirt. Heading down to the kitchen to heat up the leftover spaghetti he'd made the night before, he picked up Camelot along the way and gave her the attention she wanted, then treats when they reached the pantry. While his dinner heated and Camelot munched happily on her morsels, Ryan skimmed through the day's mail.

He set aside two utility bills, tossed out the junk mail, and opened a few Christmas cards from friends. At the bottom of the pile was a cream-colored envelope, his name and address printed with gold ink. At the sight of Haywood and Irwin's senior partner's name and *home* address affixed to the upper left-hand corner, a mixture of excitement, nerves and anticipation swarmed in Ryan's belly.

Ripping open the envelope, he retrieved the engraved card inside. Elation bubbled within him as he read the contents. "I'll be damned," he murmured with a lopsided grin, feeling as though his six years of service and dedication to the firm, all his personal sacrifices, were finally paying off.

The gilded request invited him and a guest to the private, intimate Christmas gathering the senior partners held in appreciation of their most esteemed associates. Though the firm threw a casual office holiday party for all employees, only select members were invited to Haywood's home for the black-tie affair. It was an honor to be included in the elite group, a small but significant step up the corporate ladder, and it brought him one level closer to achieving his long-term goals. This was the first year they'd included him on their private guest list, and he wasn't about to refuse the opportunity to join the ranks of his other revered colleagues.

An RSVP card was included and requested notification of one or two guests. Anxious to respond favorably, he grabbed a pen from the holder on the counter near the phone, signed his name to the card, and moved to put an X on the line for one guest.

He hesitated. From what he'd heard and knew personally, the associates that attended Haywood's party brought their wives, or significant others. While he knew it wasn't a requirement that he bring someone to the event, he was also keenly aware that he was one of the few associates in the firm who was still a confirmed bachelor. No doubt, he'd be the only single and unattached employee in attendance.

The only person he'd consider taking was the only woman he had any interest in—Jessica. He imagined her in a room full of attorneys, and winced at the possibility of her cracking lawyer jokes and insulting the senior partners. But for all her joking and teasing with him, he'd like to believe she respected him enough not to undercut him in a professional atmosphere.

If she would even agree to accompany him to the party.

The idea of inviting Jessica definitely had merit. Not only would he have a beautiful, intelligent woman on his arm and wouldn't be the odd man out, it would also afford him the perfect opportunity to show her that attorneys were civilized people and not the ruthless savages she believed them to be.

Granted, there were lawyers who took advantage of people, as in any profession. He acknowledged that, but that wasn't why *he'd* chosen a career in law. Not only did he enjoy a solid debate, but his main goal had been to help people in need, in whatever capacity possible. And while he had some clients who were vicious and wanted revenge on their spouses, he always tried to look at a case objectively and fairly.

He wanted Jessica to treat him the same way.

*Good luck in securing the date, Matthews,* he thought cynically. That in itself would be an extraordinary achievement. Yet he wasn't ready to admit defeat without at least attempting to influence her into agreeing. He'd have his answer tonight.

The microwave beeped, signaling his dinner was warm. He ate a plate of spaghetti, headed back up to his bathroom to brush his teeth, then went to his closet. Flipping on the light, he perused his collection of silk ties and selected an odd patterned one he hadn't worn in years. He folded the strip of material and stuffed it into the front pocket of his jeans for later.

Then he left the house. He stopped at the bakery to pick up his order, and followed the directions Jessica had reluctantly given him to her complex. With a lightness to his step and the handle of a paper bag in each hand, he easily found Jessica's apartment and knocked.

She opened the door, dressed in white-washed jeans

and a pale pink turtleneck, which was one of the most revealing things he'd ever seen on her. While the material covered her from wrists to throat, it was more snug than the loose sweaters and blouses she normally wore and revealed the full breasts that had pressed against his chest so deliciously that afternoon at his office.

Blocking his entrance, she crossed her arms over that lush chest, looking like a sentinel guarding priceless jewels. "I don't understand why we couldn't just handle this issue over the phone."

Knowing she'd discover his motives soon enough, he didn't bother to soothe her grumbles. Instead, he grinned, in too good a mood to let her complaint spoil what he had planned.

"Hello to you, too, Jessie." He stepped toward her, deliberately crowding her personal space. With his superior size, he forced her to back up and let him into her apartment, or end up pressed intimately against him.

With a startled gasp, she moved out of his way.

"Which way to the kitchen?" he asked, sending a quick glance around her place, which was decorated in pastels of blue, cream and bits of violet. Very soothing. Very feminine.

"Why?" She closed the door and eyed him suspiciously. "I already ate dinner."

"So did I." He lifted the bags, drawing her attention to the packages in his hands. "This is dessert."

Confusion colored her features, and obviously rendered her mute. Since she wasn't being a hospitable hostess, he headed toward the left, where he spied a small oak dining table, which led him right into the kitchen.

"I'm not in the mood for dessert, thank you," she said from behind him.

"Oh, you will be." Setting the bags on a wide chair, he stacked her quilted place mats to clear the surface of the table for their smorgasbord.

She came up beside him, and regarded his actions pensively. "I thought you were here to give me an answer on the kind of cake you think we should order."

"I am, not that what *I* think makes any difference to you and what you're determined to order." Done with his first task, he turned to look at her, letting a warm, lazy smile curve his lips. "You have it in that beautiful head of yours that being a *man* I haven't the slightest clue about cakes and desserts and what our guests might like."

A hint of a frown formed on her brows. "I never said that," she said quietly.

"Not in so many words, no, but you definitely thought it." He unloaded a number of small, square bakery boxes on the table, but left their lids secure. "I know you weren't thrilled with my suggestion of something other than plain ol' vanilla cake, so I'm here to convince you otherwise."

She stuffed her flattened hands into the back pockets of her jeans, drawing the material of her long-sleeved turtleneck tighter across her breasts. "What are you talking about?"

Masculine heat rushed through Ryan, followed by a sharp kick of desire. Judging by the faint outline of Jessica's nipples against soft cotton, Ryan guessed that she favored sheer, unpadded bras. There was nothing to conceal her body's natural response, and if he wasn't careful, his own unruly hormones were going to make his awareness of her just as obvious.

In an attempt to distract his thoughts he searched her kitchen drawers for a knife. "Out of necessity, I've become an authority on cakes, and when we're done sampling what I've brought, I'm confident that I'll have made an expert out of you, too."

She watched him set the knife on the table, then help himself to a chilled bottle of water from the refrigerator. "Ryan, you're not making any sense."

"It's simple, Jessie," he said, pushing up his shirt-sleeves to just below his elbow. "I've arranged a taste test of various cakes, and we'll see which one pleases your palate the most. And if vanilla still comes out as your top choice, we'll go with it." He rested his hands on her shoulders. "All I ask is that you give *my* flavors a fair chance."

She released a breath, and he reveled in the feel of the tension unfurling from her body. "All right," she agreed, and offered him a conciliatory smile.

Satisfied that he'd attained her cooperation, he patted the smooth, oak surface of the table. "I need you to sit right here."

"On the table?" she asked incredulously.

Unexpectedly, he touched her under the chin with his fingers, startling her. He gently lifted her gaze, so she had no choice but to look him directly in the eyes. Hers were so deep and blue he wanted to drown in their depths.

Very softly, imploringly, he said, "Just this once, make something easy on me, okay? And maybe you could trust me a little, too?"

He saw her internal struggle, and waited patiently, knowing he couldn't do this unless he had her complete and total consent. After a few heartbeats, her expression softened in agreement, and she granted him the permission he sought by sliding her bottom onto the table where he'd indicated.

"Perfect," he murmured, then withdrew the tie from his front pocket. Gradually, he let it unravel. With mesmerizing slowness, he threaded the cool silk through his hands and fingers, and finally wrapped the tapered ends around his fists.

She dampened her bottom lip with her tongue as she watched him manipulate the strip of silk. He expected her to be nervous, and he supposed on some level *she* was uncertain, but there was no mistaking the glimmer of anticipation that darkened her eyes.

It was all the reassurance he needed.

Her gaze traveled from the taut fabric in his hands, to his face. "What do you intend to do with that tie?" she asked, her voice husky.

"I'm going to blindfold you."

# CHAPTER FOUR

JESSICA SHIVERED at the direct, male look in Ryan's deep brown eyes, the unmistakable seductive intent... but she wasn't afraid. She was suddenly very aware of the heat of his body, the reckless racing of her pulse, and the spiraling warmth settling low in her belly.

He loosened his hold on the tie, and the silk whispered through his long fingers again. The erotic sound strummed along her nerve endings just as effectively, awakening an undeniable excitement within her.

She struggled to draw a steady breath. For as titillating as she found his suggestion, she wasn't sure why shielding her vision was necessary. "Why do you need to blindfold me?"

"So you'll get the full effect of my experiment."

Stepping in front of her, he leaned forward to cover her eyes. When her locked knees brushed his groin, she automatically parted her legs to make room for him... and realized her mistake. He moved closer, nudging her thighs wider to accommodate his lean hips, making her far too aware of how intimate their position was.

Their close proximity didn't seem to bother him. "Being blindfolded will heighten your other senses, like the texture of the cake, the flavor, the smell. And I don't want you cheating and knowing ahead of time what you're tasting."

He wasn't proposing anything indecent, or sexual even, yet as darkness descended over her eyes and she felt his fingers tying a knot in the scrap of silk at the back of her head, a strange, forbidden thrill rippled through her. Once he had her blindfold secure, he gently tucked the sides of her hair behind her ears—to make sure the strands didn't get sticky with cake and frosting, she was guessing. But his touch lingered longer than necessary. His fingers traced the delicate, sensitive shell of her ears, and his knuckles lightly skimmed along her jaw.

Her breasts tightened in response to his caress, and she managed a breathless laugh. "Is touching me part of your experiment?"

"I'm just making sure your senses are alert."

Her senses were electrified, and more alive than they'd ever been before. And she had no idea where his eyes were, but she felt them *everywhere.* She resisted the urge to squirm.

"How many fingers am I holding up?" he asked.

A teasing smile touched the corner of her mouth. "Two and a half."

He chuckled, and the masculine timbre of that sound shimmied down her spine with impossible pleasure. "Good. Your vision is definitely impaired."

He moved away for a moment, she heard a box opening and other sounds she couldn't identify, and then he returned to the cove between her thighs.

"Here's the first one," he said, and brushed her bottom lip with the confection.

She parted her lips at his urging and took a dainty bite of what he offered. Immediately, she identified it as the white cake. It was moist with a buttercream frosting…and very ordinary tasting. She kept her revelation to herself, still believing vanilla was their safest bet to please thirty people.

"This is the vanilla for sure," she said as she chewed and swallowed. "Are you eating it, too?"

"I'll skip this one." Another box opened. "I already know how bland and boring vanilla is."

She wrinkled her nose at him. "I can hardly wait to taste what *you* selected. Fruitcake, maybe?"

That deep, rich laugh again. And then two things assailed her senses at the same time as he took his place in front of her. The delectable fragrance of chocolate, and a burning sensation where he rested his palm on her thigh. The combination nearly short-circuited her central nervous system.

With effort, she concentrated on the scent wafting beneath her nose. "Chocolate?" she guessed.

"Ahh, but this isn't your ordinary chocolate cake."

She inhaled deeply, catching a whiff of something richer and more decadent. Since he wasn't forthcoming with the flavor, she sampled it for herself. Cocoa, a hint of coffee in the frosting and filling, and chocolate mocha candy shavings that all but melted in her mouth.

"Oh, wow," she murmured appreciatively. She licked a crumb from the corner of her mouth, feeling ravenous and greedy. "Can I have another bite?"

"I thought you might like that one." He fed her another morsel, and slowly dragged his fingers along her lower lip. "It's called Chocolate Mocha Rapture."

*Rapture.* Her eyes rolled heavenward. Oh, yeah, she'd definitely been transported to another plane. Her body felt flushed, drugged, heavy. *Aroused.*

He pressed a chilled plastic bottle in her hand and urged it up to her mouth. "Take a drink to cleanse your palate. I don't want anything to taint the next flavor."

Though the water was cold and refreshing sliding down her throat, it did nothing to extinguish the flames Ryan's "experiment" had ignited. Setting the bottle next to her on the table, she waited anxiously for the next dessert.

"Now here we have something sweet and *very* sinful."

Her nostrils flared as a luscious aroma consumed her senses. Her stomach rumbled, and she licked her lips in anticipation.

"Open up," he murmured.

She did, and groaned as an exquisite flavor filled her mouth. Ripe strawberries. Whipped cream filling. A light, fluffy frosting. Shavings of white chocolate. She was certain she'd died and gone to heaven.

"More?" he asked, seemingly knowing exactly what she liked.

She nodded, beyond caring that she wanted to overload her senses with the lush sensuality of Ryan's taste test, or that he'd probably gloat later over proving his point that vanilla was a bland choice. She'd never savored such divine recipes, never felt so seduced by tastes and textures.

"Please," she said, parting her lips for him. She took such a huge, devouring bite that the cream filling oozed out of the middle. Instinctively, she lifted her hand to stop the flow, and by luck caught the dollop in her palm, but not before she'd smeared it along her chin, too.

"Argh." The sound of distress caught in her throat. Then, unable to help herself, she laughed with frivolous lightness. "I'm making a mess. I hope you brought napkins."

"Don't need 'em," he replied, his voice infused with amusement, and something far more mischievous. "I'll take care of the spills and leftovers."

She assumed he meant to clean up later when they were done, so she wasn't prepared for his more resourceful method. He caught her wrist and she nearly jumped out of her skin when she felt his warm mouth nibble off the portion of cake stuck to her palm. A hot ache spread through her as his teeth grazed her flesh, and she all but melted when he thoroughly laved her fingers, then flicked his tongue wickedly along the crevices between. And when he was done with her hand, he went to work on her chin, eating the crumbs and licking away the frosting and filling with agonizingly slow laps of his tongue.

He indulged in her as if *she* were dessert.

"Delicious, and so sweet," he murmured, his low voice vibrating against her cheek.

A sultry pressure coiled low as she waited anxiously for him to complete his task and make his way to her mouth and kiss her deeply…

It never happened. As if he hadn't completely turned her inside out with wanting, he moved away and returned to the business at hand, selecting another cake for her to try. This one was Butter Brickle Ecstasy, and it was everything the name implied…pure, unadulterated bliss for the taste buds.

With each sampling, he tempted and teased her, and she luxuriated in the provocative pleasures he evoked. He used his lips and tongue to clean up the sticky messes she deliberately made, yet always stopped short of kissing her mouth.

Frustration nipped at her. She wanted to take off the

blindfold and participate without hindrance—and entice him in return. He insisted it remain, or the experiment ended.

He won, because she wasn't ready or willing to forfeit the delightful confections still to come.

He went on to feed her Fuzzy Navel Cake drenched with peach schnapps that she couldn't seem to get enough of, and a melt-in-your-mouth champagne cake with French buttercream frosting that made her feel giddy and drunk—not on alcohol, but the insatiable desire he was gradually building within her.

But it was the last selection that completely undid her: moist chocolate cake layered with chocolate mousse, drizzled with creamy caramel and topped with a cloud of whipped cream and chunks of butter toffee. This cake was gooey, messy, but a sumptuous feast that tantalized her mouth and pleased her belly.

She moaned deep in her throat as the contents dissolved on her tongue and slid down her throat like honeyed silk. "This cake is *incredible.* What is it called?"

He offered her another bite, knowing from previous requests that she wouldn't settle for just one taste. "Would you believe the bakery called it Better Than Sex Cake?"

She licked the corner of her mouth, not wanting to spare even a smudge of whipped cream, caramel or chocolate mousse. "Oh, God, they're right." She sighed in undisguised gratification. "This is almost… *euphoric.*"

"Do you really think it's that much better?" he asked, his tone dubious.

"In my experience, yeah," she said, realizing too late just how much she'd revealed.

There was a pause, then, "This cake, no matter how

incredible, doesn't compare to the real thing…not when you're with the right person."

And her one and only lover obviously hadn't been that right person. Suddenly feeling self-conscious under Ryan's scrutiny, she decided it was time to end their playful game, and reached for the blindfold to remove it from her eyes.

His fingers gently encircled her wrist, stopping her before she could tug the tie loose. His touch was firm, hot, branding her.

"Not yet," he said in a low, sexy voice. "Maybe you'd like more?" His comment was double edged, giving her the distinct impression that he was referring to more than just feasting on the exotically named cake she'd just eaten. "It's right here, Jessie, in the palm of my hand. Just reach out and take it, and the euphoria can be all yours. As much as you like, for as long as you want."

Cocooned in darkness, stimulated by his words and the sexual slant of their conversation, Jessica's heart beat erratically in her chest. He'd issued her a subtle dare, a flagrant invitation…beckoning her to give in to her secret desires and experience just how good sex, with the right person, could be.

She swallowed to ease the tightness in her throat. "I don't want to eat the cake alone," she whispered.

"I don't like to eat my cake alone, either," he said, humor and understanding mingling. "How about we share it, then?"

"All right," she agreed.

Standing between her legs again so she was surrounded by his scent and heat, he took her hand and slowly guided it to the side where the cakes were displayed. She had no idea what he intended, but entrusted herself to him and followed his lead.

She sucked in a quick, startled breath as he eased her fingers into the soft, silky layers of cake—all the way up to her knuckles. His own hand slid along hers as he encouraged her to play in the ingredients and feel the various textures, all of which had suddenly become very intoxicating to her senses.

Her entire body tingled with a strange excitement. "This feels…"

"Arousing?" he suggested.

*Oh, yeah, definitely that.* She grinned, not sure she was ready to admit just how much his provocative demonstration was affecting her. "I was thinking more along the lines of squishy."

He chuckled. "Then maybe we need to alter your way of thinking." He entwined their fingers, tangled them sensuously, using the mousse, caramel, and whipped cream to lubricate the rhythmic slide of his fingers between hers. He leaned into her, so his lips grazed her ear. "*This* is how good sex feels with the right person…slippery, sensual, *erotic.*"

She bit her lower lip as an illicit, liquid warmth cascaded over her and pooled between her thighs. She had no choice but to believe him. She *wanted* to believe that making love could be so thrilling, so impetuous, so rapturous.

Too soon, he lifted his hand from hers, slowly dragging it out of the cake and away. She flinched in startled surprise when his sticky, gooey fingers touched her mouth.

"And this is how good sex *tastes*," he murmured huskily as he smeared the luscious concoction along her bottom lip. "Sweet, heady, *euphoric*. Taste it, Jessie, and see for yourself."

His sexy words tempted her. Unable to stop herself, her tongue darted out, slowly licking away the confection.

*This is how good sex tastes.*

His promise rumbled through her mind, and suddenly, one taste wasn't enough. "I want more," she said in a low, breathy voice.

His finger returned, gently pressing down on her bottom lip until they parted and she took him inside the damp heat of her mouth. Removing her own hand from the cake, she grabbed his wrist so he couldn't pull back while she tormented him the same way he'd done to her. Heedless of the mess they were smearing everywhere, she nibbled the chocolate and caramel from his fingers, then leisurely stroked and swirled her tongue along each individual digit in an instinctive, up-and-down rhythm. She felt him shudder and heard him let out a hiss of breath in response.

She heard him swear, felt him try and tug his hand back, but she held firm. Her hunger had become a rapacious thing, and it wasn't for cake and sweets, but for the need to experience *slippery, sensual, erotic sex*. With Ryan.

She felt his body shift in front of her, wedging himself more intimately between her thighs, and then his mouth was on hers, urgent and insistent, and she relinquished his fingers for the pleasure of his kiss.

And from there, everything went wild and out of control. He swept an arm around her back and hauled her up against his body, forcing her legs wider to accommodate his hips and the unyielding press of his fierce erection against her aching cleft. They were fused from lips to thighs, and she still wasn't close enough.

Spearing her cake-encrusted fingers into the warm, thick hair at the nape of his neck, she arched into him, opening her mouth wider beneath his to accept the hot, sexual thrusts of his tongue. One of his hands mimicked her move, cupping the back of her head, threading through the hair that wasn't restrained by the blindfold. The fingers of his other hand caressed her jaw, her throat and skimmed lower until he held the full weight of her breast in his palm. He kneaded the mound of flesh, searing her with breath-taking heat. His thumb flicked across the diamond-hard nipple straining against her cotton shirt, plucked the tip delicately, and a needy moan escaped her.

Feverish desire clawed at her, submersing her deeper under Ryan's spell. Being blindfolded and ravished was like being swept up into a dark, forbidden fantasy. The thrill of it was liberating.

Unexpectedly, he lifted his lips from hers, putting her system in immediate withdrawal. Their breath mingled in rapid bursts, and he threw her off-kilter again when he pressed an achingly light and tender kiss to the corner of her mouth. "Go out with me," he rasped.

"No," she groaned automatically, so used to rejecting him that it had become second nature.

He swooped in for another kiss, this one slower than the last, more persuasive, more possessive. "One date," he uttered once he let her up for air.

Her resolve crumbled a fraction. "Maybe."

He took her under again, thoroughly consuming her mouth until her lips felt swollen and devoured. He brushed his knuckles over her erect nipples, teasing and tormenting her. He moved on, trailing kisses along her jaw. His fingers pulled down the collar of her turtleneck so he had access to nuzzle her throat.

She shuddered uncontrollably at the hot, wet glide of his tongue across her skin, and whimpered as he drew her flesh between his teeth for a love bite.

"Dinner and drinks." His hoarse, urgent whisper scalded her ear. "Say yes, Jessie."

Dizzy from the blindfold, faint and flushed from his sensual assault, she obeyed his command. *"Yes."*

She stiffened, just as the phone on the kitchen counter rang.

*Oh, God, had she really surrendered and said yes to Ryan Matthews?*

The phone pealed again. She didn't move, and neither did Ryan, though she could hear his heavy, labored breathing, could feel the virile heat radiating off him, and smell what she now knew was the scent of good sex...*sweet, heady, euphoric.*

Silently, she cursed the blindfold that had completely stripped away her restraints and inhibitions. Unable to see Ryan, her feminine wants and needs had taken precedence over the fact that this man before her was all wrong for her.

Her answering machine clicked on, and her voice echoed in the quiet kitchen with a brief outgoing message, followed by a shrill beep.

"Hi, Jess, it's Brooke," her sister said, sounding upbeat and cheerful. "I received an invitation in the mail today for a New Year's Eve party at Ryan Matthews', and I'm assuming you got one, too. I also wanted to talk to you about Christmas. Give me a call tonight at home or tomorrow at the office. Love ya."

The line disconnected, and the answering machine clicked off.

Unexpected guilt swamped Jessica, as if her sister had

personally caught her in a naughty act. And she was very naughty for consorting with the enemy, for allowing him to breach her well-constructed barriers. With pleasure infusing her veins, she'd forgotten one important issue while he'd coaxed her into agreeing to go out on a date with him—she didn't like divorce attorneys.

But she liked Ryan. Wanted him. Desired him.

His long fingers slipped beneath the band of silk concealing her vision and lifted it over her head. She squinted as the bright kitchen light pierced her eyes and her pupils contracted. Gradually, her gaze focused. On the man standing in front of her, who was watching her guardedly. On the disarray of baked goods around the table. Crumbs littered the table, the floor and her jeans. There was cake and filling everywhere—on his shirt, his face, arm and hands. She hadn't survived the attack, either. Her cheek was sticky, as were her fingers. And she had a white handprint on her shirt, outlining her breast.

She dragged a shaky hand through her hair, and winced as her fingers tangled in a clump of frosting stuck to the strands. "What a mess…" *she'd made of things,* her conscience finished for her.

Oh, Lord, staring into his intense, deep-brown eyes, she was so utterly confused. Undoubtedly, her emotions were tangled up in the passion he inspired, making her forget all the reasons why it would be so foolish to let herself get any more involved with him.

She fabricated a smile. "You win," she conceded, scooting off the table.

He stepped to the side out of her way, but continued to eye her cautiously, as if he knew just how skittish she'd become now that she'd had time to assess what they'd done. "What's the prize?"

"Proving me wrong." Desperately, she tried to affect a business demeanor, which was difficult to do when her body still throbbed and ached for something that would never happen with Ryan.

*Slippery, sensual, erotic sex.*

She pressed a hand to still the fluttering in her belly at that thought, and smudged more frosting on her clothing. She grimaced. She needed a shower, and she needed distance from this man who threatened everything from her sanity to her beliefs.

"Vanilla is by far the most bland and boring cake I've ever tasted," she admitted, knowing it would be ridiculous for her to say otherwise, not after being such a glutton with the flavors he'd brought. "How about we order three of those cakes. Is that variety enough for you?"

"Sure." He didn't smirk or exult over the fact that he'd gained her acquiescence. Instead, he tipped his head, regarding her with warm concern. "You pick which ones."

Ignoring the silent question in his eyes that asked if she was okay, she glanced at the assortment of half-eaten desserts on the table. She was far from okay, but she'd be much better once he left and she scrambled to put her priorities back in line.

Which didn't include *slippery, sensual, erotic sex* with Ryan Matthews.

Selecting only three flavors was a difficult task, especially when they'd all been so delicious. "How about we go with strawberries and cream, the champagne cake and butter brickle?" She deliberately kept the names short and precise, without the sexy labels he'd used to describe them.

"Good choices," he said as a too-intimate smile

curved his mouth. "Though I think the Better Than Sex Cake would be a great conversation piece for the guests."

Unwilling to let him think she couldn't handle ordering that particular cake because of the sensual memories it evoked, she gave an uncaring shrug. "I'll add it to the order."

An awkward silence fell between them, rife with sexual and emotional undercurrents—neither of which Jessica wanted to bring out in the open and discuss.

She grappled for an excuse to end the evening with Ryan. "I, uh, need to take a shower. I have frosting and cake everywhere." She waved a hand toward the mess on the table. "Just leave everything and I'll clean it up later. When you're done washing up, lock the door behind you."

Without giving him an opportunity to reply or a chance to postpone his departure, she made a beeline down the hall and sought the private sanctuary of her bedroom.

RYAN RELEASED a long stream of breath that did little to ease the self-reproach twisting inside him. He wasn't going anywhere, not until he'd cleaned up the mess *he'd* made of things. With Jessica.

He'd rushed her. Overwhelmed her. And that had never been his intent. He'd merely meant to show her how fantastic the chemistry was between them, and open her up to the possibility of giving him a fair chance at being something more than a party-planning buddy.

She'd definitely been a willing partner in what had transpired on this very table—lush, wanton and uninhibited. Her compliance had been genuine, her enthusiastic response to his kisses and caresses unfeigned.

But her body and mind weren't in harmony, and that was the crux of their problem.

While his seductive demonstration had succeeded in stripping Jessica of her physical reserve, it hadn't completely diminished her reluctance to trust him. She harbored doubts and fears that stretched beyond wallowing in sexual gratification. And for a reason that he hadn't completely sorted out yet in his own head, he *wanted* her trust—just as much as he wanted to make love to her and introduce her to all the pleasures she'd been denied.

He knew if he left now as she'd insisted, he'd give her the perfect opportunity to retreat and shore up those defenses of hers. And that wouldn't do. He'd merely scratched the surface of Jessica's complexities, and he wasn't through discovering the depth of those fascinating layers.

With his next strategy filtering through his mind, he set about tidying up the kitchen. Most of the small cakes were destroyed from their taste test, and weren't worth saving. He tossed the remnants and boxes in the trash, wiped down the table and picked up the crumbs that had fallen on the floor. Then he went into the bathroom he found off the living room and scrubbed his hands and arms free of dried frosting and cake. He rinsed the confection from his face, and decided there wasn't anything he could do about his hair until he took his own shower at home.

If things had ended more positively, he might be sharing Jessica's shower with her, he thought with a rueful smile at himself in the mirror. The image of her naked and wet, with water sluicing down the sleek curves she hid, invaded his musings. The vivid fantasy caused a liquid heat to rush to his groin. He swore and splashed cold water over his face.

A half an hour later, Jessica finally exited her bedroom and found him reclining against the tiled counter with a bottle of cold water in his hand, and the kitchen spotless.

She came to an abrupt stop when she saw him. Wariness instantly colored her eyes, made more strikingly blue by her freshly scrubbed face and the damp strands of honey-blond hair falling haphazardly to her shoulders. She wore an old terry robe that swallowed her up in the folds of worn material, from neck to ankles. On her feet were a pair of pink house slippers.

And in that moment, she appeared incredibly vulnerable to him.

Then her chin lifted a stubborn notch, reminding him of the spitfire he was used to dealing with. "You're still here," she said, her voice indicating her surprise. "I told you it wasn't necessary for you to clean up."

He shrugged a shoulder. "I contributed to the mess. It was the least I could do." Finished with his water, he tossed the plastic bottle into the recycle bin under the sink, then resumed his position against the counter.

"Well, thank you for your help." *And now you're free to leave,* her tone silently added.

"You're welcome." He didn't budge.

She released an exasperated sound beneath her breath, and tugged on the sash to her robe, tightening it around her slender waist. The lapels billowed open slightly, affording him a tantalizing glimpse of smooth skin and the beginning slope of one breast. He wondered if she was completely naked beneath the terry material, and resisted the urge to reach out, untie her belt, and find out for himself…

She crossed her arms over her chest and cleared her throat, effectively drawing his attention upward. Her eyes flared with impatience…and awareness. "Ryan… it's getting late, and you really should go."

"In a minute," he said in a slow, deliberate drawl. "You owe me something, and I didn't want to leave without it."

"Money for the cakes?" She asked the question in such a hopeful way that he knew she'd purposely misconstrued his meaning. She moved past him to open a drawer beneath the counter, leaving a scented trail of jasmine in her wake. "I don't have any extra cash on me, but I'd be happy to write you a check—"

He grabbed her hand before she could retrieve her checkbook, and closed the drawer with a bump of his hip. He waited until she looked up at him. "I don't want your money, Jessie. I want *you*," he said softly, sincerely. "And you owe me a date."

She extricated her arm from his grasp. "You obtained that date under duress, *counselor*."

He couldn't contain the laugh that escaped him. "You call the way you kissed me *duress?*"

Her mouth pursed, and he was half-tempted to haul her up against him and kiss her senseless again, until she melted and admitted the truth—that she'd been a willing participant in what had taken place on the table behind her.

"I certainly wasn't in the right frame of mind to make any kind of decision, and being the lawyer you are, you took advantage of that fact."

He shook his head at her reasoning, seeing it for the excuse it was, and a poor one at that. "So, does this mean you're reneging on your promise?"

She picked at a piece of lint on her sleeve, her gaze

downcast, her voice resigned. "I think you and I ought to just stick to party planning."

In his estimation, they'd gone too far to backpedal to platonic friends. Yet it was obvious that he still needed to tread slowly and cautiously with her. "Would you go out with me in the guise of doing me a favor?"

That captured her attention. She lifted her head and met his gaze, waiting to hear his proposition.

"I *do* need a date," he inhaled, taking a huge leap of faith, "for my firm's Christmas party."

Her incredulous expression told him his risk hadn't paid off. "Me? In a room full of lawyers?" She flattened a hand to her chest, her eyes wide, and visibly shuddered. "No, thank you."

"One date," he said, not ready to give up just yet. "No strings attached. I swear it."

A slow, devious smile played around the corner of her mouth. "How do you know when a lawyer is lying?"

Having been the recipient of that particular joke before, he knew the punch line. "His lips are moving," he replied with a grin.

"*Exactly,*" she said, obviously believing he was weaving a fib of his own.

He grabbed the tail end of her sash and gave it a playful tug. "Aw, come on, Jessie," he said in a low, deep voice. "You know you want to accept…maybe just a little?"

She shook her head adamantly and pushed her hands into the side pockets of her robe. "Not only am I refusing for personal reasons, I don't do fancy, schmancy parties. I'm sure it won't be difficult for you to find some other willing female to adorn your arm."

He still held on to the belt of her robe, suspecting if he let go she'd bolt. And he wanted to keep her near.

"I asked *you* because I don't want to go with anyone else." And that was the truth, whether she believed him or not.

"Then it looks like you'll be attending solo." The barest hint of regret tinged her voice. "I'm sorry, Ryan...I *can't* do it. It's those personal ethics of mine and all. You understand."

Her excuse was a familiar one, but this time he wasn't going to accept her obscure argument, not when he suddenly had more at stake than just securing a date to his firm's holiday party—like securing her trust. "The thing is, Jessie, I don't understand those personal ethics of yours. Not completely. It has to do with me being a divorce attorney, that I know, but *why?*"

She didn't reply. Instead, he watched those defenses of hers slowly rise, saw it in the stiffening of her spine and the guarded look in her eyes, and knew if he didn't act fast he'd lose the opportunity to reach beyond those barriers she was about to erect.

He wove his fingers casually through the end of her sash, keeping her close. "How is it that you can respond to me the way you did earlier, so openly and honestly, yet shut me out emotionally? I can't help but take that personally, Jessie."

She swallowed, hard, but her gaze remained steady on his. "I apologize if you feel that I led you on."

"No, I don't feel that way at all." He smiled gently. "I think you're scared, and maybe confused, and that's okay. But I think I've earned the right to know *what* you're afraid of."

Her chin lifted a notch, but she appeared more vulnerable than mutinous. "All right. I'm very attracted to you, but beyond the physical attraction, I'm having a difficult time getting past what you do for a living, and everything it implies."

He'd known his occupation posed a problem for her from the very beginning, but he wanted deeper knowledge. "You mean me being a divorce attorney?" he asked, coaxing her to open up even more.

"That's part of it," she said, nodding guardedly. "I'm not fond of divorce attorneys. I saw firsthand with my mother and father just how cold and calculating people in that profession can be. I watched my father's cutthroat lawyer nearly destroy my mother, and rip apart our family, all for his client's benefit. My mother struggled for years after the divorce just to make ends meet, while my father walked away with a nicely padded bank account and a charming new life without any familial responsibilities."

Her words didn't paint a flattering picture at all, and made his heart go out to the little girl who'd witnessed that devastating separation, and to the woman who was still affected by her father's abandonment. "And that's what you think I do for a living?"

"Don't you?" The challenge in her voice was unmistakable.

He paused. How to explain without incriminating himself? "What happened to your mother, your family, was very unfortunate, but there're always two sides to every case. And while some divorces aren't pleasant and amicable, I try to look at all my cases objectively and represent my clients to the best of my ability, with *facts*."

"Even if that means ruining the other person's life in the process?"

"Sometimes I represent that defendant, and women like your mother who struggle not to get shafted by their conniving husbands. It all depends on the couple and circumstances involved. Some cases are simple and friendly. Others are ugly and vicious. I have no control over the personality types I represent, and trust me when I say that there are *all* kinds."

She stepped away, and he released his hold on her sash, suspecting that she needed the emotional distance. He was stunned by the depth to which Jessica was affected by her parents' divorce. It was evident that she carried the bitterness of a childhood gone bad, and that her experiences had caused her to be wary and cautious, not just of divorce attorneys, but of men in general.

From across the kitchen, she slanted him a curious look. "So, you actually enjoy what you do?"

He slid his fingers into the front pockets of his jeans as he mulled that over, thinking about the past six years of his career, the highlights and the frustrating cases he'd had to represent. "Most of the time, I do. I'll admit that sometimes I'll take on a case that's mentally draining, but I love the challenge of my job, and the complexities involved." He thought of his long-term intentions, and shared those, too. "I'm working towards being a junior partner, and possibly heading up the family law department at Haywood and Irwin. But the main reason I chose a career in law was to help people."

The corner of her mouth quirked with a smile. "Why not be a doctor then?"

"I thought about it," he replied honestly. "But when I almost threw up while dissecting a frog in high school biology I knew I'd never make it through med school. I'm too squeamish when it comes to blood and guts." He grinned in amusement and saw her bite the inside of her cheek to keep from laughing. "So, instead, I concentrated my efforts on the debate team, and discovered that I really enjoyed disputing issues and trying to sway people to agree with my ideals and opinions."

"Which you're very good at," she admittedly wryly.

He tipped his head, acknowledging the backhanded compliment. "Yet I can't seem to convince you to go out on a date with me, or accompany me to my firm's Christmas party."

She exhaled a slow breath, and combed her fingers through her still damp hair. "Ryan…what you do for a living goes against what I believe in. Despite what my mother went through with my father, and Brooke's own divorce, I still believe in love, marriage and happily-ever-afters. It's what I want for myself one day, with the right person."

And she obviously didn't consider him a candidate for the position. Her argument was solid and indisputable. And as much as he was attracted to her, as much as he was coming to care about her, he couldn't offer her the kind of promises she demanded, and deserved. She'd given him every reason to take a huge step back, to leave her alone, but he discovered he couldn't do it, because for the first time in his adult life, he wanted to take that huge step *forward* with a woman…and see where it all might lead.

A scary prospect, even for him. But after a year of wanting Jessica, his gut twisted into a giant knot at the thought of completely severing all ties with her.

Armed with a new determination, he took that step forward, moving toward her, and she watched him close the distance between them. He smiled, and attempted to dispel the gloom their conversation had cast over the room. "Are you *sure* you won't consider coming to that

Christmas party? It might give you a whole different perspective on lawyers."

"I doubt it. I think it would be smarter, and safer, if I didn't attend something as important as your firm's Christmas party with you."

Unwilling to admit defeat just yet, he tried a different approach. "I know I hit you with this unexpectedly, and I really didn't give you the chance to consider your answer—"

"I won't change my mind, Ryan," she said, firmly cutting off his entreaty.

"I'd like to think you will." He dared to reach out and touch her, gently stroking his thumb along her cheek. A sense of satisfaction filled him when she didn't retreat. "Just think about it, okay?"

And in the meantime, if the only way to dissolve her defenses was to use seduction, then they'd at least enjoy themselves in the process.

# CHAPTER FIVE

JESSICA SAT IN FRONT of her computer, unable to concentrate on the medical reports she needed to transcribe
for the doctors that employed her services. Thanks to
Ryan's parting remark the night before, she couldn't
think about anything else except his invitation to his
firm's Christmas party.

She'd told him no, and meant it. She'd told him she
wouldn't change her mind, and she meant that, too. She
couldn't envision herself in a room crowded with attorneys, smiling and trying to make polite small talk and
acting as though she approved of what they did for a
living. She harbored too many resentments and bitter
memories to advocate the legal profession, especially
those who represented divorce cases and went against
their opponent with greedy intent.

What Ryan was suggesting was ludicrous, and impossible. The complications of involving herself with
him on such a personal level had the potential to break
her heart. Not only was his career choice a problem for
her, but his aspirations didn't leave much room in his
life to devote to building a lasting relationship. Nothing
permanent could come of them being together.

She *knew* that, so why couldn't she just consider Ryan
a friendly acquaintance and keep their association at that?

*Slippery, sensual, erotic sex.*

She groaned as those words echoed in her mind, as they had all night long and into the early morning hours. Yeah, she admitted that particular promise had something to do with her preoccupation with Ryan. He'd shown her a glimpse of that temptation, and she'd be lying if she said she didn't want to experience the full spectrum of pleasure he'd introduced her to, and take those voluptuous sensations to their inevitable conclusion.

There was no denying she was itching to try something new, to be a little rebellious and break past the caution that had ruled most of her life. She'd been a good girl for so long, and now she wanted to live a little, embrace the passion Ryan evoked, and see where it all led.

She sighed, her belly clenching with desire as she recalled the skillful range with which Ryan had used his mouth on hers. Whether long, slow and lazy, or deep, hungry and rapacious, his kisses had the ability to bring her to a fever pitch of excitement in no time flat. Her lashes fluttered closed as she imagined his mouth elsewhere, and her breasts swelled in response to the visual fantasy. She bit her bottom lip, aching to feel the heat of his breath on her skin, the silky stroke of his tongue across her tight, sensitive nipples, the wet suction of his mouth closing over her…

The phone on her desk rang, startling her out of her reverie and setting her heart to a frantic pace. Last night before he'd left her place, Ryan had told her he had a long, busy day at the office today, and had catch-up work to handle on Saturday, so he wouldn't be able to see her until Sunday. He'd requested she come by his house on Sunday so they could finalize the menu and other party matters, so she wasn't expecting him to call. She *knew* he was busy with work, and was irritated with herself for wanting it to be him on the phone.

Forcing the gorgeous, sexy rogue from her mind, she picked up the line and answered with a breathless, "Hello?"

"Hey, Jess, did you forget about me?"

Jessica winced. Her sister. She'd been too distracted by the results of Ryan's cake seduction, then their discussion, to return her call last night. And today, well, she was still distracted. "Actually, I was just going to call you back."

"I guess I saved you the dime. Where were you last night when I called?" Brooke asked, displaying those protective sister instincts that she'd honed since the age of thirteen.

*Tasting a slice of euphoria.* "I, uh, was having dessert with a friend."

The excuse slipped from her tongue, as truthful as she'd allow. Including the fact that Ryan had been her companion for the evening would only serve to rouse Brooke's curiosity, and promote questions she didn't want to answer. Once the New Year's Eve surprise reception was over, her contact with Ryan would return to a minimum, as it had always been. As it should be. And her sister would never have to know that her association with Ryan while planning the party had included his thrilling attempts at seduction.

"Well, I hope you had a fun time."

*Sexy, sinful fun.*

Knowing she'd never get any work done this morning, she saved and shut down the document she'd been typing, and turned the conversation to the reason why Brooke had called. "You mentioned that you received an invitation for a New Year's Eve party at Ryan's," she said lightly, careful not to give any part of the surprise away. "Are you planning on going?"

"Yeah, it sounds like a fun way to bring in the New Year. How about you? Are you going to go?"

She grinned at her sister's assumption, and affected a convincing reluctance on her end. "What makes you think I'd get an invitation, too? I mean, Ryan is *Marc's* friend, and it's not as though he and I are exactly buddies."

Last night, they'd come damn close to being lovers.

"Oh, come on, Jess," Brooke replied in a teasing tone. "Both Marc and I agreed that Ryan wouldn't pass up the opportunity to see you. If he's having a party, you'd be invited."

Except the whole entire party had been her idea, and if anything, *she'd* invited *Ryan*. "I was invited," she admitted, playing along for her sister's benefit.

"And?"

"I haven't RSVP'd yet," she said, forcing an indecisive tone to her voice. It wouldn't do to let her sister think she was anxious.

"Say yes," Brooke encouraged. "It'll be fun and you'll have a good time."

*Say yes.* Ryan's invocation last night whispered through her conscience, as did her pitifully easy surrender. And she *had* reneged on her promise, but with good reason.

She shook the incident from her mind, determined to put it behind her. "All right, I'll go," she said, coiling the stretchy phone cord around her finger. "Besides, it might be a great way to meet someone new and interesting."

Brooke laughed. "I doubt that's why Ryan invited you, but I'll let the two of you work that out at the party."

Jessica let the implication in her sister's comment slide. Over the past year, her sister had witnessed many encounters between her and Ryan, the sparks and teasing and flirting, as well as the attraction she'd fought to keep at bay. And in a matter of a week, Ryan had chiseled through those carefully constructed defenses. Shoring them back up after last night was more difficult than she'd imagined.

She rocked back in her chair. "So, how's married life?"

"Blissful." A content sigh echoed over the phone lines. "Absolutely wonderful."

Jessica smiled. Her sister's relationship with Marc Jamison hadn't been easy at first, and certainly had been complicated, but with the respect and love the two shared they'd managed to work through the issues and problems that had stood in their way.

"I'm glad everything worked out with Marc," she said sincerely. Her sister's first marriage had been less than ideal, and it warmed Jessica that Brooke had found a man who was her equal. It gave her hope for herself. "He's a great guy, and you deserve to be happy."

"And so do you."

Another lecture she didn't want to hear. "I'm perfectly happy with my life," she automatically said, then veered her sister onto a different topic before she had a chance to call her on that particular fib. "You wanted to talk to me about Christmas?"

"Oh, yeah. Marc and I were thinking about spending the holiday in Tahoe skiing. I wanted to make sure you were okay with that."

An odd pressure constricted Jessica's chest, and she managed, just barely, to keep her voice steady. "Why wouldn't I be okay with that?"

"Because you'd be spending Christmas without me."

For the first time ever. Every other year she and Brooke flew out to West Virginia to spend the holiday with their mother and stepfather, but this was the year they stayed in Denver—and she usually accompanied Brooke to the Jamisons' for their family get-together.

Jessica didn't miss the tinge of guilt and reluctance lacing Brooke's voice, and knew her sister would cancel her trip if she suspected that Jessica felt even a glimmer of longing to spend the holiday with her. Jessica didn't begrudge Brooke the time alone with her husband, and she wasn't about to spoil her sister's plans.

"I'll be fine, really, Brooke," she said, keeping her tone upbeat and cheerful. "It's not a big deal."

Brooke hesitated for a moment. "Well, I think you ought to consider stopping by Marc's parents' on Christmas. I know Kathleen would love to see you."

Jessica couldn't help but shake her head at her sister's protective nature. As much as she knew the Jamisons would welcome her for the holiday, it just wouldn't be the same without Brooke there. Yet, to appease her sister, she said, "I'll think about it."

"Good." Brooke sounded satisfied with that. "Now, back to New Year's Eve. How about you and I pick a day before Christmas to go to lunch and go shopping together for dresses for the party?"

Her sister's enthusiasm brought a smile to her lips. "I'd like that."

"Me, too. Let me know when is good for you, and I'll take the day off work. We'll have a girls-only outing."

They said their goodbyes, and Jessica hung up the phone. And suddenly, inexplicably, she felt very much alone…and not so perfectly happy with her solitary life.

"I FOUND A CATERER who's available for our New Year's Eve party, and they faxed me a menu of appetizers, along with the cost." Jessica slid the estimate toward Ryan, who was sitting next to her at his kitchen table. "What do you think?"

He picked up the piece of paper and considered the items in a very businesslike manner. She'd been at his house for half an hour, and so far, his behavior had been nothing short of exemplary. He hadn't issued even one sexual advance or flirtatious overture, nor had he mentioned anything of what had transpired between them the last time they'd been together. He hadn't even discussed his request for her to think about accompanying him to his firm's party. There were no casual touches, or heated glances. Indeed, judging by his pragmatic expression, he could have been dealing with one of his clients.

She told herself she was glad he was being efficient and agreeable—it made planning the party so much smoother, and kept their relationship on a more even keel. Yet his passive attitude actually bothered her. She was used to bantering with Ryan, and fending off his sexy, suggestive taunts. Though her body was still very much aware of him sitting next to her, he appeared unaffected by her presence.

She found his polite pleasantry, well, *frustrating.*

Now that he'd had time to mull over her last rejection, had he decided that she just wasn't worth pursuing? Maintaining a purely friendly relationship would be for the best, of course, and exactly what she wanted, she reminded herself.

Or did she?

She wasn't sure anymore. While she knew Ryan couldn't provide her with the happily-ever-after she wanted for herself, there was one blatant fact she couldn't refute: Ryan Matthews was the sexiest man she'd ever met, and she wanted him.

Sneaking a glance at him as he bent his head over the caterer's list, she took in his strong profile, the chiseled line of his jaw, and those firm lips that had shown her sinful delights. She blamed Ryan for introducing her to such carnal pleasures and filling her head with lascivious thoughts. She held him responsible for making her imagine night after night what it would be like to indulge in a slippery, sensual, erotic interlude with him and sample the sweet, heady, euphoric taste of sex.

He set the list back on the table and met her gaze. His eyes were dark brown and warm, but lacked the teasing sparkle she was used to seeing. "I'm impressed. There's quite a selection to choose from."

Having been taught a very memorable lesson on the effects of diversity, she'd made sure they had a wide variety at their disposal. "I thought we could get a vegetable tray, along with a meat and cheese tray, and rolls and condiments," she said. "Then we can each choose three different appetizers, and that should make a nice assortment for everyone to snack on."

"Fair enough." He rubbed his hand along his jaw, and consulted the list again. "I'll go with the chicken fingers, fried mushrooms and crab rangoon."

She jotted down his selections in her notebook to relay to the caterer next week. "And I'll pick the antipasto salad, mini quiches and pizza rolls."

He passed her the appetizer list and grinned in that easy-going manner he'd seemingly adopted for the day. "Sounds great."

They spent the next hour companionably, discussing other aspects of the party. She went over her ideas for New Year's Eve party favors, and without argument Ryan agreed with her vision. He helped her decide on the drinks and types of alcohol they'd serve, and didn't reject her decorating plans to transform his home with evergreen, twinkling lights, floral arrangements and scented candles.

All in all, they settled the planning with minimum fuss.

As she bent her head over her notepad, she felt something rub up against her calf. For a moment she thought it was Ryan's leg, until a soft, plaintive meow caught her attention. Setting her pen on the table, she glanced down to find a fluffy gray cat sitting on the tiled floor between her and Ryan.

Jessica smiled, charmed by the big green eyes staring up at her. "Well, hello there."

Another dainty meow in response.

Ryan gently scooped up the feline and settled her onto his jean-clad lap. "I don't believe the two of you met the last time you were here. This is my housemate, Camelot."

Jessica watched Ryan's long fingers stroke along Camelot's spine. The cat's eyes drooped slumberously, and a contented purr rumbled in her throat. A shiver coursed through Jessica. She knew exactly how the feline felt, because Ryan had the same effect on her when he touched her.

Which he hadn't done all afternoon.

She scratched Camelot under her chin, and the cat stretched her neck out for better access. "She's a beauty."

"And a bed hog," Ryan added, humor in his deep voice. "It doesn't matter that I have a king-sized mattress. Wherever I sleep is exactly where she wants to curl up—usually right between my feet so I can't move without jostling her."

Jessica laughed, though she couldn't help but envy the cat for having the luxury of sleeping with such a sexy man. Before her thoughts took a decidedly provocative turn, with *her* starring as Ryan's bedmate, she focused her mind back on business. "By the way, I spoke with Brooke, and she said that she and Marc will be at the party."

"And Marc left a RSVP message on my recorder, too, which is a good thing." He grinned, and continued petting Camelot, who'd gone on to lovingly knead his thigh with her paws, her adoration of her owner obvious. "We couldn't have the party without them."

She nodded, realizing their luck in that area. "Though I'm sure we would have figured out some way to persuade them to be here." She glanced over the party's agenda. "So, you're okay with everything we decided on today?"

He shrugged as if it were all of little consequence to him. "Sure."

Amazing how quickly they wrapped things up when she had his cooperation. She gathered her papers and organized them into a neat pile, unable to believe that Ryan was going to let her leave without attempting to waylay her. She should have been grateful for his courteous, accommodating conduct, but she found herself undeniably disappointed instead.

"You're making this way too easy on me, Matthews," she commented lightly. And now that they had the details nailed, there wasn't any reason for her to spend extra time with him.

"I think you learned your lesson about giving up safe and practical for variety. As well as the value of compromising."

She stuffed her party planning notes into her tote bag and glanced his way, seeing a glimmer of the Ryan she was used to dealing with in the teasing tone of his voice. "Okay, I knew this was coming," she said, reading a deeper meaning into his comment. "You're gloating."

"I am not," he replied evenly, still maintaining that relaxed, blasé composure.

His expression was completely impassive, but she was beginning to read Ryan well enough to suspect he was feeling too confident inside. "Are too."

His long fingers burrowed into Camelot's soft fur as he rubbed her back, and he tipped his head inquisitively at Jessica. "What do you think I'm gloating over?"

As if he didn't know. "The fact that you proved me wrong about the cakes."

His shoulder lifted in a casual shrug, and the corner of his mouth eased into a sexy grin. "I thought it was a lesson well learned."

*A lesson in seduction.* Heat and desire curled through her, and she fought valiantly to shake the sensation.

"And speaking of lessons," he continued in a deep drawl. "There is one more thing I want to discuss with you before you leave."

She sent him a curious glance. "What's that?"

"Have you bought your gift for Brooke and Marc yet?"

She capped her pen and dropped it into her purse. "I

picked up a few of those extra-big bath towels at a sale yesterday, but I still need to find the other items I wanted to get them."

He worked his jaw as he thought about that for a few seconds. "Are you still intent on buying your own gift for them, instead of going in together on our individual ideas?"

She sighed. So, they were back to that issue. "Yes. I still believe that my gift idea is more—"

"Practical and sensible," he finished for her, his tone indicating what he thought of her way of thinking—*boring*.

She straightened defensively. "It's what *I'd* want for a gift."

A dark brow lifted. "Really?"

The challenge lacing his voice and the glimmer of deviltry in his gaze sparked something deep within her…an illicit excitement and forbidden thrill. "Yes, *really*."

He blinked lazily, and resumed lavishing attention on Camelot. "Have you ever sat in a big bathtub with a man?"

She tucked a swath of hair behind her ear, hating that her answer would show too much of her inexperience. "No."

"Then you have no idea what it feels like to have your back scrubbed, or to have someone else soap up your body, slowly, leisurely…"

She resisted the urge to squirm in her chair. The mesmerizing huskiness of his voice and his calculated words caressed her, finding and touching all those secret warm places of hers. She watched his big hands stroke over the cat, and desire and need tightened her belly.

With effort, she flashed him a sassy grin. "My loofah works just fine, thank you very much."

He chuckled softly. The sound wrapped around her, as intimate as an embrace. Suddenly, everything about him had taken on sexual overtones.

"But it's not nearly as much fun as two slick bodies sliding against each other," he murmured. "And then there are the body paints I was telling you about, and the silky feel of fingers gliding over sleek skin as you draw funny, sexy pictures on your lover's back, then lick them off."

Her pulse skittered wildly at the image that popped into her mind. Now *this* was the Ryan she knew, taunting and teasing her with words. He wasn't physically touching her, but his words had a powerful effect on her body.

She glanced away from his direct stare, but her feminine nerves continued to tingle with awareness. "I'll have to take your word for it."

He nudged Camelot off his lap, and the feline jumped down and sauntered over to her food bowl. Ryan scooted back his chair, stretched out his long, muscular legs, and folded his hands over his flat stomach. "If you have no idea what any of that is like, how can you be so sure that you'd prefer towels and a hamper and a vanity set over more sensual pleasures?"

*Indeed.* His question was legitimately inquisitive, and she wished she had a better answer for him than the one that fell from her lips. "I suppose I shouldn't knock it until I've tried it, but what can I say? I *am* practical, always have been." And she suddenly wondered what she'd missed as a result of having grown up being so careful and prudent.

*Slippery, sensual, erotic sex.*

"And you're too damn proud of that fact." There was no criticism in his tone, just warm amusement. Standing, he held out his hand to her. "Come on, Jessie, I want to show you something."

Not budging, she eyed his outstretched hand dubiously. "Said the spider to the fly."

He laughed. "But you're curious, aren't you?"

Oh, more than he could ever know. She was tempted beyond reason, and she struggled to hold tight to her more reserved nature. "Why can't you just tell me what it is?"

"Because it would be much more fun to *show* you." He waggled his fingers, enticing her. "You can either take my hand, Jessie, or you can leave. It's *your* choice and I'll go with whatever you decide. But if I know you, it'll drive you nuts all the way home, thinking about what I wanted to show you, wondering what I had in mind…"

A tiny shiver rippled through her. He *did* know her. And it would drive her crazy not knowing where he'd planned to lead her. While her heart told her to bolt for the door and put as much distance as she could between her and Ryan, her traitorous body tended to gravitate toward the promises in his gaze.

Telling herself she only meant to appease her interest and would only spare a brief glimpse at his surprise, she stood and placed her hand in his. Immediate warmth engulfed her as he entwined their fingers. Without hesitating, she allowed him to guide her up the spiral staircase and into his master bedroom. She caught a quick hint of bold, masculine colors of hunter green and navy blue, and dark oak furniture, before he tugged her closer to the king-sized bed and the big basket sitting in the center nearly overflowing with ingredients of a sensual variety.

She took quick inventory of the items, finding bottles of bath products, candles, a bottle of wine with two crystal glasses and a rich, purple, velvet chenille robe tucked to the side. There was more, but she'd seen enough to catch the gist of Ryan's gift.

"Okay, I get the idea," she said, meeting his warm, chocolate-brown gaze. "But I still think Brooke and Marc will find my gift more useful."

"This isn't for them. This is lesson number two." He released her hand, and grinned wickedly. "My sensual versus your practical."

It took a moment for his meaning to sink in, but when it did, her eyes widened incredulously. "You want *me* to take a bath with *you?*"

"In a matter of speaking, yes." He spoke as though his suggestion was nothing out of the ordinary. "Since you're so skeptical about my gift idea, I thought we'd give practical application a try to convince you otherwise."

Too easily, she recalled his cake test, and his creative, provocative way of convincing her that variety was a very good thing. Just remembering what had transpired in her kitchen, on her table, made her feel weak in the knees, breathless, and flushed with shameless anticipation.

She shoved those thoughts from her head. "Ryan, what you're suggesting is…"

"Tempting?"

*Oh, yeah.* Knowing the state of ecstasy he could so easily bring her to, she was definitely inspired to accept his invitation. "How about *outrageous?*"

"Aw, come on, Jessie," he cajoled. "Since you've never had this particular experience, I want to show you how fun sharing a bath with someone can be. Then you might have a better appreciation for my gift."

A deep fluttering stirred in her belly, and she shook her head adamantly. "I'm *not* getting naked with you."

"Yeah, I kinda figured that was too much to hope for." A mischievous light twinkled in his eyes. "So, we switch to Plan B."

Her gaze narrowed. "Which is?"

"You leave your underwear on," he said matter-of-factly.

Abrupt laughter escaped her, full of humor. "How about Plan C, *no way?*"

He propped his hands on his hips, looking too persuasive, and way too male. "It's not a big deal, Jessie. It'll be just like you're wearing a bathing suit. And I'll wear my swim trunks. I promise you'll keep your underwear on the entire time, and if things go too far for you, all you have to do is tell me to stop, and I swear I will."

She bit her bottom lip indecisively. His brown eyes were honest and sincere, reminding her that he'd never taken advantage of her. Admittedly, she'd always been a willing participant in his various seductions.

And that's what worried her. Wearing her bra and panties and being submersed in a tub full of water might keep her safe from his gaze, but she had little defense against the other more lethal weapons he had at his disposal, like his drugging kisses, his insidious touch, his arousing words…

"Tell you what," he said, catering to her hesitancy. "If after I'm done you still feel that my gift idea doesn't have merit, I'll go in on your gift without complaint or further argument. But you can't say no to me until you at least give my idea a try. Fair enough?"

She smirked. "Does a lawyer know the meaning of fair?"

He stared at her for a long moment, looking as though he wanted to debate her distrustful comment. Then, seemingly deciding if he did so he'd risk losing her cooperation, he let it go. "How about just for a little while we forget about my profession, and reduce this to something more simplistic and basic, like a man and a woman having a little fun together. Can you do that for the sake of our experiment?"

This was it, no more hedging. Say yes and treat herself to whatever pleasures Ryan had in store, or choose no and regret losing out on the unique experience he'd offered.

Her pulse raced wildly, and her answer rushed forward, based purely on the intense need and passion clamoring within her. "Yeah, I can do that."

His smile was relieved. "Good."

She watched him head toward his dresser drawers and retrieve a pair of swim trunks. Then he pulled off his sweatshirt and tossed it on the bed. Her mouth went dry at the sight of the wide expanse of his chest, muscled and defined with a light sprinkling of ebony hair that whorled around his dark, flat nipples, then spread downward, around his navel, then on to the waistband of his jeans…where his fingers were busy releasing the snap.

Her heart lodged in her throat. "What are you doing?" she blurted.

He lifted his head and sent her a peculiar look. "Getting undressed. I suggest you do the same."

Without an ounce of decorum, he unzipped his jeans and she watched in fascination as the front placket spread open, revealing a glimpse of white cotton and other masculine assets. Before he could completely shuck his pants and briefs, she came to her senses.

"Well, if you don't mind, *I'd* like some privacy in which to strip down to my underwear." Ridiculous or not, she wasn't used to prancing around in front of a man in her bra and panties.

A wry grin canted his mouth, as if he found her request incongruous, considering he'd eventually see her in her bare essentials. "As you wish." Withdrawing the chenille robe from the basket, he dropped it on the bed. "I guess I'll leave this for you—for *modesty's* sake."

"Thank you." She made a face at him that lightened the moment and made him laugh.

Grabbing his swim trunks and the basket of goodies, he headed toward the bathroom, then stopped short of crossing the threshold. "Just come on in when you're ready."

The door closed behind him, leaving Jessica to wonder if she'd ever truly be ready for Ryan Matthews.

# CHAPTER SIX

JESSICA TOED OFF her sneakers and pulled off her socks, then froze when she heard the water in the bathroom turn on and rush to fill the tub. Her pulse skittered erratically at the thought of sharing that bath with Ryan, and her gaze darted to the bedroom door. It wasn't too late to bolt and get the heck out of there.

That would be the smart, logical thing to do. But she could no longer deny desires that had lain dormant for years—wants and needs that came alive around Ryan. Whatever he had planned with this particular lesson, she wanted to indulge her senses, wanted to play and have fun with him.

She expected touching, obviously, and maybe some kissing. Drawing on his chest with edible body paints and licking it off didn't sound half bad, either. All pleasurable stuff.

*His sensual versus her practical.*

Deciding the experience could prove to be a very illuminating one, she reached for the hem of her oversized sweatshirt and drew it over her head. After folding that article of clothing neatly and placing it on the bed, she slipped her fingers into the waistband of her baggy sweatpants and shimmied them down her legs and off. She reached for the robe Ryan had left for her, and stopped short when she caught a glimpse of her reflection in the mirror over his dresser.

Seeing herself through different eyes, she grimaced at how plain and uninspiring her choice of lingerie was. There was absolutely nothing sexy or tantalizing about her underwear, and nothing to stimulate lust in a man. Her bra was ordinary and comfortable, without a hint of lace to scallop over the fullness of her breasts, and her panties were plain ol' cotton Jockeys for women.

A sex kitten she was not. She never spent her money frivolously, and sexy lingerie was a luxury she'd never been able to justify for herself. But, it was for the best. At least her unflattering attire would help to diffuse Ryan's interest, and make it easier for her to pretend that she really was wearing an unimpressive white bikini.

Still feeling an initial twinge of modesty, she shrugged into the robe, and luxuriated in being swallowed up by soft, warm layers of chenille. Tying the sash, she headed toward the bathroom, knocked lightly to let Ryan know she was entering, then opened the door—and was instantly greeted by the delectable scent of ripe, sweet strawberries swirling from the steamed water in the tub.

Except Ryan's tub wasn't your standard fare—it was like a miniature Jacuzzi, large enough to seat more than two, and deep enough to immerse yourself up to the shoulders. Water eddied from jets situated along the rounded contour of the tub. And if that lavishness wasn't enough to throw her for a loop, then the way Ryan had transformed the bathroom into a palace of sin and seduction certainly did.

The basket of bath products sat on a ledge behind the tub, along with the open bottle of wine, and two full crystal glasses. Half a dozen candles flickered in the room, adding to the romantic atmosphere, and the fragrant scent of lush strawberries saturated her senses—all designed to influence her into agreeing to his gift idea.

"So, what do you think?" Ryan asked from behind her.

She turned and met his gaze, thinking he was on his way to contradicting her sensible nature with yet another valuable lesson—this one on the benefits of being amorous and innovative.

"I'm very impressed." With the sensual display he'd painstakingly arranged, and the magnificent, athletically built body he possessed. Wearing nothing but a pair of navy swim trunks, he was all male, virile and breathtakingly dynamic.

"That's a good start," he said, moving closer to the tub, and her. "Now off with the robe and into the water."

As nonchalantly as possible, and with a confidence that belied the anxiety thrumming through her blood, she untied the sash and let the chenille slip from her shoulders. The material pooled to the floor around her feet, baring herself to Ryan's gaze, which she felt as scorching as a brand.

"Oh, man," he groaned, the anguished sound rumbling deep in his throat.

Self-consciousness swept over her, until she looked at him, saw the pained look on his face, and found its cause in the erection straining the front of his trunks. His gaze traveled down her slender form, lingering on her bra, skimming to her panties, then taking in the length of her legs in a slow, leisurely journey.

Heat and awareness prickled her skin. "You said it

would be like me wearing a swimsuit," she said, unable to help the slight accusatory note in her voice. At the moment, she felt as if she were completely naked.

His expression turned adorably sheepish. "Well, it is…kind of."

"Kind of?" She lifted a brow and lowered her gaze to his arousal. "Do you have that kind of reaction to other women you see in bathing suits?"

He grinned unrepentantly. "Not exactly." He pushed his fingers through his thick hair and drew a deep breath. "You see, my *brain* knows that what you're wearing is equivalent to a swimsuit, but my *eyes* are finally seeing the incredible body you hide beneath loose, baggy clothing, and my hormones take over from there. I always knew you'd have gorgeous breasts and great legs, but my fantasies didn't do you justice. In reality, you're so much more perfect, in every way."

She felt her body flush from head to toe from his compliment, and his direct, candid stare caused her heart to flutter in her chest. The man was a rogue, a flirt—she knew that, but she wasn't immune to his flattery. She'd never been appraised so openly, had never felt so desirable and sexy, despite the no-nonsense cotton underwear she wore.

It was a novel experience for her to feel so attractive. All her life she'd been cautious with the opposite sex and extremely reserved, having learned through her mother's experience with her father, along with her sister's first marriage, that men weren't always what they seemed. Her brief relationship three years ago supported that theory, as well.

She'd applied the same philosophy to Ryan, more so because of his profession. His career alone, his ambition and drive, identified him as the type of guy she ought to avoid at all costs. By his own admittance he preferred short-term relationships, which went against her more traditional values.

But the man…he was kind, and caring and sincere, a direct contradiction to what his profession implied and what she'd always believed. He had a way of weakening her defenses, and tapping into intimate longings she could no longer suppress.

Unable to sort out all the confusion in her mind at the moment, she focused on the one thing that was clearcut and undeniable—her attraction to Ryan. It was an incredibly heady experience to know that she starred in his fantasies, and for today, she was going to enjoy his attention and interest without expectations or promises.

He tipped his head, causing a lock of dark hair to fall over his forehead. "Ladies first," he said, waving a hand toward the tub.

She climbed into the bubbling, churning water, and sank into its depths. She groaned as her entire body softened, lulled by the silky heat of the water, the jets pulsating gently against her muscles, and the intoxicating scent of strawberries.

"You like?" Ryan asked as he settled himself at the opposite end. Their legs tangled as they both tried to find a comfortable position, their skin slick from whatever bath product he'd put in the tub.

She rested her head against the rim, uncaring that the hair brushing her shoulders was getting wet. "Oh, I definitely like. This is *wonderful.*"

"I'm glad you approve." He handed her one of the glasses of wine, and took the other for himself. "But it gets better than this."

"Impossible," she said with a smile. She took a deep drink of the pale pink liquid, and wasn't surprised to find it flavored with a hint of strawberry, too.

He winked at her, then reached for something within the basket. "You just close your eyes, relax and let me show you how good it gets."

Taking another quick sip of her wine, she set the half-empty glass on the ledge, then did as he instructed, allowing her sumptuous surroundings to draw her into a blissful state of tranquility...until she felt Ryan's fingers curl around her ankle.

She tensed at first, then grew pliant once again as he began washing her with a silky, soapy sponge. He spent an inordinate amount of time on her legs, tickling her feet playfully until she laughed and begged him to stop, then moved on to find an erogenous zone behind her knee that made her gasp and squirm. The sponge glided upward along her thighs, dipping between them, but he didn't stroke her intimately as she expected. In fact, it seemed as though he was deliberately avoiding doing that.

Water sloshed in the tub and lapped around her shoulders as he shifted his position and moved closer. He continued to pamper her, gently scrubbing her belly, then past her heavy, sensitive breasts to her chest, her collarbone and her arms. Although he'd diligently evaded all the places that ached for his touch, he'd managed to arouse her to a breathless pitch of need.

"There's nothing like good clean fun, huh?"

She shivered at the husky timbre of his voice, and blinked her lashes open, meeting his dark brown gaze that told her he was just as affected as she was. She smiled, and made a grab for the sponge, which he relinquished with ease.

"I think it's my turn to get *you* clean," she said, anticipating the task. Sitting up on her knees for leverage, she lathered the sponge with the fragrant soap and returned the favor of scrubbing his sleek, muscled skin. She reveled in the sight and feel of the taut cords of muscles across his chest, down his belly, and along his thighs. His flesh was smooth and slick from the water and soap, and when she moved behind him, she couldn't resist running her fingertips along his perfectly sculpted back.

A shudder coursed through him, and his breathing grew shallow…the only indication that he was affected at all by her ministrations. A private, satisfied smile curved her mouth. Emboldened by a sexual confidence unfamiliar to her, and wanting to see how far he'd allow her to go, she cruised her flattened palms along his lean sides, and stole around to his chest. Her fingers stroked slowly, provocatively, over his erect nipples, and awareness sizzled. She rubbed her breasts against his back, and widened her thighs to slip closer.

His body tensed, and she closed her eyes and grew bolder. Her splayed hands roamed south, and then her fingertips grazed his fierce erection beneath the fabric of his swim trunks. With a low, vivid curse, he grabbed her wrists and turned around, nearly pulling her under the water with his abrupt move. He caught her just in time with one hand behind her back and the other grasping her bottom, and she instinctively curled her legs around his to keep her from sliding lower. She gasped as their bodies came into direct, intimate contact.

His gaze darkened, but the gold around his irises glittered with the bright flame of desire. "I think you're enjoying yourself a little too much," he murmured.

She flashed him a sassy smile while attempting to regain her equilibrium. "Wasn't that the purpose of your lesson?"

He helped her back to a sitting position, then reached into the basket and rummaged through the contents. "Yeah, I suppose it was, so pay attention."

She tried to look around him to see what he was doing, but his broad, bare shoulders provided a much more interesting distraction. "Pay attention to what?"

Producing a jar of body paint, he waggled his brows at her. "The *real* fun is about to begin." Opening the plastic container, he dipped his index finger into the thick brown substance and took a tentative sample.

Curious, she asked, "Does it taste good?"

He extended the jar toward her, a subtle, sexy challenge in his eyes. "See for yourself."

She coated her finger with the flavored body paint, but instead of licking off the delicacy, she gave in to the reckless impulse to smear the sticky syrup along his chest, then leaned forward to lap it off with her tongue. "Ummm, it tastes like chocolate." Feeling daring and naughty, she nibbled a little more, letting her teeth graze his firm flesh, his taut nipple.

Seemingly surprised by her brazen move, he sucked in a quick breath. "Hey."

Lifting her head, she affected a guileless look, though she was feeling anything but innocent. "Isn't that what the body paints are for?"

A sinful grin eased up the corner of his mouth as he set the jar nearby, then moved aside the candles sitting on the ledge behind the tub. "I always knew you were a quick study."

Without warning, he grasped her hips in his large

hands, lifted her out of the bath, and perched her bottom
on the tiled rim. A gasp of startled surprise caught in her
throat, and the immediate contrast of warm water sluicing
down her body to cool air washing over her damp skin
caused her breasts to tighten and her nipples to
pucker…which was exactly where Ryan's gaze was
riveted.

Following his line of vision, she glanced down to find
that the very sensible fabric of her bra and panties clung
when wet, leaving little to the imagination. Her rosy
nipples were clearly outlined through the cotton material,
and a darker shadow creased the V between her legs.

With effort, she managed to resist the instinctive
urge to cover herself from Ryan's bold, unabashed stare,
but an ingrained modesty prompted her to slide her legs
primly together.

Shaking his head in a silent "no," he pressed his
palms to her knees before they could touch, and gently
eased her thighs apart once again. He remained in the
tub, on his knees in front of her, with the water jetting
around his waist.

"I'm suddenly ravenous," he murmured huskily.

The look in his eyes was as hungry and primitive as
his words implied, and her pulse leapt with excitement.
In slow, mesmerizing degrees, he dragged her forward,
until her knees bracketed his ribs and she could feel the
raw, sexual heat emanating from him.

Reaching for the jar, he scooped two fingerfuls of
chocolate body paint and slashed a squiggly line down
her throat and along the slope of her shoulder. His eyes
lowered slumberously, his dark head bent toward her,
and his lips parted for a taste.

Heart pounding in anticipation, Jessica gripped the

ledge of the tub and moaned at the first silken glide of
his tongue along her neck. A shiver trickled down her
spine, and she all but melted at the light suction of his
mouth as he savored and sampled the confection he'd
smeared on her skin.

He dabbed more of the cool, slick substance down
her arm, and drew swirling, lazy patterns on her skin,
seemingly enjoying himself.

She laughed breathlessly, certain she'd never survive
this lesson, his teasing, the torment. "Didn't your
mother ever teach you not to play with your food?"

His warm chuckle was filled with wicked amusement. "Yeah, and she also taught me to eat every bite
and clean my plate." Proving his claim, all five of his
fingers smeared chocolate syrup along her collarbone,
and he followed that with arousing sweeps of his tongue
as he lapped up the mess he'd made.

Wanting to play, too, and get even with him in the
process, she attempted to confiscate the jar, but instead
bumped his elbow, which caused his sticky fingers to
graze the upper slope of her breast.

He made a tsking sound of chastisement as he
observed the dark streak of chocolate marking her. "Aw,
Jessie, now look what you've done. Between the cakes
and now this, you're one messy woman."

She laughed lightly. "Oh, no you don't," she said, unwilling to accept the blame for his error. "That was
*your* fault, not mine."

His dark brows winged upward. "And I suppose you
expect *me* to clean up the mess?" He sounded appropriately indignant, though the mischievous glimmer in
his eyes gave him away.

At the thought of what that task entailed, her breasts

strained against the confines of her bra, and her nipples drew into tight, hard peaks. She knew what he was asking held a deeper meaning, and his earlier vow filtered through her mind… *I promise you'll keep your underwear on the entire time, and if things go too far for you, all you have to do is tell me to stop, and I swear I will.*

She didn't want to stop. Not yet. Trusting him, and wanting to seduce him as much as he had her, she drenched two fingers in the edible body paint and traced the line of her sheer bra, and brushed across the tips of her nipples, making an even bigger mess for him to clean up. "As a matter of fact, I *insist,*" she whispered, granting him the permission he sought.

Sliding her free hand into the damp hair at the back of his neck, she guided his mouth to the smudges of chocolate on her chest, and let him go to work. He took his time, lavishing attention on her neck, her throat, her shoulder, until *finally* he skimmed his lips over the slope of her breast. He found her aching nipple and through the thin material he tugged on the crest with his teeth, bit gently, then opened his mouth wide and suckled her deeply.

She whimpered as pure, jolting pleasure swamped her. His tongue swirled and laved, possessing her, and she felt that exquisite, coiling sensation all the way to that empty place deep inside her. Her back arched, and her thighs clenched tighter around his waist, wanting, needing…something that seemed just beyond her reach.

Hot, wet kisses trailed to her other breast, where he feasted just as greedily on that plump flesh and her stiff nipple, elevating her to a breathless, sensual daze. She felt his fingers, slick with the chocolate body paint, glide along her abdomen between her bra and panties, and sketch what felt like a heart. His open mouth followed the lines he drew, his tongue occasionally dipping into her navel, while his hands moved on to grasp her hips and drag her closer so that her feminine softness rubbed erotically against his chest.

Her head fell back, and her fingers tightened in his hair, needing something to hold on to. She felt wild. Out of control. Unable to help herself, she widened her legs and writhed against him, increasing the pressure building in her belly, between her legs. Sweet delirium beckoned, blazing hot and rich with promise. More than anything, she wanted to experience that mindless ecstasy no other man had ever given her.

Then his hands left her, but only for seconds. They returned with more chocolate, the tips of his fingers painting the inside of her thighs with long, luxurious strokes that made her skin quiver, and made her moan shamelessly. Then came his lips, his tongue and his teeth as he treated her to random bites on her sensitive flesh. His nips grew sensuous and indulgent as his mouth inched closer and closer to that intimate part of her.

And then he was *there,* his fingers caressing, his breath hot and illicit. Shock, excitement, and fear all warred within her. Somehow, someway, he'd wedged his shoulders between her legs to keep them spread, and she suddenly felt extremely vulnerable in her thin, diaphanous panties, and very apprehensive of the forbidden pleasure awaiting her.

Realizing his wicked intent, she held him at bay with a fistful of his hair. "Ryan…no." Despite her protest, she didn't sound very persuasive.

He seemed to sense her indecision, her uncertainties, and attended to them. "I want to taste how sweet you are, how heady, how *euphoric.*"

*This is how good sex tastes.*

The heaviness in her intensified, and demanded release. Witnessing the unbridled passion etching his features—the same need that trembled within her—she knew she'd forever regret this moment if she let it pass without experiencing this erotic thrill.

Relaxing her fierce grip on his thick hair, she let her hand rest at the nape of his neck, silently offering her surrender.

She expected him to strip off her underwear, but he held true to that promise and left them on. With his hands still splayed to keep her open for him, he lowered his head and nuzzled the silky flesh of her inner thigh, starting his exploration with soft, generous, damp kisses designed to make her melt. With a shuddering sigh, the tension and apprehension drained from her body, and was replaced by a decadent languor…until he turned impatient and greedy and pressed his open mouth against that feminine cove. In one purposeful, scorching stroke, he glided his tongue upward.

She inhaled sharply, and before she could recover from that electrifying sensation, he took her intimately, thoroughly, deeply. He made a mockery of the panties she wore—the strip of cotton was a flimsy barrier against Ryan's skillful methods. With slow, deliberate laps of his tongue, combined with hot, suctioning swirls, he elevated her to that acute edge of desire.

Fearing the steep fall, her fingers dug into his shoulders for support. Her mind spun dizzily as delicious abandon took over her. A pulsing, throbbing heat settled low and deep, then burst into a pleasure so erotic, so blazing, it completely consumed her. She heard him groan deep in his throat as her explosive climax hit, and then she was aware of nothing but her soft, ragged cry and the voluptuous contractions eddying through her entire body.

And in that indescribable moment, drugged by lush sensuality, she felt herself falling for Ryan Matthews, Esquire…hard and fast and incredibly deep.

Before she had a chance to recover her breath or her bearings from that incredible experience, he pulled her down into the heated water and her knees automatically straddled his lap. She only had seconds to assimilate the hard pillar of his erection pressing between them before he tangled his hand into her hair and forced her gaze to his.

His eyes were dark, his features taut with admirable restraint. His lips were damp from his intimate assault on her. "Now, I want *you* to see how good you taste." His voice was rough, sexy, and thrilling.

With his hand at the back of her head, he drew her mouth to his and shared the taste still lingering on his tongue…the sweetness, headiness and euphoria of sex. She moaned at the eroticism of his gesture, and despite his shocking intent, his audacious words, the actual kiss he gave her was so soulful, so generous and selfless, she wanted to weep. Powerful emotions shook her, and she told herself it was just the aftereffects of the wondrous climax he'd given her. But she didn't completely believe the convenient excuse, because for as satiated as she felt physically, she felt empty deep inside, and restless in a way she'd never before experienced.

Not wanting to analyze the sentiments stealing into her heart and what they meant, she concentrated on the pleasure of Ryan's kiss. Sliding her hands along his shoulders, she wrapped her arms around his neck and pressed closer to his hard and firmly muscled body. She shivered at the slow, lazy rhythm he set with his lips and tongue, and wondered if he made love in the same exquisite manner.

And just like that, the undeniable ache of wanting him spread through her like a reignited wildfire, from her breasts, to her belly and settling once again between her thighs. His arousal strained against her still-sensitive flesh, and though he wasn't making any demands, wasn't asking for more than she was willing to give, she suddenly wanted to surrender to the passion and desire he'd merely shown her a glimpse of.

She knew she had no future with Ryan, just a few more weeks until the New Year's Eve party, and then they'd go their separate ways. He knew that, as well. So why not enjoy the sensual delights he had to offer without any strings or promises from either one of them? Undoubtedly, the gratification would be mutual, and she'd walk away with no regrets. She'd take with her the glorious keepsake and mindless pleasure of making love to him, which would replace the memory of her one awkward encounter years ago.

Heart pounding, she lifted her lips from his, and with a soft growl of protest, he let her go, though he still held her close, making her feel safe and protected in his embrace. She moved her mouth along his jaw, toward his ear, and before she changed her mind, came to her senses, or lost her nerve, she expressed her greatest need.

"Make love to me, Ryan," she whispered.

## CHAPTER SEVEN

JESSICA'S STUNNING and tempting invitation to make love to her reverberated through Ryan's mind like a seductive litany. Heat rushed to his groin, making him even harder than he'd already been. There wasn't anything he'd love more than to take Jessica to his bed, cover her lithe body with his, and lose himself deep, deep inside her giving warmth. But, he wasn't ready to take that next logical step, for practical reasons—he had no condoms on hand. And that was probably for the best, because he didn't think Jessica was ready either, for emotional reasons.

He craved more than an afternoon of wild, satisfying sex with this woman whom he'd come to care about, wanted more than her surrender to their physical attraction. For the first time in longer than he could remember, he didn't want a casual one-night stand... and he wanted her to demand and expect more, too.

Satiating desires was easy and simple—in the past he'd indulged in mutually pleasurable sex enough times to have affirmed that fact. But there was nothing easy or simple about Jessica, and once the high of physical gratification wore off, there would be emotional repercussions to consider.

And because of that knowledge, he needed her unconditional trust before they made love.

Her face was tucked against his neck, her labored
breathing warm across his flesh. He tried not to think
about the perfect fit of their position, his throbbing
arousal, and how easy it would be to give in to temptation and satisfy them both. Her body remained tense as
she waited for his answer to her request.

Very gently, he eased her head back, so she was
looking at him. Her skin was flushed from the steam
rising off the heated water swirling around them, her expression soft and slumberous from her recent release,
her blue eyes hazy. Remembering her initial reluctance
to let him give her that form of carnal pleasure, and suspecting he'd been the first to do so, he had a brief urge
to gloat, as she'd accused him of doing earlier.

Keeping his triumph to himself for now, he brushed
silky strands of hair away from her cheek, and tenderly
tucked them behind her ear. "Jessie…we can't make
love. I don't have any condoms." It was the truth, as well
as the gentlest way to turn down her request without
wounding her feminine pride.

Surprise registered in her eyes, giving him the impression that she'd expected him to have a stash of pro-
phylactics on hand.

He grinned, and leisurely stroked his palms up her
spine to the nape of her neck, enjoying the silky, damp
feel of her skin against his fingers. "Whether you
believe it or not, it's been a while since I've been with
a woman, and it's not as though I keep a supply in my
nightstand."

A becoming blush stole across her cheeks, giving
away her embarrassment. "Oh."

Finding the sponge floating on the surface of the churning water, he scooped it up and squeezed the excess liquid along her shoulders, warming her exposed skin and wiping away the smudges of chocolate that remained. She closed her eyes and sighed at the simple luxury.

"And besides, I don't think you're ready to make love."

Her lashes blinked open, and she stared at him with a combination of confusion, disbelief, and a frustration he understood too well. "How can you say that after we...after I..."

"Had such an explosive orgasm?" he supplied for her.

Obviously not used to talking about sex, she gave a jerky nod to confirm his statement.

"Yeah, your body is soft and wet and willing," he agreed, dragging the plush sponge over the swells of her breasts. "And I could slide real deep inside you right now, this very minute. But I'm not sure you're ready to make love *here*." With his index finger, he gently tapped her temple.

"In my head?" she asked incredulously. "I have to be ready for sex in my *head?*"

"Mentally, yeah. And emotionally." For once in his adult life, those things mattered to him, and he wasn't about to try and scrutinize his feelings. "I'm taking a wild shot in the dark here, but I'm guessing that your sexual experience is very limited."

She averted her gaze self-consciously. "Gee, was I *that* obvious?"

"You're very passionate, and sensual, but there's also something incredibly guileless about you when it comes to sex." Tucking his finger beneath her chin, he brought her gaze back to his. "How many lovers have you had, Jessie?"

She hesitated, then reluctantly revealed, "One. Three years ago."

"And what happened?" he prompted.

"Lane and I had been dating for about a month. I thought there was something more to the relationship, but discovered too late that he was more interested in getting me in bed. And once that happened, he decided that things were getting too serious, too fast for him, and he bailed."

And judging by the tiny crease above her brow, that relationship, no matter how brief, had left insecure scars.

She took a deep breath, and exhaled slowly. "That one sexual encounter was very unmemorable, and nothing like what you and I…well, what we just did."

He slicked the sponge down her arms, and tried not to puff his chest out too far. "I'm glad."

A look of disgust creased her features. "What, that I've only had one lover and I'm totally inexperienced?"

"No, that I was the first to give you that kind of pleasure." His hands found her hips beneath the water, and massaged the rounded curves, dipped lower and cupped her bottom. "And being inexperienced is nothing to be ashamed of. In fact, I find it refreshing, and I don't want to take advantage of the fact that you're speaking from the glow of a great orgasm when you ask me to make love to you. I don't want us being together to be a purely physical thing."

Her brows raised dubiously. "Ryan…we both know that a real relationship is impossible, that anything long-term isn't going to happen between us. So, maybe we *should* just enjoy what we know we can have, which is purely physical."

And that would make him no better than Lane. Even if she didn't realize that, he did. Her words were flippant, a pragmatic shield to protect her heart and emotions, he suspected. And for all her talk of having a brief affair, he didn't believe that she could make love with him while keeping all her vulnerabilities intact.

And he wanted her to have no regrets when it happened.

"How can you expect me to make love to you when we haven't even had a first date yet?" He injected an appropriate amount of offense into his voice, but his grin was filled with humor. "Just what kind of guy do you think I am?"

She caressed her hands over his chest, and squeezed her knees provocatively against his hips. "A very sexy, virile kind of guy."

And that virile part of him couldn't help but rise to the occasion. He groaned, in both pain and pleasure. "So, you want to use me for the sake of fantastic sex?"

She tipped her head, her gaze clear and earnest. "Would that be so bad?"

"Yes, if your mind and body aren't in sync." A year ago, he definitely would have taken her up on her proposition. Now, he felt as though there was so much more at stake between them than just sexual gratification. It was all so new to him, this protective, possessive feeling, but he didn't want to blow this chance with her. "And until that happens, you aren't ready."

She frowned at him and flicked a stream of water onto his chest. "You are, by far, the most infuriating, dictatorial man I know."

"Coming from you, I'll take that as a compliment."

She wrinkled her nose and stuck her tongue out at him.

He chuckled. "Watch yourself, Jessie, 'cause I can put that tongue of yours to real good use. You might not be ready to make love, but there's something to be said for enjoying foreplay." He touched her bottom lip and dipped his finger into the moisture within. "And I wouldn't mind feeling your mouth on me…"

As his very erotic meaning sank in, shock colored her guileless blue eyes and she jerked back, dislodging his touch.

"Now don't go and get modest on me again," he drawled in amusement. "I need you completely uninhibited when we do make love."

She heaved an impatient sigh, looking completely inconvenienced by his decision. "So, counselor, in your estimation, when do *you* think I'll be ready to make love?"

He resisted the urge to kiss that sassy mouth of hers, to strip off his swim trunks and her panties and take her right there and then in the bathtub.

Tucking that particular fantasy away for another time, he reined in his desires. "Oh, you'll know, honey," he said, deliberately using the endearment that definitely applied to her now, since ten minutes earlier she'd been as sweet and warm on his tongue as the name implied. "And when you're ready, you won't have to *ask* me to make love to you. It'll feel right and it'll just happen."

FROM ACROSS HIS KITCHEN table, Ryan watched Jessica reach for her second slice of the pepperoni-and-mushroom pizza he'd ordered for their dinner, take a big bite, and savor the Italian delicacy. He finished off his first piece, liking that she wasn't shy about her appetite, and had to admit that since their episode in the tub an hour earlier, a few notches in her reserve had evaporated, as well. There was a newfound confidence about her he found incredibly sexy, and it made him feel very optimistic about his decision to take time and care with Jessica before they elevated their relationship to a more sexual one.

They'd each taken separate showers after playing in the tub, to wash away the sticky chocolate from their bodies and hair. While he'd changed into gray sweatpants and shirt, she was wrapped in the warm chenille robe while her panties and bra tumbled in the dryer—which left her completely naked beneath the soft, voluminous folds of the robe.

At that tantalizing thought, a familiar heat rumbled through his veins, and he shifted in his chair to find a more comfortable position.

Jessica lifted her gaze to his, her eyes dancing with a carefree radiance that made his heart feel just as light. "Well, counselor, you're one tough attorney, I'll give you that. I think you can fairly claim victory over your most recent case."

He grinned, pleased that there weren't any kind of negative implications in her words against his profession, as there had been in past conversations. No matter how small the hurdle, her tentative acceptance was a promising start.

He tipped his head and regarded her curiously. "And which case is that?"

"*My* practical versus *your* sensual." She licked sauce from the tips of her fingers in long, languorous laps he felt all the way to his groin. "You win. *Again.*"

He narrowed his gaze, realizing she was testing her feminine wiles and deliberately enticing him with her slow, thorough attention to her fingers. He resisted the urge to demonstrate lesson number three—that if she teased a hungry tiger, he was certain to pounce and devour.

Exhaling a deep breath that did little to ease the coiling in his belly, he lifted another slice of pizza and set it on the plate in front of him. "That's because I *always* present my cases with irrefutable facts." He could see her absorbing the double meaning of his words, possibly realizing that he didn't purposely try to play the villain in any of his cases. "Utilizing indisputable evidence to the best of my ability is a sure way to win."

"So is knowing the other person's weaknesses, and using that evidence to take advantage of them."

Not an accusation, just a statement based on her own personal experience in the past. And there was just enough of a hint of vulnerability in her gaze to indicate that's exactly where her thoughts had wandered, to a childhood torn apart by the greed of her father and his attorney's quest to benefit his client.

Ryan thought carefully about his answer before replying. "Yes, some lawyers operate that way," he said, not wanting to lie to her, but neither did he want to incriminate himself. "But you can't judge all of us based on that one bad experience, not without giving me a fair chance and taking the time to gather some evidence of your own." Positive, enlightening evidence of him as just an ordinary, hardworking person, without the stigma of being an attorney.

It was a reasonable request, as well as a subtle challenge, and he was relieved and elated when she finally agreed with a quiet, "Okay."

He had no idea how they'd gotten so far off track, and he attempted to steer the subject back to a more pleasant one. "So, getting back to more important matters, is *my* gift idea for Brooke and Marc worthy of your approval?"

"Oh, most definitely." She took a drink of her soda, and dazzled him with a provocative smile. "I'll never be able to take a bath again without thinking about you sharing it with me."

Oh, yeah, he liked the sound of that. He might not be there physically every time, but he'd settle for being a part of her fantasies.

Done with her third slice of pizza, she put her napkin on her plate and pushed it aside. "You know, between the cakes, and the bath, I don't think I can take much more of you proving me wrong."

He chuckled at the wry note to her voice, but he was beginning to think that he had something else to prove, to her, and himself—that they could find some kind of common ground which they could build from, beyond their sexual attraction.

Having learned that Jessica responded more favorably to demonstrative measures, he considered his next plan of attack. Reclining in his chair, and stretching his long legs in front of him, he allowed an easygoing smile to curve his lips. "Considering how intimate we got in my bathtub, what do I have to do to change your mind about attending my firm's Christmas party next weekend?"

"Oh, you've done quite enough," she said, her voice husky with satisfaction.

He laughed at her brazen comment and the innuendo behind it.

As if suddenly realizing what she'd revealed, she ducked her head, hiding the adorable blush coloring her cheeks. "I can't believe I just said that," she muttered.

His heart squeezed with affection, along with something deeper and more intrinsic that took him off guard. He didn't try and block the sensation as he would have in the past, but instead allowed whatever emotion it was to settle in for a longer stay. "Well, I was hoping since you're still feeling content and satiated, that maybe I could get lucky, too."

A honey-blond brow rose over an eye. "Oh?"

"Yeah," he said, ignoring the faint skepticism in her tone. "Go with me to my firm's party, Jessie."

Jessica's heart pounded so hard in her chest it hurt. What Ryan was asking was not conducive to her emotions and went against everything she believed in. But then again, what she'd allowed to happen upstairs in his bathtub, what she'd asked of him afterward, and what she was beginning to feel for him now, felt so *right,* no matter how *wrong* it was.

She should have flat-out refused as she had the other night, but a deeper longing held her back, made her wish that things could be different between them.

Needing something to keep her hands busy, she stood and stacked their plates, then carried them to the sink. "Why is it so important that I go with you at all?" She told herself she was merely curious, but knew she was searching for a reason to accept his invitation, no matter how hazardous to her heart that kind of involvement could prove to be. No more dangerous than her sleeping with him, she supposed.

He stood, too, and helped her clear the table. "After our discussion the other day about your parents, and what I do for a living, I'd really like to show you a different side to the profession, that most of us are just hardworking people trying to make a decent living, trying to help our clients. There's no pressure or expectations involved here, but I'm hoping you'd come away from the party with a whole new outlook on the profession."

His reasoning was straightforward, his motivations basic, catering to her insecurities and doubts. The man definitely had a way of hitting her softest spots, and she realized she wasn't immune to his attempts.

He tossed the cardboard pizza container into the trash and parked his hip on the counter beside the sink where she was washing their dishes. "This is the first time I've ever been invited to Haywood and Irwin's Christmas party. It's a black-tie affair, quite a privilege and a boost to my career, and quite honestly, there's no one else I want to share the evening with but you."

He wanted to share the *evening* with her. How could she have forgotten that his career was his main focus, not developing a lasting relationship? Not that she was asking him for a commitment, but the reminder did help to put things back into perspective—that her time with Ryan was only temporary.

That fact gave her the perfect excuse to accept his invitation and spend that much more time with him before they parted ways. She gave her head a rueful shake— she was crazy for considering his overture, crazier still for wanting to be with him, despite every reason she had to stay away. Yet just like the situation with the cakes, just like the seduction in his bathtub, she was helpless to resist him.

She struggled between following her desires, and listening to her conscience. Done with the dishes, she turned toward him and accepted the terry towel he gave her to dry her hands, and tried to do the smart thing.

"You know, I'm really not a party type of person, Ryan, and I definitely don't have anything fancy to wear to a black-tie affair—"

He pressed two fingers over her lips as a lopsided grin creased his features. "If that's the best excuse you can come up with, then it's pretty lame."

She circled his wrist, pulled his hand away from her mouth, and immediately missed the warmth he generated. "It's the truth."

"Then leave the details to me and I'll make sure you have something appropriate to wear." Before she could argue, he slipped his hands into the front opening of her robe, just below the tie, and grasped her naked hips.

She inhaled a sharp breath, shocked at his bold, unexpected move, and at the fact that she was completely exposed from the waist down. She latched on to his forearms, uncertain what he intended. "What are you doing?" she asked breathlessly.

His dark brown eyes held hers, never looking lower, while his palms and fingers measured the indentation of her waist, the curve of her hip, and the slope of her bare bottom. The earlier warmth he'd created became a raging inferno, curling low in her belly and spreading outward with every languorous stroke of his hands. Yet though she wore not a stitch of clothing, he refrained from caressing her intimately, which seemed to make the experience more sensual, more arousing, more erotic.

His fingers grazed up the sides of her thighs, causing a shiver to skip along her spine. "Size six?" he guessed, his voice a low, rich murmur.

It took her a moment to realize he was referring to her dress size. "Size eight," she clarified, and smiled. "But thanks for the boost to my self-esteem."

"You're perfectly proportioned." He blinked lazily, and dipped his finger into her navel in a very provocative way, making her stomach muscles clench in response. "And your shoe size?"

"Eight again."

"That's easy enough to remember." Withdrawing his touch, he let the folds of the robe fall together again without taking a peek at what had been so openly revealed. "Expect a package by the middle of the week."

Without his hands supporting her hips, Jessica's legs suddenly felt wobbly, and she had to lean against the counter or risk falling in a puddle at his feet.

He padded across the kitchen in his bare feet, opened a drawer, and rummaged through the contents. Finding whatever it was he was searching for, he returned and held a key out to her. "By the way, I wanted to give you this."

She stared at his offering, and knew without asking what it was—a key to his house. She kept her fingers curled around the ledge of the counter and raised her questioning gaze to his. "What do I need that for?"

"So you'll have access to the house, since you'll probably start decorating for the party next week."

She shook her head. "I'll just let you know when I plan to be here, or work it out so you're home."

"Take it, Jessie." He grabbed her wrist, and pressed the key into her palm, the metal warm from his own touch. "You never know when you might need it. And you're welcome here, *anytime,* without asking or calling beforehand."

Emotion clogged her throat as she stared into his sincere gaze. His words held a wealth of meaning, implying an exclusivity to just her, and seeking her trust. For as much as she knew she should balk and adamantly refuse the intimate gesture, she couldn't bring herself to do so, because in that moment she felt wanted and secure, and no other man had ever made her feel that way.

And even though she knew her emotions were most likely a figment of her overactive imagination, she curled her fingers around the key and held it tight.

WITH A BIG, FLUFFY TOWEL wrapped around her body after her relaxing shower, Jessica took inventory of the items laid out on her bed, which had been delivered to her apartment earlier that week with a note from Ryan in bold, masculine script stating: *I can't wait to see how gorgeous you look. I'll pick you up at 5 PM on Saturday.*

The man had impeccable taste, and an eye for what appealed to a woman's feminine side. Not only had he bought her a complete head-to-toe ensemble to wear to his firm's Christmas party, but he'd included more sensual indulgences, too. Jasmine-scented body wash had accompanied her long, hot shower, and was followed up with fragrant lotion and powder that lingered in the air around her and made her skin silky-soft to the touch.

She felt pampered and spoiled, and admitted that it was a very nice feeling having a man take care of her— a luxury she'd best not get used to, she reminded herself.

With a half hour left until Ryan arrived, she knew she had to make haste or she'd make them late for the party. Not a great impression to make on the occasion of Ryan's first invitation to his firm's elite holiday get-together. He'd obviously worked hard to earn the recognition, and the last thing she wanted to do was mar his first appearance to such an important event. The man took his professional goals seriously, and this was, undoubtedly, a major milestone in his career.

And she'd be on his arm when they walked in the door together.

Her stomach dipped at the thought. Releasing the end of the towel tucked between her breasts, she let it fall to the floor, wishing she wasn't so nervous about the evening still to come. While a part of her was anxious about rubbing elbows with all those attorneys and trying to make polite talk when she had absolutely nothing in common with any of them, she couldn't deny that she wanted to enjoy the evening with Ryan.

Determined to have a good time tonight regardless of the circumstances, she shoved those thoughts from her mind and reached for the small pile of intimate apparel Ryan had purchased for her. She selected the pair of black cotton panties cut high on the thigh and trimmed in lace, and smiled when she realized he'd taken into consideration her practical nature. As she pulled on the pretty underwear, she discovered that the combination was sexy, yet surprisingly comfortable. The translucent, stretch-lace black bra went on next, and the garment was such a perfect fit she knew he must have peeked at the label in her bra last weekend when he'd retrieved it from his dryer.

Instead of panty hose, he'd chosen sheer, shimmering black stockings with an elasticized band of lace that hugged her thighs, and when she turned to look in her mirror to see the full effect of the lingerie, she almost didn't recognize herself. A smile curved her mouth, and her pulse picked up its beat.

She'd become a sex kitten. And she liked the transformation, as well as the incredibly arousing feel of the sexy lingerie against her skin.

Finally, she slipped on the knee-length dress Ryan had bought for her, concealing the provocative under-garments. But knowing what she wore beneath the sheath of black velvet made her feel utterly feminine and decidedly risqué. The dress shaped to her curves, the sleeves were long and warm, and the neckline scalloped low enough to show a tasteful hint of cleavage.

As a whole package, with her freshly washed hair falling softly around her face, her diamond studs sparkling in her ears, and makeup lightly applied to enhance her blue eyes and features, she appeared so-phisticated and elegant. All a temporary fantasy, she knew, because beneath the trappings she was just plain and sensible Jessica Newman. A woman with simple dreams of stability and security with a man, and emo-tional needs that didn't coincide with Ryan's future plans and his dedication to his career.

The doorbell rang, interrupting her thoughts. Quickly, she slipped her stockinged feet into the matching black velvet heels, grabbed the beaded handbag with the silk corded strap, and headed into the living room.

Giddy with the anticipation of seeing Ryan, she opened the door, saw how striking and gorgeous he looked in black-tie attire and greeted him with a breath-less, "Hi."

He stepped inside her apartment, and the subtle scent of his cologne wrapped around her. "Hi, yourself," he drawled, his voice as dark and rich as the appreciation glimmering in his deep brown eyes. "You look... *stunning.*"

His warm, sincere compliment caused her heart to flutter in her chest and boosted her confidence another notch. "Thanks to you."

"Partly." Pushing back his well-cut jacket, he slid his hands into the front pockets of his trousers, and inclined his head. "I have to confess that I took Natalie with me to the boutique to help me pick out the dress, but what's beneath it was all my choice. I take it everything fit okay?"

She nodded. "Perfectly, and very comfortably, I might add."

"I tried to keep in mind your sensible attire, but you deserve pretty, feminine things, and I liked buying them for you." A wolfish grin curved his lips, and he stepped closer, tracing the scalloped edges of her bodice with a long, tapered finger. Her breasts swelled at that tantalizing caress, her nipples hardened and he watched her body's response to his touch. "And I'd be lying if I didn't say that just imagining you in that sheer bra, those lacy panties, and those thigh-high stockings is enough to make me want to strip away your dress and look my fill."

Desire curled in her stomach, prompting a brazenness to match his mental seduction. Dampening her bottom lip with her tongue, she smoothed her hand along his lapel. "Yeah, well, maybe we can turn that particular fantasy into reality."

A dark brow winged upward, accentuating the heat blazing in his eyes. "You know, if we didn't have a very important party to attend, I'd accept that challenge."

Wanting to tempt him as much as he did her, she leaned into him and whispered huskily in his ear. "The challenge stands, counselor, all…night…long."

He groaned, the sound both agonized and aroused. "You are a *very* wicked woman, Jessie."

She'd never been wicked before, not until Ryan. He made her feel inflamed and restless and daring, and for now, she'd luxuriate in the sensations because, too soon, she'd be alone again.

He drew a deep, steady breath, and cast a glance at the fancy black-and-gold watch strapped to his wrist. "As much as I'd like to stay and explore the endless possibilities of your intriguing invitation, we need to be on our way. Are you ready to go?"

Back to reality—his party, his world, which was so far removed from her own simple life. Reaching for her long, black wool coat, she flashed him a smile that belied the sudden apprehension infusing her veins. "Ready as I'll ever be, I suppose."

With nothing left to stall the inevitable, Jessica let Ryan escort her to his Lexus and buckled in for the ride. The half-hour drive to Phillip Haywood's estate passed quickly with Ryan keeping up a steady stream of inconsequential conversation, which she suspected was designed to put her at ease. She appreciated the gesture and thought she was going to be just fine until they started wending their way up a long, winding driveway to a huge, stately mansion. She suddenly felt as though she was way out of her league and had no business being there.

Her stomach churned with uncertainties, but she had little time to dwell on them. A valet promptly appeared to park Ryan's car, and she was forced to exit the vehicle. Ryan met up with her on the sidewalk, tucked her hand into the crook of his arm, and led her toward the enormous double doors inlaid with etched glass.

With every step, her legs felt weighed down by lead. Tension tightened every molecule in her body, and with every breath she gulped her chest burned and seemed to compress.

Oh, Lord, what was she doing?

Stopping at the front door, Ryan rang the doorbell. He glanced her way with a sexy smile, and must have seen the panic in her eyes, because concern instantly touched his features. "Hey, are you okay?"

*No, I don't belong here with you.* As honest as that knowledge was, she couldn't bring herself to say the words, knowing that he'd take her back home rather than force her to stay. Unwilling to ruin this night for him just so she could wallow in her own insecurities, she settled for an understated version of the truth and prayed that she'd survive the evening. "I'm just a little nervous."

He brushed his knuckles softly over her jaw, his gaze both tender and understanding. Lowering his head, he placed a quick, but infinitely sweet kiss on her lips that lingered long after he pulled back.

"I'll be right beside you the entire time," he murmured reassuringly. "You're going to be just fine, Jessie."

And then the door opened and they were greeted by a warm, friendly man that Ryan introduced to her as his boss, Phillip Haywood. As Phillip's hand engulfed hers in a warm handshake and the older man chastised Ryan for keeping such a beauty all to himself, Jessica had no choice but to trust Ryan and believe his promise that she really was going to be just fine.

# CHAPTER EIGHT

AFTER FOUR HOURS of exchanging pleasantries and formalities with attorneys, Jessica couldn't help but let loose a little humor now that the evening was over. "How do you save a lawyer from drowning?"

Ryan glanced her way, seemingly trying to gauge her mood. "I haven't a clue," he murmured.

She allowed a tired smile to touch her lips. "Take your foot off his head."

His deep, rich chuckles filled the close confines of his car as he navigated his way back to the main road from Haywood's estate. "Thank you for saving that joke for a more private moment."

"You're welcome." The chill cloaking the inside of the vehicle stole beneath her long, wool coat and caressed her legs, making her shiver. "I don't think your bosses or colleagues would have appreciated my brand of humor quite the way you do."

He flipped on the heater, then turned to meet her eyes, visible by the illumination radiating from the dash. "Was the party that bad for you?"

With a sigh, she rested her head against the back of her seat and thought about his question. "Actually, it wasn't as bad as I imagined it would be. Everyone was friendly and warm. Any discomfort I experienced was strictly my own." And, surprisingly, it had been minimal.

She'd survived the evening, and had even enjoyed herself at times, regardless of knowing the occupation of half the guests at the party. She'd seen a different side to what she'd always believed was a hard-edged profession. The associates who worked at Haywood and Irwin were hardworking men and women who just happened to have chosen law as a career, as Ryan had suggested. People with humor and emotions. People with families of their own. People who represented the good and evil of the world because it was their sworn duty to help others and assure them of a fair trial.

But what had made the greatest impact on her was an idle, but profound comment that one of the female attorneys in the firm had made to her while Ryan had been talking to his boss. Having worked in law offices for the past twenty years, the woman found Ryan refreshing as a lawyer. According to her, Ryan was a lawyer who cared about people and catered to his client's needs, rather than focusing on his own personal gains.

And despite her bitter childhood memories, Jessica came to accept on a tentative level that not all lawyers were as cutthroat and merciless as her father's had been. Ryan certainly didn't fit the mold, and she'd been wrong for ever believing he could deliberately hurt someone with selfish intent.

"You did great, Jessie." He reached across the console and settled his hand on her leg. Though a heavy layer of wool separated her flesh from his fingers, she could feel the supportive squeeze he gave her thigh. "And I'm very glad you came with me."

She was glad, too, for purely selfish, personal

reasons. Ryan had been so attentive—touching her without reserve, holding her hand, gazing at her with affection—that she'd briefly enjoyed the fantasy of being more than just his date for the evening. But just like Cinderella, by tomorrow morning the fairy tale would be over and reality would return.

She recalled the various comments revolving around her and Ryan that she'd overheard during the course of the evening. "You do realize, don't you, that your bosses and colleagues think we're an item," she said.

He transferred his gaze from the road to her. "Does that bother you?"

"Only because I'll probably never see any of them ever again, and I got the impression that they expect me to be around in the future." Which she wouldn't be, *couldn't* be.

He shrugged off her concern. "I'll handle any questions anyone might ask about our relationship."

And he'd make it clear that they weren't an item, that she'd just been a date for the evening. The pang of regret she experienced over that thought took her off guard, and she berated herself for being so foolish, for wanting something that was completely impossible with Ryan. And while she'd seen this evening that most of his colleagues juggled a career and a long-term relationship, she knew Ryan's main focus was his commitment to his career. Judging by Haywood and Irwin's enthusiasm toward their young associate, it was obvious that Ryan's goals weren't far from his reach.

*You should be proud of Ryan. He's one of our up-and-coming attorneys, and has a very promising future ahead of him at Haywood and Irwin.*

Phillip Haywood's praise filtered through Jessica's

mind. For as much as Ryan's future goals would consume more time than a relationship or family would permit, she couldn't begrudge him the success he sought, and deserved.

Her fingers slid along the strap of her purse, and she swallowed to relieve the odd pressure that had gathered in her chest. "Your bosses think very highly of you," she said, trying to sound optimistic for him.

He grinned, appearing pleased that he'd gained Haywood's approval. "After six years with the firm, it's nice to get the recognition I worked so hard for. The next couple of years will definitely be interesting as far as advancements go."

He had his heart set on a promotion to junior partner, which was an admirable goal, as well as one that would entail more work, more hours, and no time to cultivate a strong, lasting relationship. His commitment would be to his job, and maintaining his position within the firm.

Not that that issue mattered to her, she tried to convince herself as she glanced out the side window to the twinkling lights of the city beyond the freeway. After a few minutes of silence passed, she looked back at Ryan's strong profile and summoned the courage to express a question she'd been curious about for a while now. "What made you decide to be a divorce attorney?"

Now that the interior of the car was warm, he turned down the heater. "Honestly, it wasn't *my* decision to be a divorce attorney," he replied easily. "I originally wanted to get into corporate law."

She wasn't expecting that response, and found it interesting that he'd settled for a position so different from his primary choice. "What happened?"

"Before I graduated from law school, I was hired on at Haywood and Irwin as a law clerk until I passed the bar and became an associate. The only opening they had at the time was as a divorce attorney in the family law department, and because I had bills to pay, and Haywood is such a reputable firm, I accepted the position and made the best of it." He shrugged, and cast a quick glance at her. "Honestly, now I can't imagine doing anything else."

The message he relayed with his eyes was unmistakable—he was silently asking her to accept him for who and what he was. And in that moment, she realized somewhere along the way she'd done just that. As much as his choice of career made her too aware of her turbulent childhood, she knew they'd remain friends once the New Year's Eve party was over and they went their separate ways. And despite the sudden ache near the vicinity of her heart, she knew she had no choice but to end this tentative, sensual relationship of theirs…before things became any more emotionally complicated for her.

The Lexus came to a smooth stop, and he shut off the engine, bringing her back to the present. She glanced out the window, expecting to see her complex, and was surprised to find them parked in front of his office building. The lot was empty, and the only source of illumination came from the dim lighting in the lobby.

"What are we doing here?" she asked, curious.

He unsnapped his seat belt and turned toward her. "I need to pick up a file on a case that's going to court on Monday so I can review a few things over the weekend." He hesitated a brief moment. "Do you mind?"

Of course weekend work would consume his extra time. She experienced a twinge of regret she immediately dismissed and shook her head. "No, go ahead. I'll wait here."

"I was hoping you'd come with me." Reaching out, he fingered a strand of her hair, which she was coming to realize was a source of fascination for him. "I also wanted to show you the fabulous view from my office in the evening."

Heat seeped through her veins, and a smile tugged at her lips. "Ahh, I should have known you had ulterior motives."

He chuckled, and ran his fingers along her cheek. "Yeah, I'll do just about anything to get you alone and all to myself."

Unable to resist that sexy smile of his, and what his words implied, she accompanied him up to his office, very aware of just how alone they were in the deserted building.

He turned on the overhead lights and strolled toward his desk. "Give me a few minutes to find what I need."

"Sure."

The room was pleasantly warm, and she took off her heavy coat and hung it on one of the brass hooks by the door. While he sorted through files and paperwork stacked on his desk, she drifted toward a credenza along the wall holding framed photographs.

Passing idle time, she gazed at each one, most of which were group shots. Recognizing Ryan and Natalie in one of the larger gatherings, she picked up the professional portrait to take a closer look at the older couple surrounded by six adults and five young children.

Seeing a striking resemblance between Ryan and the older man in the middle of the photo, she turned the picture toward Ryan and asked, "Is this your family?"

"Yep." Setting aside a few file folders, he shrugged out of his jacket, hung it next to hers, and came up beside her. "There are Mom and Dad in the middle, and you know Natalie, of course," he said, then went on to point out his two older sisters by name, and their respective husbands and children.

The photo, as simple as it was, encompassed a wealth of emotion Jessica couldn't help but envy. An abundance of affection radiated from everyone's smiles, happiness shone in their eyes, and love was evident in the strength of the familial bond they shared.

A pang of longing struck near her heart, so strong it nearly stole her breath. "You're very lucky to have such a close-knit family," she said, her voice a whisper of sound in the quiet room. "Don't *ever* take that for granted."

Ryan recognized the vulnerability that etched Jessica's features and tinged her voice—he'd seen and heard that emotion with some of the women he'd represented in divorce cases. While he'd always managed to remain immune and objective with his clients because he had a job to do, he felt Jessica's pain like a vise around his heart.

Jessica was a casualty of divorce, having been deeply affected by her father's betrayal. She'd lost the stability and security of a complete family in one fell swoop, and apparently was still struggling to find what her father had carelessly ripped apart.

*A family.* Something he *did* take for granted because all he'd ever known was the love and support of his mom and dad, and his siblings. He'd never lacked for affection, had never gone to bed as a child feeling alone, and had never questioned either of his parents' love.

Ryan drew a deep breath, knowing it was time to discuss her past, that in order for her to trust him as he wanted, they had to cross this hurdle together. And maybe, during the course of their conversation she could purge some of the bitterness and resentment caused by one's man lack of compassion.

"How old were you when your parents divorced?" he asked quietly.

She looked at him, initially startled by his question. "I was nine, and Brooke was thirteen." She gave the photo in her hand one last lingering glance before setting it back on the credenza. "I think the most difficult part of the divorce was that before my father left and my parents separated, everything seemed so perfect. I was definitely Daddy's girl, and I adored him. He was always so larger than life for me."

He slid his hands into the front pockets of his trousers to keep from touching her, comforting her. "I'm sure whatever problems your parents had didn't happen overnight." From his experience with clients, the strife within marriages sometimes festered for years before married couples split up—which accounted for many unpleasant divorces. He'd witnessed amicable separations, as well as vengeful ones.

"You're right, of course, and I realize now that my father must have been having an affair for quite a while before my mother found out. But as a little girl, I was so wrapped up in feeling secure, that when my dad just packed up and walked out one day, I was devastated." She shook her head, her velvet blue eyes brimming with shadows of old misery. "I just couldn't understand what went wrong, what *I* did wrong to make him leave."

Ryan balled his hands into fists, aching deep inside

for the innocence she'd lost at such an early age. He imagined her at nine, carefree and filled with girlish dreams, and blinded by fantasies of happily-ever-afters, only to have them crushed by the one man she'd trusted to always be there for her.

She moved away from him and stopped in front of the huge plate-glass window overlooking the city. With the lights on in his office, though, all she could see was the reflection of herself, and the room around her. He didn't approach her, suspecting that she needed to work through this particular event in her life without interference. And so he gave her what she needed—someone to listen to her rid herself of her painful past.

"Then my father filed for divorce, and he wasn't satisfied with half of everything," she continued. "From yelling matches that I overheard between my parents, I learned that he felt he deserved everything, because he'd been the sole breadwinner. When my mother disagreed, that's when things got real ugly with my father. Come to find out, his new girlfriend was twenty-two years old and very high maintenance, and he was out to get whatever he could from the marriage at our expense."

Her shoulders lifted as she drew a deep breath, and relaxed when she exhaled, though her spine remained stiff with tension. "He hired a cutthroat divorce attorney who took advantage of my mother's emotional state and took her for everything he could, and since my mother couldn't afford a powerful lawyer, she lost just about everything to my father and his new lover.

"My mom was a mess after that ordeal," she went on, her voice hoarse. "All I can remember is her constantly crying, and staying in her bedroom with the shades drawn. It was awful, and if it wasn't for Brooke taking control and pushing my mother to snap out of her depression, I'm sure we would have ended up on welfare—or worse, Brooke and I would have gone into a foster home."

He watched a shudder wrack her slender form, and she wrapped her arms around her middle as if to hold herself together. "We moved our meager belongings from the house my mother was forced to sell, the one I grew up in, and into a one-bedroom apartment because that's all she could afford. My mother took on two jobs to support us, and because Mom was hardly ever home, Brooke pretty much raised me. We went from dining on solid, nutritious meals to eating macaroni and cheese and hot dogs because it was filling, and cheap."

"What about child support?" he asked. Surely they'd had that extra income to rely on and to help them with expenses.

She turned to look at him, and laughed, but the sound held no humor. "What about it? According to my sister, the checks came sporadically, then stopped altogether, as did my father's infrequent phone calls. I haven't seen or heard from him in over thirteen years."

She was trying so hard to remain composed and strong, when he knew beneath the surface brewed dark, bitter emotions. "It's okay to be angry, Jessie," he said softly.

"Is it okay to hate him for what he did?" Moisture glimmered in her eyes, contradicting the defiant lift of her chin. "For making a family, then walking away from it?"

"No man should ever forsake his children," he said, vehemently believing that.

Divorces happened, it was a sad fact of life. And if

there was one thing he disliked about his profession, it was that the children involved were sometimes embroiled in their parents' spiteful attempts to hurt one another. He'd never given the long-term effects of that any thought while handling his cases, but was coming to realize through Jessica that the impact of a nasty divorce on a child left lifetime scars.

Compassion and an inexplicable tenderness welled within him, and it took concentrated effort to remain where he stood, when he wanted to close the distance between them. "I'm sorry that you had to go through that."

She turned back to the window. "Yeah, me, too," she said, her voice a mere whisper.

The office grew quiet and still, and little by little, understanding trickled through him, as well as a deeper insight into Jessica. After everything she'd endured as a child, was it no wonder that she'd never allowed a man to get too close emotionally?

Obviously, his profession had been the initial deterrent for her, but it wasn't the sole reason she'd built a wall of reserve. He suspected that her father's abandonment and the crass way Lane had treated her had left her feeling insecure and unable to put faith in any man's promise.

Dragging a hand through his hair, he tried focusing on the positive. "Your mother is remarried and happy, isn't she?"

She hesitated before answering. "Yeah, she is."

"And Brooke, too," he added.

She glanced over her shoulder at him, her mouth pursed with impatience. "Can you just get to the point you're trying to make with this line of questioning?"

"The point I'm trying to make," he replied very calmly, "is that maybe it's just a matter of finding the right person."

From across the room, he could see her gaze searching his, deep and intense. "And how do you know when it's the right person?"

"You trust your instincts."

She scoffed at his simple response. "That didn't work for my mother or Brooke's first marriages."

"Then maybe you have to trust your heart." Just as he was beginning to put complete faith in his, and what he was beginning to feel for Jessica.

A glimmer of fear flashed across her features. She was scared of risking her heart again, scared of giving, and losing, and having to start all over again alone. But life, and relationships, didn't come with guarantees, and she had to trust in her emotions before she could believe in him.

Knowing there wasn't anything more he could say or do, not on the heels of this particular discussion, he turned off the overhead lights, let the blanket of twinkling lights from outside be his guide, and approached her.

He held out his hand for her to take. "Come on, sweetheart, I believe I promised you a fabulous view."

A tentative smile touched her mouth. "Yeah, you did."

Slipping her fingers into his, she followed him to the high-back chair behind his desk. He settled himself in the seat, and she didn't protest when he pulled her down to sit across his lap, then draped her legs over the armrest while his other arm curved around her back to support her.

He turned the chair to the side to make it easier for them to enjoy the diamond-studded landscape of the city and skyline. Much to his surprise and pleasure, she curled into him, placing one hand on his chest, easing the other around his neck, and rested her head on his shoulder. He could feel the warm gust of her breath against his neck, could smell the light scent of jasmine radiating from her hair and skin.

He closed his eyes briefly, and reveled in the small gesture of trust she'd given him, especially after their emotional discussion. They remained quiet, and he absently stroked the curve of her hip with his palm. Never in his life had anything felt so perfect and right as the feel of her in his arms. And never had his soul encountered such contentment as it did in this moment.

The revelation stunned him. His career and ambition had always satisfied him on a physical, intellectual level, and although he'd always enjoyed the opposite sex, he'd never needed a woman to make him feel whole and complete, had never found one who made him question the tight focus he had on his future.

Until Jessica.

He'd always known that one day he'd settle down, get married, and have a family of his own, but he'd never been in a rush to start that particular phase of his life, not with his career on the verge of taking off. He was still too uncertain of making a lifetime commitment to a woman when he knew how difficult it was to sustain a relationship under the best of circumstances.

Yet, after spending time with Jessica the past few weeks, he wasn't ready to let her go, either. What he felt for her was rare and special—he knew that, and wanted to take the time to see what developed. Without a doubt, he wanted her in his life in some capacity. He liked spending time with her. He liked the way she challenged him. And he loved how she could make him laugh at her ridiculous lawyer jokes, yet want her at the same time.

With her bottom pressed against his groin, he wanted her now. In an attempt to distract his libido, he grasped the first bit of conversation that entered his head. "Sometimes, when I'm working really late, before I go home I'll just sit here in the dark like this, just to relax and unwind."

"I can see why." She lifted her head, and smiled at him. "The view is breathtaking."

"*You're* breathtaking," he corrected, and ran the pad of his index finger down the slope of her nose. "But I'm glad you like the view, and that I could share it with you."

She drew lazy, swirling patterns on his chest with her finger. "It's a nice way to finish up the evening."

One he didn't want to end. Neither did she, if the wistful note to her voice was any indication. Tonight would eventually come to a close, that much was inevitable, but he wanted something more to look forward to.

He made a split-second decision. "I spoke to Marc a few days ago, and he told me that he and Brooke are going to Tahoe over the Christmas holiday."

"Yes."

"What do you plan on doing for Christmas?" He felt her stiffen against him, and suspected he'd tapped into a sensitive subject. Guessed, too, that she'd planned to spend the holiday alone.

She transferred her gaze to the panoramic view, and though it was dark in his office, the glow from the lights of the city silhouetted her profile, and gave him a shadowed glimpse of the raw emotions touching her features. "I haven't decided yet," she said, the words deliberately vague.

He knew better, and couldn't stop the tide of possessiveness that swept over him. "Well, since you have no firm plans, why don't you come with me to my parents' for Christmas Eve? My whole family is there, and it's this fun, lively sleepover."

She shook her head, making her hair shimmer around her shoulders. "Oh, I couldn't."

"Oh, you can." He grinned, and slowly glided his palm from her thigh to just beneath the swell of her breast, tantalizing and teasing her with a light brush of his thumb. "If I remember correctly, I just invited you."

She sighed as he continued to stroke along the graceful, slender line of her body. His caresses were chaste, yet aroused her, if the subtle arching of her back into his touch was any indication. "Ryan...I don't think going to your family gathering is a good idea."

The more he considered the suggestion, the more perfect it sounded. "And why not?"

"I just don't want to give your family the impression that you and I are..."

"Dating?" he supplied.

She ducked her head. "Yeah, something like that."

He heard the regret in her voice, and he didn't like it. Not one bit. "I thought we'd established that tonight was definitely a date, so technically, we *are* dating." No way was he going to let her write this night off when it had been so meaningful and insightful. "But as far as Christmas and my family go, if it relieves your mind and makes you feel better, I'll introduce you as a friend."

Interest and curiosity mingled in her gaze. "Have you brought many female *friends* to your parents for the holidays?"

He rested his head against the back of the chair, and

regarded her with a deceptively lazy smile. "You're the first since high school."

She laughed, and the husky sound filled something within him he hadn't realized was empty until that moment. Then her smile fell away, and he knew in that instant she'd realized the importance of his statement— and just how serious he was about her. He saw a flicker of panic, but before it could spread like wildfire to her brain and prompt her to retreat, he acted.

He cupped her cheek in his palm, wanting this acquiescence, wanting *her* in ways that defied his emotions. "Say yes, Jessie," he whispered.

A frown creased her brows. "If you're doing this because you feel sorry for me..."

A frustrated groan rolled up from his chest. "Good Lord, you're stubborn. I'm asking because I *want* you there, but mostly I want to share my family with you."

She bit her bottom lip, and her expression softened with gratitude, and a good dose of desire and wanting, too. She touched her fingers lightly to his mouth, their gazes locked, and something sizzled in the air between them.

A naughty twinkle entered her eyes. "Do you think you could coerce me into saying yes?" she asked huskily.

Molten heat spread through his blood, hardening him in a flash. Remembering other times he'd resorted to cajoling tactics, he knew what she was alluding to, knew what she wanted. And no way was he going to refuse her request, not when obliging her was such a pleasurable experience.

A wicked smile eased across his face. "I can certainly give it my best shot."

Delving his fingers into her soft, silky hair, he guided her mouth to his. Her lips parted on a shuddering sigh, and he took advantage, gliding his tongue deeply, touching hers, tangling seductively, stroking her in a slow, lazy rhythm. He thoroughly possessed her mouth, just as he wanted to possess her body and soul.

But that wouldn't happen tonight, he knew. With her so emotionally drained from their conversation, he refused to heap the intimacy of making love into the mixture. But also, he still didn't have any protection with him. The condoms were now at home, in his nightstand, waiting for the perfect moment, the *right* moment—when Jessica decided she wanted to take their relationship to that next level.

Accepting that he'd most likely have to resort to a cold shower when he got home, he decided to enjoy their necking and petting, and take their tantalizing foreplay as far as Jessica wanted it to go.

With a sultry moan, she shifted restlessly on his lap, turned toward him so her breasts crushed against his chest, and rubbed against him. With extreme effort, the hand he'd parked at her hip remained there, even though primitive male instinct urged him to caress and explore feminine hollows and curves.

He pulled back and looked up into her face, and from the glow of outside lights he could see the flush of passion on her skin. Her lips were damp and swollen from his kiss, her gaze slumberous, her breathing just as ragged as his own.

"Tell me yes, Jessie," he rasped. "Tell me you'll go with me to my parents' on Christmas Eve."

She shook her head and dragged her hands over his chest, finding his stiff nipples with the edge of her nails beneath his starched white shirt. "I think you need to be more persuasive."

Her lips moved up to his ear, and she traced the shell with her tongue, making him imagine her mouth and tongue elsewhere. "I *dare you* to look your fill," she said, her voice low and throaty and every bit the tease.

Her brazenness scalded his senses. He closed his eyes on a groan, recalling their sexy banter at her apartment when he'd picked her up.

The opportunity was his, and he wasn't about to refuse her audacious dare. Meeting her gaze, he reached behind her, found the tab of the zipper securing her dress, and slowly slid it down, down, down, all the way to the base of her spine. The shoulders of the gown fell off her arms, and the material draped around her waist, revealing full, perfect breasts nestled within sheer black lace, her erect nipples begging for the caress of his lips, the slow lap of his tongue.

*Soon.*

"Very nice," he breathed, and touched his fingers to her knee. Her eyes darkened to a smoky shade of blue, and without a hint of modesty her legs eased apart for him as he slid his palm up the inside of her thigh. The hem of her dress pooled around his wrist, and he looked down to watch the gradual unveiling of her stockings, and the lacy band that gave way to a strip of pale, soft flesh and finally a pair of black panties.

His lungs pumped hard and slow, as he concentrated on tracing the elastic band along her thigh and up to her hip, teasing her, arousing her, using pure seduction to get the answer he sought, the answer she deliberately withheld. "Well?"

She caressed a hand along his jaw, and played the game to her full advantage. *"Maybe."*

He chuckled, liking this playful side to her, and how

uninhibited she'd become with him. Very slowly, he slid each of her bra straps down her arms, until the only thing holding up the lacy cups was the tips of her rosy nipples. "You do realize, don't you, that you're forcing me to extreme measures?"

The warning only served to spark excitement in the depths of her eyes. "A man's gotta do what a man's gotta do."

He gave a tug, and the lacy webbing slipped lower, giving her perfect, lush breasts freedom. They swayed forward, her nipples tight, and he wasted no time in bending his head to taste her. She cried out as the wet heat of his mouth engulfed her, and he opened wider still to suckle her as deep as he could. His tongue swirled around her nipple, his teeth added to the sensation. She speared her fingers through his hair and sobbed—the sound rife with a combination of pleasure and sexual frustration.

He understood her discomfort, knew what she wanted, what she *needed.* And he planned to give it to her.

Severing their contact for two seconds, he turned her so she sat with her back against his chest, her bottom nestled against his rock-hard erection. Before she realized what he'd intended, he'd slipped his hands into the sides of her panties and dragged them down her legs and off, but left her stockings intact. Then he lifted her knees and draped her spread thighs over the chair's armrests.

She gasped at the wanton position he'd so easily maneuvered her into on his lap. The window in front of them was like looking into a hazy mirror, and she was all but naked except for the dress bunched around her waist, and her sexy stockings.

"Ryan?" An uncertain tremor laced her voice.

Closing his eyes to block the erotic image reflected on the window in front of him, he buried his face in her hair, and inhaled her delectable scent. "Trust me," he whispered. "And watch how responsive you are, how sensual and beautiful."

She relaxed against his chest, granting him the acquiescence he sought. Their new position freed up both his hands, and he pressed his warm palms to her breasts, kneaded the plump flesh, and groaned right along with her when she arched her back and wriggled against his throbbing groin.

Grasping every ounce of control at his disposal, and praying *he* survived this ordeal, he moved one hand gradually lower, moving over her quivering belly, up her trembling thighs, while trailing kisses along the soft flesh at the back of her neck. She continued to watch as he'd instructed, swallowing convulsively, her eyes heavy-lidded as he lazily, leisurely, built the thrill of anticipation within her.

And then, he finally touched her intimately for the first time, with absolutely nothing to hinder the feel of her slick heat and the suppleness of her softly swelled flesh against his fingertips. She was so hot, so wet, and as he eased two fingers deep within her he discovered that she was incredibly tight, as well.

The knowledge made his entire body shudder.

She whimpered as he filled her, and reached back to wind an arm around his neck, as if needing some kind of anchor to hold onto because she was on the verge of flying apart. His breathing turned harsh, and a muscle in his jaw clenched with the effort it took not to pull her to the floor and completely ravish her.

With monumental discipline, he ignored his own raging needs and concentrated on hers. He plied and stroked and escalated her to a delirious fever pitch of desire, which was right where he wanted her…on the edge of exquisite release.

She tilted her head to look up at him. Her eyes, glittering in the darkness, begged for what he withheld. "Ryan…*please.*"

The hand lavishing attention to her breast plucked at her hard nipple, rolled it between his fingers until pleasure became near unbearable pain. "Tell me what I want to hear, Jessie."

This time she didn't hesitate. *"Yes."*

Victory was sweet, and excruciating for him, but he accepted the consequences of where her dare had led. Dipping his head, he captured her mouth in a deep, hungry, rapacious kiss, as if filling her mouth with the thrust of his tongue could somehow make up for the loss of not being able to do the same within her pliant body. He increased the pressure to that exquisitely sensitive flesh between her legs, and felt her tense as her orgasm hit.

She moaned long and low as a tremor rippled through her, sweeping her up in a whirlwind of sensation. He took her as high as he could, then brought her back down with a gentleness that belied the raw, untamed fury of his own suppressed climax.

When it was over, she slumped against him, trying to regain her breath…and all he could think about was how easy it would be to unzip his pants, free his rampant erection and enter her from behind while she sat on his lap.

Much to his relief, after a few quiet moments she slid off him and stood to straighten her outfit. Unable to watch her provocative actions, he leaned back in the chair, and slung his forearm over his eyes. The sound of her zipper echoed in his ears, and he heard the shimmy of her panties sliding up her stockings as she put them back on. His belly clenched, and his nostrils flared. Hell, he could smell the honeyed musk of her release still clinging to his fingers.

Then her soft, husky voice wreaked additional havoc with his senses. "Ryan, are you okay?"

Her guileless question almost made him laugh, but it took too much effort. No, he wasn't okay—he was certain he was going to expire from sexual frustration. "Give me a few minutes," he rasped, desperately needing time for his libido to cool.

She gave him five seconds before she touched him, and he nearly jumped out of his skin when he opened his eyes to find her kneeling in front of him and pushing his knees apart for her to fit in between. Stunned and mesmerized, he watched her skim her palms up his thighs, and gulped when her fingers worked to unbuckle the thin leather belt around his waist.

His heart drummed in his ears, and his entire body throbbed with each beat, pumping blood straight to the one organ that didn't need the extra stimulation. She unfastened his black dress slacks, lowered the zipper over the thickest, longest erection he could ever remember having, then grasped the elastic band of his briefs to lower them.

Her fingers grazed the bulge straining the confines of cotton, scorching him, setting his nerves on fire. Sucking in a quick intake of air, he grasped her wrists to stop her. "Jessie, if you so much as touch me, I'll go off."

His blatant warning didn't seem to faze her. Instead, an amused, lopsided grin tipped her lips. "Do you think you could give me maybe a minute or two to play first?"

A deep, guttural groan vibrated in his chest. "Sweetheart, you don't have to do this."

She looked up at him, her eyes shimmering with desire, and the need to know him as intimately as he'd known her. "I know I don't *have* to do this. I want to touch you, and taste you. Will you let me?"

He struggled with her request and what it would entail, not sure he could handle such an all-out assault. He was, after all, just a man—one who was hanging on to his last thin thread of control.

And then she took the decision out of his hands and put it directly into hers. *Literally.* And he was lost, unable to deny her anything, especially this.

Her nimble fingers granted him freedom and curled around his shaft snugly, measuring his breadth and length. He gritted his teeth while she explored, and squeezed his eyes shut so he didn't have to watch. Except he could feel…and when she took him into her warm, wet mouth and swirled her tongue around the swollen tip, he shook with the effort it took to restrain his natural impulse to thrust.

He swore when she deepened her intimate kiss and applied the same techniques he'd used on her… suckling sensuously, stroking rhythmically, taking time and pleasure in discovering the taste and feel of him with her fingers, her supple lips, her wicked tongue.

Heat flared. Carnal gratification beckoned. His stomach muscles clenched, and knowing he was fast approaching the point of no return, he tangled his fingers in her hair to ease her away. She stubbornly remained, making hungry little sounds in the back of her throat that reverberated along his shaft. Desperate, certain this wasn't what she meant to do, he uttered a final warning she blatantly ignored.

And then it was too late, and all he could do was surrender to her selfless offering, her inherent sensuality, and her giving, generous heart.

# CHAPTER NINE

"ARE YOU COMING?"

Startled by the question and the connotation behind it, Jessica snapped herself out of the private, erotic fantasies that had consumed her thoughts ever since her tryst with Ryan at his office five days ago. She glanced toward her sister, who was looking at her oddly.

Those sexy daydreams were going to get her into trouble, if they hadn't already. Had Brooke recognized the flush on her skin as sexual arousal, which she seemed to be in a constant state of lately? Had she made some kind of peculiar noise that had tipped her sister off to the provocative scenarios filling her head?

Jessica's heart beat triple time. Her body tingled with a desire that had yet to be fully appeased, and her face inflamed with guilt at being caught making love to Ryan in her mind—with her sister standing three feet away, her expression now concerned.

"Excuse me?" She winced as her voice came out as a high-pitched squeak.

Brooke's frown deepened. "I said, I'm going into the dressing room to try these on." She indicated the outfits hanging over both of their arms that they'd chosen for Ryan's New Year's Eve party. "Are you coming?"

"Oh," she breathed, the sound relieved. Her sister's

question was completely innocent. It was *her* brain that was overloaded with sinful, lustful scenarios.

She glanced at her own selection, and knowing she wasn't in the frame of mind to continue searching through the racks in the boutique, she nodded in answer. She followed Brooke into the changing area, and they each took their own spacious rooms next to the other. Jessica hung her dresses on the hook by the door, refraining from looking into the two-way mirror because she didn't want to get lost in another fantasy, and pulled her sweatshirt over her head to change.

"You know, you've been distracted all day," Brooke said, her voice drifting over the partition separating them. "First at lunch, and now here. Is everything okay, Jess?"

"I'm fine," she said automatically, and reached for the first dress, a red sequined number that sparkled and shimmered and had a life of its own. Her assurance was meant to appease her sister, because Jessica wasn't ready to divulge the truth, that emotionally she'd been feeling mixed up and confused over Ryan Matthews. Not to mention feeling so sexually charged, she was sure her years of deprivation had finally caught up to her with a vengeance.

She wanted to make love with Ryan, and after what they'd shared at his office, she knew she was ready to take that next step. Except she'd started her period, and still had another three days to go before everything was back to normal, which meant she wouldn't be able to seduce him until after Christmas. It had been incredibly frustrating two days ago, when things had gotten hot and heavy between her and Ryan at his house and she'd had to put the brakes on any intimate foreplay. He'd been understanding, and incredibly patient, but she couldn't say the same about herself.

The thought of going all the way with Ryan was both a scary and exciting prospect—scary because he made her feel more than any man ever had, cherished and desired. Yet despite how compatible they were, she'd witnessed his dedication to his job, in the time he spent at the office after hours handling a case, and weekend work. She knew his career would always come before her, or a relationship, and she accepted that, too. Ultimately, that knowledge kept her from doing something incredibly foolish…like depend on him. Or worse, fall in love with him. In the meantime, she was determined to indulge in everything he had to offer, because in another week and a half, their affair would be nothing more than a glorious memory for her.

"Are you *sure* you're okay?" Brooke persisted.

Ignoring the emotion knotting her throat, Jessica slipped the fancy dress on and adjusted the material over her hips. Drawing a deep breath, she summoned a light tone. "Brooke, stop worrying about me."

"You know I can't help it," her sister replied affectionately.

Jessica smiled, accepting that her sister's protective habits were ingrained since childhood, and Jessica would probably live the rest of her life with Brooke fussing over her. "Yeah, I know."

They exited the rooms to admire each other's outfits in the large, communal mirror in the dressing area. Brooke agreed with Jessica's assessment that the beads and sequins on her dress were too much for her taste, and the gold dress Brooke had selected did nothing to accentuate her figure.

They returned to their rooms for round two.

"So, what did you decide to do for Christmas?" Brooke asked.

Jessica winced. It had been too much to hope that her sister wouldn't inquire about her plans. "Actually, I was invited to spend the holiday with a friend's family." When in reality, she'd been *coerced* into it in a very delicious, tantalizing manner.

"Oh." Brooke sounded surprised. "Anyone I know?"

Jessica closed her eyes, silently asking for forgiveness for her fib. "No, it's a friend from one of the medical offices I do transcripts for." She had no choice but to stretch the truth, because her sister would be all over her for details if she so much as suspected that something was going on between her and Ryan. And there was no sense involving Brooke when the relationship was only temporary.

They met at the mirror again, this time with Brooke wearing a leopard print dress that was too tight across the bodice and puckered at the zipper, and Jessica in a pale gray jersey that did nothing for her complexion. With a shake of both of their heads, they returned to change into their next outfits.

Jessica slipped into her next dress, a vibrant, royal-blue silky sheath that caressed her skin in a very luxurious way. She thought about Ryan, and what he'd think of the dress, and suspected he'd be more interested in finding out what she wore beneath it.

A shiver stole through her, and without thinking she asked her sister a question that had been on her mind since her discussion with Ryan in his office about relationships. "Brooke...how did you know that Marc was *the one?*"

.There was a quiet pause from her sister's dressing room, then, "Why do you ask?"

"Just curious," she replied, though she knew her inquiry wasn't as simple as that. She needed to know what made a woman give her heart to a man, not that she intended to give Ryan hers, of course.

"Well, quite honestly I didn't know Marc. was *the one,* not until I'd almost lost him and came to realize just how much I loved him." Brooke laughed lightly. "And it took him a while to come around, too, if you'll recall."

Jessica smiled, remembering Marc's reluctance, and his belief that Brooke was better off without him. Now, it was hard to imagine the two ever being apart. "But didn't you love Eric, too?" She had to bring up Brooke's first husband, unable to stop her own personal doubts from creeping into the conversation.

"Well, of course I did, but sometimes people don't have the same expectations of a relationship, and Eric and I realized that we married for the wrong reasons. Unfortunately, it happens sometimes, just like with Mom and Dad." There was the faint sound of material rustling and settling into place, then Brooke continued. "It's hard to explain, Jess, but I love Marc in such a way that I can't imagine living without him. When you meet the right guy, you'll just *know.*"

A lump formed in Jessica's throat, one she had trouble swallowing back. She absorbed her sister's words, wondering if maybe her expectations were unrealistic. Wondering, too, if she'd ever be able to put such unconditional faith and trust in a man for her happiness, as Brooke had with Marc. The prospect made her stomach clench, and brought on a tidal wave of fears and insecurities she'd been clinging to since the day her father had turned his back on their family. She'd trusted him, believed in him, and she'd never forgiven him for callously destroying her safe, secure haven.

Brooke knocked on her door, jarring Jessica out of her painful memories. "Hey, are you changed yet?" she asked.

"Just a sec." Pushing those disturbing thoughts from her mind, Jessica exited the dressing room and met Brooke at the mirror.

She gazed at their reflections, seeing past the outfits they wore. While she and Brooke were similar in looks, and they'd gone through the same childhood turmoil, they'd both reacted differently to the experience. Brooke made the best of situations, opting toward making responsible, sensible and pragmatic decisions. Jessica was practical, too, but had discovered it was easier, and less painful, if she safeguarded her heart and emotions.

And that explained why she was still alone and single, she knew. And she also knew and accepted that with Ryan's goals, profession and carefree outlook on relationships that he wasn't the kind of man she could have a future with, either. He'd made her no promises, and that was probably for the best, for both of them.

But that knowledge only served to make her more determined to take what Ryan was offering, and enjoy what she could of their affair.

She focused on the images of her and Brooke and the dresses they wore, both of which complemented their figures and complexions perfectly. Jessica smiled. "Well?"

"What do you think?" her sister asked at the same moment.

They both looked into the mirror, then at each other.

"You look fabulous," they echoed in unison, and laughed.

"HO, HO, HO! Merry Christmas!"

The deep, baritone voice resounded in the Matthews' spacious family room where everyone was gathered. Jessica watched in amazement and delight as Ryan's five nieces and nephews stopped whatever they were doing and turned wide-eyed to the jolly man in red standing in the doorway, wearing a full white beard, gold-rimmed glasses, and carrying a bulging, red velvet sack over his shoulder.

"It's Santa!" three-year-old Alyssa breathed, as if she couldn't quite believe her eyes.

"He's here, he's here!" Six-year-old Richie squealed in unabashed excitement.

Total chaos erupted as four little kids stampeded toward "Santa" and clamored around him for attention. Max, the youngest at two, decided to observe from a distance, his gaze narrowed, as if he wasn't quite sure who the big, boisterous stranger was, or if he wanted to approach him just yet. The adults sat back and watched, letting the little guy make the decision for himself.

Courtney, one of Ryan's older sisters, slid into the empty seat beside Jessica and spoke out of the corner of her mouth. "You'd think that Jackie would figure out that Santa is really her uncle Ryan, but for two years now she's been just as enthralled as the other kids."

Jackie, Jessica had learned, was seven years old, and though she seemed very mature for her age, when it came to believing in St. Nick, she was just as gullible as the others. "Sometimes it's hard to let go of that illusion," she replied, knowing she was speaking from her own childhood experiences. "And it's nice to see them enjoy it for as long as possible."

Courtney agreed, and they both turned their attention back to the Christmas Eve surprise unfolding for the little ones, none of whom had seemed to notice that Ryan had slipped out of the room twenty minutes ago, or that he wasn't currently present. Once "Santa" calmed the excited kids, he addressed them one at a time, letting each one sit on his lap and tell him what they wanted for Christmas. Then, he pulled out a special gift for them from his velvet bag, and went on to the next captivated child. His patience and affection for his nieces and nephews was apparent and made Jessica experience an odd tug near the vicinity of her heart.

Jennifer ripped open her present and gasped when she revealed what Santa had given her, which had been one of the things she'd just asked him for. Jessica smothered a grin—she and Ryan had gone toy shopping a few days ago with a list from his sisters of what the children wanted.

"Mom, Dad! Santa brought me the Herbee I asked for!"

Jennifer cried jubilantly as she held up a small square box for everyone to see the furry, animated creature that spoke nonstop and was no doubt designed to drive an adult certifiably nuts.

"Thank you, Santa," Courtney said wryly, and Ryan replied with a hearty, "Ho, ho, ho," that had the other adults chuckling.

As Richie hopped off Santa's lap with his own gift and Alyssa climbed on, Ryan glanced Jessica's way, and their gazes met. His brown eyes twinkled just as merrily as his namesake, and the wink he gave her was very private and made her cheeks warm. Fortunately, everyone else in the room was preoccupied and hadn't witnessed the intimate exchange.

. When they'd arrived at Ryan's parents' house four hours ago, Nancy and Conrad Matthews had welcomed her as if she *were* part of their family, despite that Ryan had held true to his word and had introduced her simply as a friend. And though everyone had accepted his introduction without question, Jessica was fairly certain that his mother and sisters were wondering about the real scoop between her and Ryan. Knowing she'd probably never spend Christmas with his family again, she preferred that they believed his explanation.

She outright envied the love and security so evident in his family, how warm and supportive they seemed to be. They had fun together, they laughed and teased, and it was apparent that Ryan's mother took extra care in creating a holiday atmosphere meant to make lasting memories. Before Santa's arrival, the kitchen had been bustling—with finger foods and holiday treats to snack on, and with Jessica and Natalie helping the children to bake cookies to leave for St. Nick when they went to bed for the night.

The whole evening was magical and something Jessica knew she'd never forget. And for the first time since she was a little girl, she was wrapped up in the sense of belonging—and had to firmly remind herself that although Ryan had shared this holiday and his family with her, it wasn't something she'd be a part of in the future.

Jessica pulled her thoughts back to the present, and realized that all the kids had taken a turn with Santa, except for Max, who was still eyeing him warily from across the room. Wanting the little boy to share in the fun and spirit of St. Nick, she leaned forward until she caught Max's mom's attention.

"Can I take him to see Santa?" Jessica asked Lindsay.

The other woman smiled and nodded. "Go right ahead."

Jessica approached the toddler, and his big brown eyes, the same shade as his uncle's, darted from her to his mother. Lindsay must have silently reassured him somehow, because he visibly relaxed.

She squatted in front of him and gentled her voice. "You know, I've never met Santa personally, either, so what do you say we go together?"

Max swallowed and sneaked a peek at Santa, the yearning in his gaze clear. Seemingly deciding that he'd be safer with an escort, he nodded his head jerkily, and placed his tiny hand in hers.

Jessica accompanied Max to the man in red, and sat him on Ryan's knee, but remained close so the little boy didn't panic.

Santa patted Max's thigh in a gesture meant to reassure him. "I hear you've been a very good boy this year," Ryan said, his voice deliberately gruff to disguise it.

Max, eyes round as he stared at Ryan's huge white beard, nodded mutely.

"Would you like to tell me what you'd like for Christmas?"

Max shook his head "no" in response, still uncertain of this jolly, strange man.

"Well, I think I might have something in my bag that you'd like." Ryan withdrew the last gaily wrapped present, and handed it to Max.

"Thank you," the little boy whispered, then scrambled off Santa's lap and bolted for the safety of his father, Clive, who sat across the room watching the show.

Jessica stepped away to return to her seat, but a white-gloved hand caught her wrist, gently tugged her back, and she found herself sitting on Santa's very hard, muscular thigh. She gasped in surprise that he'd so openly flirt with her in front of his family when his behavior toward her had been platonic all evening.

A dark brow quirked over the rim of his ridiculous-looking spectacles. "So, has Jessica been naughty or nice this year?" he murmured, his deep, rich voice sending a shiver rippling down her spine.

She could feel a blush tingling along her skin, as well as the curious stares of his mother and sisters. Luckily, the kids were being so loud that it was impossible to hear her and Ryan's conversation.

"I've been so good that I'm probably one of the top ten names on your list." She grinned, and decided to turn the tables on him. "And what about yourself, Santa?"

He looked surprised at her direct challenge, then his eyes sparkled with a wicked, unrepentant light, and she knew trouble was heading her way. "Oh, definitely naughty. I'm expecting a lump of coal in my stocking this year, but all the fun I've had has been worth it."

She laughed, not wanting to think about the kind of "fun" Ryan might have indulged in. She was certainly well aware of how naughty he'd been with her. Feeling a little mischievous herself, she leaned close and whispered in his ear, "Naughty and nice can make for a very interesting combination."

He released a very hearty "ho, ho, ho," then added more privately, "I'll certainly keep that in mind when I bring you *your* gift."

'TWAS THE NIGHT before Christmas, and all through the house, not a creature was stirring, not even a mouse…just Ryan.

It was a quarter until midnight, the house was dark and silent, and Ryan stealthily crept upstairs, avoiding the wooden planks he'd discovered as a teenager that creaked. He snuck past his parents' closed door, and continued down the hall past his sisters' rooms, where they slept with their husbands and kids, to his old bedroom where Jessica was sleeping for the night while he took the couch downstairs. Slipping quietly into the shadowed room, he moved toward the bed.

"Ryan?" came Jessica's husky whisper.

"Yeah, it's me," he confirmed, sitting on the edge of the mattress.

"What are you doing in here?" She propped herself up on her elbow, and the moonlight filtering through the window made her tousled, honey-blond hair shimmer around her shoulders. "It's nearly midnight, and your parents are right down the hall—"

He pressed his fingers to her lips, stopping her chastisement. "Yeah, and you're gonna wake everyone up if you don't be quiet."

Her eyes widened slightly, and she pulled his hand away. "Ryan, I was just teasing about that naughty and nice thing. I mean, we can't do anything *now,* and especially not under your parents' roof."

She sounded so prim and proper, he couldn't help but grin. "Oh, I plan to take you up on your naughty and nice comment, but that's not why I'm here," he said, keeping his voice low. "I want you to come with me." He stood, and waited for her to do the same.

She frowned up at him. "Why?"

He propped his hands on his hips and exhaled a breath, summoning patience. Would she always question his motives? Would she ever believe and accept that his interest in her went beyond his original plan of seducing her?

"Because I asked," he said, deliberately vague. A simple issue of trust was at stake, and he wanted her to acknowledge that she trusted him, even on this small, insignificant issue.

After a brief hesitation, she tossed back the covers and slipped off the bed, garbed from neck to toes in a long-sleeved nightshirt, bottoms and socks.

"Nice pajamas," he teased.

She scrunched her nose at him as her gaze took in his cotton shorts and T-shirt. "If you haven't noticed, it's winter, and flannel is warm."

"As an alternative, I suppose it suffices," he murmured. "But body heat can be just as effective."

She rolled her eyes at his innuendo, but accepted the hand he held out to her. Then, like two little kids wanting to catch Santa in action, they snuck back downstairs to the dark family room. Ryan hit a switch on the wall, and the lights on the Christmas tree came on, their twinkling colors providing a dazzling, magical atmosphere.

"What are you going to do?" Jessica asked in a hushed voice filled with amusement. "Find out which ones are your gifts and shake them?"

He chuckled. "No, you and I are going to put Santa's

gifts under the tree, which has somehow become my job over the years. And then we have cookies to eat and milk to drink so the little imps upstairs will know that Santa was really here."

She glanced at the coffee table, where the kids had left a plate piled high with the sugar cookies they'd made that evening, and a glass of milk that had no doubt turned warm. A brief glimpse of melancholy flickered over her expression, but by the time she met his gaze again whatever emotional memory she'd been caught up in was gone.

She smiled at him. "Well, let's get started," she said, enthusiasm infusing her voice.

She followed him to the coat closet that doubled as a storage area under the stairs, and they spent the next half hour hauling presents out and placing them under the tree until the corner of the room was overflowing with gaily wrapped gifts. His sisters had left small bags of items to stuff in the kids' stockings, and by the time he and Jessica were done, it appeared that Santa had, indeed, paid a visit to the Matthews home.

"And now for the cookies," Jessica reminded him, caught up in the spirit of things, just as he'd intended.

After the snippets she'd revealed about her childhood, he'd suspected that it had been a long time since she'd enjoyed such frivolous fun, and it made his heart swell that he was able to share this with her. "Let me go get a fresh glass of milk."

He returned a minute later and sat beside her on the couch. The blinking lights from the tree cast pretty highlights in her hair, and made her eyes shimmer with the delight still lingering from their escapade of playing Santa's helpers.

He picked up a cookie sprinkled with red and green sugar, and popped the entire thing into his mouth and chewed. "I think this is the best part of Christmas."

She slanted him a curious look as she selected her own baked confection, then nibbled on it. "What? Eating the cookies?"

He shook his head, and washed down his bite with a drink of milk. "Knowing that the kids are going to come downstairs in the morning and see the gifts under the tree and the plate with crumbs on it, and truly believe that Santa was here." He filched another cookie, and thought about himself as a young boy on Christmas, so filled with energy and excitement, until he'd discovered the truth about St. Nick. "I remember I was so crushed when I learned there was no Santa Claus."

"How did you find out?" She shared his glass of milk, then licked the remaining droplets off her lips.

Ignoring the automatic desire that flared to life within him at Jessica's innocent gesture, he reminded himself that this weekend wasn't about the seduction they'd yet to consummate. Averting his attention, he took one of the remaining cookies between his fingers and crushed it to leave visible crumbs on the plate. "Well, I thought I'd be creative and test the Santa theory, and instead of leaving cookies for him, I insisted on making him a peanut butter and sardine sandwich."

"Oh, yuck." She blanched, her expression reflecting her disgust at the combination. "Were you trying to assure that Santa never paid another visit to your house?"

He chuckled. "Well, I remember thinking if the sandwich was gone, then there really was a Santa because he'd be so hungry from his trip around the world that he'd eat it, or feed it to Rudolph. But if it was still there in the morning, then there wasn't really a Santa, because no normal person would eat something so awful."

"Interesting theory," she said, her tone wry. "And what happened?"

"In the morning, it was gone." He licked the remnants of sugar from his fingers.

"Your parents ate it?" she asked incredulously.

"Not exactly." Grinning, he reclined against the sofa cushions and stacked his hands behind his head. "I found it in the trash. I was eight, and I think I was ready to discover the truth, but I was still crushed."

She nodded in understanding, and there was that melancholy again.

"What about you?" he asked, tugging on her pajama sleeve before she could emotionally retreat from him. "When did you discover that there wasn't really a Santa Claus?"

Sitting back, she drew her knees up on the couch and wrapped her arms around her legs. "Well, it was the year my parents divorced." She gave him a sad smile that made him ache for her. "I was nine years old, and after losing my father, believing in Santa Claus was just so important to me. A part of me knew he wasn't real, but I clung to the fairy tale."

With a soft sigh, she rested her chin on her knees and focused on the Christmas tree lights. "I remember asking for the newest, latest Barbie playhouse that was out at the time. It was really expensive, and Brooke kept giving me the spiel that Santa has a lot of kids to bring gifts to, and not all kids get what they want. She knew where the presents came from, and also knew I was in for a big letdown. Still, that was the only thing

I put on my list, because I wanted so badly to believe that Santa was real, and that he'd bring me that one toy because I knew it was too expensive for my mother to afford."

She ducked her head so he couldn't see her face, but her trembling voice gave her away. "My mother was hardly ever home because she was working two jobs, and when I heard her come in on Christmas Eve after working her late shift at a restaurant, I snuck out to the living room and saw her sitting on the floor wrapping presents. And there, among a few inexpensive trinkets for me and Brooke was the Barbie playhouse I'd asked for. And in the morning, it had a tag on it that said, 'From Santa'."

Finally, she turned and looked at him, the moisture in her eyes revealing her inner pain. "As much as I loved my mother for scrimping and saving to give me my one wish, I stopped believing in a lot of things that Christmas."

Her anguish seemingly became his own, squeezing his chest tight, and the only thing he could think of was chasing away her misery and bad memories and giving her something she could cling to and depend on. Him.

"Jessie, sweetheart," he whispered, and reached for her, because mere words were inadequate to soothe her. She came into his embrace without resisting, burrowing into him like a lost soul seeking comfort. Wrapping an arm around her back and holding her close, he eased them both down onto the couch so she was lying between him and the cushions, cocooned in his warmth and strength.

She buried her face against his neck, and a great, big shuddering sigh wracked her entire body. Then, he felt the hot dampness of tears seeping through his T-shirt, and knew all he could do was just be there for her while she came to terms with the pain of her past.

He cuddled her close and watched the tree lights dance in front of them, stroking her side and hip through her flannel pajamas until her breathing grew deep and even and he knew she'd succumbed to peaceful sleep. In a few minutes, he'd wake her up and take her back to her room. In the meantime, he savored the feel of her, the jasmine scent of her hair and skin, and how perfectly she fit into his life…and he came to realize with a calm acceptance that despite not looking for love, he'd found it with her. And no matter what he had to do, he wanted to make room for her in his life, his future.

If only she'd allow him into her heart.

JESSICA SNUGGLED closer to the warm, masculine body next to hers, luxuriating in the sense of complete contentment and security enveloping her. Their sleeping quarters were cramped, but she didn't mind. Her head rested on Ryan's chest, her arm was slung over his stomach, and her legs entwined with his. A sleepy smile touched her lips when she realized that one of Ryan's hands was tangled in her hair, and his warm breath brushed across her temple.

She'd never *slept* with a man before, nor had any man ever held her so tenderly, without expecting a sexual favor in return. And despite the desire that Ryan inspired, she liked the feeling of just being held in his arms, especially after last night and the desolate memories that had swamped her. He'd silently consoled her and allayed the loneliness that had been her constant companion for far too long.

Yet, she knew the isolation and solitude would return

once he was no longer a part of her life. And as much as the thought of letting Ryan go hurt, she accepted it as inevitable, knowing their lives, their aspirations and dreams for the future, didn't mesh.

Ignoring the ache in her heart, she sighed and rubbed her cheek against his chest, focusing on the present and what they had in common—their attraction, desire and passion. And for now, for today and the next week, she planned to be greedy and experience it all. And then, when that awful loneliness settled in, she'd have wondrous memories to draw on, to keep her warm on the long, solitary nights ahead.

The sound of hushed whispers and stifled giggles reached past Jessica's musings, and brought her back to the present. She blinked her eyes open and found herself staring at Ryan's three nieces, who stood in front of the couch watching them sleep. From the other room, she could hear the adults approaching, too. Not sure how to handle the situation or explain their dilemma, even though they'd done nothing wrong, she gave Ryan a firm shake.

He awoke, slowly and lazily. His slumberous gaze met hers, and a sexy smile eased up the corners of his mouth. "Morning," he murmured.

Trying not to let that husky, intimate voice of his and just how gorgeous he looked first thing in the morning distract her, she nodded toward the trio in front of them. "Uh, we've got company."

Ryan turned his head, and though his body tensed with instant awareness, his expression gave nothing away. "Morning, girls," he said cheerfully.

"Uncle Ryan," Jackie said, a slight frown marring

her brows. "How come you and Jessica are sleeping on the couch?"

"Well…" His voice trailed off as he obviously tried to conjure an excuse. Taking more time, he sat up, just as the rest of the Matthews clan converged in the family room. Surprise and speculation registered across everyone's faces at seeing them together, and Jessica felt her face flush at being caught in such an embarrassing predicament.

"Hey, did you two get to see Santa last night?" Ryan's sister Lindsay asked, amusement lacing her voice.

Alyssa's eyes rounded with hope at that thought. "Did you?"

Richie dashed past his father and raced into the room, dancing around the coffee table, pointing to the plate with the crumbs on it, and the empty milk glass. "Look, Santa ate the cookies and drank the milk! Did you see him, Uncle Ryan? Did you?"

Ryan dragged a hand through his tousled hair and grinned. "The thing is, Jessica and I snuck down here last night and tried to stay awake for Santa, but we were so tired that we just didn't make it." He shook his head regretfully.

"But look at all the presents he left," Jennifer said, scrambling over to the tree and the overflow of gifts. "Here's one for me, and one for Max and one for Grandma…"

As the kids squealed in excitement and huddled around the tree, and the adults moved in to help sort and pass out the presents to the eager children, Ryan took the opportunity to grasp a private moment with Jessica.

"I'm sorry," he whispered, appearing contrite at the

awkward situation he'd put her in. "I swear I didn't mean for us to fall asleep together and wake up with an audience."

She smiled to reassure him. "It's okay."

Uncaring of who might see the affectionate gesture, he stroked his knuckles down her cheek, then tucked a wayward strand of hair behind her ear. "You ready to enjoy Christmas morning, Matthews style?"

She shivered at his touch, reveling in the warmth and tenderness in his gaze. "Yeah, I am."

And as she watched Ryan with his nieces and nephews, and was accepted so completely into the fold of his family, she knew this sense of belonging would be her most precious memory of all.

# CHAPTER TEN

*TONIGHT'S THE NIGHT.*

Rod Stewart's raspy voice and the classic lyrics to that sexy song reached Ryan just as he stepped into his house from the garage after an unexpectedly long day at the office. Having seen Jessica's car parked out by the curb, he knew she was decorating for the New Year's Eve party, which was tomorrow night.

Using the key he'd given her, she'd spent the past two afternoons setting up chairs, bringing in party supplies, and embellishing the bottom level rooms of his house with twinkling lights and flora. They'd been so busy since Christmas, both of them preparing for the surprise party and him wrapping up loose ends on a few cases at work, that they hadn't had any private, intimate time for *them*.

Tonight, there was something different in the air, an undeniable sensuality and desire that made his blood warm in his veins and his heart beat faster. Feeling drawn in by the sultry mood of the music, and seduced by the sexy lyrics that seemed so fitting to what Ryan felt for Jessica, he headed toward the front room in search of the only woman who'd ever managed to capture a significant piece of his heart.

She'd also managed to charm his family, too, as he'd known she would. His mother had specifically called him at work to tell him how much she'd enjoyed Jessica's company, and that she hoped to see more of her in the future. Though Ryan would have liked to assure his parents that Jessica would be a part of his life, he knew he couldn't make that promise. Not yet, but maybe after tonight that would change, because he planned to take a huge risk and wear his emotions on his sleeve.

With Rod Stewart's raspy voice swirling around him, he turned the last corner into the living room, and came to an abrupt stop. Because of the music, Jessica hadn't heard him enter the house from the garage. She was busy twining a string of white lights along the bottom of the spiral staircase railing, but what captured his attention were her uninhibited, sinuous movements as she danced to the classic tune. Her husky voice sang the suggestive lyrics, while her hips swayed to the beat of the music, slow and enticing. Then she closed her eyes, lifted her arms, and undulated—a full-bodied shimmy as captivating as any exotic dancer's move.

He grew hard just watching her, wanting her with a hunger and need that superceded anything he'd ever experienced. And then it hit him…the pure rightness of the moment. Despite all he'd achieved professionally, *this* is what had been missing from his life. Jessica, with her sass and laughter and warmth. Jessica, filling his soul, his waking hours. *She* was who he wanted to come home to every day. *She* was who he wanted to sleep with at night.

And then that revelation faded as she twirled around and gasped in breathless shock to find him standing less than five feet away, watching her. Her face flushed pink, and instead of the embarrassment he'd expected, her eyes turned a dark, velvet shade of blue. The color of desire and passion.

He blinked lazily, and allowed a rakish grin to tip the corner of his mouth. "Don't stop on my account." He heard the deep, male nuances of arousal in his voice, despite his casual tone.

With a beguiling smile, she stepped into the living room, grabbed the remote for his CD player, and pressed the Repeat button to play the last song again. He thought she planned to give him another provocative show, but instead of gyrating those hips for his sole pleasure, she turned and held out her hand to him.

"I've got a better idea," she said, meeting his gaze steadily. "Why don't you join me?"

A deliberate dare, an irresistible challenge, one he was fully prepared to accept because he knew that everything that had been building and growing between them for the past year had led to this moment. Shrugging out of his sports coat and tossing it onto the couch, he closed the distance between them. He gathered her in his arms, nudged a thigh between hers and pulled her flush against his hard length until the only thing separating them was the one inch of space between their parted lips.

But she didn't kiss him, and he didn't kiss her—though not for a lack of desire. If tonight *was* the night, it belonged to Jessica, and she'd be the one to make the physical connection between them finally happen.

She seduced him in subtle ways. To the alluring beat of the music, she teased him with the erotic brush of her body along his, tempted him with the crush of her full breasts against his chest. He followed her lead, tantalizing her with the stroke of his hands along her lithe hips, her bottom, and along the backs of her thighs encased in form-fitting black leggings.

She closed her eyes on a soft moan and moved rhythmically, sensually, against his muscular thigh. He clasped her hips tighter, dragged her closer, increasing the friction and pressure until her breathing hitched, an unmistakable sign that a climax was imminent.

The music stopped, and so did Ryan, leaving Jessica on edge and just as aroused and inflamed as he was. Her lashes fluttered open, and there it was in the depth of her eyes, the complete and total acquiescence he'd been waiting for since that afternoon in his bathtub when she'd asked him to make love to her. Now, the request wasn't necessary, because the moment was *right,* and she was ready for it to happen.

She knew it as well as he did.

Without words, she ran her palm down his arm to his hand, and entwined their fingers. Then, with Rod Stewart singing "You're In My Heart, You're In My Soul," he followed her upstairs to his bedroom. He shut the door behind them, not wanting anything to intrude on their first time together, nor did he intend to share his bed with anyone but Jessica. Camelot would have to find other lodgings for the night.

He turned on the bedside lamp, wanting to see everything…the unveiling of Jessica's supple curves, her incredible blue eyes when he finally came inside her, and her expression when he revealed just how deeply his feelings for her ran.

There wasn't a hint of modesty about her now, just a feminine confidence he'd spent the past month cultivating. His patience had been worthwhile, because he wouldn't accept anything less than her full surrender.

Easing his warm hands beneath the hem of the sweater she wore, he slowly skimmed along her sides as he pulled the top up and over her head, then let it drop to the floor as his gaze discovered a delightful surprise…a flesh-tone, stretch-lace, low-cut bra that lifted and shaped her breasts.

He lifted a brow in teasing inquiry, boldly traced the scalloped edge of the bra that dipped into very enticing cleavage, and watched her nipples tighten for him. "What's this?"

She drew a breath that made those full, perfect mounds of flesh quiver. "I've taken a liking to pretty lingerie."

Smiling, he skimmed his finger down her abdomen, to the waistband of her leggings. "You know you turn me on in your cotton underwear, but I like the way this looks on you. And it makes me wonder what you're wearing beneath these pants." In time, he'd find out.

But first things first. Reaching behind her, he unclasped the hooks of her bra, then eased the straps off her shoulders until the lacy garment joined her sweater on the floor. Because words eluded him, he groaned to express his appreciation of what he'd revealed, then he lowered his head and *showed* her. Burying his face between her lush breasts, he inhaled her scent, then lapped his warm, wet tongue over the full slopes, grazed his teeth over the tight crests. On a startled gasp, she fisted her hands in his hair and let him taste his fill of her.

It was only the beginning. Slipping his hands into the waistband of her leggings, he dragged the stretchy fabric down her slender legs, and moved his mouth lower, too, kissing her smooth, silky belly, the insides of her thighs, and lingered there as she stepped from her pants. Then he took in the matching, lacy, beige panties she wore, and couldn't resist pressing a hot, open-mouthed kiss to the satin covering her mound. She moaned, and trembled, and before he gave in to the urge to indulge in a more intimate exploration, he straightened to his full height, toed off his shoes, and pulled off his socks.

The rest was up to her.

He spread his hands in front of him. "I'm all yours, sweetheart," he said, meaning it in more ways than the obvious.

Grabbing his tie, she wrapped the strip of silk around her fist, drawing him closer. She cast him an upswept glance, full of sass and feminine wiles…and just the barest hint of vulnerability. "How can you tell if a lawyer is well hung?"

Before he could recover from his surprise at her question, she replied with, "You can't fit a finger between the rope and his neck."

His mouth quirked with amusement, but he wasn't about to let her retreat or hide behind her brand of humor. Not here and not now. "There's another way to tell if he's well hung," he said, and guided her free hand to the fierce erection straining the front of his trousers.

Dampening her bottom lip with her tongue, she squeezed the length of him, stroked him through his pants until he groaned, shuddered and had to grab her wrist to halt her caresses.

"*Very* impressive, counselor." She tugged him closer with her grip on his tie, and settled her mouth over his, drugging him with her deep, leisurely kiss.

He let her set the pace, knowing his turn would come later. She proceeded to undress him, taking her time stripping off each article of clothing until he was completely naked. Then, starting at his neck and traveling south, she explored his hard, hot skin with the glide of her palms, her soft lips, and the wet warmth of her tongue until his breathing grew ragged, his body throbbed with need, and his control and restraint teetered on the verge of snapping. He had to stop her, or he wasn't going to last.

"Jessica…" he groaned her name, and threading his fingers through her silky hair, he drew her up against his body and slanted his mouth across hers, tasting the salty, musky essence of him on her tongue. As one kiss inevitably, enticingly melted into another, he guided them toward his bed, until the backs of her thighs met the mattress.

Reluctantly, he let her go, knowing he needed to put on protection while he was still able to think with a semblance of clarity. As she settled on the bed, and he moved away, an uncertain look passed over her features, as if she thought, *believed,* that he was leaving her. As if he ever could.

"Give me a sec," he rasped, and opened the nightstand drawer to grab a condom.

She lay back against the pillows, watching him though lashes that had fallen to half-mast. Her lips were pink and swollen, her hair tousled around her face, and her lithe body was flushed with feminine desire. She looked so incredibly inviting, so sensual, that he had a difficult time concentrating on his task.

Finally, he managed the deed, and the brief separation from Jessica gave him the reprieve he needed to continue things slowly. She smiled at him as he climbed onto the bed, and she went to remove her lacy panties—the only barrier between them—until he stopped her.

"I want to take them off," he said huskily. But first, he lavished attention on her breasts, curling his tongue along her nipples, taking her deeply into his mouth until she shivered beneath him. His lips tasted her belly, the curve of her waist, while his fingers found the waist-band of her panties and slowly drew them down her slender hips, over her mound, and left them tangled around her thighs for a moment, which restricted the spread of her legs to only a few inches.

She whimpered, the sound filled with frustration. Her hand slid along his shoulder, then curled around the nape of his neck, urging him toward the very heart of her. His mouth followed the path he'd bared, the one she dictated, until her heady, aroused scent filled his every breath. A raw, primitive hunger shot straight to his groin, and he gave in to the instinctive need raging within him. Tucking his chin between her confined thighs, he delved his tongue between her softly swelled flesh and found the sensitive nub hidden within. She gasped and writhed, but he kept her hips pinned to the mattress as he stroked, suckled, and lost himself in the sweetness of her response.

Then, her climax hit. Her back arched and she cried out, loud and unabashed, and before the convulsions rippling through her ebbed, he had her panties stripped off and was kneeling between her legs, his own breathing labored. Hooking his fingers beneath her knees, he dragged her down so she lay flat on the mattress and her spread thighs draped over his, the tip of his erection teasing her glistening, slick folds.

At that moment he looked into her velvet blue gaze, and the acceptance he saw there arrested him, made his heartbeat quicken and his chest fill with a multitude of emotions that humbled him, and made him wonder, for a split second, if he could be everything Jessica needed him to be. Strong. Reliable. A man who could promise her forever.

He could be, if she *let* him.

And then the fleeting thought receded as Jessica whispered invitingly, "Come inside me, Ryan."

Unable to deny either one of them what they both wanted, he settled his body over hers until they were face to face, guided himself into the hot, liquid center of her, and filled her with one fluid thrust. She gasped sharply, and he groaned deep in his throat at the sweet, tight clenching of her body.

He'd primed her well, yet she was incredibly snug, and the erotic rush of it nearly had him unraveling. With effort, their labored breaths mingling, he moved his hips, withdrawing and surging back into her slowly, feeling her soften around him, beneath him. As she adjusted to the fit of him, her expression turned rapturous. He savored the languorous drift of her hands down his spine, the instinctive way she lifted her hips and wrapped her legs around the back of his thighs to allow him deeper still.

She'd given him her body, and there was only one other place he needed to be. In her heart.

Burying himself to the hilt in one long, smooth stroke, he stilled over her, his pulse racing erratically. He tangled his fingers into the hair at the side of her face, making sure that he had her complete and total attention. She gazed up at him, a sultry smile on her lips, her eyes hazy with passion.

"I love you, Jessica," he said, his voice unmistakably clear.

He felt her tense, saw the panic and denial that flashed across her features, and wasn't surprised at her reaction. While he'd had time to come to terms with his feelings, she'd only had a few seconds. And he didn't expect her to return the declaration, only knew that she needed to hear the words, and believe in them.

With a gentleness that belied his body's need for release, he lowered his head and kissed her, and then she *did* surprise him, opening her mouth wide beneath his and responding with a greed and urgency that shot his plan for tenderness to hell.

A sense of desperation cloaked her, made her as wild and tempestuous as a summer storm...and all he could do was ride the intense waves of pleasure consuming them both. She reached the crest with a shattering cry, and he followed, surrendering to the hot, carnal flames of his own explosive climax.

*I LOVE YOU.*

Curling up in the old, soft, comforting chair in her living room, Jessica swiped at the tears lingering on her cheeks, acknowledging the words that had haunted her all night long. The same words she'd whispered to a sleeping Ryan in a tight, aching voice just before she'd slipped from his bed in the early-morning hours before dawn.

Not only had she snuck out on him, but she'd left the key to his house on the nightstand, along with a hastily written note that she'd see him tonight at the party. Her manner of leaving said what she couldn't put into words—she was ending their affair. After the New Year's Eve party they'd revert to the friendly acquaintances they'd been before.

He wasn't going to be happy to find her gone, or with the cowardly way in which she'd executed her departure—a move born of pure self-preservation, because in that moment when he'd declared his love, she'd finally accepted that she'd fallen for Ryan Matthews deeper than she'd ever intended. And although it was too late to protect her emotions, she could still safeguard what was left of her heart, which hurt as it had never hurt before.

She swallowed back another well of tears and rubbed her hand along the chair's armrest. Without a doubt, she'd wanted Ryan. She'd wanted last night with every fiber of her being. So she'd selfishly taken from him when she'd *known* she couldn't give back—because openly loving him, trusting him with her future, was a heartbreaking combination. It was a harsh lesson taught to her by her father and backed up by her short-lived relationship with Lane. And with Ryan's career being his foremost priority, along with his profession contradicting her need for stability and security, she couldn't depend on him to be there in the long run. By his own admittance, long-term relationships weren't his forte, and she wasn't willing to be the casualty of a failed experiment.

So, she was cutting her losses, letting him go, and taking with her all the glorious, wondrous memories he'd given her. It didn't compare to the real feel of being held in his arms, hearing his deep laughter, or seeing the sexy gleam in his eyes as he attempted to seduce her with one of his erotic shenanigans. She'd never be able to look at a cake without remembering his *slippery, sensual, erotic* promise, which he'd more than fulfilled last night. And taking a bath would be an excruciating reminder of how much fun and pleasure he'd shown her when a couple shared the experience.

She drew a deep, shuddering breath, knowing she'd miss him, knowing she'd *never* regret what they'd shared.

A loud pounding on her door made her jump and jostled her back to the present. She'd known this confrontation was coming, and though she'd resigned herself to facing him, she just hadn't expected the encounter to be at six o'clock in the morning.

"Dammit, Jessica," he said, his deep, gruff voice muffled through the door separating them. "I know you're in there so open up. I'm not leaving until we talk."

She wouldn't expect him to. He wasn't a coward as she'd been. Ryan wanted answers, an explanation, and since he'd been nothing but sincere with her, he deserved her honesty in return. And maybe, if she was lucky, once their discussion was over he'd understand her position and they'd be able to part as friends.

He pounded on the door again, making the whole apartment seem to shake with the wrath that stood out in the hallway. Before he could wake her neighbors, she unlocked and opened her door, feeling surprisingly calm after having had two hours to purge herself of her tears and misery.

He brushed past her into the living room, then stopped, jammed his hands on his hips, and *glared* at her. Not only was he not happy, he was *furious*.

Judging by his appearance, she guessed he'd woken up, realized she was gone, and had grabbed the first article of clothing he'd come into contact with, which was the shirt and slacks he'd worn last night, now wrinkled from being tossed haphazardly to the floor. He'd been in such a hurry that he hadn't bothered to tuck in the tails, nor had he put on any socks. His dark hair was still tousled from her running her fingers through the strands last night, his unshaven jaw was clenched, and his eyes were dark, but rimmed in a bright shade of gold that seared her straight to her soul.

Praying that he wouldn't hate her for what she had to do, for what she'd done, she closed the door, leaned against it, and waited for him to unleash the anger raging just below the surface.

The tempest didn't take long to erupt. He swept a hand in the air, his expression thunderous, showing her a very different side to the sexy, teasing, tender man she knew. "What the hell was that all about, you sneaking out in the middle of the night like I was some kind of one-night stand?"

Even though she knew his question was born of anger, she inwardly winced at his tawdry reference, when last night—the whole month they'd spent together—had been anything but a cheap tryst. The time with him had been magical, sensual, unforgettable.

And temporary.

"I'm sorry," she whispered around the tight knot of emotion in her throat, belatedly realizing the apology was inadequate for her departure, which had been instigated by pure panic.

She drew a breath and flattened her palms against the cool door. "I thought me leaving would be the easiest way to…"

"End things between us?" he finished for her.

The man was very perceptive, but she'd discovered that characteristic about him the past month, among others. "Yes."

"You thought *wrong,* Jessica," he said, his tone vibrating with resentment, and a deeper layer of hurt. "I don't take what we did last night lightly, not after wanting you for the past year. When I went to bed with you, when we made *love,* I expected to wake up with you next to me. Instead, I find the key to my house, and a facsimile of a 'Dear John' letter on my nightstand."

The pressure in her chest felt near unbearable, but she lifted her chin and clung to her convictions. "I know I didn't handle this morning the best way—"

"No, you didn't," he interrupted heatedly, and slowly stalked toward her, a ruthless light in his eyes. "And I don't appreciate you making decisions for me when I'm capable of making them for myself."

Her stomach clenched as he neared. She didn't fear *him,* just his arguments. He was a man used to debating, and winning, and this was one issue on which she had to stand firm. "I made the decision to leave, to end our affair, for myself *and* for you."

He stopped two feet away, the heat and energy radiating off him nearly palpable. "How...*considerate* of you. But what makes you believe I want us to end?"

There was the rub in their situation. Right now, he was so caught up in the physical aspect of their relationship, the new and fresh emotions of love, that he didn't want the euphoria to end. Neither did she, but she was a realist and knew better, and sustaining what was between them now into the distant future was another matter altogether. And too huge a risk to her heart.

Before she could formulate a response, his gaze narrowed and he continued in a demanding tone. "I want reasons, Jessica. Are you ending things because I'm a divorce attorney?"

His question wasn't unwarranted. From the first time

she'd met him at Brooke's cabin a year ago she'd clung to that excuse to keep her attraction to him at bay. She'd been successful, until this month. During the course of the past four weeks, she'd discovered all her preconceived notions about him, about lawyers, had been a defense. She'd always felt the need to blame someone for destroying her family, and blaming her father, and his attorney, had been the easiest route.

There was so much more to Ryan than his profession, and that's what made her choice so difficult. She'd seen many facets to his personality, and beneath the charm and flirtatious manner was a good, kind, caring man. One who enjoyed his family and friends, but ultimately loved his job.

She shook her head in answer to his question, and tried to explain. "No, it's not because you're a divorce attorney, but your career, your ambition and drive, don't leave much room in your life for a committed relationship." The stable, secure kind of relationship she needed.

"How do you *know* that?"

The challenge was unmistakable, and she couldn't help but think of what a formidable opponent he'd be in the courtroom. "I've seen your dedication to your job. I know where you're heading in your firm, and what it's going to take to get there. Long hours. Personal sacrifices. Possibly no extra time to nurture a new relationship. Can you deny that?"

He stared at her for a long, hard moment, then exhaled a harsh breath. "No, I can't deny any of that, but I'm willing to find some kind of balance."

"Well, I can't risk that you might not be able to find that balance, that your goals won't mesh with what I need from a relationship, and that you'll decide after a few months or a year that it's so much easier and simpler remaining single and unattached. Which brings us back to ending our relationship now, before things get any more complicated."

"I love you, Jessica," he said, frustration and tenderness mingling in his voice. "That's about as complicated as it gets."

Her knees nearly buckled at the declaration, made in the light of morning. She didn't doubt his sincerity, not for one second, but the emotional blackmail was excruciating. "I know you do."

He shook his head in confusion. "Doesn't that mean anything to you?"

She couldn't answer him, because his love meant too much. Rejecting it was the most difficult thing she'd ever had to do.

A low, frustrated sound erupted from his chest, and he spun around and paced to the other side of the small living room. Then he abruptly stopped and turned back to face her. "I get it now," he said, a dawning realization touching his features. "You're leaving *me* before I can leave *you,* aren't you?"

Her heart thudded in her chest, and she moved away from the door, but kept her distance from Ryan. "I have no idea what you're talking about."

"Don't you?" A dark brow winged upward. "I'm talking about the fact that you're scared I'll leave you at some point in our relationship, so you're doing it first. It's easier for you not to invest your emotions and not to believe what I feel for you is real, than to trust that I won't hurt you."

She bristled defensively. "You can't make that kind of promise."

"Can anyone?" he countered. He waited a tension-filled minute for her to answer. Then he smiled grimly. "Judging by your silence, I'm taking it that you agree the answer is no. Which means that although you're afraid of being abandoned and alone, that's exactly where you'll stay, because no man will be able to make you that promise. The only guarantee I can give you is how I feel about you. The rest is up to you to trust me."

Despite loving him, she wasn't sure she had the strength and emotional fortitude to put her faith in his hands. Doubts and uncertainties overwhelmed her, tugging her in two different directions. Hot, scalding tears burned her eyes, and she valiantly blinked them back. She pressed her fingers to her trembling lips and turned away so he wouldn't witness her insecurities, even though he knew every single one of them.

A long moment passed, and she flinched when she heard the front door open then close behind Ryan, leaving her completely and utterly alone. The quiet and solitude wrapping around her was absolute, more so than it had ever been.

HE'D DONE ALL HE COULD. Ryan knew that, but it didn't stop him from replaying his conversation with Jessica over and over in his mind, scrutinizing the rebuttals he'd issued to her arguments, trying to figure out what he could have said to sway her, to make her realize his intentions were pure.

There was nothing else he could do. The realization was tough to swallow. For the first time in his life he felt utterly defeated, not over a case, but a woman. A very special, beautiful, sassy, stubborn woman. He'd given Jessica factual evidence of his devotion, not only in words, but in actions, and none of his efforts had made a difference.

Unable to concentrate on the speech he needed to write for tonight's surprise party for Brooke and Marc, he set his pen aside and scrubbed both hands down his face. The knot in his chest hadn't abated since he'd walked out of Jessica's apartment, and he doubted he'd find relief any time soon. Especially not tonight, when he'd be so close to Jessica, but unable to touch her, tease her, and revel in the fact that she was exclusively his.

He'd never intended to fall in love with her, but she'd shown him what was missing from his life…love, laughter and shared intimacies with one very special person. True, he'd managed to remain uncommitted since he was eighteen, but he was coming to believe that being a bachelor hadn't been a conscious choice as much as not finding the right person to complement him.

Jessica complemented him, physically, emotionally and intellectually, in a way that made her feel like his other half. His soul mate. A piece of himself that he hadn't known was missing until she'd entered his life. And deep inside, beneath layers of doubts and uncertainties instilled by a negligent father and an unstable childhood, he suspected that she felt the same.

With a weary sigh, he sat back in his chair and rolled the pen between his fingers. Despite his earlier debate with Jessica, he knew he couldn't force her into believing he'd never deliberately hurt her, or walk out on her without a backward glance. She had to realize his sincerity came straight from his heart, driven by an emotion that was turning out to be more painful than joyful.

After another half hour of brooding over his situation, Ryan resigned himself to the inevitable. There was nothing else he could do to convince Jessica of his love, except let her go. There was nothing else left to say... except goodbye.

And with that aching thought filling his head, he put pen to paper and wrote the toast to Brooke and Marc, using the speech as a way to congratulate the happy couple, put his own feelings down on paper and issue a final farewell to Jessica.

# CHAPTER ELEVEN

"*SURPRISE!*" a loud assembly of guests chorused as Brooke and Marc walked into Ryan's house right on schedule a half hour after everyone else had arrived.

Standing at the front of the group in the silky blue dress she'd bought for the occasion, Jessica watched as Brooke gasped and pressed a hand to her chest, her eyes wide with confusion. Beside her sister, Marc looked on with bemusement as he helped Brooke take off her coat, seemingly unsure of what he and his wife had just stepped into.

Brooke's gaze found Jessica in the gathering of friends and family crowded in Ryan's foyer. "What's all this about?" she asked, bewilderment coloring her voice. Her fingers fluttered self-consciously down the front of her slim black dress, smoothing out imaginary wrinkles. "I thought this was a New Year's Eve party."

Ryan stepped forward before Jessica could respond, and her heart twisted painfully in her chest, adding to the constant ache she'd experienced since arriving two hours ago to help him with the last-minute preparations for the party. Despite what had transpired between them last night, and this morning, he'd been polite and cordial, almost indifferent, and whenever possible he'd kept his distance. He acted as if they'd never spent the past month getting to know each other. As if they'd never indulged in sensual fantasies and made love last night. As if he'd never told her he loved her.

And even though Jessica acknowledged that it had been her choice to end their affair, that she'd been the one to drive him to such extreme measures, the distance he'd already established between them added to her misery. If she was fortunate, in another twenty years the memories they'd created together would no longer smother her. And she'd be able to say his name without feeling as though a piece of her soul had been ripped from her. And maybe, just maybe, she'd be able to live through a whole minute without being consumed by thoughts of him.

"It *is* a New Year's Eve party," Ryan confirmed with an easy grin. He shook Marc's hand in greeting, then placed a chaste kiss on Brooke's cheek. "But it's also a surprise party for you and Marc since you had a small wedding and no reception."

Sentimental emotions touched Brooke's features, and she once again sought Jessica. "Did you know about this, Jess?"

She nodded, her throat too tight to speak.

"Actually, it was her idea," Ryan said, slipping his hands into the front pockets of his black trousers that complemented his black-and-beige pinstriped shirt. "I just supplied the house for the party."

He'd done more than that, and they both knew it. He'd been responsible for a good many of the decisions that had gone into the planning, from the decorations, to the menu, to the huge gift basket overflowing with sensual items, which was sitting on one of the tables laden with presents from the other guests.

"Well, you two shouldn't have," Marc said, though it was obvious he appreciated the gesture, as well.

Jessica forced a cheerful smile. "I wanted to do something special for the both of you." She enveloped each of them in a warm hug, then grabbed her sister's hand and tugged her toward the waiting guests. "Now come on in, and enjoy your evening."

Now that the guests of honor had arrived, the party atmosphere turned lively, loud and fun. Laughter and conversation filtered through the house, the buffet enticed people to eat, and Jessica did her best to have a good time and keep her gaze off Ryan. Yet out of sight was not out of her mind. And every time she thought about not seeing him after tonight, she felt herself die a little more inside.

A few hours later, everyone gathered in the living room to watch Brooke and Marc open their gifts. They received everything from kitchen appliances, to basic accessories and other practical items. The sensual bathroom products she and Ryan had selected were a hit, and caused a bit of ribald teasing. While Marc fended off good-natured ribbing from the male guests, Jessica glanced across the room where she knew Ryan was standing, with his shoulder braced against the wall and a drink in hand.

Her breath caught when she found him watching her, a flicker of warmth in his eyes, as if he, too, was remembering the fun they'd had testing their own supply of those items. She recalled how incredibly patient he'd been with her...and she'd repaid him by rejecting his love.

He looked away when his sister, Natalie, came up to his side and said something to him. Ignoring the sense of loss settling over her, Jessica returned her attention to her sister and Marc, and was chagrined to realize that Brooke had caught the exchange between her and Ryan. Her sister's brow quirked curiously at her, and Jessica pretended not to understand the questioning look.

Once the gift opening was over, Jessica mingled with the guests, then met up with her sister, who was enjoying a slice of one of the cakes. Brooke took a bite of the confection and rolled her eyes heavenward as she savored the taste.

"Oh, wow, this cake is *incredible,*" Brooke said, and held out a forkful to Jessica. "Do you want a bite?"

The dessert Brooke offered was the Better Than Sex Cake. Jessica suppressed a shiver of recollection and shook her head. She'd be so grateful when the evening was over and she could escape everything that reminded her of Ryan and the time they'd spent together.

She'd return to her quiet, lonely apartment and continue her quiet, lonely, solitary life, a little voice in the back of her mind taunted. Before she could stop herself, a painful sigh unraveled out of her.

Brooke tipped her head, regarding her with concern. "Hey, are you okay?"

"Sure. I'm great." Her voice vibrated with false lightness, and she added a quick smile as backup. "Why?"

"You just seem, well, upset about something." Brooke took another bite of the dessert, and seemed to contemplate Jessica's mood. "Did you and Ryan have an argument?"

Oh, yeah, a huge, life-altering one.

"I mean, you must have had to spend some time together while planning this surprise party," Brooke went on while finishing her cake. "And I know how the two of you are around each other. The air fairly crackles with tension when you're together. But now it seems like you're avoiding each other."

"Don't we always?" she quipped.

"Not like this, Jess. You're *deliberately* avoiding each other, and despite your lawyer jokes and Ryan's teasing, that's never kept the two of you *apart* when you're in the same room." She set her plate aside. "Is something going on between the two of you?"

She wanted so badly to confide in her sister, but her emotions were in such turmoil, she didn't know where to begin, or what to say.

And then she lost the opportunity as the *ping, ping, ping* of silver against crystal captured everyone's attention. The guests grew quiet, and all eyes turned to Ryan, who stood in the middle of the living room with a glass of champagne in his hand.

He smiled, but his eyes lacked their normal sparkle. "It's ten minutes to midnight, and before we bring in the new year, I'd like for everyone to grab a drink so I can make a toast to Marc and Brooke."

It took nearly five minutes for family and friends to grab their choice of drink and settle back into the room. Once everyone was present, and Marc and Brooke were situated next to Ryan to receive his best-man speech, he cleared his throat and began.

"I've known Marc for quite a few years now, and I always thought he'd remain a bachelor forever, or at least that was his plan." Chuckles rippled through the small audience before Ryan continued. "When Marc fell in love with Brooke, I knew that she had to be a really special woman, one with a giving heart and the capacity to accept Marc for who and what he was. I knew she'd be the kind of woman who'd be his best friend through trials and triumphs. It is said that no man is complete until he finds the right woman to marry, and it's clear that Brooke has made Marc's life complete. Every man should be so fortunate."

Jessica stood behind Brooke and Marc, and belatedly realized her mistake in positioning herself so close to the bride and groom when Ryan's gaze subtly shifted to her. A frisson of awareness shot through her, and her insides began to tremble.

He didn't look away, and she couldn't either. "I've only been in love once, but I understand how powerful that emotion can be. I also know that there are times when love can be painful and trying, so I'd like to say a few things for you to keep in mind for the years ahead. Love without fear. Trust without questioning. Accept without change, and desire each other without inhibitions. Always believe in one another, and always have faith." He raised his flute of champagne to the happy couple, and everyone followed his lead. "Here's to love and laughter, and your happily ever after."

"Hear, hear," the guests echoed jovially, and Jessica was hardly aware of someone next to her clinking their glass against hers as she watched Marc kiss her sister with the kind of the love and tenderness Ryan had shown her.

Emotions clamored in her chest, her mind spun and she struggled to keep herself grounded. Tears tightened her throat and burned the back of her eyes. Though Ryan's toast was for Brooke and Marc, the profound words beckoned to her, and made her realize what she'd never, ever have in her life—love, laughter and her own happily ever after.

"Hey, everybody," someone in the room called out. "It's the countdown to midnight!"

The guests began counting down from ten, until finally the old year rolled into the new one and everyone cheered, hugged, and wished one another a happy new year.

Unable to participate in the ritual when she had absolutely nothing to celebrate, Jessica slipped from the room as inconspicuously as possible, taking her heartache with her.

BROOKE FOUND HER in the downstairs study minutes later. Jessica barely had time to swipe the tears from her cheeks before her sister laid into her.

"I *knew* something was going on between you and Ryan. He might have made that toast to Marc and me, but he was looking at *you,* Jessica." Brooke crossed her arms over her chest, exerting her big-sister presence. "Out with it," she demanded.

Jessica didn't bother to pretend she didn't know what Brooke was referring to. This time, she let the floodgates open and told her sister about the past month with Ryan, how she'd seen such a different side to him than she'd always believed, how she'd fallen in love with him, and ultimately, how she doubted her ability to trust in him because of her fears.

Brooke grabbed her hands and gave them a gentle squeeze. "Ah, Jess, sometimes following your heart is one of the most difficult things you'll ever do."

"But what if—"

Brooke shook her head, cutting off her sister's argument. "There are no 'what ifs' when you're in love. It just *is.* And despite what you might believe, not every man is like Dad."

"You know," she breathed, not at all surprised that her sister understood her so well.

"Yeah, I know that his leaving devastated you and made you feel insecure about so many things. I know our life was tough, but we made it just fine, Jess." Brooke smiled, and brushed a stray strand of hair off her cheek. "*You* made it just fine. And I don't want to see you lose the best thing that has ever come into your life because you're afraid of trusting your true instincts."

She moved away from her sister and glanced at the hardbound books tucked in an oak bookshelf, unable to relinquish deeper insecurities. "What if I want more from Ryan than he can give me?"

"How do you know what he's capable of giving unless you give him a chance?" she countered.

And that meant trusting Ryan to put her first, and on those occasions when he couldn't because of the demands of his career, trusting herself to be strong enough to believe he'd always be there for her. To have faith that he'd find that balance.

"I don't think you'll ever forgive Dad for what he did to the family," Brooke said softly from behind her. "But don't let him sabotage your chance to be happy and possibly have a family of your own."

With that, her sister left the room to return to the party, leaving Jessica to contemplate her past, the present, and the future. And as she let go of bitter, resentful memories, she discovered a fortitude she never realized she possessed. A strength born of love. And the courage to grasp the kind of happiness Brooke had found for herself.

The kind of happiness Jessica had denied herself for far too long.

It seemed like forever before everyone cleared out of Ryan's house and she was alone with him. She was exhausted, but determined to speak with him. And she was nervous. Oh, Lord, especially that. So much was at stake. So much was at risk. Her heart. Her body. Her soul.

The rest of her life.

He frowned when he saw her standing in the entryway all by herself, clearly not happy to find her still around. "What are you still doing here?" he asked, his tone flat and emotionless. "I thought you left when Brooke did."

"No, I only walked them out." Feeling her tenacity slip a serious notch, she blurted out her request before she lost her nerve. "Ryan...I'd like to talk to you."

He stared at her for a long, hard moment. "After this morning, I don't think there's anything left to say."

His reply startled her, rattling her composure and the carefully thought-out discussion she'd had planned. An awful sense of foreboding closed in on her like a vise around her chest. "What about..." *Us.* She nearly wept as the one word got tangled around those damnable insecurities of hers.

He jammed his hands on his hips, his expression impatient. "What about what?" he prompted gruffly.

She couldn't think straight. She needed time, time to gather her thoughts again. Her gaze swept the area, and she grasped the first excuse that came to mind. "What about the mess?"

Her offer to help only seemed to aggravate him more. "I have a cleaning crew coming in the morning, so go on home and don't worry about it." He paused for a moment, then said in a low, rough tone filled with too much emotion, "Goodbye, Jessica." With that, he turned and headed toward the kitchen.

She watched him go, her heart aching so fiercely she could hardly breathe. He didn't want her anymore. And she had no one to blame except herself.

All because she hadn't been able to bring herself to trust in Ryan and his love.

RYAN HEARD THE FRONT DOOR open and close, and felt the finality of Jessica leaving right to the very depths of his soul. Bracing his hands on the kitchen counter, he squeezed his tired eyes shut and berated himself for being such an ass. The least he could have done was walk her to her car, but he hadn't been able to perform that simple gentlemanly task. It just hurt too damn much to be around her, and he hadn't wanted to stretch out their final goodbye.

All night he'd suffered with her being in his constant line of vision, of being wrapped in her scent when she happened to pass him. He'd tormented himself with private fantasies that included stripping off that sexy, silky blue dress she'd worn, fantasies of having her in his bed, his life.

And there, for a moment, he'd thought, hoped, that her reasons for wanting to stay behind had to do with them…not the mess.

Yeah, he was a mess all right, he thought with a disgusted snort. And he had no idea how he was going to get over loving and losing Jessica. One day at a time, he supposed.

A half an hour later, dead tired and weary to the bone, he locked up the house, turned off the lights, then dragged himself upstairs. By the time he'd reached his bedroom he had his shirt unbuttoned. Shrugging out of the garment, he tossed it over the end of his bed. He toed off his shoes, pulled off his socks and replaced his dress pants with a pair of sweat shorts.

He went to retrieve a T-shirt from his dresser, and that's when he caught sight of the pool of shimmering blue silk on the carpeted floor. His pulse raced as he followed a trail of silky stockings, a lacy black bra and panties that led to the bathroom door, which had been left open a crack.

He pushed slowly against the door, and was greeted by the lush scent of strawberries, the flickering illumination of candlelight and a woman lounging in his bathtub with a froth of bubbles coating the surface of the water. His gut clenched, with anxiety, and a hope so excruciating it nearly stole his breath.

Somehow, some way, he found his voice. "What are you doing here?"

Big blue eyes met his, and a tremulous smile touched her lips. "I'm attempting to prove a point."

Not sure where her scene for seduction was leading, he frowned down at her. "Excuse me?"

She drew a deep breath, and he watched in too much fascination as the bubbles quivered around the soft rise of her breasts. "You've shown me many times in the past month that actions speak louder than words. And since I was having trouble speaking downstairs, I thought I'd give *your* tactic a try to get your attention."

"You definitely have that." He rubbed a hand along the back of his neck, unable to relax the tense muscles bunching across his shoulders. "I thought you left."

"I never left, Ryan," she said, her voice as soft as the shadows in the bathroom. And just as vulnerable. "When it came right down to walking out your door, I couldn't do it. And I'm not going to leave until we talk."

Remembering how his bruised pride had prompted him to tell her they had nothing left to say to each other, this time he couldn't refuse her, not after she'd found the fortitude within herself to stay.

"All right," he conceded, and settled himself on the ledge of the tub. "Since you know exactly what I want from you, exactly how I feel about you, the floor is yours."

"I do want you, Ryan Matthews. More than I've ever wanted anyone in my life, and in ways that scare me."

"And what are you afraid of?" He knew her fears, but he had to know she'd resolved them for herself.

"I'm afraid of trusting a man for my happiness. Scared of giving in to the things I feel for you, and ending up being alone anyway." Her hands fluttered over the surface of the water, making it ripple enticingly. Making him wonder if she was completely naked beneath. "It's been very difficult for me, but I've come to realize that my expectations of you were unrealistic, and were just a way for me to maintain an emotional distance. As much as I wanted to when I first met you, I can't condemn you for being a divorce attorney, because you've shown me how kind, caring and fair you are, and that you'd never deliberately hurt someone for your own selfish gains. I have to believe what you do for a living, you do because you truly want to help people, because there is nothing egotistical or self-absorbed about you."

As much as her revelation pleased him, he remained quiet, needing more from her than that acceptance.

She seemed to sense that, too. "I know I can never forget what my father did to our family, the pain he put us through by abandoning us so completely, but I'm ready to put that resentment behind me, because I can't bear the thought of losing you."

"And what about my career?" he asked, knowing her insecurities extended to that, too. "Are you able to accept the long hours ahead, the late nights and the balance between my work and our relationship?"

"I'm willing to try," she replied honestly. "Knowing you love me makes a big difference, because I know you don't take something like that lightly."

His gaze held hers steadily. "No, I don't."

She bit her bottom lip, and reached out and touched a wet hand to his cheek. "You make me feel safe, and secure and protected," she whispered in an aching voice. "And it's been so long since I've felt that way."

"I'll be here for you, Jessie." Gently capturing her wrist, he pressed a kiss in the center of her damp palm. "All you have to do is trust me, and believe in me."

"Oh, I do." The candlelight flickered, illuminating the beauty of her face, the vulnerability still lingering in her eyes. "And that's part of what frightens me so much. The depth of my feelings for you is very over-whelming, and like nothing I've ever experienced."

"And what do you feel?" The question prompted her to take that final leap of faith, to risk all.

She did. "I feel a richness and contentment I never knew was possible until you came into my life. I'm ready to trust my instincts, and I'm ready to trust my heart." She paused for a moment, then seemingly drew on that well of strength and confidence he always knew she possessed. "I'm naked beneath these bubbles, Ryan. Physically and emotionally. I didn't want anything between us when I told you that I loved you so you'd know that I'm not hiding behind anything, that what I feel for you comes straight from my heart and soul."

He let go of her hand, briefly severing the connection between them, knowing when they came together again the bond would be stronger than before. "Stand up and show me."

A sensual dare. A provocative challenge. A final dissolving of those barriers that had kept her from being completely his.

Without an ounce of modesty, she stood, baring herself to him. His mouth went dry as he watched the slick water sluice down her naked body. Her skin glowed from the candlelight, and bubbles clung to her breasts, her belly, her thighs. He grew hard with a wanting and hunger he knew would never abate. Not in this lifetime.

She slipped her fingers beneath his chin and raised his gaze back to hers. "I love you, Ryan Matthews," she said, her clear voice and velvet blue eyes filled with the sentiment she spoke of.

His chest tightened, seeming to spill over with emotions for this woman who'd filled his life to overflowing. Straightening, he stripped off his shorts, not wanting her to be the only one naked—physically and emotionally. "I love *you*, Jessica Newman," he returned.

A sultry smile curved her mouth as she took a moment to appreciate the length of his body, and his obvious need for her. Passion and tenderness brightened her eyes when she met his gaze again.

"I love you without fear," she said, reciting the toast he'd written and had meant, on some level, for her. "I trust you without question. I accept you without change, and I desire you without inhibitions."

He stepped into the tub, but didn't touch her. "Will you always believe in me, and always have faith?"

"Yes," she breathed.

It was all he needed to hear. He sank into the warm, silky water, braced his back against the side, and pulled her with him so she straddled his hips. She gasped as his erection slid against the heat of her, and for as much as he ached to complete their union, he held back.

He smoothed damp, unruly strands away from her face. "Then I promise to give you love and laughter, and a happily ever after."

She stiffened, her eyes widening in shock. "Are you…"

"Proposing?" he suggested.

She settled her hands on his shoulders and nodded, hope and uncertainties mingling in her gaze.

He lazily, leisurely stroked his hands along her spine to her hips, loving the feel of her. "Yes, I am."

"You really want to marry me?" Disbelief tinged her voice. "I mean, that's a big step, a huge commitment—"

"One I'm finally ready for," he assured her. But doubts still lingered for her—he could see them in her expression, and suspected those uncertainties tied in to his profession. "Would you believe that working on divorce cases makes me more aware of how difficult it is to make a relationship work? I've felt that way for years, and I've developed an appreciation and respect for my parents' strong marriage. Those traditional values are what I want for myself. With you. And just so you know going into this, I want kids, too." He grinned, knowing that wouldn't be a problem for her at all. Knowing, too, how much fun they'd have making those babies.

A joyful moisture filled her eyes. "A family," she whispered.

"Yeah, a family," he agreed. "One for us to love, and share and grow old with."

She wrapped her arms around his neck and held him close. "It scares me how much I need you, Ryan," she said after a poignant moment had passed.

Her open honesty humbled him. Tangling his fingers in her hair, he gently pulled her back, just enough to look into her eyes. The water lapped between them erotically, her taut nipples brushed against his chest, but Ryan resisted the urge to give in to the tantalizing delights beckoning to them. *Soon.*

"Hell, Jessie, this is all new to me, too." He smiled in understanding. "I was hoping we could figure out this love and forever thing together."

A shiver passed through her body, and a hint of remorse creased her delicate brows. "You're right, of course. We'll work on it together. I guess old insecurities die hard. Can you forgive me?"

"Ah, sweetheart, there's absolutely nothing to forgive." He caressed a thumb along her frown, making it disappear beneath his touch. "Just say you'll marry me so I'll know you'll always be mine."

A sassy, naughty sparkle suddenly entered her gaze. Sliding intimately closer, she squeezed her knees shamelessly against his hips. "Umm, do you think you could *coerce* me into saying yes?"

He groaned as his erection strained between them. Knowing her innocent request would lead to a thrilling build-up to her ultimate surrender, he played along. "I'll certainly do my best," he drawled, and guided her warm and willing mouth to his.

Her lips parted, soft and welcoming. His tongue dipped and parried and swirled with hers in a slow, deep, rapacious kiss. Beneath the water, he glided his flattened palms up her thighs, until his thumbs parted her slick flesh, stroked rhythmically and expertly brought her to that exquisite crest.

Stopping his illicit caresses before she fell over the edge, he lifted his head and met her heavy-lidded gaze. "Marry me," he murmured.

Her face was beautifully flushed with arousal and the heat of the water, her breathing heavy. "Maybe," she said huskily, then dampened her lips with her tongue. "I think you need to be more persuasive."

He grinned wickedly, and slanted his mouth possessively over hers. With his hands on her hips, he lifted her, brought her flush against his length, then let her sleek, wet body slowly glide back down his chest, his belly, until his hard, aroused flesh demanded entrance between her silky thighs. She moaned and shuddered, and with excruciating slowness, he impaled her on his shaft, sheathing himself in measured, gradual degrees until he was deep inside her.

He inhaled sharply as she rocked urgently against him, intending to coax him to a quick climax. He stilled her seductive movements with his hands on her waist and struggled for a semblance of control.

"Before I let you take advantage of me like you intend to, I need an answer first," he rasped, trying not to lose himself in the dark desire shimmering in her eyes. The pure adoration. "Be my wife, Jessie. My lover. My best friend."

Framing his face between her hands, she captured his gaze in the romantic candlelight. "Yes," she said without hesitation. "I'll be all those things for you…your wife, your lover, your best friend."

A cocksure grin tipped his mouth. "It's nice to know I haven't lost my touch."

She rolled her eyes at his teasing comment. "Considering all the years ahead of us, I'll make sure you have plenty of practice."

Oh, he didn't doubt her claim for a second. And as he seduced her body with pleasure, and she gave of herself with abandon, he knew he was a lucky man, indeed.

*Everything you love about romance...*
**and more!**

*Please turn the page for Signature Select™*
*Bonus Features.*

A LITTLE BIT
Naughty

BONUS
FEATURES
INSIDE

## Author Interview:
### A Conversation with
# Janelle Denison

**What's your idea of the ultimate seduction?**

For me, the ultimate seduction is being with the person you love the most and having a great time, which can lead to all kinds of sensual fun. Then there's always a romantic night out, complete with chocolate dessert and an entire night without kids!

**What tempts you?**

I'm tempted by a sexy smile, and a slow, knowing look. When you're crazy about someone, it doesn't take much to be tempted, or seduced! Though chocolate does help!

**Why did you become a writer?**

I started reading Harlequin romances when I was just out of high school, and I was swept away by so many of those incredible stories. The more I read, the more I wanted to write a story of my own, and I wouldn't consider writing anything other than romance! It's been a long, wonderful and very rewarding journey as a published author. I absolutely love what I do, and can't imagine doing anything else.

**What matters most in life?**

My husband and kids matter the most to me—their health, their happiness and overall well-being. Then my immediate family and close friends. Surrounding yourself with people who love and care about you is what's most important in life.

**What gives you pleasure?**

Chocolate is pretty close to the top of the list! Actually, I love spending time with my husband. He's my very best friend, and I enjoy being with him, even if it's for something as simple as watching a TV show together. I'm very easy to please!

**When you're not writing, what do you enjoy doing?**

I enjoy hanging out with my two teenage daughters. I love being with friends, laughing and having a good time. I enjoy watching movies, reading good books and taking naps!

**Do you believe in love at first sight?**

Absolutely! I also believe in soul mates. I met my husband when I was sixteen years old, and there is no doubt in my mind or heart that we were meant to be together. At sixteen, it was definitely love at first sight. Now, nearly twenty years later, I can still look at him and fall in love all over again. It's the best feeling in the world knowing that I'm going to be spending the rest of my life with this wonderful man!

**Is there one book of yours in particular that stands out in your mind?**

There is one book that is very near and dear to my heart, since it deals with an issue I'm familiar with. That book is *Ready-Made Bride,* a Harlequin Romance novel published back in 1998, which deals with illiteracy. The hero of the story is modeled after someone I know personally, and writing that book really helped me to understand what he deals with on a daily basis. It's a story that shows a hero facing huge odds, and with the help of a very loving heroine overcomes those fears and insecurities. It's one of my personal favorite stories!

## What are you working on right now?

I just finished a Harlequin Blaze novella for the Sinfully Sweet anthology, out in early 2006. Now I'm starting my next single title, *Born To Be Wilde*, which is part of my "Wilde" series. I hope you'll give both books a try!

# Romance Guide
## Erogenous Zones:
## Going Off the Beaten Path
### by Diane Peters

*Does your lover know all your "Mmm" and "Wow!" zones? Do you know all of his? Chances are, you've both spent some long, luscious time in the tried-and-true erogenous zones. But there are many more nooks and crannies on both of your bodies worth exploring. Here are a few out-of-the-way erogenous zones you may want to visit.*

**The Skinny on Skin**

Carol Queen, staff sexologist at San Francisco's Good Vibrations, says we often ignore the biggest erogenous zone on our body: our skin. "The skin is completely covered with nerve endings that appreciate touch. It can blow people's minds and really expand people's definition of what's erotically possible," says Queen.

An all-over body touch sends out the message "I can't keep my hands off you." It's a loving, intimate way to show your partner how much you love his or her body. All of it. To seduce the skin, start with long strokes using a medium-firm amount of pressure. Don't go too light or it might feel ticklish. As things get more passionate, feel free to be more energetic: pressing hard and grabbing can feel amazing when someone's really aroused.

Dry hands are fine (but you might want to douse them in body powder if you've got clammy palms) but using scented massage oil is even better. During your exploration of his body (and his exploration of yours), you may even stumble on some unknown, shiver-inspiring spots.

**Footloose**

Stuffed into shoes and trod on all day, our feet are hardly pampered or revered in daily life. But they're actually one of the most wonderful pleasure zones on the body.

"Many people find that nice firm strokes on their feet, especially if oil is involved, feel delicious," says Queen. That's because the nerve endings in our feet are actually connected to our genitals. Queen's even heard of people who've had an orgasm from a killer foot massage.

To turn the feet into a more sexy body part, however, you might want to try this one out after a hot sensual bath together. Post-soak, either using scented oil or not, set to your partner's heels, soles and toes with strong, massaging pressure.

### *Back* to Basics

Most of the time when we make love we're face-to-face. But if you turn things around and start approaching your partner's back as an erotic zone, things can get exciting. "The nape of the neck, the shoulders, the backs of the thighs, all of these places don't ordinarily receive a lot of touch," says Queen. The nape, especially, is often covered by hair or our shirt collars, but it's as sensitive to kissing and stroking as our throats.

Exploring your partner's back can be a surprise, and something different is *always* exciting. Plus, we often feel vulnerable when our back is exposed, so this is an amazing way to build trust.

### Off the Beaten Path

But the best out-of-the-way erogenous zone on your body and your lover's is best discovered in private. If you keep trying out new places and new ways of touching, you're sure to find that perfect stroke guaranteed to drive him mad, that little corner you just adore having stroked. And when you do make these discoveries, they create a bond between you that keeps your sex life intimate and *always* interesting.

# All Night Long

by Janelle Denison

KRISTIN TAYLOR RODE the elevator up to the thirty-sixth floor of the Chicago high-rise where as of five o'clock that Friday evening she *used* to work. While today had been her last day on the job for Corgan Architectural Group, she still had unfinished business to resolve. If Michael Karr was game for the provocative seduction she had in mind, tonight they'd take a foray into the forbidden.

Biting her lower lip, she absently slid a black silk scarf through her slender fingers, the texture cool, sleek and highly seductive to her senses. Especially when she thought about what she planned to do with the scrap of material. Would Michael find her erotic request equally stimulating and agree to be hers for one night only? Or would he refuse and send her on her way, leaving unfulfilled this deep, consuming craving she'd developed for him?

There was no denying the chemistry and attraction between them, which had grown stronger and hotter over the past few months. They'd indulged in a sexy but harmless office flirtation, but in order to keep their relationship from developing into anything more serious, she'd been the one to turn down two separate invitations to join him for dinner.

Her career came first. Always had, always would. Which was why she'd accepted a very generous offer to head up the restoration division at another architectural firm. The new firm provided a better position, more money and plenty of opportunity to advance within the company. At twenty-eight years of age, she knew security and total independence were within her grasp.

But before she immersed herself in her new job, she wanted an unforgettable night with the one man who attracted her like no other.

The elevator came to a gliding stop, and with a soft "ping" the doors slid open into a luxurious reception area, quiet and empty now except for the soft glow of light illuminating the corridors leading to two separate wings of the firm. Taking off her shoes and leaving them by the bank of elevators to slip back on later, she headed left and silently made her way down the hall toward Michael's office.

At a quarter to eight, all the rooms were dark and empty, except for the one at the very end of the corridor. She'd been counting on his late-night work habits to act in her favor, and she'd been giddy with relief when she'd seen his Lexus in the parking struc-

14

ture below. One obstacle had been cleared, but another still remained.

She stood in the doorway to his office, her heart beating hard and fast in her chest, the scarf clenched tight in her fist. He sat across the room on a stool in front of his drafting table, his concentration focused on the set of blueprints open on the surface. Soft rock music played from the stereo he'd had installed, which would help to drown out any noise she might make as she approached him from behind.

She glided quietly across the room, admiring the great view she had of his strong, broad shoulders that tapered to a lean waist and an ass that looked tight and firm, even in khakis. His dark brown hair was mussed, as if he'd repeatedly combed the thick strands with his fingers, and he'd rolled up the sleeves of his dress shirt, revealing corded forearms. His hand, splayed on one corner of the plans, was big and masculine, his fingers long, virile and no doubt very capable of making a woman's body respond to his will.

She shivered in anticipation, until a hint of insecurity nudged its way to the surface. She was confident at work, aggressive when the need arose, but she'd be lying if she didn't admit that she was a teeny-tiny bit nervous about kidnapping Michael for an evening of satiating desires. Before she could change her mind, she came up behind him, slipped the folded scarf over his head and covered his eyes.

His entire body immediately tensed and he

grabbed at the material she'd used as a blindfold. "What the hell?"

Her hand caught his wrist, stilling him before he could rip off the scarf. "Leave it on," she said, her breath stirring the strands of hair near his ear.

Hearing her soft command, he lowered his hand and cocked his head. "Kristin?" His low, rough tone held both surprise and incredulity.

He didn't sound angry, which she took as a positive sign. "Yes, it's me," she said, and tied the ends of the fabric into a secure knot behind his head.

He relaxed and turned around, blindfold in place, his trust in her automatic and unconditional. "I thought you were gone. For good."

16

She might have covered those compelling green eyes of his that always seemed to see too much, but now his sexy, kissable mouth was more prominent—the sensuous curve to his lips, the soft fullness that beckoned her to taste with her tongue…

Inhaling a deep breath, she stated her intentions before she lost the nerve. "I came back to take care of some unfinished business."

Dark brows rose above the strip of black material, giving him a very rakish appeal. "With me?"

His disbelieving tone was warranted, considering how long she'd been fighting her fascination with him, and his sexy charm. "Yes, with you. I was hoping we could do something about this attraction between us before I move on." She slowly circled him, brushing her body subtly against his, tempting and teasing him. "That is, if you're up to accepting the invitation."

"Sweetheart, I'm as up as a man can get right now." A devastatingly wicked grin slid into place. "Don't you know the sound of your voice is enough to make me hard?"

Her face heated at his candid remark, and one quick glance at the front of his trousers verified his claim. He was impressively aroused, and her own body grew damp at the thought of finally indulging in a fantasy or two of her own with him.

He leaned his backside against the drafting table. "So what's with the blindfold?" he asked, patient but curious.

She'd spent hours coming up with a tantalizing answer for the prop she'd selected, a reply that would excite him yet allow her to protect her heart and emotions. "The blindfold makes tonight more exciting and adventurous, and it allows me to be more uninhibited."

All true. So was the fact that he wouldn't be able to look into her eyes, watch her expression and see that she'd been half in love with him for months now. She couldn't afford that kind of emotion distracting her on a long-term basis. Not with her own personal goals within her reach.

"I give you permission to do anything you want

with me tonight, ask anything you desire. Anything at all. And vice versa."

His breathing deepened, a sign that she'd definitely intrigued him. "Talk about a fantasy come to life."

She smiled to herself; he was her fantasy come to life, as well. "There is one condition you have to agree to before we go any further. The blindfold stays in place…at all times. You can use your imagination, of course. Just think how much your other four senses will be heightened." Closing the distance between them, she placed her hands on his chest, finding his nipples as hard as her own beneath the fabric of his shirt. "*I'll* be your eyes for the night."

"Mmm, I like the sound of that," he murmured.

"So what do you say, Michael?" She skimmed her lips along his jaw and up to his ear, where she whispered huskily, naughtily, "Are you willing to be mine tonight, all night long?"

Michael Karr had never been so illicitly propositioned in his entire life. Not that he was complaining about Kristin's shameless proposal, or the fact that she fit so perfectly against the length of his body as she leaned into him. If there was anything he objected to, it was her insinuation that they had only one night together. And that was an assumption he had every intention of correcting…*tomorrow*.

After spending months pursuing Kristin in a fun, flirtatious manner, only to have his advances gently turned down, he'd thought he'd lost every chance to

18

sway her to his way of thinking, especially when she'd announced that she'd accepted an offer to go to work for another architectural firm. Michael wanted her badly, but he wasn't about to stalk her to another company.

Now she was offering him the opportunity to be with her and show her that their attraction went deeper than the physical desire she wanted to satisfy. He had less than twelve hours to change her mind about them, and he planned to use that precious time wisely.

Starting with agreeing to her seductive request. "Yes, I accept your invitation."

Her warm sigh of relief wafted across his throat. "Great."

She started to move away, but he wrapped his arm around her back, keeping their bodies aligned and her secure in his embrace. "There's something I have to do before we go any further."

"What's that?" she asked curiously, though her voice had taken on an unmistakable edge of excitement.

Framing her face in his hands, he found her mouth with his thumbs, traced the damp softness of her lips with the pads of his fingers. "I have to kiss you, because it's something I've wanted to do for a very long time and I can't wait a minute longer to taste you."

Without hesitation she slid her arms around his shoulders, her own fingers caressing the nape of his

BONUS FEATURE

neck. "Me, too," she whispered, and slowly drew his head down to hers.

Michael experienced his first urge to rip off the blindfold that kept him from catching a glimpse of her features and seeing what she was feeling—pure passion, or something deeper? The blindfold served as a safeguard, a barrier that kept her emotions to herself. Frustrated as hell, he managed to resist the impulse to break her rule, realizing he'd fallen victim to her strategy in this game of seduction.

Which forced him to use other means to gauge her feelings and response to him. As soon as her lips touched his and parted eagerly for him, he slid in, slow and deep, and his senses took over from there. She tasted hot and sweet, like freshly spun cotton candy that melted on his tongue. Her skin was soft and warm, and the unique, feminine scent he inhaled made him light-headed.

He didn't need to open his eyes to see her flowing blond hair tumbling to her shoulders, or to witness the hazy desire no doubt darkening her blue eyes. He'd etched everything about her to memory months ago, but the reality of kissing her, of feeling her lush curves against him and her mouth so tempting beneath his, was nothing short of pure heaven.

And he couldn't seem to get enough of her.

His free hand stole between the press of their bodies, skated over her ribs and cupped a generous breast in his palm, kneading and stroking the pliable flesh. She wore a cotton T-shirt and a bra with no substance, and he plucked at the hardened nipple begging for its share of attention. With a moan of pleasure that reverberated in the back of her throat, she stood on her tiptoes, angling closer, causing his fierce erection to nestle in the crux of her thighs, right where he ached to be.

He knew if didn't stop this nearly out-of-control madness, and quickly, he'd end up making love to her on his drafting table, hot and fast and deep. And he wanted to experience every detail of her erotic seduction too much to take her in such a rush.

He lifted his head, breaking the kiss, and she pressed her forehead against his cheek. "Oh, wow," she murmured.

"I second that," he said, amusement and arousal deepening his voice. "And just think, that's only the beginning."

A shiver coursed through her. "Then let's not waste another minute here." She slipped from his arms.

He immediately missed her softness, her warmth. "Where are we going?"

He heard the "click" of her turning off the light above his drafting table as she began shutting down his office. "It's a surprise."

He had a feeling it was just the first of many for the evening.

KRISTIN'S FINGERS CURLED around the steering wheel of her conservative Honda Accord as she headed toward downtown Chicago and their final destination for the night, with her soon-to-be-lover seated beside her. She licked her bottom lip, still tasting Michael, still reeling from the kiss they'd shared. She'd known the sexual chemistry between them would be incendiary once ignited, but she'd been stunned by the intensity of need that had risen within her, so immediate and blistering hot it threatened to consume her.

After making a right turn onto North Lake Shore Drive, she cast a glance at the man sitting next to her, so good-natured and gorgeous, so willing to go wherever she led him.

Thank goodness he'd been wearing the blindfold during and after that kiss. He was a man who was always very aware of everything around him, always watching her, studying her with his gaze, and tonight she didn't want her actions and emotions to be dissected and analyzed by anyone but her.

"So, do you do this kind of thing often?"

Michael's casual and humorously asked question pulled her out of her private musings. As serious and dedicated as he tended to be at work, he obviously knew how to enjoy himself outside the office, whereas she was too afraid that fun and relaxation might veer her off the course she'd set for herself at the age of eighteen.

"What, kidnapping men for my own personal pleasure?" she replied, giving playful a try herself and liking how it felt.

"And theirs," he drawled, a sexy male smile on his lips. "I'm enjoying this very much. I'm just curious if I'm your first."

"My first kidnap victim, yes." Admittedly, she'd never been so bold with any man before, but then, Michael wasn't just *any* man. He was the one she'd fantasized about for months. "I've never done this kind of thing before, but we're both physically attracted to each other, and you have asked me out a few times before. Now the timing seems right with me moving on to another company. And best of all, we won't have to worry about any awkward encounters at the office after tonight."

"That's…convenient." He was quiet for a moment, then said, "So we spend one night together and in the morning we just go our separate ways."

She wished he didn't make it all sound so sordid. She wished she didn't ache for more. "Yes."

"Why?" He stretched his arm across the back of their seats and threaded his fingers through her hair. "Do you think tonight is going to be that bad?" he joked.

She laughed. "If that kiss was any indication, I'm sure it'll be very, very good." Her truthful nature prompted her to be completely honest, to make sure he understood what he was getting into before they stepped out of this car. That tonight she'd give him anything he asked for sexually, but it was a one shot deal. "I'm not looking for any kind of commitment right now. Not for a long while. Especially not with a new job, new responsibilities and my desire to move up the corporate ladder without anything distracting me from my goals."

She brought her vehicle to a stop in front of the entrance to the Four Seasons Hotel, grabbing the few seconds of privacy they had left before the valet opened her door. "Michael, are you having second thoughts about us being together? Because if you are, we don't have to go through with this. But tell me now before we go any further." She held her breath as she waited for him to answer.

"There's not a chance I'm going to give up this night with you." With his palm cupping the back of her head, he brought her mouth to his and proved his interest with a deep, scorching kiss.

Michael knew how to kiss. Soft, nibbling bites that turned into the slow, erotic glide of wet lips, the deep tangling strokes of tongues. She could have spent the next hour making out with him in her car, letting him lavish her with such exquisite, mindless pleasure. Except a man dressed in a black tuxedo interrupted the heated moment by opening her door and letting the outside world intrude. Much to her relief, the valet was trained to be discreet, and didn't comment on her passenger's blindfold as he helped her out of the car.

Grabbing her overnight bag, Kristin entwined Michael's fingers with her own and ushered him into

24

the hotel and across the elegant lobby, ignoring the curious stares cast their way. She caught an empty elevator and hit the button for the top floor.

His thumb rubbed along the crease in her hand, and he smiled lazily. "Why do I get the feeling that you drove me around the block and we're on our way back up to my office?"

She brushed a soft kiss on his jaw, just because she wanted to. Just because he was hers for the night and she could. "We're not, I promise."

The ride to the top went smoothly, and less than a minute later they were standing in a marbled foyer, in a magnificent room that overlooked Lake Michigan. Dropping her bag, she pulled Michael deeper into the room, in awe of all the rich elegance surrounding them. The suite hadn't been cheap, but for once she'd decided to splurge and spoil herself with the frivolous and sensual amenities the hotel had promised. She'd spent years being frugal with her money, saving for the future and the financial security she'd never had growing up. But tonight she'd spare no expense and would experience whatever her heart desired.

Including Michael Karr.

She spun around to face him, her heart fluttering wildly in her chest. "We're here," she announced.

He tipped his head, causing a lock of sable hair to fall across his forehead. "Where's *here?*"

She trailed a finger along his collar and down the front of his shirt, anxious to feel his warm, bare flesh beneath her hands. "We're at a suite at the Four Seasons, and it appears we've got our own den of iniquity for the night."

MICHAEL LIKED this very sensual, uninhibited side of Kristin. Normally she was reserved and serious at work, though he'd always suspected that a very passionate, playful woman lurked beneath the surface of her self-contained facade. The past hour with her had confirmed his hunch, as did her animated tone as she gave him a verbal tour of their own private palace designed for an evening of sin and seduction— complete with their own Jacuzzi out on the enclosed balcony.

26

"Can I get you something to eat?" she asked once they'd returned to the main area of the suite. "I had room service deliver finger foods for us to munch on if you're hungry."

Her arm slipped from the crook of his elbow, but before she could move away he managed to reach out and by sheer luck grabbed her wrist. Lifting her hand, he pressed a lingering kiss in the center of her palm, then gently bit the soft flesh just below her thumb. Her breath caught in her throat, the kind of erotic sound he imagined she'd make at the crest of an orgasm.

Tonight he intended to find out.

"It's not food I'm hungry for, Kristin," he said meaningfully.

"Then what would you like?"

Her voice was husky, her tone a suggestive challenge he wasn't about to refuse. "I'd love for you to strip for me, slow and sexy," he said.

Her soft laughter wrapped around him like a caress. "What's the point of doing a striptease for you when you can't see me?"

"*You're* going to be my eyes, remember? Tell me what you're doing, as you're doing it, and my imagination will fill in the rest."

"All right," she agreed, and catered to his second request to find him a seat while she performed her show.

Settling into a straight-back, armless chair, he stretched his long legs out in front of him and made himself comfortable. "Now hand over your shirt, and I want *details*." He grinned.

"I'm pulling the shirt over my head and taking it off," she told him seductively, and a moment later he felt the garment land on the top of his head as she tossed it his way. "And here's my white lace bra." That piece of lingerie fell over his shoulder like a well-placed slingshot. "Now my breasts are bare."

A hot, aching need surged through him as he removed both articles of clothing from his person and dropped them to the floor. He pictured Kristin standing a few feet away, her full, rounded breasts thrusting toward him. He wished he could see them for himself, their shape and texture, but for the moment he had no choice but to live vicariously through her.

"Since I can't see your breasts, you're gonna have to tell me what they look like."

"Mmmm…" The provocative sound rolled from her throat like a purr, giving him the distinct impression she was stroking her breasts, and enjoying the sensation. "They're smooth and taut, and my nipples are hard and very sensitive to the touch."

He groaned, feeling as though he was going to burst through the front placket of his slacks. Even shifting in his seat didn't help to relieve the throbbing pressure in his groin. He couldn't ever remember being so hard and thick. So intensely aware of a woman he couldn't even see. It was an exhilarating feeling, and frustrating as hell.

"And now my jeans are coming off." He heard the slow drag of a zipper, along with the rustle of denim as she shoved the heavy material down her legs. "And at last, here are my panties."

Said item hit him in the middle of his chest and dropped to his lap, right on top of his pulsing erection. He picked up the scrap of silky material, still warm from her body and damp with her own arousal. Her rich, feminine scent set off a wild, primitive urge.

His heart pounded an erratic rhythm. "God, you smell good," he said with a low, rough timbre to his voice that he almost didn't recognize as his own. "I bet you taste even better."

"You're welcome to find out," she dared, a come-hither smile in her tone that stoked the fire building inside him.

He couldn't stand the distance separating them, the solitude he felt wearing the blindfold. The visual fantasy she'd created in his mind wasn't nearly enough when he wanted, *needed*, a physical connection. He craved to discover every dip, swell and curve of her shape with the slow glide of his hands. To learn what foreplay she liked best with the caress of his fingers, the hot, wet lick and swirl of his tongue.

No more games, no more waiting. "Come here, Kristin," he murmured, and crooked his finger in her direction. "It's my turn to feel and touch and taste."

Completely naked and unbearably aroused by her own striptease, Kristin obeyed Michael's command and glided toward him, until her knees bumped his, indicating that she was only an arm's length away.

His big hands remained splayed on his thighs, his restraint causing the muscles in his arms to flex. "Closer," he instructed.

A tight knot of laughter escaped her. "Any closer and I'll be straddling your lap."

"Exactly." A shameless grin canted his mouth, and when she hesitated too many seconds, he drawled, "Don't go all shy on me now, sweetheart, unless *you're* having second thoughts?"

Second thoughts, no. A little nervous about him touching her intimately for the first time, yes, because she knew that no matter how hard she tried to categorize this night with him as nothing more than anything-goes sex, her heart and emotions were already mocking her attempt to keep things between them purely physical.

She'd started this whole charade, and she was damn well going to enjoy every bit of it, without regrets. Ignoring those niggling doubts, she widened her stance and moved over him until her legs bracketed his thighs and her breasts were level with his face.

She started to lower herself, but his hands gripped her waist, stopping her before she could sit astride his lap. "Not yet," he said, rasping as his thumbs brushed along her flat stomach, over her hipbones and down to where the crease of her thighs led to a thatch of curls.

She felt so exposed, and was grateful for the blindfold protecting her from his hot, penetrating gaze, though she knew he could feel her trembling. Every nerve in her body seemed suspended as she waited for him to make the next move, and then he leaned forward and touched his lips to her belly.

She gasped. His damp mouth was like fire, his breath feathering across her skin like a slow, burning caress. He traced the indentation of her hips and waist, then glided his palms back down to her thighs and up and around to her bottom. He cupped and squeezed her flesh, licked her stomach as if she were a sweet treat he wanted to savor. His wicked tongue found her navel and delved inside, tasting her as she'd dared him to do.

The pleasure spiraling through her was too much…and not enough. She wanted to clench her thighs to help ease the throbbing ache in between, but his legs kept hers spread open for him. So she did the only thing she knew would grant her the release she craved.

"Touch me," she said on a ragged breath.

"Where?" he rasped as he nuzzled her belly, grazed her soft flesh with his teeth, laved her with his tongue. "How?"

After those provocative kisses they'd shared, she had no doubt he knew exactly where she wanted to be stroked, and how. She'd promised herself that the blindfold he wore would allow her the freedom to be brazen and bold, and she grasped the opportunity to be a complete wanton. For once, she'd deny herself nothing when it came to indulging in sensual delights. The memories of this one erotic night would have to last her through years of private fantasies, and she was determined to store a dozen for those lonely nights ahead.

Removing one of his hands from her bare bottom, she placed his heated palm on her thigh and guided him upward. "Right…*here*," she said on a shuddering sigh when his long, warm fingers found her slick, tender flesh. "Slow at first, and gradually increase the pressure."

Despite his request for her to tell him what she wanted, the man didn't need any instruction when it came to heightening her need. He finessed her with a lazy, rhythmic skill that kept her on the razor-sharp precipice of release and made her restless and wild.

Desperate and beyond ready, she threaded her fingers through his hair and clenched the silky strands in her fist. Pulling his head back, she bent over him and brushed her breasts against his mouth. His lips parted, and he immediately latched on to a stiff nipple and drew her in, flicking the rigid crest with his tongue, suckling her greedily.

And still, she needed more. "Michael...*please*."

This time he didn't ask what she was pleading for. He knew. And he gave it to her, deepening his exploration with two thick fingers while rubbing his thumb along her cleft. The breathtaking sensations went to her head in a dizzying rush. Her legs quivered and went weak, and she cried out as pure, fiery bliss engulfed her.

With one last shudder, she sank down to straddle his lap and expressed her gratitude with a long, lingering kiss that quickly turned hot and deep. His hands stroked her bare back, and instead of soothing her desire, her recent orgasm had ignited a smoldering hunger to return the favor, to know him just as intimately as he'd just learned her body.

Her lips remained locked with his as she worked the buttons of his shirt free and pushed the material over his broad shoulders, down his arms and off. She rubbed her breasts against his chest while she unbuckled his belt, unfastened the clasp and pulled the zipper down and over the enormous bulge straining the front of his trousers.

Still sitting on his thighs, she caressed him everywhere with her hands, and with her lips…starting with his neck and moving lower. She tongued the erratic pulse at the base of his throat, and flicked her thumbs over his erect nipples, making his chest rumble with a sexy groan.

Spurred on by her own quickening pulse and his encouraging response, she slid to her knees in front of him and grabbed the waistband of his pants. "Lift your hips for me," she ordered, and he obeyed.

In one fluid motion she dragged his slacks and briefs down his legs and tossed them aside, leaving him magnificently naked. Pressing his thighs open, she moved in between and pushed against his engorged shaft with her thumb and index finger. She devoured him with her gaze, squeezed his heavy sacs gently in her grasp, heightening his anticipation, and her own.

Michael's hands curled against the edge of his chair, the muscles in his stomach rippling with every choppy breath he drew. "Touch me, Kristin," he said, his tone tinged with desperation.

She remembered issuing the same plea earlier, and his teasing reply. "Where?" she asked, and glided

BONUS FEATURE

her thumb over the tip of his erection and the silky fluid gathering there. "How?"

His hips bucked and he laughed, the sound torn from his throat. "Stroke me with your hand." He showed her the tight grip and slow, firm motion he liked best, then tangled his fingers in her hair and urged her closer. "Take me in your mouth."

She did so willingly, the carnal act the most erotic, intimate thing she'd ever done for a man. She loved the male taste of him. The heat he exuded. The strength of his body and the control and power she held in her hands.

It didn't take long before she heard his labored breathing, felt his fingers tighten against her scalp and imagined his cool green eyes changing to a slow burning flame of passion. She took him deeper, and his hips rocked forward. His head fell back, his entire body tensed and a low, animal-like roar ripped from his chest as his climax shuddered through him like a visceral wave.

Long moments later he recovered enough to untangle his hand from her hair and cradled her cheek in his palm, his touch infinitely tender. "You didn't have to do that."

"I wanted to." The truth came easily. There wasn't anything she didn't want to experience with him tonight. "Consider it an appetizer," she teased.

He chuckled and shook his head. "If that was an appetizer, I can't wait for the main course."

34

Michael spread his arms along the rim of the tiled whirlpool bath, feeling as though he were sitting in a cauldron of boiling water. After his encounter with Kristin he could have used a cold shower, but she'd insisted on taking advantage of the amenities the suite offered, and he hadn't been able to refuse her request. According to her description, they were out on a private enclosed balcony, complete with a full service bar, which is where Kristin was at the moment—getting them something to drink.

The impulse to lift his blindfold a few inches and take a peek at her was strong, but he wouldn't betray her trust that way, no matter how much he hated wearing the stupid thing. No matter how much he wanted eye-to-eye contact with her. To see if what they'd shared had made as much of an emotional impact on her as it had on him.

The foreplay they'd indulged in had been incredible and mind-blowing, his arousal all the more acute because his mind had conjured up what he couldn't see for himself. His mouth and hands had been his eyes, learning the shape of her body, gauging her candid and passionate response to him. And in return, she'd been so giving and generous with his pleasure, more than he'd ever expected from her.

Sexually, they complemented each other perfectly, but there were other bonds he was interested in forging that went beyond the physical. Emotional ties she wouldn't be able to walk away from easily

BONUS FEATURE

after their night together. Which meant discovering what made this woman tick outside the office and beneath her disciplined facade so that he could use that information to his advantage later.

"Here's something to drink," Kristin said as she joined him in the churning water and pressed what felt like a flute-type glass in his hand, then settled in next to him.

The contents were cold and refreshing against his warm palm, and he took a sip, surprised at what he tasted. "Mmm, sparkling cider. Is this your substitute for champagne?"

"Do you mind?"

Her tone was slightly defensive, giving him the distinct impression she was hiding something deeper than a dislike for the bubbly drink. "Not at all." He swallowed another mouthful of the cool, tart liquid to back up his claim, then asked casually, "You don't like champagne?"

She paused, then said, "I don't drink anything alcoholic."

Intrigued by her answer, and interested in anything that would give him a deeper insight into her psyche, he pressed the issue. "Can I ask why?"

Again she hesitated, this time long enough to make him think she wasn't going to share her personal, private reasons for avoiding liquor, which left him to come to his own conclusions. "Are you a recovering alcoholic?" he asked, without censure.

36

"No, I'm not." Her reply was quick, followed by a sigh that unraveled out of her, releasing a bit of the tension lacing her voice. "My father was a heavy drinker, and I saw what it did to my mother, and our family."

When she hesitated, he prompted her further. "Tell me more about your dad."

She cleared her throat. "My father worked for a steel mill, and for as long as I could remember he spent most of his time off at the local bar instead of at home. My mother didn't work, and we didn't have a lot of money to begin with, and a good chunk of the money he made went to booze instead of groceries."

Listening quietly, attentively, he rubbed his instep over her arch and used his toes to slip and slide between hers—maintaining a physical contact with her to keep her from withdrawing emotionally.

His strategy seemed to work, because she continued. "I was an only child, and growing up, I watched my father's health deteriorate, along with his marriage to my mother. But despite the way he treated her, she stayed with him until the very end. He died of chronic liver disease when I was sixteen, and after that my mother fell into a deep depression, ignoring everything and everyone around her, including me, and she died two years later. It was as if she'd been so dependent on my father she didn't know how to live without him."

The sadness in her voice tore at him. As did the fact that she'd been alone and on her own for so long that she didn't realize what she was missing. "I'm sorry."

"There's nothing to be sorry for. Both of my parents chose their own fates." He heard her teeth click against her glass as she took a drink, her toes absently playing with his beneath the water. "Their choices made me realize that it was up to me to make a difference in my own life, to make something of myself and never depend on a man the way my mother did."

Which explained her drive and desire to be successful and self-sufficient. She was scared of falling into the same trap as her mother. He admired her strength and fortitude, but knew that while money and independence might bring her the security she craved, the solitude in which she lived wouldn't provide ultimate happiness. Didn't she know she could have it all, a successful job and a committed relationship, and not sacrifice anything that would compromise her own personal values? Apparently not, and he realized it was up to him to show her differently if he wanted more than one night with her.

Knowing it was past time to change the direction of their current conversation, he set his empty glass away from the hot tub and blindly stretched out his arm. He found her damp shoulder and used his fingers to draw squiggly patterns on her wet skin that caused her to shiver. "So, what's it like out here?"

38

"The view is incredible," she said, her tone awed, as well as grateful for the switch in topic. "The city below is all lit up, and the stars above make it look like there are a thousand diamonds twinkling up in the sky. I've never seen anything quite like it before."

He drew his thumb along her neck and followed the line of her jaw up to her ear. Just touching her made him want her all over again. "Didn't you ever just sit outside at night as a kid and make up silly pictures out of the stars by connecting the dots?"

He felt her shake her head. "Never."

Considering her tumultuous family life, she'd probably missed out on most fun childhood antics. "Me, my brother and sisters did it all the time. I still do it sometimes."

"Really?" she asked incredulously.

"Sure." He grinned, determined to share something special with her. "Look up at the sky and stars and tell me what you see."

The water around him swished as she turned to brace her elbows on the edge of the tub. She was quiet for long moments, then she said, "I see a butterfly, and a heart. And over there I see a serpent."

He chuckled at the excitement she exhibited, glad that she still had a bit of kid left in her after her suppressed childhood. She spent the next half hour playing connect the stars, their time together lighthearted, silly and carefree in a way he'd never seen from her before. And with every second that passed, his desire for her escalated.

While she continued to spout off imaginary, star-studded pictures, he moved along the edge of the Jacuzzi until he found her. He settled in behind her, her rounded bottom nestling against his groin, his erect penis sliding between her thighs. He massaged her shoulders with strong hands, eased his thumbs along the taut tendons in her neck.

"Michael," she breathed, and attempted to turn around.

He stopped her before she could fully execute the move. "Shh, just relax and enjoy."

40  Her head lolled forward, giving his fingers access to more muscles, more sensitive flesh. "Umm, this hardly seems fair."

"Do you hear me complaining?" He pressed a kiss to her exposed neck, nipped at her shoulder and soothed the love bite with his tongue. "When was the last time you let anyone pamper you?"

She groaned as he kneaded the taut muscles bisecting the slope of her back, all the way down to the base of her spine. "Never."

That's what he'd thought. She was too busy taking care of herself. "Then let me take care of you for a change."

As soon as the comment fell from his lips, he felt her stiffen...and immediately knew he'd used the wrong choice of words for a woman who prided herself on depending on no one but herself.

Kristin didn't want to be taken care of by any man. Ever. For any reason. She struggled internally against Michael's words and what they implied, but his hands were pure magic and her body contradicted the lecture in her mind. She came vibrantly alive at his tantalizing touch, and there wasn't a damn thing she could do to stop the jolt of pleasure that surged through her veins. Or the deep-rooted longing that tied her emotions into a tangled knot of confusion and burning need.

She wanted to be cherished and desired, and she felt all that and more with Michael. As if what she said mattered to him. As if he cared deeply for her, despite her insecurities. Knowing she was crazy, she pushed fears aside and dropped her guard, letting him indulge her in a way she'd never allowed another man. In a way she knew she could get used to, very easily.

He flattened his chest against her back, and his palms cupped and kneaded her breasts, his parted lips leaving a trail of hot, damp kisses along the side of her neck. The position was erotic. Thrilling. With one hand plucking at her hard nipples, his other fingers strummed lower, over her belly and between the thighs he widened with his own.

Long fingers glided, probed, finding the sleek friction and rhythm that made her instantly wild. She

BONUS FEATURE

moaned, the tickling vibration of the bubbling water adding to the breathless sensations. Feeling the last thin threads of her restraint unfurling, and refusing to come apart this time without him, she grabbed his wrist, forcing him to stop his ministrations.

"I want you inside me this time," she said, and he agreed with a low, guttural "Yes."

The condoms were in her overnight bag, and she helped him from the Jacuzzi, pulling him back into the suite's living room, both of them naked and dripping wet and not giving a damn. She dug out a foil packet, and no sooner had she rolled on the protection for him than he grasped her face in his hands and was kissing her. Deeply. Hungrily. Greedily. She backed up, needing the nearest wall for support, knowing he would, too, because they were never going to make it to the bedroom for a nice, soft bed. Not this time.

His hands skimmed down to the backs of her thighs, and he lifted her, spreading her legs, tipping her hips until his erection pressed against sleek feminine folds of flesh. She wrapped her legs around his waist, and with a harsh growl he buried himself inside her, all aggressive male and unyielding heat and strength. His entry was hard and swift, making her suck in a startled breath as her body adjusted to the invasion of his thick shaft. Then he moved, slow at first, then faster, his hips pumping, straining, lifting her higher, until the only thing she was aware of was him inside her, filling her completely.

Sweet, sharp pleasure engulfed her, and she came on a high-pitched cry. She held on tight as he drove into her one last time, raw and primitive, nearly crushing her with the force of his own release. He shuddered and groaned her name, a possessive sound of utter male satisfaction that rocked her entire world.

"WHAT WOULD YOU LIKE TO EAT?" Kristin asked as she glanced at the tray of finger foods she'd ordered from room service earlier. She was sitting on Michael's lap in a chair at the dining table, both of them wrapped in thick terry robes supplied by the hotel, replete and relaxed after making love. "We've got fruit salad, cold cuts, cheeses, chilled shrimp and cheesecake for dessert."

Grinning, he slipped his hand inside the front opening of her robe and rested his palm just above her knee with his thumb stroking her sensitized skin. "I'm starved, and everything sounds good to me."

"That's what you get for not eating dinner before I arrived at your office." She fed him a shrimp dipped in cocktail sauce, and he insisted on licking her fingers clean, one at a time.

"You've worked late nights before," he said with a shrug. "And I know you've skipped a meal or two because of a project with a tight deadline."

"Yes, I have." She wouldn't have moved up the

ranks so quickly without making late-night sacrifices. "With plenty more to come with the new job, no doubt." She slipped a wedge of sweet cantaloupe into his mouth.

He chewed and tongued a dribble of juice from the corner of his lips. "Speaking of which, tell me about your new job."

She warmed to the subject, proud of her accomplishments. "I'll be heading up the restoration division, which is something I've been working toward for years now. I love historic preservation, and while Corgan gave me a few opportunities to dabble in that area with a few oddball jobs they took on, it wasn't enough. When I received a generous offer from Bennett to go to work for them, it was something I couldn't pass up, personally or professionally."

He reached in front of her and skimmed his fingers over the array of foods on the tray, choosing a cube of cheese. He took a bite, and lifted the other half to her lips, which she nibbled at leisurely until it was gone.

"So now you're going to spend the next few years making a new name for yourself with Bennett," he said, and licked the traces of smeared cheese from his thumb. "More late nights and weekends filled with projects that need to come in on deadline."

She picked up a cherry and plucked the fruit from its stem with her teeth. "I don't mind." At least, she never had before. Now the words stung her throat like

44

a lie, startling her, forcing her to truly acknowledge the fact that the only thing she had in her life was her job. No dog or cat because she was too wrapped up in her work to give it the attention it deserved, and no special man to spend time with because she feared where a relationship could lead, of all that she could lose—her independence and the security of knowing she could take care of herself.

She swallowed hard, the cherry more bitter than sweet because of her stunning thoughts. "Erratic schedules are common. It's that way with any architectural firm I've ever worked for. Besides, moving up as high as I can within a company has always been my main focus. If I'm offered something better elsewhere, I'll take it."

He considered that while eating a rolled slice of ham. "What about a social life and dating?"

"Most men don't seem to understand my dedication to my job."

"Do you really give them a chance to get used to what you do for a living, or do you just assume that they can't adjust to your schedule?"

She frowned at him, even though he couldn't see her. "What is that supposed to mean?"

"I was just wondering if you'd make time for a man or a relationship in your busy life, or if you'll always choose to be alone?"

Annoyance rippled through her at his casually

BONUS FEATURE

asked question, which made her feel too defensive. "Being alone is a choice I've made for myself."

"But not a very practical one, sweetheart." A smile eased up the corners of his sexy mouth. "That job of yours isn't going to keep you warm at night, and all the money in the world won't buy you happiness."

He was getting too close to uncovering too many secret yearnings. Whimsical dreams and wishes she'd dismissed long ago because they weren't realistic or sensible and could only lead to pain and heartbreak. And now he was ruthlessly unearthing those suppressed desires, the need she harbored to be loved and adored, to let a man fill her soul with joy and give her life real purpose.

46

Confused and torn, she moved to scoot off his lap, *retreating,* doing the only thing she knew that would protect her heart and emotions from this man who wore a blindfold but saw much deeper than any other person ever had.

He tightened his arms around her waist, holding her in place. He tipped his head and asked gently, "Where are you going?"

"I think we're done here," she said with more authority than she felt, and prayed he'd let her go.

Dread seeped into every pore in Michael's body. Did Kristin mean that *they* were done, or that she was finished eating? Either way, he refused to let her withdraw from him. Refused to let her put any more distance between them that he'd never be able to scale in such a short amount of time. He had to act fast or risk losing the ground he'd made with her thus far.

She was ready to escape as soon as he released her, her entire body stiff as she sat on his lap. Undoubtedly, he'd pushed her too far with their last conversation, but he was determined to make her see that her life could revolve around more than just her job—if she was willing to take chances. Specifically, with him.

He decided to use the best arsenal he had at his disposal to chase away the tension vibrating through her: seduction.

"We're far from done," he drawled, a distinct double meaning lacing his comment. "We haven't had dessert yet, and I was really looking forward to having some of that cheesecake. Mind passing me a piece?" Relaxing his hold on her, he held out his hand and waited for her to trust him enough to surrender to his request, or give in to insecurities and bolt.

Triumph coursed through him when he felt her place a small sticky square of cheesecake against his fingers. He took a bite, savoring the rich taste, and let a wicked thought prompt him to indulge in a bit of erotic foreplay.

"Sit on the edge of the table for me, Kristin," he said, and this time when she slid off his lap he knew it wasn't to flee.

He heard her move the tray of food and settle on

the table. "What are you going to do?" she asked, her voice both expectant and curious.

He stood, moving forward until her knees widened and flanked his hips. With his free hand he tugged at the belt holding her robe together and pushed the lapels aside until his fingers made contact with her warm, smooth flesh. "I want *you* to be my dessert."

She didn't object, and using two fingers he blindly painted the cheesecake over her breasts, her belly, her slender thighs…then followed the path with his lips and tongue, nibbling and licking the confection off her skin until she was moving restlessly against him, urging him to enter her. After sheathing himself he did just that, and she shattered moments later, her heat and warmth taking him over the crest with her.

She was a feast to every one of his senses, and he couldn't get enough of her. And for the next eight hours he made sure she realized that, too.

KRISTIN STARED at her reflection in the bathroom mirror at the break of dawn the next morning, unable to believe the disheveled woman with flushed cheeks and bright blue eyes staring back was her. She'd never looked so wanton in her entire life. Had never felt so sensual and desirable and physically satisfied.

Her one night with Michael had been as memorable as she'd hoped it would be. She closed her eyes and shivered as she recalled last night's episode on the table, with her as dessert. She knew he'd meant to distract her after their too-serious conversation about her job and goals, and she'd let the ruse work.

The man was an incredible lover, so generous and attentive, and completely insatiable, and she hadn't been able to resist him. Afterward they'd taken a long, hot shower together, another provocative experience she wouldn't soon forget. They'd ended up in the big king-size bed with her cuddled up to his side, his blindfold still in place, and just *talked*. This time about his parents, his brother and sisters, and crazy childhood antics that had made her smile and laugh and envy the closeness his family shared. Then they'd made love again and she'd fallen asleep in his arms, surrounded by his strong embrace, feeling secure and cherished in a way that had eluded her all her life.

And this morning she was going to walk away from him. Her heart gave a painful lurch, and she fought the doubts crashing over her, the enormity of her actions striking her hard. Instead of satisfying the craving she'd developed for Michael, the night had made her feelings for him far more intense. The intimacy they'd shared went beyond sex and had been rooted in emotion. And knowing she was about to leave him and never see him again made her feel empty and hollow inside…a huge, consuming ache that threatened to overwhelm her.

Pushing that weakness aside, she brushed her teeth and splashed cool water on her face. It was time for her to go, before she did something incredibly stupid. Like tell Michael that she'd fallen in love with him. Which didn't completely surprise her, since she'd been halfway there before last night.

Tugging the collar of the robe closer to her throat to ward off the chill settling within her, she opened the bathroom door and quietly stepped back into the master bedroom. She needed to find her clothes so she could change and leave before Michael woke up so they didn't have to deal with an awkward morning-after scene.

Except her eyes were drawn to the big bed and the gorgeous man sprawled on the mattress. She let her gaze linger one last time, committing everything about him to memory. He still wore the blindfold that she'd foolishly believed would keep her emotions hidden from this man. His thick, silky hair was tousled from her fingers, his chest was bare and the sheet draped low on his hips, which did little to hide his morning erection. She smiled, admiring everything about him, and felt her skin tingle in awareness and renewed desire.

Resisting temptation, she turned to head out to the living room to get her clothes.

"Are you going to leave me like this?" his deep, sleep-husky voice asked.

She jumped in startled surprise, wondering exactly what he meant. Was she going to leave him blindfolded? Aroused? Aching the way she did?

There were so many ways to interpret his question, and her traitorous heart and body battled with the difficult decision to stay or go.

"C'mere, Kristin," he said, the crook of his finger beckoning to her, mesmerizing her.

And like a woman lured by the spell he'd cast, she found herself slipping out of her robe, wanting one last time with him. One last goodbye. Crawling across the mattress, she pulled away the sheet and slid the length of her body along his. He wrapped his arms around her, holding her close, the heat they generated together making her shiver.

She lowered her head and parted his lips with her tongue. They kissed, long and deep, a slow, sensuous exploration that matched the caress of his hands down her spine. Their limbs entwined and heartbeats quickened. She tasted his hunger, felt the urgency build, his need as great as her own. Physical desire made itself known and she was beyond ready for him, but there was so much emotion to their embrace, as if their hands and mouths and bodies spoke the words she held locked in her heart.

*She loved him.* Unexpected tears burned the backs of her eyes and she somehow managed to keep the moisture at bay. She'd have plenty of time later to wallow in misery.

The tenor of their kiss changed, turning hot and dominant, and his hold on her tightened. She gasped as he abruptly rolled and dragged her beneath him, pinning her to the bed with his hard, muscular body. He wedged her legs apart with his thighs, settling his hips in between, right where he belonged. She held her breath, waiting for that first thrust that would make her forget everything but this man's possession.

It didn't come. Instead, he did the unthinkable. He reached up and pulled the blindfold off, breaking her rule. He glanced down at her, his fiery green gaze making direct eye contact with her for the first time since she'd kidnapped him.

Michael watched Kristin suck in a deep, startled breath and struggle beneath him, her panic a tangible thing. She closed her eyes and turned her face away, hiding her plain-to-see feelings and emotions. She shoved at his shoulders to push him off her, all to no avail. He wasn't going anywhere. At least not until he made sure she knew how much she meant to him.

Pinning her arms on either side of her head, he entwined their fingers so that they were palm to palm and he was in complete control. Still she refused to look at him, so he took a few precious seconds to drink in the glorious sight of her. Her tangled blond hair tumbled across his pillow, and her skin was flushed with passion, her lips pink and swollen from his kisses. Even without makeup she was incredibly beautiful, so fresh and honest, inside and out. And everything he wanted and needed in his life.

"You promised to keep the blindfold on," she whispered.

She sounded so betrayed, and guilt reared within him. But not regret. This was an obstacle they had to hurdle together if he had any chance at all at a future with her. Her trust was imperative.

"If this is all you're going to allow me, then let me watch you when you come this time." He nudged the head of his penis against her slick flesh, sliding in a few excruciating inches. "Let me have that memory of you, at least."

With a flex of his hips he sank all the way into her, and she moaned softly, raggedly, accepting him. He left the decision to look at him solely up to her, and with every stroke of his body within hers he felt the strain ease from her muscles and another kind of tension take over, felt the rapid beat of her heart matching his, felt her melt beneath him....

Slowly she turned her head. Slowly her lashes fluttered open, and while the moisture shimmering in her expressive blue eyes tore at him, it also offered him a whole lot of reassurance. There wouldn't be tears if she were indifferent to him.

Their gazes locked as he slid back into her, pressing higher, harder, angling his body for maximum friction and pleasure. He watched her every reaction, reveling in her response and her gradual climb to an intense climax. And when the spiraling sensations finally came to a peak she held nothing back. Her lips parted as she sighed his name, and her head rolled back on the pillow. Clutching their clasped hands, she arched into his hips, taking as much of him as she could. And still he watched, until her shudders subsided and he couldn't hold back his own release any longer.

When their passion was spent, he moved off her, giving her space, valiantly resisting the urge to pull her into his arms to keep her from bolting from their very emotional lovemaking. She didn't immediately scramble from the bed, and he took that as a very positive sign.

Propping himself up on his elbow beside her, he pulled the sheet up around her naked breasts and tenderly brushed wisps of hair off her soft cheek. Morning sunlight streamed through the sheers covering the window, making her skin glow. Making the vulnerability in her eyes more prominent. "What are you thinking?"

She inhaled a deep breath, let it out slowly, but her gaze never wavered from his. "That I'm scared to death."

That wasn't the answer he'd anticipated, and he frowned. "Of me?" he asked cautiously.

She bit her bottom lip, and it took her a few extra heartbeats to admit, "Of what you make me feel."

She was being truthful, with him and herself, and that was a start. "And what do I make you feel?"

She skimmed her fingertips along the stubble lining his jaw, her touch reverent. "Adored and cherished."

"Let me see if I've got this right," he said, a

lopsided grin curving his lips. "You're scared to death because I make you feel adored and cherished?".

"Yes." She ducked her head, but not before he caught the tinge of warmth pinkening her cheeks. "I know it sounds silly to you, but nobody has ever made me feel that way before. I've never let anyone close enough."

Was she letting *him* that close? Hope and elation mingled. Tucking his index finger beneath her chin, he brought her gaze back to his. "The way I see things, sweetheart, you have two choices. You can walk away and chalk up this incredible night to one hell of a provocative affair, or you can take a chance on me. On us. Either way I'll accept your decision." His chest tightened as he waited for her to answer.

"I don't want to give up my new job." A wealth of doubts chased across her features. "My aspirations. My goals. I've worked too hard to walk away from what I've achieved."

Now that he knew her deepest fears, he felt better equipped to cater to her insecurities. "Nobody ever said you had to give up anything, Kristin. I've never been one of those macho guys who makes unreasonable demands. And one of the things I love about you is your determination and drive to succeed, and your independence. Those are admirable traits, and I know that given time, you'll use that same persistence to make sure our relationship works, too."

BONUS FEATURE

"I'm willing to try, because I can't bring myself to walk out that door and never look back."

"We'll take this relationship slow and easy. One day at a time," he reassured her. He ran a gentle finger down the slope of her nose, his heart overflowing with so much passion and affection for this woman that he couldn't contain it. "I love you, Kristin."

Her eyes grew wide, her expression tentative, fragile. Disbelieving. "You love me?"

He wondered if anyone had ever said those words to her before. "Yeah, I love you." His voice was strong and sure. "Is that going to be a problem?" Because he planned to tell her often.

"No, not at all." Her voice caught as her eyes grew misty once again, but this time her tears were born of happiness. "How did I get so lucky with you?"

He grinned down at her. "Don't ever doubt for one second that *I'm* the lucky one."

She laughed, the sound incredibly sweet to his ears. "I love you, too, Michael Karr."

He didn't have to ask if she meant the declaration, because the emotion shone bright in her eyes for all the world to see. And it was all he needed to know— that she was his, now and forever.

**THE END**

*Originally published online by eHarlequin.com*

Take a trip to the sensual French Quarter with
two favorite stories in

# NEW ORLEANS NIGHTS

*USA TODAY* bestselling author

# Julie Elizabeth Leto

The protector becomes the pursuer in two
editorially connected tales about finding
forbidden love with the bodyguard amidst
murder and mystery in New Orleans.

"Julie Elizabeth Leto always delivers sizzling,
snappy, edgy stories!"—*New York Times*
bestselling author Carly Phillips

**May 2006**

# The much-anticipated conclusion to this gripping, powerful continuity!

THE
FORTUNES
OF TEXAS:
Reunion

# The Reckoning

by

**national bestselling author**

# Christie Ridgway

Keeping a promise to Ryan Fortune,
FBI agent Emmett Jamison offers his help to
Linda Faraday, a former agent now rebuilding
her life. Attracted to him, yet reluctant to
complicate her life further, Linda must learn
that she is a stronger person than she realizes.

**On sale May.**

If you enjoyed what you just read,
then we've got an offer you can't resist!

# Take 2 bestselling love stories FREE!

# Plus get a FREE surprise gift!

**Clip this page and mail it to Harlequin Reader Service®**

| IN U.S.A. | IN CANADA |
|---|---|
| 3010 Walden Ave. | P.O. Box 609 |
| P.O. Box 1867 | Fort Erie, Ontario |
| Buffalo, N.Y. 14240-1867 | L2A 5X3 |

**YES!** Please send me 2 free Harlequin Presents® novels and my free surprise gift. After receiving them, if I don't wish to receive anymore, I can return the shipping statement marked cancel. If I don't cancel, I will receive 6 brand-new novels every month, before they're available in stores! In the U.S.A., bill me at the bargain price of $3.80 plus 25¢ shipping & handling per book and applicable sales tax, if any*. In Canada, bill me at the bargain price of $4.47 plus 25¢ shipping & handling per book and applicable taxes**. That's the complete price and a savings of at least 10% off the cover prices—what a great deal! I understand that accepting the 2 free books and gift places me under no obligation ever to buy any books. I can always return a shipment and cancel at any time. Even if I never buy another book from Harlequin, the 2 free books and gift are mine to keep forever.

106 HDN DZ7Y
306 HDN DZ7Z

| | | |
|---|---|---|
| Name | (PLEASE PRINT) | |
| Address | Apt.# | |
| City | State/Prov. | Zip/Postal Code |

*Not valid to current Harlequin Presents® subscribers.*

*Want to try two free books from another series?*
*Call 1-800-873-8635 or visit www.morefreebooks.com.*

\* Terms and prices subject to change without notice. Sales tax applicable in N.Y.
\*\* Canadian residents will be charged applicable provincial taxes and GST.
  All orders subject to approval. Offer limited to one per household.
® are registered trademarks owned and used by the trademark owner and or its licensee.

PRES04R                          ©2004 Harlequin Enterprises Limited

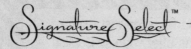
Signature Select™

# COMING NEXT MONTH

**Signature Select Spotlight**

ANGEL EYES by Myrna Mackenzie

Her special clairvoyant ability has led to painful betrayal for Sarah Tucker, leading her far from home in search of peace and normalcy. But an emergency brings her back, throwing her headlong into her past—and into the passionate but wary arms of police officer Luke Packard.

**Signature Select Collection**

PERFECT TIMING by Julie Kenner, Nancy Warren, Jo Leigh

What if the best sex you ever had was two hundred years ago... or eighty years ago...or sixty years ago? Three bestselling authors explore the question in this brand-new anthology in which three heroines travel back in time to find love!

**Signature Select Saga**

KILLING ME SOFTLY by Jenna Mills

Brutally attacked and presumed dead, investigative reporter Savannah Trahan assumes a new identity and a new life—but is determined to investigate her own "murder." She soon learns how deep deception can lie...and that a second chance at love should not be denied.

**Signature Select Miniseries**

NEW ORLEANS NIGHTS by Julie Elizabeth Leto

The protector becomes the pursuer in two editorially connected tales about finding forbidden love with the bodyguard amidst murder and mystery in New Orleans.

**Signature Select Showcase**

ALINOR by Roberta Gellis

Ian de Vipont offers marriage to widow Alinor Lemagne as protection from ruthless King John. His offer is sensible, but Alinor cannot deny the passion that Ian arouses within her. Can their newfound love weather the political unrest within England?

**Fortunes of Texas Reunion, Book #12**

THE RECKONING by Christie Ridgway

Keeping a promise to Ryan Fortune, FBI agent Emmett Jamison offers his help to Linda Faraday, a former agent now rebuilding her life. Attracted to him yet reluctant to complicate her life further, Linda must learn that she is a stronger person than she realizes.

SIGCNM0406